791.45

HOW WELL DO YOU KNOW THE CASTAWAYS?

- What was the Skipper's real name?
- Why did Ginger bring so many clothes on a three-hour cruise?
- Why were the Professor's and Mary Ann's names originally left out of the popular theme song, and then added later?
- What was Lovey's favorite perfume?
- What mix-up resulted in the sudden cancellation of one of the most popular shows in television history?

You'll find the answers to these and many more tantalizing questions in this fabulous, one-of-a-kind guide.

TV TREASURES

A companion guide to

GILLIGAN'S ISLAND

Sylvia Stoddard

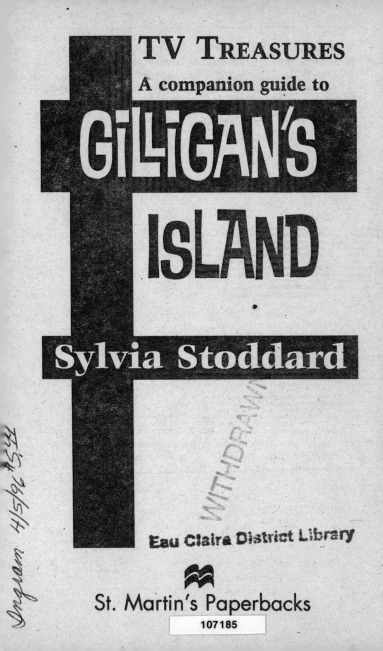

St. Martin's Paperbacks

TV TREASURES: A COMPANION GUIDE TO GILLIGAN'S ISLAND

Copyright © 1996 by Sylvia Stoddard

Cover photograph by Photofest.

ISBN: 0-312-95797-1

Printed in the United States of America

St. Martin's Paperbacks edition/May 1996

10 9 8 7 6 5 4 3 2 1

CONTENTS

CONTENTS

LIFE RAFTS

Acknowledgments

This book would have been impossible to write without Tom Wilson. His generous loan of files, photos, video, collectibles and enthusiasm were invaluable. And a special nod to Chelsea and Candace Geolfos, who started it all.

I would also like to thank my agent, Ellen Geiger, who believed, Shawn Coyne and Todd Keithley at St. Martin's, and the friends and mentors who have helped along the way.

Invaluable to the process were Guy Riddick, Yvonne Bachem, Greg Mackellan, Richard Green, Ann and Chas. Floyd Johnson, Jeri Taylor, Don Cannon, Max Preeo, Mike Powers, Jim Novack, Chris Abbott, T. S. Lamb, Dr. Marilyn Solsky, Dr. Alex Taylor, Dr. Melvin Nutig, H. T. Bear, Richard T. Jordan, J. Randy Taraborrelli, Bruce Cervi, and Karen Harris.

Thank you to Sherwood Schwartz and Russell Johnson.

Blessings to Fran Creevy for her prodigious memory and her knowledge of CBS Radford.

I'm also indebted to Claire, Heidi, and Donovan at an oasis for TV lovers, Eddie Brandt's Saturday Matinee in North Hollywood.

Nothing with kings,
Nothing with crowns.
Bring on the lovers, liars and clowns!
Old situations
New complications
Nothing portentous
Or polite;
Tragedy tomorrow,
Comedy tonight!

—STEPHEN SONDHEIM,
    "Comedy Tonight,"
    *A Funny Thing Happened
    on the Way to the Forum*

A companion guide to

GILLIGAN'S
ISLAND

A VAST OCEAN

Introduction

In 1964, our president was dead, Congress enacted bitterly-fought civil rights legislation, the Russian premier was deposed, our sons were dying in Vietnam, and hippies were turning our cities into centers of free love and flower power. There were sit-ins, love-ins, dropouts, and freak-outs. We wore buttons that said, "Black is Beautiful," "Ban the Bra," "Turn on, Tune In, Drop Out," "Make Love Not War" and "Do Not Fold, Spindle, or Mutilate." Is it any wonder that everyone wanted to escape to a desert island with a movie star, the girl next door, a couple of millionaires, and a smart guy?

The world was changing. The euphoria of the postwar years was over and the future seemed uncertain for the first time in many years. Television, as it often does, reflected our lives. When we wanted an escape into fantasy, TV provided it.

As we look back at classic TV shows, we often see them as little worlds of their own, but *Gilligan's Island* didn't exist in a vacuum. On the contrary, it was just one bush on the overall television landscape.

Until I began work on this book, I didn't realize how unfamiliar that landscape is to a new generation. A friend told me that his young nieces frequently asked him questions after they watched *Gilligan's Island*, about a line, a word, a joke they didn't understand. Their questions made me realize that I watched the show when it was first on and all those cultural references were common knowledge then. But for the many generations of viewers who now watch the show, this isn't true.

Gilligan's Island was written by intelligent, funny, and talented people. The writers put in references to their world just as TV writers do today. At the time, no one dreamed it would become the most rerun of all television shows, ever. It passed *I Love Lucy* several years back.

I've put the episodes in the order in which they aired. Several of the books on *Gilligan's Island* have them listed in the order they were filmed, which is meaningless, since shooting schedules are adjusted for weather, guest star availability, and script availability, not for story continuity. The Turner networks, TNT and WTBS, run *Gilligan's Island* episodes in the order they are listed in this book.

Also note that although *Gilligan's Island*, like most situation comedies, did not use episode titles onscreen, all the shows have them. Most one-hour drama series use their titles onscreen, with *Gunsmoke* and *Mission: Impossible* among the rare exceptions. It probably has something to do with length. A one-hour drama has a lot more time for credits and establishing footage than a half-hour sitcom does. You'll notice that now, Nickelodeon and the Sci-Fi cable networks have added titles and original airdates before many of their classic TV shows.

This book should give you (and my friend's

nieces) the context of this show . . . the times, the events, the way we felt when we watched it. The Castaways may have been in the middle of nowhere, but the world still touched their lives. As with so many things from limericks to Shakespeare's comedies, humor can be timeless.

Sylvia Stoddard
Los Angeles, 1996

LAYING THE KEEL
The Beginning

"If you were alone on a desert island, what one thing would you like to have?" That was a question in *Gilligan's Island* creator Sherwood Schwartz's college public speaking class. He says in his book, *Inside Gilligan's Island* (St. Martin's Press, 1993), that if there was a beginning for the idea of *Gilligan's Island*, perhaps that was it.

But that was just an idea. It was nothing without the writers, the cast, the set, the jokes, all the various elements that made it a hit.

And, as you will see, the long road from concept to television show was particularly arduous for *Gilligan's Island*.

SHAKEDOWN CRUISE

The Pilot

Most TV series introduce their characters with a pilot which relates the "backstory" of where they came from and how they happen to be assembled in the place or situation that becomes the show's "franchise." In the case of a comedy series, that franchise dictates the type of stories to be told, the way the characters interact and sets up the locale.

In *The Odd Couple*, for instance, the franchise is the inherent chaos of a neat freak and a slob living together. In *I Dream of Jeannie* it's the relationship of Jeannie and Tony as well as her magical powers. When a series's producers tamper with the franchise, the results are usually disastrous—for example, when Jeannie and Tony got married, or when *Moonlighting's* Maddie and David had sex and stopped bickering.

Gilligan's Island began with Sherwood Schwartz pitching the idea to his agent, who hated it. Schwartz got a new agent. In May 1963, that agent took it to actor Phil Silvers's production company at United Artists, and they liked it and gave Schwartz the go-ahead to put the idea together and try to sell it to CBS, which was airing *The Phil Silvers Show*.

A month later, Schwartz got a pitch meeting

5

at CBS Television City in Los Angeles. Schwartz told the story of the Castaways to CBS honchos William Paley, Dr. Frank Stanton, Michael H. Dann, and the controversial programming chief, James T. Aubrey, who had propelled fourteen CBS shows into the top fifteen (NBC's *Bonanza* was the lone representative of another network). It was June 1963.

Sherwood Schwartz had a very definite idea of what he wanted the show to be. "Getting the show on was not difficult, but getting it on in the shape that I wanted it to be on was very difficult. When you sit down with a network—a network is a lot of people—and every one of those vice presidents knows how you should do the show better than you want to do it. Different than you want to do it.

"My idea of *Gilligan's Island* was a group of people who, because they were shipwrecked, had to learn to get along with each other. It was a character interrelationship show. CBS loved the idea of the Skipper and Gilligan but their idea of the show was that this little charter boat, which was wrecked in the first episode, would be refitted in the following episodes to take different people on different adventures. Which is a very different show. That's a comedy-adventure show and my idea was a comedy-adventure-interrelationship show.

"And that was the important problem that I had with the network. It may sound simple. But there were thirty meetings that I went through trying to make the network understand that what I was saying is important not just for those seven people, but on a philosophic level, which is very much underneath the comedy level of the show. Just as these seven people were on this little island, the nations of the world are on the Earth, which is a little island in space.

"And just as those Castaways had to learn to get along with each other, that's how the countries of the world eventually are going to have to get along with each other. Now that was never openly stated, but with comedy you can sometimes have a subliminal message and that really was the message of the show. And that's why my version of the show was so far different from CBS's because they didn't want or they didn't have those ideas in their view of the show."

Schwartz believed in this so deeply that he used a phrase in his first CBS meeting that might have killed the show. He said he wanted the island to represent a "social microcosm." (Remarkably, one of the people at that first meeting was Dr. Frank Stanton, then president of CBS. Though he didn't say a word during the meeting, he later sent Schwartz a copy of a lecture he delivered in 1962. The topic—of all things—was social microcosms!)

But Jim Aubrey wanted to tinker with the idea. Aubrey wanted to call the show *Gilligan's Travels* with Gilligan and the Skipper taking a new group out each week.

Schwartz badly wanted to use a theme song he'd written to introduce the show. It was a calypso, a very hot rhythm at the time, and appropriate for the show since it was to be set on a Caribbean isle. He wanted it so much he even sang it himself in a later pitch meeting— and he's the first to admit he's no singer. Aubrey hated the idea of the theme song. He hated the song.

But Silvers, United Artists, and CBS all liked the concept and told Schwartz to write the pilot.

He hired his younger brother Elroy Schwartz and his partner, Austin "Rocky" Kalish, to do it with him.

Schwartz embarked on a marathon round of meetings. He argued plot points and fought for his ideas with Hunt Stromberg at CBS in L.A. He bounced back and forth between L.A. and New York like a yo-yo, meeting with Dick Dorso at UA and Aubrey, et al., at CBS in New York.

Finally, in August, the script was approved to be made into a pilot. The location managers decided the pilot would be filmed in Hawaii, since California beaches either didn't look tropical enough or had a modern highway nearby. Shooting would begin in November 1963.

Now Schwartz had to cast his seven characters. With so few guest stars, these actors would have to carry the show week after week and viewers had to like each of them.

Schwartz first thought of Jerry Van Dyke for Gilligan but Van Dyke's agent was Schwartz's former agent (the same one Schwartz had dumped because he didn't like the concept of *Gilligan's Island*) and he talked Van Dyke out of doing the pilot. Another agent suggested Bob Denver, who had nearly stolen *Dobie Gillis* out from under Dwayne Hickman. It had just gone off the air after a successful four-year run. Denver was perfect.

The Skipper was harder to cast. Viewers had to like him in spite of the way he treated Gilligan. Schwartz even wrote a special scene just to test the actors for likability, but none passed the test. The date for shooting the pilot was fast approaching and Schwartz had no Skipper.

Then one night, Schwartz and his wife went out to dinner near Twentieth Century–Fox Studios and saw four actors in Civil War costumes at another table. One was Alan Hale, Jr. One look at him, and Schwartz knew he had found his man.

When Hale read the script, he was enthusiastic enough to extricate himself from an inaccessible gorge in Utah (where he was filming location scenes for the Civil War picture—*Advance to the Rear*—coincidentally costarring Jim Backus) to come to Hollywood to test with Bob Denver.

Schwartz had written the role of Thurston Howell III with Jim Backus in mind (they worked together on *I Married Joan*), but Backus was unavailable and he was a bigger star than their budget could afford. Schwartz was resigned to using someone else but couldn't seem to find the right actor.

Then just six days before filming was to begin, Backus suddenly became available and Schwartz grabbed him. CBS came up with the extra money. Backus signed without seeing the script, since the part would be enlarged now that they had a major actor to play it.

Hunt Stromberg at CBS suggested Natalie Schafer for Lovey Howell. Everyone agreed she was perfect and strong enough to play opposite the energetic Backus.

The other three roles were minor ones in the pilot. Kit Smythe played Ginger, John Gabriel the Professor, and Nancy McCarthy played Bunny, the Mary Ann prototype.

The pilot for *Gilligan's Island* was filmed in Hawaii in November 1963. The location was in a remote part of the island of Kauai, which had served as the major location for the film, *South Pacific*. The beach scenes were shot on the bay where the swabbies had sung "There is Nothing Like a Dame," and the cast and crew stayed at a hotel built for *South Pacific's* cast and crew, adjacent to the set of Emile Debeque's gorgeous estate in the film. Everything on the *Gilligan's Island* set went well.

Friday, November 22, was to be their last day on Kauai. They were supposed to finish filming, then fly to Honolulu Friday night and shoot the departure of the *S.S. Minnow* on her "three-hour tour" on Saturday in Honolulu harbor.

They had just started the day's shooting that Friday morning when the horrible news was received from Dallas: President John F. Kennedy had been shot. Because of their tight schedule, the *Gilligan* group had to continue shooting while waiting for bulletins and updates, and had to swallow their grief and feelings of helplessness in order to go on after their worst fears were confirmed. Somehow, the company finished and flew to Honolulu that night.

But in the morning, Schwartz was told that the harbor, a military installation, would be closed all weekend in tribute to the fallen president. Then when Monday was declared the official day of mourning, the filming was pushed to Tuesday.

This meant putting up the whole cast and crew in a very expensive resort area for three extra days—and United Artists said they just couldn't come up with the extra money. Schwartz called CBS, and the network agreed to pick up the additional cost.

They finally filmed the *Minnow*'s departure on Tuesday, unable to disguise the fact that there were several flags in the shots which were flying at half-staff. This footage survived in the opening credits during the entire first season, until it was replaced when the show switched to color.

You might think this was the end of the rugged road to success for *Gilligan's Island*, but it wasn't. For one thing, Schwartz hated the way the pilot had turned out. He'd given in on a number of things CBS or UA wanted changed and was regretting it.

Schwartz particularly disliked the opening, which had each Castaway getting ready for the cruise. He'd arrived in Hawaii to discover that Hunt Stromberg at CBS had actually hired other writers to create four extra minutes worth of these scenes.

Jim Aubrey had also insisted on a "tag," a scene tacked on the end alluding to future adventures with the Skipper and Gilligan. For this pilot, the scene involved gangsters commandeering the *Minnow* at gunpoint.

The theme song was gone.

But the finished pilot was shipped to CBS in New York.

Jim Aubrey didn't like much about it, perhaps half of the scenes. Schwartz and one of his producers recut the pilot several times in response to notes from various people, but nothing worked. Schwartz put back the calypso theme song he'd first sung at a CBS meeting, but CBS still said no. Dick Dorso even suggested Schwartz make ukulele picks out of the (celluloid) film stock. But Schwartz didn't give up.

Schwartz decided—without telling CBS or UA or even his own agent—to recut the show the way he originally wanted it, and get it to the network the following week. He and his film editor worked day and night and reedited the pilot.

Schwartz was determined to use a theme song, but the old calypso didn't fit now that the show was set in the South Pacific. He hired composer George Wyle and together they wrote a new song and coerced a trio of little-known singers to sing it, but there was no money to record it. Schwartz called a friend who had a makeshift recording room at his home. The only problem was, they had to do it on Sunday, and the friend was having a huge catered party that night.

But there, on a Sunday, in the middle of caterers, waiters, and preparations for a big charity affair, the Wellingtons recorded the song now recognized far and wide as "The Ballad of Gilligan's Isle." It not only introduced the show in the way Schwartz always hoped, it told a little of the backstory.

Schwartz's agent was very excited when he saw the recut pilot and moved heaven and earth to get it to New York before CBS unveiled its fall schedule. They had to smuggle the film off the lot when no union drivers were available, get the film on a midnight flight, track down Dick Dorso at a New York restaurant, and get him to show it again to CBS.

The network shipped the new pilot back to L.A. the next night and tested it before a preview audience, which loved it. And, that day in May, when the fall schedule was announced, there was *Gilligan's Island* set for Saturday nights!

The entire original pilot, as summarized below, finally aired on TBS in October 1992, only twenty-five years late. It also has been released on videotape as part of the Columbia House Collector's Edition of *Gilligan's Island*.

"Marooned"—The Lost Pilot

First broadcast: October 16, 1992

Created and Produced by
  Sherwood Schwartz
Written by Sherwood
  Schwartz, Austin
  Kalish, Elroy Schwartz
Directed by Rod Amateau

Bob Denver as . . . . Gilligan
and
Alan Hale as . . The Skipper
Also Starring
Jim Backus as . . . .
 . . . . . . Thurston Howell III
and
Natalie Schafer as . . . .
 . . . . Mrs. Howell
Featuring
John Gabriel as . . . .
 . . . . The Professor
Kit Smythe as . . . . . . Ginger
Nancy McCarthy as . . Bunny

Associate Producers
  Norman Henry and
  Larry Heath

Director Rod Amateau directed some of the best comedy shows in television, including Dobie Gillis, The George Burns and Gracie Allen Show, Mr. Ed, The Patty Duke Show, *and* Private Secretary. *He also directed low-budget feature films, including* High School, USA.

Johnny Williams, who composed the music for this pilot, is the now-famous John Williams, composer of many renowned modern film scores, including Star Wars, E.T.—The Extra-Terrestrial *and* Jurassic Park.

John Gabriel, who plays the Professor, went on to play a recurring role as Andy Rivers, one of Mary's handsomest beaus on The

Mary Tyler Moore Show. *He starred in* El Dorado *with John Wayne. He also played Teddy Holmes on* General Hospital, *a handsome newspaperman who romanced Jessie Brewer (Emily McLaughlin) when she was dumped for the umpteenth time by erstwhile husband Phil. He was also Dr. Seneca Beaulac on* Ryan's Hope *and Link Morrison on* Love of Life. *He is currently the producer of Charles Grodin's CNBC nightly talk show, and sings every summer in a New York nightclub, Danny's. He was young and devastated when he was fired from* Gilligan's Island, *but today says, "It turned out to be a very lucky thing that happened. The show ran for three years. Because the costumes were so unique and identifiable, it really locked these very gifted people into the* Gilligan's

Production Manager Bill Porter
Music by Johnny Williams
Director of Photography Charles Van Enger, ASC.
Art Direction John H. Senter
Film Editors Robert Moore and Jim Faris
Set Decoration Norman Rockett
Assistant Director Miles Middough
Supervising Music Editor Kenneth Runyon
Sound Effects Supervisor Richard Sperber
Costumer Ray Summers
Dialogue Supervisor Ray Montgomery
Script Supervisor David Davis
A Gladasya–United Artists Production

The plight of the *S.S. Minnow* and its passengers is described in a calypso song:

> *In tropical sea is a tropic port*
> *Vacation fun is the favorite sport*

This is the place where the
    tourists flock
Renting the boats at the
    busy dock

Two secretaries from
    U.S.A.
Play on the Minnow this
    lovely day
A high school teacher is
    next aboard
All taking trip that they
    cannot afford

The next two people are
    millionaires
They got no worries, they
    got no cares
They climb aboard and
    they step inside
With just enough bags for
    a six-hour ride

Tourists come, tourists go
tourists touring to and fro
These five nice tourists,
    they take this trip
Relaxing on deck on this
    little trip
The weather is clear and
    the sun it is hot
The weather is clear?
I think it is not.

Tourists come, tourists go
Tourists tossing to and fro

Island mode. They never
had an opportunity to get
out. It turned out to be
an enormous break for
me."

Harry Belafonte's calypso
records were very
popular in the early
sixties. Schwartz's original
theme song was a calypso
because the first two lines
originally were:

> Off Florida coast many
>   hundred miles,
> Is tropical sea full of
>   tropic isles.

When the location of the
Castaways' island was
switched to the Pacific,
this style of music was no
longer appropriate.

When the Howells
demand that the Skipper
take them to the Hilton it
reflects the fact that Hilton
was one of the first
American hotel chains to
expand worldwide. In
1964, it did seem

that Hilton had hotels
everywhere. The huge
chain was run by Conrad
Hilton, the "Mr. Hilton"
to which Mr. Howell
refers.

The captain is brave. . .
Carramba! What a storm!
The captain is brave, he's a
  fearless man
And Gilligan helps him all
  that he can
The wheel she break and
  lose all control
S.S. Minnow do the rock
  and roll

The sea is calm and the
  weather grand
Where is the Minnow upon
  this sand?
What happen now will
  bring you a smile
The adventures of Gilligan
  and the Skipper
and the Millionaire and
  Mrs. Millionaire
and the other tourists
On Gilligan's Isle

The Castaways awaken on
the battered Minnow, which is
beached in a pretty lagoon.
The Skipper is the first to ven-
ture out on deck and realize
they're shipwrecked. Gilligan
wakes and is worried about
what the passengers will say.
But they all seem pretty glad
to be there—wherever there is.
The two secretaries aboard,
Ginger and Bunny, seem
thrilled at the adventure, as is

the Professor. The Howells just want to be taken to the nearest Hilton.

They all listen to the radio, which reports that efforts to rescue them are being abandoned. The Skipper finds a very tall coco palm and suggests that Gilligan climb it to get a view of the whole island. Gilligan eventually braves the heights and yells that he sees people and a boat. He slides down and runs off. He goes to the beach, only to realize it's their own passengers and the wrecked *Minnow* that he saw.

Gilligan goes to fish for their dinner and the Skipper tries to get Mr. Howell to fetch some water, but he's retired . . . though he's never worked. The Professor fixes the transmitter, but then it mysteriously disappears. They find that Gilligan has accidentally hooked it with his fishing line and has cast it into the ocean.

Gilligan redeems himself somewhat that night when he produces bullets for the Skipper's gun that he salvaged from the wreck. But he spills all the bullets into their campfire and it becomes a rather explosive situation.

The next day, the Skipper

won't even let Gilligan help
because he's bad luck. He says
he's sorry he gave Gilligan the
job on the *Minnow*. He's even
sorry Gilligan saved his life
when then were in the navy.
The Professor won't let Gilligan
help either.

> We leave all our friends on
>   this tropic shore
> Perhaps they will be here
>   forevermore
> Maybe a rescue will set
>   them free
> Tune in next week and then
>   you will see.

THE WORLD
1964

Nineteen sixty-four was the last year of a post-war era and the first year of a changed world where the impact of events thousands of miles away could be felt almost instantly. Marshall McLuhan named this phenomenon the "global village." Other 1964 milestones included:

- At the New York World's Fair, Billy Graham narrated a film called *Man in the Fifth Dimension*, which had a sound track simultaneously translated into six languages. We could watch news events live on television on both sides of the Atlantic, thanks to Syncom, the first geosynchronous satellite that duplicated the Earth's orbit and therefore always stayed in the same place.
- On July 31, two TV transmitters aboard Ranger 7 sent over four thousand photos back to Earth from space and they appeared on national television less than twenty-four hours later.
- St. Louis got its arch and Los Angeles got Dodger Stadium. The monorail at the World's Fair seemed to be the mass transit of the future.
- The most successful film studio of the year was United Artists. It released Academy Award–winner *Tom Jones* as well as *A Shot in*

the Dark, It's a Mad Mad Mad Mad World and the Beatles' *A Hard Day's Night*. But the single most successful film of 1964 was from Warner Bros.—*My Fair Lady*. Also in release were *Dr. Strangelove, Fail-Safe, Mary Poppins, Goldfinger, The Unsinkable Molly Brown, Lilies of the Field, Hud,* and *The VIPs*.

• A hotline between the White House and the Kremlin had been working for a year. Traditionally portrayed as a red telephone, it was actually a teletype machine.

• Everyone was talking about pop art, and Andy Warhol became a cultural icon, leading a movement which included Roy Lichtenstein, Claes Oldenburg, and Jim Dine. Warhol's images of soup cans, Marilyn Monroe, and car disasters were scenes from daily life and were appealing to the general public.

• The Beatles reached a such a level of worldwide popularity in 1964 that a new word was coined, *Beatlemania*, to describe the phenomenon. Capitol Records released the first Beatles recording, "I Want to Hold Your Hand," in December 1963. The British group made its first American appearance on Ed Sullivan's television show in February 1964. The group was nearly drowned out by the screaming fans in the audience. "Can't Buy Me Love" was the number one song of the year.

• Ford introduced the Mustang. The company hadn't had a sports car in its line since the Thunderbird (which had been introduced to compete with GM's Corvette) had evolved into a luxury car in 1958.

• U.S. athletes brought home thirty-six gold medals from the Tokyo Olympiad, but only one from the Innsbruck Winter Games. Still reeling from the 1961 loss of the entire U.S. figure skating team, coaches, and referees in a plane crash, Team U.S.A.'s traditional supremacy in figure skating was only a memory.

- Lunar probe Ranger VII took the first close-up photos ever of the moon. However, it failed to answer the question of how thick the dust on the moon's surface was. Meanwhile, the Soviets launched the first two-man space capsule, Voskhod.

- The St. Louis Cardinals beat the New York Yankees four games to three in the World Series. Michigan beat Oregon State in the Rose Bowl, 34–7. The Cleveland Browns beat the Baltimore Colts in a 27–0 upset for the NFL title. The Buffalo Bills defeated the San Diego Chargers 20–7 to top the AFL. Bob Cousy retired after thirteen years from the Boston Celtics, who still went on to defeat San Francisco in the playoffs. In college basketball, U.C.L.A. were the NCAA champs after pounding Duke 98–83, letting John Wooden's team finish the year undefeated.

- Valium was introduced, but in general, the tranquilizers, antidepressants, stimulants, hallucinogens and other so-called miracle psychotropic drugs were not proving as effective as hoped in reducing the number of mental patients clogging the nation's hospitals.

- Cassius Clay defeated Sonny Liston to win the world heavyweight title, then two days later, announced his conversion to the Black Muslim faith, changing his name to Muhammad Ali.

- Lasers had been around for a couple of years and were just finding commercial and military applications—and a laser beam threatened to split James Bond in half in *Goldfinger*.

- The two worst disasters of the year were earthquakes. An 8.5 temblor struck in Prince William Sound, Alaska, causing widespread damage even in Anchorage, and a series of fifty-four tremors within seventy-eight hours in Niigata, Japan, killed twenty-seven, split city streets, and destroyed thirty thousand structures. An 11-1/2-foot tsunami resulted and destroyed more than 241 roads and fifty bridges.
- TWA put movies on its flights in 1963, and a year later, all the other major airlines joined in, providing another bonanza for the motion picture studios.

WHAT STUFF COST IN 1964

McDonald's hamburger	15¢
McDonald's fries	12¢
McDonald's milkshake	22¢
Del Monte Catsup—14 oz. bottle	2 for 25¢
Chuck Steak—USDA Choice, lb.	59¢
Quart of milk	20¢
Motel 6—one night	$6.00
Regular gasoline—gallon	25.9¢
TV picture tube (installed in your old set)	$16.95
Western Airlines airfare from Los Angeles to San Francisco	$11.43
Average weekly wages for a telephone worker	$102.44
Week-Ender boots for men	$14.98
Firestone auto brake reline	$13.88
Deluxe Champion whitewall tires	4 for $49.49
8mm. movie of the Beatles	$2.00
10' × 10' aluminum patio cover, installed	$60.00
Hourly rate for heavy equipment construction worker	$4.21

Woman's nylon jersey dress	$14.98
One issue of *TV Guide*	15¢

TELEVISION
1964

Like it or not, TV was part of our lives. Its influence was pervasive, and it was blamed for nearly every ill affecting society. Intellectual snobs claimed they watched nothing but public television.

Everybody thought television had murdered the printed word. The *Saturday Evening Post* was dead, as were many newspapers, both legendary and not: the *Boston Traveler*, *Houston Press*, *Pittsburgh Sun-Telegraph*, *Los Angeles Examiner*, *Indianapolis Times*, and the *San Francisco News-Call-Bulletin*. New York had seven daily papers in 1960. By 1970, there were three.

The motion picture industry also had been moaning for years that TV would be the death of it. Threatened by free pictures on the box, the film industry had tried widescreen movies, Cinerama, 3-D, and other gimmicks to pull audiences away from the mesmerizing eye in the living room. But television proved to be a boon instead of a threat to the motion picture industry. A large portion of TV programming now consisted of older motion pictures.

Pay-TV was a hot concept in 1964, but it didn't really take hold for many years. The only game in town, as usual, were the three networks. CBS,

NBC, and ABC were more powerful (and more profitable) than is imaginable today. They were megacompanies controlling much of our lives in the way that Bell Telephone did, or the electric company or the post office. This was an era of governmental regulation and it seemed as if certain institutions of our lives would always be there—companies like Pan Am, Bell Telephone, General Motors, Motorola televisions, etc.

Urban dwellers had always had several independent TV stations to augment their viewing, but what we watched in prime time, what we talked about at the watercooler, what we planned our week around, were the network schedules. People stayed home on Saturday nights to watch *Perry Mason* or *Gunsmoke*. When our president was assassinated, we got our information and comfort from Walter Cronkite.

Newton Minow, president of the Federal Communications Commission, had taken television to task, calling it a "vast wasteland." Partly in response, partly because that was what big companies did, the networks usually tried to enlighten us while they entertained. They made sure we had our dose of cultural programming even while giving us shows like *The Beverly Hillbillies*. The networks shut down each night (with a prayer and the national anthem) at the time good folks should be in bed, they gave us inspirational programs on Sunday mornings and sports on Saturday afternoons. The networks had censors—their standards and practices offices—and men who could still put a program on the air simply because they liked it and cancel one because they didn't. The bottom line was important, but it wasn't all-important. In the booming economy, profits could be made more than one way.

The leaders of the networks, like the great movie studio chiefs, put their personal stamp on their products. We could expect a CBS show to look like a CBS show. Each network had an identity and attracted a certain type of viewer. There were no remote controls. Chances were, if we turned on CBS at 7:30, the TV stayed on CBS all evening. TV was still novel enough, new enough, that it was something we *did*—sitting down to watch a program. We dimmed the lights, gathered the family, and watched. It wasn't just on in the background. And the networks tried not to let us down.

Incidentally, prime time in 1964 was a half hour longer than it is today, extending from 7:30 P.M. to 11 P.M. in most time zones.

Other milestones in 1964:

- A home TV tape recorder was developed in England and sold for two hundred dollars.
- A law was passed requiring all TV sets be capable of receiving both the twelve VHF channels plus seventy UHF channels.
- California voters outlawed pay-TV of any kind by a two-to-one margin.
- There were 62.6 million television sets in use in the U.S.—with at least one TV set in 92.8 percent of all homes. We watched an average of six hours and forty-eight minutes of programming every day. The FCC began to regulate cable TV and pay-TV for the first time because everyone feared the premier services would buy up all the good stars and shows and there would be nothing to watch on free TV.

- There was a new wrinkle in audience measurement techniques. Weak radio signals are emitted from all TV sets and were measured by trucks roaming neighborhoods with rotating dishes on top of them. Everyone thought the trucks could listen in on their dinner conversations and worried that "Big Brother" had arrived twenty years early.
- The presidential campaign of 1964 was waged primarily on TV. There was nearly gavel-to-gavel coverage of both the Republican and Democratic conventions.
- Most local TV newscasts expanded from fifteen to thirty minutes in length.
- CBS spent $28.2 million (three times as much as the previous contract) for two years of NFL games and presented two games back-to-back on many Sundays.

GILLIGAN'S ISLAND
1964

The January 25, 1964, issue of *TV Guide* was a special one, including a section chronicling the nation's common vigil in front of its television sets the weekend of November 22 following the assassination of President John Fitzgerald Kennedy. Readers might have missed an unrelated article about business as usual—the new network comedies which were in various stages of development for the fall season. Among those listed:

- *Tycoon*, starring Walter Brennan as a cantankerous CEO of the Thunder Corporation. Brennan was coming off six years as the cantankerous Grandpa on the immensely popular rural comedy, *The Real McCoys*, yet this new show (which was eventually called *The Tycoon*) lasted only a season.
- *Take Me to Your Leader*, starring *Sugarfoot*'s Will Hutchins, concerned the ultimate GATT agreement—two entrepreneurs from Venus come to Earth to hawk their planets' products. It never made it to the fall schedule.
- *Kentucky's Kid* never made it to the starting gate. It was supposed to star Dennis Weaver

(fresh from *Gunsmoke*) as a horse trainer who adopts a Chinese son.

- *The Jones Boys* was a comedy about a home maintenance crew. It was never heard from again.
- Mickey Rooney was slated to star in a sitcom about a Midwestern redneck who inherits a luxury hotel.
- *Google*, a comedy starring Jerry Van Dyke.
- *Valentine's Day* was about a New York bachelor in the publishing business, starring Anthony Franciosa. It never made it to TV, but interestingly, in 1968, Franciosa would costar with Gene Barry and Robert Stack in NBC's *The Name of the Game*, about the magazine publishing business.
- *Please Don't Eat the Daisies*, a book by Jean Kerr, playwright and wife of *The New York Times* drama critic Walter Kerr, had already spawned a film (starring Doris Day and David Niven) and it was announced as a television show to star Eleanor Parker. It did go on to be a successful show, but it starred Patricia Crowley.
- *Kibbee Hates Fitch* was a New York–based comedy that sounds suspiciously like *The Odd Couple*, and was to star Don Rickles and Lou Jacobi as firemen who don't get along.
- *Three on an Island* sounded a lot like the comic strip *Apartment 3-G*, with three young women sharing a New York apartment.
- *Pioneer, Go Home!* was about a family that moves to Florida.
- *Cap'n Ahab*, starring comic Judy Canova, singer Jaye P. Morgan, and a parrot.
- *Duncan—Be Careful!* was to star comic Marty Ingels as a (presumably bumbling) forest ranger . . . in Brooklyn.

- *Broadside* was a comedy about an all-female Navy motorpool on a South Pacific island during WW II. Don't let the politically incorrect title mislead you, it was a clever, funny show and starred Kathy Nolan (of *The Real McCoys*), Dick Sargent (of *Bewitched*, Sheila James (of *Dobie Gillis*), and a number of other talented actors, but it only lasted one season.
- And, a new comedy [then] called *Gilligan*, starring Bob Denver. All *TV Guide* said about the show was that it was to be "set in Hawaii."

Among the "chase and intrigue" shows on tap for the fall was *Solo*, starring Robert Vaughn as a spy (it became *The Man from U.N.C.L.E.*), Robert Horton in *John Stryker*, Victor Buono in *Mr. Man*, Darren McGavin in *Hide and Seek*, a new Rod Serling show called *Jeopardy*, and *Yellowbird*, about three spies who worked out of a boat by that name in the Caribbean.

The Fall Season

Twenty-one of thirty-seven new fall shows were comedies. After the huge success of *The Beverly Hillbillies* on CBS in 1962, comedies moved from the cities to more rural settings. CBS was the top network in prime time, and a young man named Fred Silverman was hired in 1963 to give the daytime schedule a shot in the arm. By 1964, CBS's daytime shows won every time period. Silverman would go on to be regarded as a programming genius, and eventually worked for all three networks.

SATURDAY NIGHTS—FALL 1964

	ABC	CBS	NBC
7:30	The Outer Limits	The Jackie Gleason Show	Flipper
8:00			The Famous Adventures of Mr. Magoo
8:30	The Lawrence Welk Show	GILLIGAN'S ISLAND	Kentucky Jones
9:00		Mr. Broadway	NBC Saturday Movie
9:30	Hollywood Palace		
10:00		Gunsmoke	
10:30	local		

New TV shows that did make the 1964 fall schedule included *Voyage to the Bottom of the Sea*, *The Man From U.N.C.L.E*, *The Addams Family*, *Bewitched*, and *The Munsters*. A large number of new shows failed, including the forgettable *Karen*, *Harris Against the World*, and *Tom, Dick, and Harry*, all of which ran on Monday night in a ninety-minute slot called *90 Bristol Court*. Daytime serials were adapted to prime time for the first time, and *Peyton Place* steamed up ABC twice a week.

The show now named *Gilligan's Island* premiered (in glorious black-and-white) in the 8:30

P.M. slot on Saturday night, September 26, 1964, following *The Jackie Gleason Show* on CBS. It was followed by another new show, *Mr. Broadway*, which starred Craig Stevens as a public relations man to the stars, politicians, and phonies. That show expired by December, and was replaced by another fall show, *The Entertainers*, a schizophrenic variety show that had either Carol Burnett, Bob Newhart, or Caterina Valente as each week's host. The 10 P.M. slot was occupied, as it had been since 1955, by the venerable *Gunsmoke*.

Opposite the CBS lineup in Saturday nights that fall, ABC presented *The Outer Limits*, *The Lawrence Welk Show*, and *Hollywood Palace*, while NBC aired adventure with *Walt Disney's Wonderful World of Color*, comedy with *The Bill Dana Show*, the western *Bonanza*, and *The Rogues*, a comedy-drama about two families of "scoundrels" which starred Gig Young, David Niven, Charles Boyer, and Gladys Cooper.

RATINGS
October 1964–April 1965
TOP 25 SHOWS

1.	Bonanza	36.3
2.	Bewitched	31.0
3.	Gomer Pyle, USMC	30.7
4.	The Andy Griffith Show	28.3
5.	The Fugitive	27.9
6.	The Red Skelton Hour	27.4
7.	The Dick Van Dyke Show	27.1
8.	The Lucy Show	26.6

9.	Peyton Place II	26.4
10.	Combat	26.1
11.	Walt Disney's Wonderful World of Color	25.7
12.	The Beverly Hillbillies	25.6
13.	My Three Sons	25.5
14.	Branded	25.3
15.	Petticoat Junction	25.2
	The Ed Sullivan Show	25.2
17.	Lassie	25.1
18.	The Munsters	24.7
	GILLIGAN'S ISLAND	24.7
20.	Peyton Place I	24.6
21.	The Jackie Gleason Show	24.4
22.	The Virginian	24.0
23.	The Addams Family	23.9
24.	My Favorite Martian	23.7
25.	Flipper	23.4

*Ratings represent the percentage of all TV-equipped households watching this particular show. Thus, an average of 36.3% of all homes with televisions were tuned to *Bonanza* every week during the season.

1964—LAUNCH

So, Sherwood Schwartz had sold his pilot. But he couldn't celebrate. He discovered, as producers always do, that the time between May and September is an awfully short time in which you must find a studio to film your show, hire a crew, build sets, hire writers, and get enough scripts ready to shoot one episode per week from July to April. On top of that, CBS insisted Schwartz recast three roles, the Professor and the two young women.

Schwartz looked for a place to film *Gilligan's Island*. He settled on CBS Studio Center—known in the industry as CBS Radford because that's the street in Studio City where the facility is located. As the entertainment industry consolidated in the sixties, the major studios and networks took over various small backlots, ranches, and production facilities that had been owned in the heyday of the movies by smaller companies. CBS Radford had belonged to silent movie king Mack Sennett, then Mascot Studios, Republic Studios, and the small but prestigious TV production company owned by Dick Powell, Charles Boyer, Ida Lupino, and David Niven, Four Star Studios.

Schwartz hired Tina Louise (expanding the

part of Ginger into a movie star), Russell Johnson, and Dawn Wells. Then, all the scenes with the three other actors had to be redone.

They filmed the replacement scenes on California's Zuma Beach because the set and lagoon were not finished yet. The scenes match the ones done in Hawaii remarkably well, partly because matching film is far simpler in black and white than it is in color.

Schwartz was astonished when CBS told him they wanted a "regular" episode to launch the show and would not use the pilot. CBS wanted the first show to be one where the Castaways were trying to get off the island, and the network decreed "Two on a Raft" would be the first episode. Schwartz felt strongly that this type of show *had* to tell its audience how the Castaways got to the island, but CBS wouldn't budge. This awkward start may be part of the reason why *Gilligan's Island* took such a critical drubbing.

In 1964, it was still common for a show to have just one or two sponsors. *Gilligan's Island*'s sponsors were Proctor and Gamble and Phillip Morris (yes, tobacco advertising was still permitted, and the tobacco companies were extremely active in television, sponsoring some of the most beloved shows in history). These sponsors had a lot of clout and when CBS contemplated major creative changes in *Gilligan's Island*'s characters and storylines, it was the sponsors who demanded the show be left just as it was. The ratings for this first episode were so good, CBS left well enough alone.

Note that the opening scenes of this, the first episode broadcast, are from the original pilot shot on Kauai, with the original cast. The scene where they listen to the radio was reshot with the new series cast.

Over the three years, nearly all of the information about the outside world the Castaways heard came from their radio. The radio announcers on the series included Charles Maxwell, sportscaster Chick Hearn (who appears in several episodes and the third reunion film), and Larry Thor, who also appears in episode number 40.

Ginger claims to know a little Hawaiian and says Wahine wiki huki luki nu means "This bar is off-limits to all military personnel." It doesn't, nor is it an actual Hawaiian phrase. Wahine means

1.
Two on a Raft
September 26, 1964

Created and Produced by
   Sherwood Schwartz
Written by Lawrence J.
   Cohen and Fred
   Freeman
Directed by John Rich

The Castaways are washed up on a deserted tropical island. Gilligan and the Skipper are horrified to see the extent of the damage to the *Minnow*. They all gather on the beach and listen to the radio, which includes a report on efforts to find and rescue them. It's feared they've all perished at sea.

The Castaways begin to build a raft. Ginger and Mary Ann make a sail with a large S.O.S. on it spelled out in socks. The Professor finds a scarifying primitive mask and an arrowhead that he thinks are evidence that members of the Marubi tribe—headhunters—have been there. He thinks they might inhabit a nearby island.

Gilligan and the Skipper

depart on the tiny raft, though Gilligan has an accident with the anchor. After paddling for three long days, they're becalmed and hungry. They find a bottle with a note in it, but it's one they prepared themselves before they left the island.

Then a shark appears, looking for lunch. The shark eats Gilligan's paddle, then starts on the raft. They take apart the raft to bash the shark, but without much success. They finally get rid of the shark and after being thrown around in a terrible storm, they're eventually washed up on a beach.

Meanwhile, the other Castaways are worried when they see a fire on the other side of the island. The Professor fears the Marubi have returned and finds a cave where they all prepare for imminent attack. The Professor sets up a booby trap which he hopes will immobilize the headhunters and they all head out, looking for Marubi tribesmen.

2.
Home Sweet Hut
October 3, 1964

woman and wiki means quick, but the phrase is just for fun—intentional gobbledygook.

When rescued from the cave, Ginger moans that her only dress—the beaded evening gown—is ruined. She does get a little more wear out of it—about three years' worth. This gorgeous dress—singularly inappropriate for a three-hour tour on the Minnow—was explained in the show by the report that she boarded the craft immediately after completing a nightclub engagement.

Sherwood Schwartz, in Inside Gilligan's Island, describes his difficulties with the huts. He found the studio carpenters, used to making something out of nothing, had trouble making the huts look "bad" enough, and Schwartz had to insist they be built to look like the untrained Castaways actually had built them from materials found on the island.

Director Richard Donner moved from television to feature films with a great deal of success. He is the director of Superman, *the three* Lethal Weapon *films,* The Goonies, The Toy, Maverick, The Omen, Tales From the Crypt, *and* Wanted: Dead or Alive.

We learn the Skipper's name in this episode: Jonas Grumby.

Created and Produced by
  Sherwood Schwartz
Written by Bill Davenport
  and Charles Tannen
Directed by Richard
  Donner

A sudden tropical storm and a thorough drenching convinces the Castaways that the first order of business on the island is shelter. Since the Professor predicts an early storm season is likely, they agree on one permanent hut for everyone, which dashes the Howells' hopes for a mansion with a verandah and Ginger and Mary Ann's hopes of privacy. That night, Gilligan and the Skipper have a little trouble coping with their double-deck hammocks, but they eventually settle in, though the Skipper ends up on top and nearly crushes Gilligan.

It's soon apparent that the palm frond walls are lousy sound barriers. They all end up yelling at each other and each one decides to take that part of the hut he or she personally built and start individual huts. The next day, all the huts are going splendidly except Gilligan's and the Skipper's, which is delayed by Gilligan's inept work and everyone else borrowing his tools. Mr. Howell announces five o'clock cocktails at Howell Manor.

The Professor settles into his hut and begins to write a chronicle of his adventures when Gilligan visits. He fiddles with one palm frond and the whole place collapses. One by one Gilligan manages to accidentally destroy every hut. The storm's almost upon them.

3.
Voodoo Something to Me
October 10, 1964

Created and Produced by
  Sherwood Schwartz
Written by Austin Kalish
  and Elroy Schwartz
Directed by John Rich

Gilligan is making a mess of his stint of sentry duty, falling asleep and spraying the place with bullets (which are in short supply) whenever he's startled. He's there to protect the supplies and to fire flares in hopes a ship in the area will

The title is taken from Cole Porter's song, "You Do Something to Me." It was written in 1929 and was introduced in the musical Fifty Million Frenchman. It has been sung in a half dozen other movies including the Shirley MacLaine and Frank Sinatra film, Can-Can, in 1960. It remains one of the all-time standards of pop music.

Mr. Howell's joke about giving to "the community hut every

year" refers to the predecessor to United Way charities, Community Chest, a phrase that survives only in Parker Brothers' Monopoly game.

Mary Ann talks about a film she saw once called The Land of the Vampires. *It is not a real movie.*

spot them. In the morning, the Skipper notices their supply hut has been burgled and accuses Gilligan of sleeping on guard duty. Their food supplies, the flare gun, and a flashlight are missing. Ginger moans, "If we had to get marooned on an island, why didn't we pick Manhattan?"

For reasons he doesn't share, the Skipper thinks voodoo is involved. He just says, "Let's not upset the women." Gilligan suggests, "Let's not upset the men either." Mr. Howell installs bars on their hut windows. He jokes, "That's what we need, some neighborhood bars," but knows it's serious.

That night, Gilligan's on guard duty again and he hears a terrible sound in the supply hut. Something attacks him. He calls the others, who run in and find nothing. The Skipper still insists it's voodoo. The Professor scoffs. The next day, Gilligan falls into a mud hole and is washing off when a monkey sneaks out of the bushes and grabs Gilligan's clothes.

That night, the chimp goes into camp wearing Gilligan's clothes and the Skipper thinks a voodoo spell has turned Gilligan into a monkey.

4.
Goodnight Sweet Skipper
October 17, 1964

Created and Produced by
  Sherwood Schwartz
Written by Dick Conway
  and Roland MacLane
Directed by Ida Lupino

One night, the Skipper sleepwalks and seems to be reliving a wartime experience. A bewildered Gilligan tags along as the Skipper converts a radio into a transmitter, sees bombers in the sky, and pushes Gilligan in the lagoon. Then the Skipper goes back to his hammock and goes to sleep. Gilligan returns and drips all over the peacefully-snoozing Skipper. The Skipper wakes and insists Gilligan's the one who was sleepwalking.

On the radio, the Skipper and the Professor hear about a woman—the "Vagabond Lady"—setting off on a round-the-world flight. The Skipper

The title is from Shakespeare's Hamlet, act *V, scene ii. It is Horatio's final epitaph to his friend Hamlet, Prince of Denmark, as he dies:*

Now cracks a noble heart. Good night, sweet prince; And flights of angels sing thee to thy rest!

The Skipper tells the Castaways he fought at Guadalcanal, a small island in the western Pacific Ocean, part of the Solomon Islands group. During World War II, the Japanese set up a strategic airfield there, and in 1942, a group of American Marines seized the airfield and battles raged in the area for months. After six months of heavy fighting, the Japanese had lost over thirty thousand men in the area and withdrew.

figures she'll pass right over them. They discuss ways to alert her. Gilligan mentions the dream and the Skipper realizes it *was* his dream, of his actual experience at Guadalcanal. If only he could remember how he converted the radio into a transmitter. They all insist he go to sleep again and try to rerun the dream. Gilligan gets some of Mr. Howell's tranquilizers.

Gilligan puts some tranquilizers in the Skipper's drink and goes to get him. Mary Ann adds some, then Ginger adds some, then the Professor adds some. The Skipper finds the bottle and adds a couple more. He gulps the drugged mango juice and falls asleep right at the table. They all wait and watch and finally he gets up and wanders around. He's like a bag of Jell-O, and Gilligan and the Professor try to hold him up but he collapses in a stupor.

The model for Wrongway Feldman is American pilot Douglas Corrigan. In the summer of 1938, he flew from New York to Ireland, but claimed he

5.
Wrongway Feldman
October 24, 1964

Created and Produced by
Sherwood Schwartz

Written by Fred Freeman
   and Lawrence J. Cohen
Directed by Ida Lupino
Guest
Hans Conreid as . . . .
. . . . . . Wrongway Feldman

Gilligan discovers an old plane in the jungle, marked SPIRIT OF THE BRONX on its fuselage. Mr. Howell remembers its pilot, "Wrongway" Feldman, an ace from World War I who got his nickname when he bombed his own base. He went down on a round-the-world flight in the thirties and was never heard from again. Just when they're wondering what happened to Wrongway, he appears. He's been on the island all these years. He has gasoline, but gave up trying to fix the engine after three years.

Feldman's amazed to hear Gilligan talk about planes with no propellers that go six hundred mph, no rumble seats in cars, no *Liberty* Magazine, and no World War II. Gilligan also enjoys Feldman's wild tales.

The Professor thinks he can fix the plane. Feldman agrees to let him try and does his own preparations, which sets off a

was actually heading for California. The newspapers dubbed him "Wrong Way Corrigan," a name which has since been applied to a number of people, including several football running backs who ran the length of the field and carried balls across their opponents' goal lines.

Ida Lupino is a member of a family with theatrical roots that go back to the seventeenth century. Her father was British vaudevillian Stanley Lupino, her mother actress Connie Emerald. Ida came to Hollywood in 1933, but never achieved the success in acting she felt she should have. She was given the New York Film Critics best actress award for a 1943 film, The Hard Way, but she is known more for They Drive by Night, While the City Sleeps, The

Adventures of Sherlock Holmes, and The Big Knife. *She became a writer, producer and director in the fifties and did a great deal of work in television. She costarred with husband Howard Duff in an early series,* Mr. Adams and Eve, *and then produced and starred in an anthology series,* Four Star Theatre.

The reference to "Lindy" is pilot Charles "Lindy" Lindbergh, who was the first man to fly solo across the Atlantic. He took his monoplane "The Spirit of St. Louis" from New York to Paris and captured the fancy of the public.

A "rumble seat" was common to the one-seat roadsters in the thirties. Because there was only one seat in the sporty convertibles, there was a panel in the large,

rash of bribes and coercion among the Castaways, all of whom want him to take them along even though it's just a one-seater. Ginger promises him "glamorous evenings," Mr. Howell promises him the presidency of Howell Aircraft or even his teddy bear. Feldman ends up taking no one, though he does try to smuggle Mary Ann into the cockpit. "But Lindy had sandwiches," he rationalizes.

The engine blows as he starts it. Late that night, someone saws a wing support clear through. The next day, the engine starts and the wing strut splits. The Professor spots it instantly: sabotage. The Castaways all insist they didn't do it—they *want* to be rescued.

That night, Gilligan guards the plane with a bow and arrow. The next day, Wrongway has disappeared. The camp's been trashed and Gilligan finds only Wrongway's aviator's scarf. He's gone.

rounded trunk that lifted up and became an auxiliary seat that could hold several people.

6.
President Gilligan
October 31, 1964

Created and Produced by
   Sherwood Schwartz
Written by Roland Wolpert
Directed by Richard
   Donner

Gilligan is helping the Howells plan their "Howell Hills" estate—a small fifteen-room cottage—when the Skipper insists he needs Gilligan to dig a well. This gets the Skipper and Mr. Howell into a spat over who's running the island. Ginger suggests they have an election. Mr. Howell vows to spend

When Mr. Howell refers to "the power seekers," he uses a phrase popularized in the fifties and sixties by author Vance Packard, who wrote a series of sociological studies written for the general public with titles like The People Shapers, The Naked Society, The Status Seekers, The Ultra Rich, *and* The Wastemakers.

millions on his campaign or maybe to buy votes.

The campaign begins and the mud starts flying. Mr. Howell wants to debate the Skipper on "public transportation, coconut conservation, and high-rise dwellings." The Skipper's motto is "Don't change leaders in mid-ocean." When Mr. Howell says he's thinking of buying Hollywood, Ginger falls squarely in his camp. Then everyone tries to coerce Gilligan to their side. Mr. Howell offers him the post of secretary of the navy.

The Professor builds a voting booth and all the Castaways enter and cast their ballots. The Professor counts them and it's two for Howell and two for the Skipper and two for Gilligan. One of the votes for Gilligan is Mrs. Howell's. She explains that if her husband wins, she's afraid he'll be so busy he won't ever have time for her. Gilligan's elected.

The Skipper warns President Gilligan to look out for "the power seekers." Sure enough, Mr. Howell gives him a set of solid gold cufflinks. The Skipper (who's made himself vice president) and Mr. Howell are still going at it.

7.
The Sound of Quacking
November 7, 1964

Created and Produced by
  Sherwood Schwartz
Written by Lawrence J.
  Cohen and Fred
  Freeman
Directed by Thomas
  Montgomery

There's a blight on the island's food supply and all the edible plants are dying. Everyone's hungry and worried. When they introduce rationing, Mr. Howell's concerned that he'll be "drummed out of the social register" for getting in a soup line. He offers Ginger a thousand dollars for her olive. She's amazed. "Without a martini?" The Professor returns from a survey of the island crops and has no hope to offer the hungry group.

Gilligan spots a plant that looks nourishing and asks the Professor about it, but he says most of that species is poison-

The music as the dream starts is Gunsmoke's theme and the establishing scene is unmistakably "Dodge City, Kansas." All the sets used here belong to Gunsmoke. This episode is the first of what would become an enduring tradition of spoofing the long-running Western. Not only did Gilligan's Island precede Gunsmoke on Saturday nights on CBS, the two shows filmed side by side at CBS Radford. Like Gilligan, the main set for Gunsmoke, the main street of Dodge City, was actually inside the soundstage. But where Gilligan used a "cyc"— a painted backdrop or cyclorama—for the distant details and the sky, Gunsmoke used "matte paintings"— backgrounds painted on glass then a matching mask is made on the camera when the scene is filmed and the two are put together in post production. Other Gunsmoke-isms: The Skipper, as Marshal Gilligan's (read Dillon) sidekick, limps, just like Chester (as originally played by Dennis Weaver). Ginger plays "Miss Ginger," in the manner of Amanda Blake's Miss Kitty, proprietress of the Long Branch Saloon.

Note that in the dream sequence, Gilligan has a mysterious white X on his back pocket, which is never explained.

When Mr. Howell says "the o-o-o-only way to fly," he's imitating a popular airline advertisement of the time. It was Western Airlines' slogan for many years, spoken in TV commercials by "Wally," an animated

ous so they can't risk it. Just then, a duck flies overhead and lands in the lagoon. With visions of duck dinner, everyone follows. The Professor tells them to hold it. It's a migratory duck from North America and they've got to affix a message and let him go.

Gilligan makes a decoy out of an old shoe covered with feathers, and the duck adores him immediately. He names the duck Everett, after his grandfather. The Professor's afraid the duck isn't healthy, so they put him in a cage and fatten him up. Gilligan exercises him like a kite on a string.

Some days later, they decide Everett's ready, put a message on the bird's leg, and send him aloft. But the bird flies in a circle and lands. Gilligan is shocked when Everett suddenly lays an egg. Gilligan renames him Emily. That's why she couldn't fly.

But when she's fed, Emily still won't fly. That night, the ravenous Castaways try to steal Emily.

DREAM SEQUENCE

Gilligan dreams he's Marshal Gilligan in the Old West, protecting Emily in her jail cell. Mr.

Howell, a notorious gun-slinger, threatens to pump Gilligan full of gold. The Professor asks if he doesn't mean lead. He replies, "A Howell use lead? Such a vulgar metal." Miss Ginger tries to convince Gilligan of the joys of a roast duck dinner.

Mary Ann reports the lynch mob is a-comin' and the marshal lets Emily go. The town watches as the marshal is stalked by the Professor and Mr. Howell. It's *High Noon* as the men face each other on the main street. They're only inches apart when the two varmints fire like crazy, but miss Marshal Gilligan. He fires his gun in the air as the bad guys flee. The shot brings down Emily.

bird who relaxed against a fluffy pillow propped against the plane's tail, holding a glass of champagne and a cigarette in a long holder.

8.
Goodbye Island
November 21, 1964

Created and Produced by
  Sherwood Schwartz
Written by Albert E. Lewin
  and Burt Styler
Directed by John Rich

The Professor has calculated that there will be a high tide

When Mr. Howell jokes about making ropes out of vines and says, "That little old vinemaker, me," he's imitating a television commercial for Italian Swiss Colony wine, a popular, inexpensive brand of rosé. Their commercial featured an animated grandfatherly man who said, "That little old winemaker, me."

in six days and he thinks they should try to repair the *Minnow* in time to take advantage of it. The main problem all along has been to get metal to make nails and he has just found an outcropping of ferrous oxide and uses it to make a nail to board over the hole in the *Minnow*'s hull. But the nail breaks like it's made of plaster.

Gilligan trips and makes another hole in the boat's keel. To keep him from doing any more harm, the Skipper sends him to work with the Professor. The next nail version melts. So Gilligan goes to help Ginger and Mary Ann, who are making dinner. They've made pancakes out of breadfruit, but they have no syrup. Gilligan says that lots of the island's trees have sap.

Gilligan finds one, taps it, and collects the sap. The Professor's next nail explodes. Everyone's thrilled to see pancakes but the syrup is like glue. The Professor takes it to the lagoon and finds it's waterproof. Now they can patch the boat with Gilligan's magic glue. The next day, they glue boards over the hole with the substance and it works.

The Skipper recaulks the

entire boat with the stuff. Nobody will let Gilligan help. He wanders off to the lagoon and picks up his original plate of pancakes. He's talking to his reflection when the "syrup" dissolves into dust.

9.
The Big Gold Strike
November 28, 1964

Created and Produced by
  Sherwood Schwartz
Written by Roland Wolpert
Directed by Stanley Z.
  Cherry

Gilligan caddies for Mr. Howell, who hits a ball into an underground cavern and they both fall in. Mr. Howell asks what that streak of yellow stuff is, and they determine it's gold. Mr. Howell says he has a "gold syndrome" and shakes when he's near "anything over 24-carat." He insists they must keep it a secret. And he insists Gilligan mine the gold.

Ginger and Mary Ann fish for dinner and catch something huge and heavy. The Skipper takes over the pole and pulls up a rubber life raft—the *Min-*

When Mr. Howell thinks Gilligan is wildly double-jointed (actually, it's the Professor's feet that stick out from under the raft next to Gilligan's head), he suggests he'll get him on The Ed Sullivan Show, *which was a very popular variety show on CBS every Sunday night from 1948 to 1971. Sullivan frequently booked acrobats, novelty acts, and people who could do interesting things in addition to a steady stream of the top entertainers of the day.*

America was still on the gold standard in 1964 (all our currency was backed by sufficient gold reserves to redeem it) and the price of gold was fixed at thirty-five dollars per ounce. It was also illegal for U.S. citizens to posses gold in any form other than jewelry, which is why so many of our grandparents had their gold coins set into necklaces and rings.

now's own life raft. The Skipper looks for Gilligan to help him start immediate repairs. Oddly, Mr. Howell is not very anxious to leave the island.

Mr. Howell makes Gilligan work every night in the mine after he's worked a full day on the raft, and he's exhausted. One night the suspicious Skipper follows Gilligan and the jig is up. The rest of the Castaways want a share of the gold. They stake claims and start digging, but they find nothing while the Howells strike another rich vein. The Skipper gives up and Mr. Howell asks if he can rent or buy his mining tools.

The title brings to mind Samuel Beckett's avant garde 1952 play, Waiting for Godot, *which was very popular with intellectuals and college students in the sixties. The existential play consists of two men sitting around talking about pretty much nothing. Godot never arrives. There is also a famous play from the*

10.
Waiting for Watubi
December 5, 1964

Created and Produced by
  Sherwood Schwartz
Written by Lawrence J.
  Cohen and Fred
  Freeman
Produced and Directed by
  Jack Arnold

The Skipper, Gilligan, and the Professor are digging an

underground storage pit for their food when the Skipper unearths an idol, which he says is Kona, the god of evil. The superstitious Skipper says, "Whoever disturbs his rest is cursed forever." The Professor thinks it's all bunk, but just then, a small earthquake hits. Sure enough, the Skipper keeps having accidents, which the Professor reminds him are simply a "statistical probability."

The Skipper insists that Gilligan help him rebury the idol. The Howells see them and assume the statue is valuable and steal it. Later, the Skipper and Gilligan go to the Howells' hut and find it where they've hidden it. The Skipper's really spooked and thinks the god's following him around. He begs Gilligan to rebury it. Another earthquake hits and then lightning strikes a tree near Gilligan, who tosses the idol away and flees.

The Skipper insists they find it and rebury it. Then he falls in quicksand. They can't find Kona and the Skipper's really depressed. Gilligan suggests they throw a surprise party for his boss. Ginger and Mary Ann

thirties, Waiting for Lefty, by Clifford Odets. Lefty is a popular cabdriver and the members of his union discuss social injustice and their labor problems while they wait for him to arrive. Word comes that Lefty's been killed and the other members vote to strike.

The Skipper isn't alone in his superstitions. Seamen are traditionally so, indulging in all manner of ceremonies and rituals to ward off all manner of imagined threats. The Skipper is also a resident of Hawaii, where residents are also very aware of the power of the ancient gods, as civilization is more recent there than on the mainland. Most people respect Pele, the goddess of volcanoes, and there are numerous documented cases of disasters when people try to build on ancient temple sites.

find the idol and think it will be a perfect present. When Skipper opens it, he freaks out. Gilligan and the Professor bury the idol in a deep pit. But before they can fill it in, the Skipper falls in. He crashes into a tree as he runs away.

Financial backers for all manner of theatrical endeavors are traditionally called "angels," hence the episode's title.

Mr. Howell invokes the name of Richard Burton when exasperated with the Skipper's performance as Marc Antony because Burton was a splendid actor, well known for his superb interpretations of Shakespeare's classical heroes. He played Marc Antony in the film, Cleopatra, with Elizabeth Taylor. That was the occasion when he fell in love with his leading lady, and after the press breathlessly reported

11.
Angel on the Island
December 12, 1964

Created and Produced by
   Sherwood Schwartz
Written by Herbert Finn
   and Alan Dinehart
Produced and Directed by
   Jack Arnold

Ginger is miserable because tonight was supposed to be her opening night on Broadway in a play written especially for her. Everybody's worried because she's so depressed and Mary Ann takes her a tray of special food. Gilligan finds Ginger's script and gives it to Mr. Howell, who says he's backed some shows in his time. Gilligan suggests he put it on there and if it's a success, he can take it to Broadway when they're rescued.

Mr. Howell decides to produce Ginger's play, *Pyramid for Two*, and she's very grateful. The Professor paints sets with jungleberry paint and Mary Ann makes costumes. Ginger's playing Cleopatra and Mr. Howell's directing. He's quite entranced with Ginger, and his wife is jealous. Mrs. Howell is not a bit happy playing the maid. She forces him to dump Ginger and let her play the lead. Ginger runs off in tears.

scandalous doings on the set, she divorced husband Eddie Fisher shortly after the film was completed and married Burton.

Ginger, distraught by being replaced, compares Mrs. Howell to another performer—Mr. Ed, the talking horse of sitcom fame. Mr. Ed was on CBS from 1961 to 1965.

When Mrs. Howell fakes laryngitis and Gilligan suggests Ginger could take over, he mentions a movie where an understudy goes on for a sidelined star. That film is 42nd Street, *the classic 1933 backstage musical from which all future making-it-in-showbiz clichés would be drawn and which starred Ruby Keeler and Dick Powell.*

Sherwood Schwartz says about seventy-five percent of the pilot was used in this episode. Though most of the scenes with the new cast members were reshot, in the scene where the Skipper awakens on the island for the first time, you can see Kit Smythe as Ginger and Nancy McCarthy as Bunny asleep on the Minnow.

The title brings to mind "Fish gotta swim, birds gotta fly, I gotta love one man 'til I die," the opening lines in the song, "Can't Help Lovin' Dat Man," from Oscar Hammerstein and Jerome Kern's landmark musical Show Boat, which had a revival production on Broadway in 1961.

12.
Birds Gotta Fly, Fish Gotta Talk
December 19, 1964

Created and Produced by
    Sherwood Schwartz
Written by Sherwood
    Schwartz, Austin
    Kalish, and Elroy
    Schwartz
Directed by Rod Amateau

The Castaways are decorating their Christmas tree with bamboo. But they stop what they're doing when the radio reports a navy weather plane has spotted them and a destroyer has been dispatched to rescue them. The Skipper and Gilligan remember their first day on the island.

FLASHBACK

The Skipper and Gilligan are glad to be there—wherever "there" is. The Howells demand to be taken to the nearest Hilton. The Professor tries to fix their transmitter so they can radio for help.

The Skipper finds a very tall coco palm and he suggests Gilligan climb it to get a view of the whole island. Gilligan eventually braves the heights and yells that he sees people and a boat. He slides down and runs off. He goes to the beach, but it's only their own passengers and their own boat he saw.

The Skipper and the Professor work on the transmitter while Gilligan goes to fish for their dinner. The Professor fixes the transmitter, but then it mysteriously disappears. They realize that Gilligan has accidentally hooked it with his fishing line and has cast it into the ocean.

THE PRESENT

The radio broadcast reports that the destroyer is nearing the Castaways' island. They all pack and get dressed up for departure and wait on the beach. Mr. Howell remembers how furious they all were with Gilligan that first day.

FLASHBACK

The Skipper and the Professor salvage all they can off the *Minnow*. They send Gilligan to start a fire. He louses up as always. The Skipper won't even let him help because he's bad luck. He says he's sorry that when they were in the navy, Gilligan saved him from a depth charge that broke loose on a destroyer.

Gilligan goes fishing again. In fact, he's nailed some huge ones, including the one that swallowed the radio. The Skipper hopes they'll catch the transmitter. They all talk into each fish Gilligan's caught, trying to find it, with the Professor listening in on the radio. They find the transmitter, which the Professor tries to fix. He gets it running and the Skipper radios a mayday. Gilligan's collecting firewood and drops all his logs onto the transmitter and crushes it.

THE PRESENT

The navy has still not arrived, but then the radio reports some people have been picked up. They weren't the *Minnow* passengers, but a group that had been stranded for eleven years.

When Ginger thinks Gilligan is rich, she suggests Hollywood will make a movie of his life starring her as his wife and Rock Hudson as Gilligan. Hudson was the

13.
Three Million Dollars More or Less
December 26, 1964

Created and Produced by
    Sherwood Schwartz

Written by Bill Davenport
and Charles Tannen
Produced and Directed by
Thomas Montgomery

Gilligan's been practicing his putting on the sly and when he gets into a putting contest with Mr. Howell, it turns into the bet of the century. They're still at it at 10:30 P.M. The bet has escalated to six million dollars. The Skipper puts a stop to it, but Gilligan's now worth the three million he won on the previous bet and everybody's anxious to be his best pal.

The Skipper tells Gilligan to look out for the change in the other Castaways because he's now wealthy. Of course, the Skipper's treating him differently too; he calls Gilligan "son."

Mr. Howell brings Gilligan the check and a lot of gobbledygook about income taxes. He suggests Gilligan would be better off, fiscally, if he accepts one of Mr. Howell's corporations. The Skipper comes in and finds out Howell gave Gilligan one of his oil companies which consists of two hundred acres in Dustbowl, Oklahoma. The Skipper, Mary Ann, Ginger,

number one leading man in films in 1964, thanks to a string of successful romantic comedies with Doris Day, including Send Me No Flowers *in 1964.*

Dawn Wells recalls an incident when she was filming another television show, long after Gilligan's Island *was off the air. "We were out on a location on a ship and a very young man about twenty-three was one of the boom operators and he was too shy to talk to me. People said, 'Dawn, he's had a crush on you forever.' And he wouldn't talk to me until the very last day and his name was Bam Bam and he was six foot three, and about two hundred and thirty pounds and he picked me up and put me on his lap and put his arms around me and said, "I just want you to know, you got me through puberty in the nicest of ways."*

and the Professor are angry with Mr. Howell for rooking Gilligan.

Then, on the radio, there's news of a huge oil strike on the Howell holdings in Dustbowl, Oklahoma. Gilligan gets the royal rush again. He plans the presents he'll buy for everyone, including a science lab for the professor, the state of Kansas for Mary Ann, and a boat for the Skipper. Now everybody gets greedy.

The title is a famous quote from Samuel Taylor Coleridge's The Rime of the Ancient Mariner, *"Water, water everywhere, and all the boards did shrink; water, water everywhere, nor any drop to drink." The epic poem was written in 1798 and concerns a man who kills an albatross after it leads his ship through a horrible storm. The mariner learns the error of his ways and journeys from land to land, teaching reverence for all God's creatures.*

14.
Water Water Everywhere
January 2, 1965

Created and Produced by
  Sherwood Schwartz
Written by Tom Waldman
  and Frank Waldman
Directed by Stanley Z.
  Cherry

The Professor's working on the garden and Gilligan's pumping water, but their spring seems to have dried up. The Castaways consolidate the fresh water they've got and start a rationing program. The Professor suggests they start looking for a place to dig a new well. The Skipper's got a new divining rod. It seems to work as it points out Mr. Howell's secret flask of water. At least it works until Gilligan breaks it.

That night, Gilligan guards the water supply. The Skipper marks the level on a stick. Mr. Howell distracts him while Lovey steals some water. Then Ginger hypnotizes him while Mary Ann steals some. The Skipper catches both Mrs. Howell and Mary Ann and chews them out. Gilligan's made a new divining rod, but he punches a hole in their communal water supply and spills all the remaining water.

The Howells do a rain dance. Gilligan's really depressed and writes a letter home about all his mistakes. He's interrupted by a frog with wet feet. He trails him. Mary Ann finds Gilligan's letter and thinks it's a suicide note and she and the Skipper go looking for him. Meanwhile, Gilligan follows the frog into an underground cave filled with water. He's excited, but can't find a way out.

Gilligan's little routine with the frog ("S'all right? S'all right.") brings to mind a ventriloquist/comedian named Señor Wences who appeared regularly on The Ed Sullivan Show *in the fifties and sixties. He did this routine with a very simple hand puppet, simply a lipstick mouth, hair, and eyes applied to his own hand.*

The title is based on an old joke which is too politically incorrect to tell today.

Alan Crosland, Jr., was a premier director of television. He shot many episodes of TV shows such as Ben Casey, 77 Sunset Strip, Alfred Hitchcock Presents, The Bionic Woman, Bonanza, Emergency!, Maverick, Mr. Lucky, The Outer Limits, Peter Gunn, Rawhide, The Six Million Dollar Man, The Virginian, Wonder Woman, *and* Voyage to the Bottom of the Sea.

When Ginger tells the Japanese soldier she'll make him a star, he asks about Robert Taylor, Robert Montgomery, and Lloyd Bridges, actors who were famous at the time of World War II. Robert Montgomery was a leading man in the thirties and forties, starring in

15.
So Sorry, My Island Now
January 9, 1965

Created by Sherwood
   Schwartz, Executive
   Producer
Produced by Jack Arnold
Written by David P.
   Harmon
Directed by Alan
   Crosland, Jr.
Guest
Vito Scotti as . . . .
. . . . Japanese Sailor

Gilligan's emptying his lobster traps when a barnacle-encrusted periscope sticks itself up in his face. He thinks it's a sea serpent.

What Gilligan saw is a one-man sub, driven by a Japanese sailor. The sailor docks and immediately captures Mr. Howell. He seizes Ginger next, then Mary Ann, the Professor, and Mrs. Howell. He locks them all in an ingenious bamboo jail (which he learned how to make from a John Wayne movie). The captives are amazed to learn the sailor's radio broke in 1942 and he has no idea World War

II is over. He was educated at U.C.L.A. (which is why he speaks English).

Meanwhile, the Skipper and Gilligan find the sub and realize what's happened. The Skipper notes that you read in the paper every year about Japanese sailors on remote islands who don't know the war's over. They decide to use the sub to sail to Hawaii for help, but it's tiny and the Skipper can't squeeze in. He pops Gilligan into the sub, but the directions are all in Japanese. He makes an abortive trip around the lagoon. They go looking for the sailor and the missing Cast-aways.

Here Comes Mr. Jordan *(the movie remade as* Heaven Can Wait *with Warren Beatty),* The Lady in the Lake, Private Lives, *and* Riptide. Bewitched*'s Elizabeth Montgomery was his daughter. Robert Taylor was billed as "The Man with the Perfect Profile" at MGM and competed with Clark Gable for prime roles. Taylor made films from the thirties well into the sixties, including* The Law and Jake Wade, A Yank at Oxford, Waterloo Bridge, The Crowd Roars, Tip on a Dead Jockey, Quo Vadis, Ivanhoe, *and* Camille. *Lloyd Bridges will soon do a new version of his syndicated hit series from 1957–1961,* Sea Hunt. *Bridges was signed in 1941 by Columbia Pictures and appeared in over twenty-five low-budget westerns and action pictures before becoming a star. Today* *he's known as the star of High Noon, Hot Shots, Airplane!, East of Eden, the miniseries Roots, and Honey, I Blew Up the Kid. He's father to film stars Jeff Bridges and Beau Bridges. Our Japanese sailor must have spotted Bridges in some of his first minor film roles!*

BOB DENVER

Bob Denver was kicked in the butt by the acting bug while a sophomore at Loyola University in Westchester, near the L.A. airport. His speech teacher twisted his arm to audition for a part in a school production of *The Caine Mutiny Court-Martial* and to Denver's horror, he got the part.

He performed it with the worst case of stage fright in recent history but the audience response kept him coming back for more. By the time he finished school, he chose acting as a career. During school and after, he had a lot of part-time and temporary jobs, including coaching, teaching, and working in manufacturing and for the post office.

"I delivered mail in the Pacific Palisades to Jerry Lewis and Mel Blanc and thought I was hot stuff. Boy, at 5:30 in the morning, delivering specials to Jerry Lewis's house is not a thing you want to do. 'What do you want?!' Mel Blanc's house you got Bugs Bunny, Porky Pig at the door."

It was while working this job that he got the call from 20th Century–Fox. His sister Helen worked there and had slipped his name on a list of actors to be called for a new TV series based on Max Shulman's best-selling book, *The Many*

Loves of Dobie Gillis. He managed to get a screen
test and when he went to the studio, the schedules were mixed up and the resulting confusion
convinced somebody he might be right for
Dobie's dumb pal, Maynard G. Krebs.

Denver did the screen test with Dwayne Hickman, whom he knew slightly from Loyola, and
it went very well, but he didn't hear anything for
months. Finally, a call came that he was in the
running. He got the part and shot the pilot in
1958. He did some research and put a lot of
authenticity into the beatnik character.

The pilot sold, and 20th started production on
the series in the spring of 1959. Denver quit his
teaching job (to the anger and consternation of
his students) and the post office job and signed
a studio contract.

Denver's student deferment had ended when
he finished college and he'd only shot three episodes of *Dobie Gillis* when he was drafted. Studio
pressure and the fact that Denver supported his
mother didn't faze the army and he was ordered
to report. Fox hired Michael J. Pollard to replace
Denver.

But Denver had broken his neck in 1956 and
it got him out. He dashed back to the studio,
which had already signed Pollard for thirty episodes. Leaving Bob in limbo for a couple of days,
20th finally decided to pay off Pollard and bring
Bob back. In the grueling schedule of the times,
they shot thirty-nine episodes of *Dobie Gillis* that
first season. Michael J. Pollard went to Broadway
and starred as Kim MacAfee's boyfriend Hugo in
Bye, Bye Birdie with Chita Rivera, Dick Van Dyke,
and Paul Lynde.

Dobie Gillis ran four years and when it finished
in the spring of 1963, Denver was out of work

just as his daughter Megan was born. He and his wife Maggie had a son, Patrick, as well as her son by a previous marriage, Kim. Several months later, Sherwood Schwartz called him and asked if he was interested in doing a pilot and he jumped at the chance.

"I met with Sherwood Schwartz and I said what the network said, 'It sounds good for one episode and maybe one more, but after that, it sounds pretty dull—seven people stuck on an island.' He said, 'No, we have guest stars.' I laughed and said, 'For instance?' 'Well, there's a surfer who takes a big tidal wave from Hawaii who surfs to the island and lands there.' And I said, 'Interesting, but now we have eight people on the island.' He says, 'No, no. A reverse tidal wave takes him back to Hawaii and he bangs his head on a rock and can't remember where he was.' And I said, 'I want to do the show. That I can understand.' It was just great."

After *Gilligan's Island* was unceremoniously canceled, Bob Denver went on to yet another series, *The Good Guys*, which is nearly forgotten today. He played Rufus Butterworth, a cab driver. The cast included veteran character actor Herb Edelman as a diner owner, Burt, and Joyce Van Patten as his wife. Burt and Rufus were long-time best friends and Rufus was a schemer who came up with hair-brained money-making schemes for the two of them. The show was mildly popular.

He found it a grueling experience, for though it was shot on the same soundstage as *Gilligan*, it was done before a live audience and when the taping is done each week, the cast spends hours and hours reshooting scenes and angles missed during the live taping. When it ended two years later, Denver was anxious to get out of L.A.

Denver immediately headed east and took over for Woody Allen on Broadway in *Play It Again, Sam* and never looked back. He and his wife Dreama moved to Kauai, then a Nevada desert, then to a West Virginian mountaintop, where they live today.

Denver still loves it. "Beautiful West Virginia, in the Poconos, in one of the hills. I think the retirees are going to find it soon. I live at the end of a dirt road. I'm up in the mountains. One day I opened the door and there was a fan who said, 'I drove a hundred and eight miles from Kentucky just to say hello to you.' I couldn't believe it. He said, 'And I respect your privacy.' And I said, 'What are you doing on my front porch?' He said, 'Oh, I'm sorry,' and he left. It's really beautiful and I just love it."

In addition to regional theatre and occasional appearances at a *Gilligan* event, he'd like to organize an organic cooperative farm in Princeton, start a chain of tropical putt-putt golf courses, and has formed a foundation named for his young son Colin to benefit the handicapped.

Most people think Denver and the cast made fortunes doing *Gilligan's Island*. Not true. "We all got paid off in two years. By '68, residuals were done. It's true. It'd be nice if we were collecting a nickel on every rerun, we'd be rich. It picks up more people every year because the two-, three-, four-, five-year-olds, it's new to them. And the parents get a half-hour break and sit down and watch with them. There's nothing in there that's offensive."

And Bob Denver's memories? "I really loved it. Doing *Gilligan* was like doing all the physical jokes I always wanted to do, falling down, running into the palm tree. I never hurt myself."

Credits

Broadway and Regional Theatre
Play It Again, Sam—Broadhurst Theatre
Murder at the Howard Johnson's—regional theatre
The Owl and the Pussycat—regional theatre

Films, TV series, Telemovies, and Specials
A Private's Affair 1959
The Many Loves of Dobie Gillis—series 1959–1963
Take Her, She's Mine 1963
For Those Who Think Young 1964
Gilligan's Island—series 1964–1966
Who's Minding the Mint? 1967
*Did You Hear the One About the Traveling Sales-
    lady?* 1968
The Sweet Ride 1968
The Good Guys—series 1968–1970
The Bob Goulet Show—variety special 1970
Dusty's Trail—series 1973
Far-Out Space Nuts—animated series
    1975–1977
Wackiest Wagon Train in the West 1977
Whatever Happened to Dobie Gillis?—pilot 1977
Rescue From Gilligan's Island—telefilm 1978
The "Castaways" on Gilligan's Island—telefilm
    1979
The Harlem Globetrotters on Gilligan's Island—
    telefilm 1981
The All-Star Salute to Mother's Day—special 1981
Scamps—pilot 1982
Gilligan's Planet—animated series 1982–1983
The Invisible Woman—pilot 1983
High School, U.S.A.—telefilm 1983
Back to the Beach 1987
Bring Me the Head of Dobie Gillis—telemovie
    1988

Guest-Starring Roles

The Roaring 20s "War with the Night Hawkers"
Maverick "The Deadly Image"
Tales of Wells Fargo "Kelly's Clover Girls"
87th Precinct "Out of Order"
Lawman "No Contest"
Joey Bishop Show "A Young Man's Fancy"
Surfside 6 "A Private Eye for Beauty"
Bonanza "The Way Station"
It's a Man's World "The Bravest Man in Corde-
    lla," "Chicago Gains a Number"
Hawaiian Eye "The Sign-Off"
Laramie "The Violent Ones"
Redigo "Papa-San"
Channing "Swing for the Moon"
The Invaders "Dark Outpost"
Wild Wild West "Night of the Headless Woman"
Perry Como
Farmer's Daughter "An Enterprising Young Man"
I Dream of Jeannie "My Son, the Genie"
The Andy Griffith Show
Bonanza "The Burning Sky"
The FBI "The Attorney"
Hagen "More Deadly Poison"
The Love Boat "The Judges," "Ticket to Ride,"
    "A Dress to Remember"
Fantasy Island "The Way We Weren't," "The
    Eagleman," "House of Dolls," "The Magic
    Camera," "Love Island"
Love, American Style "Love and the Cake,"
    "Love and the Hitchhiker"
Matt Houston "The Visitors"
Matlock "The Therapist"
Growing Pains "Carnival," "Broadway Bound"
Alf "Somewhere Over the Rerun" (rerun as
    "The Ballad of Gilligan's Isle")

Evening Shade
Roseanne "Sherwood Schwartz: A Tribute"

Autobiography

Gilligan, Maynard & Me, Citadel Press, 1993

Willie Gilligan

Gilligan is really the man with whom we'd all like to be stranded on an island. Who needs a millionaire who won't do any work and whose money is worthless? Or a self-absorbed movie star? Or a scientist who can't even build a boat? What you need is Gilligan, to dig the wells and build the huts and catch the fish and take sentry duty all night.

After all, he can mine gold, fly an old plane, do the laundry, make friends with the local apes, chimps, spiders, and birds. He's a great golf caddie, doesn't seem to mind running errands, and is generally agreeable. He'll take the top hammock and doesn't snore.

He reveres his family, remembers his friends, and is loyal and true to a fault. He's so tenderhearted, he can't even kill a bird when they're all starving. He doesn't want wealth or fame, he just wants to be himself. He'll follow his friends anywhere and will save your life if you're in danger. What more could anyone ask of a fellow Castaway?

16.
Plant You Now, Dig You Later
January 16, 1965

Mr. Howell knows all the legal terms, because he says he "watched Perry Mason for six years."

The most popular legal show ever, Perry Mason, starring Raymond Burr, Barbara Hale, and William Hopper, ran on CBS from 1957 to 1966 (not including the dozens of telemovies which were done later).

Mrs. Howell says Mr. Howell should be on The Defenders, *his legal form is so good.* The Defenders, *another CBS courtroom drama, starred E. G. Marshall and Robert Reed* (The Brady Bunch) *as father and son lawyers.*

Mr. Howell, while bowling, says "The family that bowls together, splits!"
This is a parody of a slogan used at the time by churches, "The family that prays together, stays together," which was widely parodied.

WHAT'S MISSING?
If you're watching this episode in syndication, one scene that is often cut are the scenes from the night after Gilligan finds the chest. Nobody can sleep

Created by Sherwood Schwartz, Executive Producer
Written by Elroy Schwartz and Oliver Crawford
Directed by Lawrence Dobkin

Gilligan finds a treasure chest while he's digging a barbecue for the Howells. The first problem is how to get it open. The Skipper tries everything: breaking it, sawing it, prying it. The Professor's away exploring, so he can't help.

The second problem is ownership of the chest. Mr. Howell claims that since Gilligan was working for him when he found it, he's the owner. Gilligan claims it. They decide to settle the ownership in a poker game, but the Professor returns and insists they hold a legal proceeding to determine ownership.

As they prepare for the hearing, Mr. Howell realizes he never paid Gilligan for the work on the barbecue. He tries to remedy this, but the Skipper, who's representing Gilligan, tells Gilligan not to take the money. Then each litigant tries to coerce the other and there's a great deal of spying and bribing going on. They all file charges against each other.

for curiosity about what's in the chest. Each of them tries to sneak down to work on the chest, but each one is caught.

17.
Little Island, Big Gun
January 23, 1965

Created by Sherwood Schwartz, Executive Producer
Produced by Jack Arnold
Written by Dick Conway and Roland MacLane
Directed by Abner Biberman
Special Guest Star
Larry Storch as . . . . Jackson Farrell
[Uncredited] Guests
K. L. Smith as. . . . . Farrell's Accomplice
Jack Sheldon as . . . . Lucky (Indigo Mob)
Louis Quinn as . . . . Hank (Indigo Mob)

Gangster Jackson Farrell lands on the island with the loot from a bank robbery. His accomplice takes their boat back into the shipping lanes so it will be boarded and

When Ginger tries to seduce the gun away from Farrell because they can "make beautiful music together," and Farrell tells her the music will be "And the Angels Sing" if she tries it, he's referring to the 1939 big-band standard by Johnny Mercer and Ziggy Elman. The song was popularized by Benny Goodman's orchestra and was used in the film, The Benny Goodman Story.

Louis Quinn, who plays one of the Indigo Mob gangsters, played racetrack tout Roscoe on 77 Sunset Strip *which ran from 1958 to 1964 on ABC. Quinn guest starred on many other television shows.*

The Indigo Mob gangsters are entranced with Ginger and one of them says, "Hello, Dolly," referring to the biggest smash hit musical in years which opened on Broadway in January 1964, starring Carol Channing.

searched. Then they can pick up Farrell (and the loot) and head to South America. The next morning, Gilligan smells the bacon Farrell is cooking and finds the gangster. Farrell claims to be a shipwrecked doctor (his clothes—and shoes—are drip-dry). He was heading for another island to rid it of tropical diseases.

Gilligan shows him how he shoots dates out of the trees with a bow and arrow, and accidentally shoots down the bag of loot Farrell's hidden. The gangster claims it is an endowment for a hospital.

The rest of the Castaways all buy Farrell's story. The Howells even offer to contribute to his hospital and the Skipper insists he take Gilligan's hammock. Then Gilligan hears about the robbery and Jackson Farrell on the radio. He tells the others and then Farrell hears a repeat of the news bulletin and he holds them all at gunpoint.

According to the map used in the opening, the location of the warhead test—and, therefore, the island—is about equidistant between

18.
X Marks the Spot
January 31, 1965

Created by Sherwood Schwartz, Executive Producer

Written by Sherwood
  Schwartz and Elroy
  Schwartz
Produced and Directed by
  Jack Arnold

Guests

Russell Thorson . . . .
. . . . General Bryan
Harry Lauter . Major Adams

A decision is made at the Pentagon. A new warhead will be tested in a remote section of the South Seas because "no people, no habitation." Meanwhile, Gilligan and the Skipper begin building a playroom. Later Ginger and Mary Ann are listening to the radio, and just as there's a news bulletin from Honolulu about the bomb test, the batteries die. The Skipper's got extra batteries but they're dead too. The Professor recharges them with sea water.

When the radio's fixed, they hear about "Operation Powderkeg," the test originating at Vandenburg AFB. The Professor and the Skipper figure out that ground zero is the Castaways' island.

Facing possible annihilation, the Castaways begin to apologize to each other for past slights and mistakes. Ginger's

Mexico City and Hilo, Hawaii, just above the equator. The radio bulletin says the test will be conducted at one hundred forty degrees latitude by ten degrees longitude.

Mary Ann's favorite radio program is Young Doctor Malone, an immensely popular radio soap opera which aired from November 20, 1939, until November 25, 1960. It ceased production on "the last day of radio soaps" when six long-running programs were all canceled.

Ginger mentions she played a nurse on Ben Casey, ABC's popular medical show starring Vince Edwards. It ran from 1961 through 1966.

We learn that the Howell family motto is: "Honesty, Fidelity, Integrity."

The colorizing on this episode as it's running on the Turner networks is off—the two Air Force officers in the Pentagon scenes wear identical uniforms (except for rank insignia), yet one has been tinted blue, one brown.

musings remind the Professor the military always sends out a search plane to check the area before bombing it. He'll signal it with the mirror he's been making for Mrs. Howell. The plane comes, but Gilligan breaks the mirror before they can signal. They use the shards. As the plane leaves the area, Mr. Howell calls out, "Come back, I'm your biggest taxpayer." They don't.

The Castaways listen to the missile launch and watch as it heads for the lagoon. It doesn't detonate. But it heads for the beach and stops on the sand. The Professor begins to disarm it, using Gilligan inside to execute his instructions. He clips the wrong wire and the missile takes off, scooting across the ground and spitting sparks. It heads off across the lagoon. The Castaways are planning memorials to Gilligan when he staggers back.

Yeah, this is the Kurt Russell, who went on to become the star of The Computer Wore Tennis Shoes, Escape From New York, Silkwood, Tango & Cash, and The Thing.

19.
Gilligan Meets Jungle Boy
February 6, 1965

Created by Sherwood
  Schwartz, Executive
  Producer

Produced by Jack Arnold
Written by Al Schwartz,
    Howard Merrill, and
    Howard Harris
Directed by Lawrence
    Dobkin

Guests

Kurt Russell as. .Jungle Boy

Gilligan hears what he thinks must be a wild monkey and is astonished to see a jungle boy swinging from tree to tree. Nobody believes him. Later, the boy finds him and wants to play catch. He can mimic Gilligan's speech, but can't understand English. They manage reasonably well with sign language and the boy shows Gilligan a small volcanic cone with hot steam hissing out.

Back at camp the Castaways finally see him. Mary Ann charms him first. They all want him to tell them how to get off the island but, of course, he speaks no English. The women try to teach him the basics, but fail. That night, Mrs. Howell's worried when the boy sleeps in a tree. She gives him Mr. Howell's teddy.

The next day, Gilligan shows the Professor and the Skipper the hot-air vent, which con-

Alan Hale, the Skipper, remembers seeing the boat used for the show's Minnow. "I don't know whether it's still there or not, but that boat for a long while was actually down at Wilmington. I went down personally to see it. Still had a hole in it. They weren't able to fix it down there either, so that kind of lets us off the hook."

tains either helium or hydrogen. The Professor suggests they use it for a hot-air balloon. They sew together everybody's raincoats and rig the balloon over the vent. It works very well.

Now comes the debate about who's going to go. The men draw straws and the Skipper wins. They cast him off but the Skipper breaks through the floor of the basket. The Professor figures out all the weight requirements and the boy is the only one light enough. But how's he going to tell the world about them?

The title refers to the legend of St. George and the Dragon. St. George is the patron saint of England, and has been popular since the Crusades. Scholars agree that he's a real historical character, probably based upon a martyr who lived about 303 A.D. The legend of St. George and the Dragon is merely a fable intended to show the triumph of good over evil.

20.
St. Gilligan and the Dragon
February 13, 1965

Created by Sherwood
Schwartz, Executive
    Producer
Produced by Jack Arnold
Written by Arnold and Lois
    Peyser
Directed by Richard
    Donner

The women decide to go off on their own, fed up with the

men making all the decisions and pushing them around. They build huts of their own. The men quickly get sick of doing their own cooking and cleaning, and try to think of ways to lure the women back. They finally decide to make a monster costume and scare them into coming back. But Ginger and Mary Ann overhear their plan and they're ready when the Skipper and Gilligan show up looking like a cross between a mammoth and a ficus bush. They beat it with sticks.

Gilligan ruins their laundry and Mr. Howell burns their dinner to ashes. The men all sleep in the same hut, and as they drift off, the Skipper pleads, "If women would just act the way we wanted them to . . ."

DREAM SEQUENCE

The Skipper dreams he is sultan and Ginger, Mary Ann, and Mrs. Howell do his every bidding. It's heaven. Mr. Howell dreams he's in a deluxe manicure parlor with Ginger, Mary Ann, and his wife treating him tenderly. Gilligan dreams he's a famous matador, tended by the three women as he prepares for the bull ring.

Back to reality, the men can't sleep. Gilligan suggests they tell the women they admit defeat and beg them to come back. They're not happy about it, and it turns out, neither are the women.

Denny Miller, who stars as the surfer in this episode, is married to Kit Smythe, the actress who played Ginger in the original pilot.

This was the age of surfing movies, started by Sandra Dee in Gidget *in 1959,* Beach Party *in 1963, and* Ride the Wild Surf *in 1964.* Gidget *became a television series starring then-unknown Sally Field in 1965, so audiences were familiar with the strange language of surfing:*

SURFER LINGO GLOSSARY

Gremmie—young, inexperienced surfer.

Gidget—a contraction of the words girl *and* midget *coined by Frederick Kohner in his novel which was the basis for the film and TV series.*

21.
Big Man on a Little Stick
February 20, 1965

Created by Sherwood
    Schwartz, Executive
    Producer
Produced by Jack Arnold
Written by Charles
    Tannen, Lou Huston,
    and David P. Harmon
Directed by Tony Leader
Guest
Denny Scott Miller . . . .
. . . . Duke Williams

The Castaways are astonished when a muscle-bound surfer rides into the lagoon and collapses on the beach. After he recovers, he tries to communicate with the Castaways, but his surfer lingo is a tad confusing. They make contact at last and learn he's Duke Williams and he caught a thirty-foot wave on Waimea Beach in Hawaii and here he is.

Shortly, the women are all

slobbering over the handsome hunk. He's equally entranced with Ginger and Mary Ann, but he's pretty dumb and when he comes on to her, Ginger's not very cooperative. "Believe me, Mary Ann, while we've been admiring his muscles, we've been ignoring his fangs."

The Castaways want to get Duke on his board and headed back to civilization—they're sick of him, and he's got the stamina to make it and send help. But he isn't thrilled about leaving Ginger and Mary Ann. So they come up with a plan. They let Duke "catch" them in other romantic situations. The Professor and Ginger talk about the stars with gusto and Mary Ann and Gilligan pretend to be besotted.

The next day, Duke goes out surfing, catches a wave, and he's on his way to Honolulu. The radio tells them the bad news. Duke got to Hawaii but has amnesia after hitting his head on a rock.

Hot Dogger—*surfer who takes risks.*
Riding the nose—*having your board on the front of the wave's crest (hanging ten is having your feet at the board's front).*
The tube—*when a wave is so large, it forms into a tunnel as it crests.*

Duke Williams makes the Castaways think of other Dukes. The "Duke who started World War I" was Archduke Ferdinand of Austria whose assassination in Sarajevo triggered the war.

The most famous surfing Duke was Duke Kahanamoku, a nearly legendary Hawaiian who won gold medals for the U.S. in the Olympiads of 1912 and 1920.

Note the bamboo backscratcher Mr. Howell has in his tropical drinks. At that time, the

Hawaiian Village Hotel in Honolulu created an infamous cocktail, the "Tropical Itch," served in a huge hurricane lamp–shaped goblet with a souvenir backscratcher sticking out. The drink was composed of five shots of various whiskeys and rums (including 151-proof Demarara rum) and a blend of tropical fruit juices. It had a lethal kick.

The title brings to mind "Diamonds are a Girl's Best Friend," which became a common expression and a song (by Leo Robin and Jule Styne) from a book, play, and movie, Gentlemen Prefer Blondes, *which all originated from a story by Anita Loos. The play (1949) made a star of Carol Channing. The film was made in 1953 and Marilyn Monroe and Jane Russell sang the song. The Gabor sisters made*

22.
Diamonds Are an Ape's Best Friend
February 28, 1965

Created by Sherwood Schwartz, Executive Producer
Written by Elroy Schwartz
Produced and Directed by Jack Arnold
[Uncredited] Guest
Janos Prohaska as . . . . . Ape

Gilligan thinks he's having a nightmare when he sees a gorilla in the hut window. The ape next visits the Howells and takes a diamond brooch from the bedside table. In the morning, Gilligan tries to shake a coconut loose for some milk for his pancakes and inadvertently disturbs the sleeping ape. Mr. Howell reports Mrs. Howell's missing brooch, implying one of the other Castaways stole it. He finally apologizes and offers a ten-thousand-dollar reward.

They're all searching for the brooch when Gilligan and the Skipper see the gorilla. Then it kidnaps Mrs. Howell. The Professor and Gilligan figure out where the gorilla might live and head off around the island. Meanwhile, Mrs. Howell is appalled at the gorilla's manners. The men do find them, but the gorilla won't let Mrs. Howell out of his cave.

The men try to get the upper hand, but the ape picks up the Skipper and tosses him in the brush. Since the ape already stole one of the women, Mr. Howell suggests they use Ginger and Mary Ann as bait and drop a net over the beast. He presents his case, but both the girls are too scared. But when he appeals to Ginger's career drive, she assents. Ginger vamps the gorilla as the men

the sentiment their life's work.

Gilligan gets syrup for their pancakes from a tree. After the disaster in episode number eight ("Goodbye Island") when the sap turned into a non-permanent glue which destroyed the Minnow, we must assume a better syrup has been found.

When Mr. Howell tells the gorilla he's a Harvard man and the gorilla attacks him, and Mrs. Howell notes the ape must be a Yale man, they're referring to the long-standing rivalry between the two Ivy League universities that began when they were both all-male institutions. A "Yale Man" frequently would have nothing to do with a "Harvard Man." This distinction blurred and the rivalry became more ritual than way of life when the schools admitted women in the seventies. This rivalry was still very strong in the sixties.

Anton M. "Tony" Leader directed films, TV movies, and many, many episodes of television series including Hawaii Five-O, The Virginian, Ironside, It Takes a Thief, I Spy, Lost in Space, Perry Mason, *and* Tarzan.

Gilligan talks about his uncle Ramsey, who was a guide in the Great War's (World War I) "lost" battalion.

get ready. The gorilla comes after her but then runs back to Mrs. Howell.

23.
How to Be a Hero
March 6, 1965

Created by Sherwood
  Schwartz, Executive
  Producer
Produced by Jack Arnold
Written by Herbert Finn
  and Alan Dinehart
Directed by Tony Leader
[Uncredited] Guest
Eddie Little Sky . . . as
  Headhunter

A headhunter sneaks onto the island, hiding his outrigger canoe. Gilligan's chasing butterflies when Mary Ann yells for help while swimming in the lagoon. The native watches as Gilligan dives in, but Gilligan can't swim either and the Skipper must save them both. Afterwards, Gilligan's feeling small and insignificant and the Howells are worried about him. Mrs. Howell talks to the Skipper and they decide Gilligan needs to feel like a hero.

The Skipper rigs up a fake

accident, pretending he's caught under a fallen tree. Ginger gives him groaning lessons and he's ready. Ginger gets Gilligan, who rushes (well, he does get hung up on the clothesline first) to the Skipper's aid. Unknown to all of them, the headhunter watches and he is about to attack the fallen Skipper when Gilligan and Ginger return. The Skipper extricates himself, then Gilligan gets stuck under the fallen tree.

The native again approaches when they all run to get the Professor. They rescue Gilligan who then sees the headhunter. Mrs. Howell thinks Gilligan is delusional and gives him a sedative. Later, he's asleep when he hears Mrs. Howell calling for help. He doesn't know it's another rigged rescue. She shows him a tarantula on the floor. He says it's a plain old beach spider and bashes it with the broom. But he bashes himself too and knocks himself out.

The Skipper plots a new rescue and this time, Gilligan overhears him tell Mary Ann and Ginger about the plan, which is for the Skipper to dress up like the headhunter Gilligan keeps talking about. Ginger thinks the idea's kind of dumb and later tells the head-hunter (who she thinks is the Skipper) and he captures them all and ties them to stakes.

What is the first thing each Castaway wants when he or she gets back to civilization? Mr. Howell plans to double the rents on their apartment buildings; Mrs. Howell plans to triple the rents; the Professor wishes for a soft bed; Ginger dreams of having her name in lights (Ginger Guggenheimer —"If my name's gonna be in lights, I want as many lights as I can get"); Gilligan and Mary Ann want to see their mothers; and the Skipper wants a steak and a beer.

Hans Conried worked extensively in films and television. He guest starred in nearly every television series of the fifties, sixties, and seventies, including I Love Lucy; U.S. Steel Hour;

24.
The Return of Wrongway Feldman
March 13, 1965

Created by Sherwood Schwartz, Executive Producer
Produced by Jack Arnold
Written by Lawrence J. Cohen and Fred Freeman
Directed by Gene Nelson
Special Guest Star
Hans Conried as . . . .
. . . . . . Wrongway Feldman

Wrongway Feldman returns (from episode number five) to the island and is greeted like a prodigal son. But he keeps changing the subject when they ask about rescue plans. He finally admits he didn't tell anyone about them. He says they're crazy to want to leave. Civilization stinks. He's settling permanently on the island.

He complains about all the steaks he ate in New York and

the pastries covered with chocolate, and drives the Castaways nuts. Mr. Howell tries his usual routine of bribery. But he hardly gets his proposal out when Feldman tells him the Howells' New York apartment building has the lowest rents in the city because they haven't been there to raise them.

Wrongway tells Ginger about her roommate Debbie Dawson's success. She's the toast of Broadway. The rest don't know what to do. Gilligan reminds them Wrongway taught him how to fly. But the Skipper and Professor don't think that's such a good idea. They try to think of a reason Wrongway would *have* to go back. The Skipper pretends he has appendicitis until Wrongway prepares to perform the operation himself. Then Gilligan pretends to have Bola Bola Fever and seems to convince Wrongway that he's truly ill.

The next morning, they find a note from Wrongway that makes them think he's gone for a doctor. Gilligan's glad—he was sick of faking the symptoms. The Castaways pack and wait at the airfield, dreaming of civilization. Wrongway returns. He's brought the Bola

Disneyland; Make Room for Daddy; Love that Bob; Maverick; Donna Reed; Adventures in Paradise; Bullwinkle; Have Gun, Will Travel; Love, American Style; Laverne & Shirley; Fantasy Island; *and* Lost in Space.

Bola syrup cure. He made sure no one saw him.

They come up with a fool-proof plan: Make Wrongway miserable with the kind of noise and hustle and bustle he wants to get away from. The Castaways hammer, pound, nail, and generally make a ruckus. They tell him everyone works—they're building a city. They run the man to a frazzle. Among the projects they assign to him are a freeway, a music center, and a slum clearance project. He's beat. And starving. He starts craving "real" food, not just coffee made from fish.

Joanna Lee produces and writes afterschool specials for young people. She also wrote the TV movies Mary Jane Harper Cried Last Night *and* The Waltons Thanksgiving Special.

The Tour d'Argent wasn't a real restaurant in New York. However, d'Argent translates from the French as "of money."

25.
The Matchmaker
March 20, 1965

Created by Sherwood
   Schwartz, Executive
   Producer
Produced by Jack Arnold
Written by Joanna Lee
Directed by Tony Leader

Mrs. Howell misses the social season, especially the weddings. She glances out the window and sees Gilligan carrying Mary Ann and has an inspiration. Planning a wedding would be just perfect! But Mary Ann and Gilligan just don't have any interest in each other. Mr. Howell tells his wife to forget it. But she insists he "work on" Gilligan. He does it, but without enthusiasm.

Mrs. Howell works on Mary Ann. Gilligan brings Mary Ann flowers. Ginger reminds her he's a "shy, frightened fawn." When Ginger talks to Gilligan around the issue of love, he thinks she's flirting with him. Then Gilligan tells the Skipper and Professor that Mrs. Howell picked the flowers and had him deliver them to Mary Ann, and he's realized it might be misinterpreted.

The Howells have a candlelight dinner for Gilligan and Mary Ann. She finds out about the flowers. Gilligan's real uncomfortable. But he's nice to her and the Howells return with some champagne. Mrs. Howell tells them it's the twenty-year anniversary of the night Thurston proposed at the Tour d'Argent restaurant on 47th Street. But they start disagreeing about silly little things and then it progresses to picking on each other's little

Very clever, Ms. Lee and/ or Mr. Schwartz!

Ginger reveals the name of another one of her cinematic gems, the movie, The Hula Girl and the Fullback. *We can assume she played the former.*

faults. Some ad for wedded bliss. Then the fight really starts. They end up not speaking.

Mrs. Howell tells Mr. Howell he has Leonard Bernstein's wrists and Mr. Howell wonders what the famous composer is using to conduct at Lincoln Center, which is the nonprofit center of cultural life in New York City, the home of the Metropolitan Opera, the New York Symphony, and several other theatres.

Longtime radio and television bandleader Lawrence Welk was known for his fractured English as well as his music. He began conducting most numbers with "A-one and a-two," which Mr. Howell imitates as he begins a number.

26.
Music Hath Charms
March 27, 1965

Created by Sherwood Schwartz, Executive Producer
Written by Al Schwartz and Howard Harris
Produced and Directed by Jack Arnold
[Uncredited] Guests
Paul Daniel, Russ Grieve, and Frank Corsentino as ..
.................Natives

Mrs. Howell is "hungry for music." She hears Gilligan pounding a rhythm on a tree stump and has an idea. They'll form their own symphony orchestra.

Somewhere across the waves—there is another island. The natives hear Gilligan practicing his drums and think they are enemy war drums.

Back on Gilligan's Island, Mrs. Howell has asked Mr. Howell to be the orchestra's conductor ("You have Leonard

Bernstein's wrists!"). The trouble is, the Skipper thinks *he* should be conducting. After all, he led the navy band on his destroyer for five years.

Mr. Howell is practicing Beethoven's *5th Symphony* and the Professor is making a flute. Then the Skipper arrives and asks who made Mr. Howell conductor. Mrs. Howell ends up leading their little group on a wild variety of homemade instruments. They practice "The Blue Danube" and it's not too bad until the Skipper blows his foghorn. Gilligan plays on a wide variety of interesting drums. Meanwhile, a horde of natives arrive in outriggers.

The Castaways flee to the other end of the island. They decide to try to convince the savages that they're all primitive gods. The Professor and Gilligan try to wow them with the radio. The natives are in awe until the battery dies. They capture the Professor. The Skipper tries to dazzle the natives with the flashlight next. But those batteries are dead, too. The natives capture the Skipper.

The Castaways copy a battle plan from Beau Geste, a novel by Percival Christopher Wren, a British soldier and adventurer who spent many years in India and wrote a number of tales about the French Foreign Legion. Beau Geste was his most popular novel and it was later dramatized on stage and screen. The story concerns three brothers who join the Foreign Legion and die defending a desert fort from marauding Arabs. It was first made into one of the best-remembered silent films in 1926 starring Ronald Coleman. A remake in 1939 starred Gary Cooper and opened with the famous scene of the dead soldiers propped up to look like an army defending the desert fort. An inferior 1966 remake starred Telly Savalas and Guy Stockwell, notable only for the fact that the story was given a happy ending. Beau Geste is also one of

27.
New Neighbor Sam
April 3, 1965

Created by Sherwood
   Schwartz, Executive
   Producer
Produced by Jack Arnold
Written by Charles Tannen
   and George O'Hanlon
Directed by Thomas
   Montgomery

Gilligan hears voices in the jungle. He listens as two men plot a murder. He takes the Skipper to hear the voices. They tell the others, who are convinced they'll all be killed. The Professor figures the plotters must have arrived by boat, which the Castaways could steal. He and Mr. Howell and the Skipper try to find the gangsters' camp. Gilligan is sent back to set up a booby trap to protect the women. The men hear the gangsters' voices coming from a cave. The discussion is about killing someone and a jewel theft and their boat. The men go back to camp to formulate a plan.

Ginger suggests they adopt the plan from the movie, *Beau Geste*. They plan to stuff Mr.

GILLIGAN'S ISLAND 93

Howell's clothes so it looks like they have more men. This accomplished (it looks like the attack of the elephant people with long-necked gourds as heads), the Castaways take a position behind the dummies and watch for the gangsters. A great rustling in the bushes heralds their arrival. A parrot marches out and announces his name is Sam.

Sherwood Schwartz's favorite books.

The title brings to mind the 1964 movie Good Neighbor Sam, *starring Jack Lemmon. It was based on a popular novel by Jack Finney, who wrote the classic time-travel novel,* Time and Again, *and* Invasion of the Body Snatchers.

28.
They're Off and Running
February 2, 1965

Gilligan names the Skipper's turtle after his friend from home, Rex Stoneseifer.

Created by Sherwood Schwartz, Executive Producer
Written by Walter Black
Produced and Directed by Jack Arnold

The Castaways hold a turtle race. Mr. Howell's turtle beats the Skipper's handily. For the thirty-ninth time. The combatants pledge to hold another race in a few days, but the Skipper moans that he's got nothing left to wager. Mr. Howell has won it all. Mr. Howell

The title brings to mind Hollywood Park, a Southern California horse racing track, which used a catchy jingle in its radio and television ads during the sixties and seventies. Its first line was "They're off and running at Hollywood Park."

muses that Mrs. Howell would really like a houseboy—after all, she has many servants at home. He says he'll wager his yacht against Gilligan's services as a houseboy.

Gilligan insists that the Skipper take Mr. Howell's bet. He does, then Mr. Howell finds out the Skipper's turtle likes carrots and buys up every plant in Mary Ann's vegetable garden.

The Skipper orders Gilligan to find something the turtle likes as well as carrots. They try seaweed, grass, and plants. Nothing works. They try moss and the turtle likes that.

The race commences but the turtle's so full of moss, it can't move. Mr. Howell's turtle wins. Later, Gilligan appeals to Mr. Howell's better nature, which doesn't work, and offers his most prized possession—his Boy Scout knife—which does.

That night, Mrs. Howell switches the turtles in their pens to "make Thurston be the kind of man he really is, despite himself." Then Mr. Howell switches them, also for noble motives. Gilligan sees him and tells the Skipper. But the Skipper only wants to win honorably. They switch them back. Gilligan wakes Mr. Howell (and his teddy) to tell him. But Mr. Howell orders Gilligan to switch them again.

The next day, the Howells' speedy turtle with the "H" on his back wins, to everyone's dismay. Later, Mr. Howell asks the Skipper to choose which of his hands has the pebble in it. The Skipper loses but Mr. Howell says he's giving Gilligan's services back anyway. Gilligan's lousy washing and ironing is ruining his wardrobe.

29.
Three to Get Ready
April 17, 1965

Created by Sherwood Schwartz, Executive Producer
Written by David P. Harmon
Produced and Directed by Jack Arnold

Gilligan finds a large, shiny stone while digging. The Skipper insists it's the legendary "Eye of the Idol" and the Professor says it's a common quartz cat's eye. The Skipper is sure the stone means he's got three wishes before sundown.

A joke is made confusing yoga and Yogi Berra (for whom the Hanna-Barbera cartoon bear was named), who was a legendary baseball player with the New York Yankees from 1946 until 1963. His 358 home runs set a record for a catcher. He later managed the Yankees and the New York Mets and was elected to the Baseball Hall of Fame in 1972.

The title refers to the old nursery rhyme, "One for the money, two for the

show, three to get ready,
and four to go."

Mr. Howell's expression
"Heavens to Fulton
Fish" refers to the Fulton
Fish Market, a famous
wholesale emporium on
the docks in New York
City, now part of the
renovated South Street
Seaport.

Gilligan takes it and wishes for a gallon of ice cream. He runs to the lagoon where a five-gallon container of chocolate ice cream (still frozen) drifts in.

Gilligan tries to figure out what else to wish for and it's making him nuts. Everybody tries to help. Mr. Howell wants him to practice yoga, Ginger tries massage, the Skipper tries role-playing. While Gilligan stands on his head, Mr. Howell steals the stone from him. Mr. Howell wishes for twenty billion dollars. Nothing happens. He keeps lowering the amount, but nothing happens. The Skipper says it only works for the one who found it. While demonstrating, Gilligan wishes for vanilla ice cream, it comes floating up and he's wasted the second wish. But he'll use the third wish to get them off the island. Then Gilligan loses the stone.

When Mrs. Howell says
there are some things
money can't buy, and Mr.
Howell says, "May J. P.
Morgan have mercy on
your soul," he refers to the
real wizard of Wall Street,
John Pierpont Morgan

30.
Forget Me Not
April 24, 1964

Created by Sherwood
   Schwartz, Executive
   Producer
Written by Herbert
   Margolis

Produced and Directed by Jack Arnold

Gilligan and the Skipper are working on a signal tower because the radio reports the navy's planning maneuvers in the area. Gilligan accidentally knocks the Skipper unconscious and when he comes to, he has amnesia. Gilligan alerts the Professor. The Skipper's not himself. He leers at Ginger and bites her neck. Everyone's worried, partly because he's the only one who knows how to signal with semaphore flags.

The Professor reads up and finds amnesia's still a medical mystery. Perhaps another blow on the head. . . . The Howells decide to take care of that but brain Gilligan instead when he switches hammocks with the Skipper. Mrs. Howell comes in to try again, but they've switched back and Gilligan gets it yet again. The Professor tries hypnosis, but when regressed, the Skipper sees the Castaways as small children too. The Professor tries again, but the Skipper thinks it's World War II and the Castaways are all Japanese soldiers. He flees and hides.

(1837–1913). Morgan was a second-generation banker and founded his own firm, which became one of the most powerful banks in the world. He helped found U.S. Steel, created the first combined British/American Atlantic shipping line, saved several major railroads, and was the principal donor of the Metropolitan Museum of Art. When he died, his estate was valued at more than $69 million. His son, J. P. Morgan, Jr., organized a hundred-million-dollar fund to bail out New York City, which found itself in financial ruin at the start of World War I. Then the house of Morgan worked with the British and American governments to coordinate all sources of industrial supply for the war effort.

ALAN HALE, JR.

"I knew from the outset the two characters that were the comedy base for the show were the Skipper and Gilligan," says Sherwood Schwartz. "Gilligan in my mind was always inept, thin, scrawny. . . . Now, when you have this kind of sympathetic character who's always doing something wrong, the big heavy, his superior, was going to bawl him out for everything he did wrong, which meant every step of the way. Somehow I had to find a man who, big, gruff, and vigorous though he was and would have to be, nevertheless you would love him because there was no room for hatred on this island. And their problems were engineered by the fact that they were on the island and I wanted everybody to be sympathetic. So I had to find somebody to play the Skipper who was absolutely a teddy bear of a man. And that the audience would immediately know no matter how he yelled or beat Gilligan, that he really loved him underneath it all. And the search for that man was very, very difficult."

"When I [first] saw Alan Hale, it was in a restaurant. I had tested fifty different men with Bob. Nobody measured up when it came to a certain test scene that was written specifically to weed

out those that turned evil or dark when they
yelled and browbeat Gilligan. One night, my wife
and I were in a restaurant and I looked across a
crowded room—like the song says—and there
was Alan Hale, who had never been in to be
tested. He was in a Civil War uniform, which may
sound surprising, but the restaurant was behind
Fox Studios, so apparently he was having dinner
then going back to work.

"So I could hardly wait until the next morning
to call his agent to talk about Alan being in the
show. And the next morning, I did call Alan's
agent and said I would very much like to discuss
Alan Hale. They said 'Fine,' and I asked if he was
available for a series and they said 'Yeah, but
right now he's in a movie.' I asked if I could talk
to him and they said he's in St. George, Utah. I
said I just saw him last night in Hollywood. They
said, 'That was last night. He left at six this morning for Utah and is going to be there for a couple
of weeks to finish the movie'—an Audie Murphy
western. Now St. George, Utah, is at the bottom
of a canyon and the only way to get to it is by
horseback. And the complications of just getting
a script to Alan Hale by horseback down the canyon . . .

"Shooting in Hollywood means shooting six
days a week and that meant that there was only
one possible Sunday where I could test Alan Hale
with Bob Denver. That meant that Sunday, I had
to keep the CBS facilities open, which took some
doing. Alan Hale, in order to test for the part of
the Skipper on *Gilligan's Island*, got his friend
Skip Homier to get some horses and together
they came up from the bottom of St. George up
the trail to the highway where Alan Hale hitched
a ride to Las Vegas, took a plane to Hollywood,

did the test, got back on a plane, hitched a ride back to where Skip Homier was waiting with Alan Hale's horse, and took the two of them back down to finish the picture. Nothing is easy."

Because Alan Hale, Jr., resembled his father so closely, it always seems as though he was in films forever. He actually made his debut in *Wild Boys of the Road* in 1933. His father, who was in over a hundred films, changed his name from Rufus Edward MacKahan to Alan Hale and his son was named Alan Hale MacKahan. He dropped the last name and added a jr. when he began acting.

The six-foot-two Hale moved from juvenile to adult roles after 1940 and acted in some memorable films, including *It Happens Every Spring*, a charming movie where a science professor invents a substance that makes wood repel baseballs and becomes a star pitcher. Hale also appeared in *The West Point Story*, *Springfield Rifle*, *Destry*, *Advance to the Rear*, and *Johnny Risk*.

Hale made a lot of westerns, playing mostly good-guy sidekicks as well as appearing on all the major TV westerns including *Cheyenne*, *Maverick*, *Gunsmoke*, *Wanted: Dead or Alive*, and *Rawhide*.

Hale served in the coast guard during World War II and made several anti-Hitler propaganda films as well as a number of movies which addressed the problems and joys of the vast numbers of returning servicemen.

Up Periscope is one of the most exciting submarine movies ever made and Hale costarred in it with James Garner and he appeared with Lana Turner and Jeff Chandler in *The Lady Takes a Flyer*.

The medium where Alan Hale, Jr. surpassed his father (who died in 1950) was television. He was a natural TV actor, and made dozens and dozens of guest-star appearances on everything from the early anthology shows in the fifties to eighties sitcoms. He made a number of pilots and a couple of series but nothing clicked until *Gilligan's Island*.

His universal recognition as the Skipper was his joy. Though typecast like the others after the show finished, he seemed to thrive on the identification and used it to make frequent visits to children's hospitals and to start a successful seafood restaurant on Los Angeles's La Cienega Restaurant Row, Alan Hale's Lobster Barrel.

There was little that seemed to delight him more than making the rounds of the restaurant, making each diner feel like part of his family, and the Skipper's booming laugh was a constant dinner companion. He said, "Nonsense—that's one of the ingredients that made the show so successful. People do need nonsense. You know, through all the years . . . going all over the world, people reach out and they have to touch you. There's a genuine fondness for the show."

In later years, he ran a travel agency and had plans for several other ventures when he passed away on January 2, 1990, at the age of sixty-eight. Hale was married to Naomi Hale and had four children and three grandchildren.

Hale had little time for the critics of *Gilligan's Island*. "Every knock was a boost. The more people read about how bad it was, the more they liked it."

Credits

Films, TV Specials, Series and Pilots
Wild Boys of the Road—1933
I Wanted Wings—1940
All-American Coed—1941
Watch on the Rhine—1943
Sweetheart of Sigma Chi—1946
It Happened on 5th Avenue—1947
Sarge Goes to College—1947
Spirit of West Point—1947
One Sunday Afternoon—1948
Music Man—1948
It Happens Every Spring—1949
Rim of the Canyon—1949
Riders of the Sky—1949
The Whipped—1950
The Gunfighter—1950
Kill the Umpire!—1950
The West Point Story—1950
The Underworld Story—1950
The Blazing Trail—1950
Short Grass—1950
Home Town Story—1951
Sierra Passage—1951
Honeychile—1951
The Big Trees—1952
At Sword's Point—1952
And Now Tomorrow—1952
Lady in the Iron Mask—1952
Springfield Rifle—1952
Arctic Flight—1952
Man Behind the Gun—1952
Trailblazers—pilot, 1952
Biff Baker, U.S.A.—series, 1952–1953
Trail Blazers—1953
Captain John Smith and Pocahontas—1953

Captain Kidd and the Slave Girl—1954
Silver Lode—1954
Rogue Cop—1954
The Law vs. Billy the Kid—1954
Destry—1954
Young at Heart—1954
The Iron Glove—1954
Many Rivers to Cross—1955
The Sea Chase—1955
A Man Alone—1955
Indian Fighter—1955
The Killer is Loose—1956
Canyon River—1956
The Cruel Tower—1956
Battle Rhythm—1956
True Story of Jesse James—1957
Affair in Reno—1957
All Mine to Give—1957
Casey Jones—series, 1957
The Lady Takes a Flyer—1958
Johnny Risk—pilot, 1958
Up Periscope—1959
Thunder in Carolina—1960
The Long Rope—1961
The Mighty O—pilot, 1962
The Crawling Hand—1963
Advance to the Rear—1964
Bullet for a Badman—1964
The Swingin' Maiden—1964
Company of Cowards—1964
Gilligan's Island—series, 1964–1966
Hang 'em High—1968
Dead Heat—1968
Tiger by the Tail—1969
There Was a Crooked Man—1969
The Giant Spider Invasion—1975
Rescue From Gilligan's Island—telefilm, 1978

The North Avenue Irregulars—1979
The "Castaways" on Gilligan's Island—telefilm, 1979
The Fifth Musketeer—1979
When the West was Fun—variety special, 1979
The Harlem Globetrotters on Gilligan's Island—telefilm, 1981
Gilligan's Planet—animated series, 1982–1983
Johnny Dangerously—1984
Hambone & Hillie—1984

Guest-Starring Roles

Fireside Theatre
Wild Bill Hickok "Hepsibah," "Johnny Deuce," "Hands Across the Border"
The Loretta Young Theatre "Son, This is Your Father"
Public Defender "The Hitchhiker"
Navy Log "The Pollywog of Yosu"
Crossroads
Matinee Theatre "The Big Guy"
The Millionaire "The Story of Professor Amberson Adams"
Cheyenne "Hired Gun," "Road to Three Graves"
Wanted: Dead or Alive "Shawnee Bill"
Northwest Passage "The Redcoat"
Bat Masterson "A Personal Matter"
Restless Gun "Incident at Bluefield"
Colt .45 "The Saga of Sam Bass"
Bronco "Bodyguard," "A Sure Thing"
The Texan "Dangerous Ground," "End of Track," "Buried Treasure," "Captive Crew," "Showdown," "Widow of Pardise"
Man from Blackhawk "The Three Thousand Dollar Policy"
The Alaskans "Partners"

M Squad "Two Days for Willy"

Johnny Ringo "Reputation for Murder"

Maverick "The Deadly Image," "The Troubled Heir"

Walt Disney Presents "Moochie of Pop Warner Football"

The Outlaws "The Waiting Game"

Adventures in Paradise "The Serpent," "Captain Bucher"

Acapulco "The Gentleman from Brazil"

Hawaiian Eye "Dragon Road"

Gunsmoke "Minnie," "Champion of the World," "Jubilee"

G.E. Theater "Louise and the Horseless Buggy"

The Jim Backus Show "The Texas Millionaire"

Whispering Smith "The Idol"

Andy Griffith Show "The Farmer Takes a Wife"

Hazel "The Burglar in Mr. B's PJs," "Hazel Scores a Touchdown"

Rawhide "Incident of the Woman Trap," "The Bosses' Brothers"

Follow the Sun "The Irresistible Miss Bullfinch"

Frontier Circus "The Inheritance"

Route 66 "Narcissus on an Old Red Fire Engine"

Hondo "Hondo and the Death Dive"

Daktari "A Man's Man"

The Good Guys [three episodes]

The Flying Nun "The Great Casino Robbery"

Wild Wild West "Night of the Sabatini Death"

Green Acres "A Prize in Each and Every Package"

Here Come the Brides "The Fetching of Jenny"

Land of the Giants "Our Man O'Reilly"

Lucy Show "Lucy and Wally Cox"

Alias Smith and Jones "The Girl in Boxcar Number Three"

Men from Shiloh "Tate, Ramrod"

The Paul Lynde Show "Everything You Wanted to Know About Your Mother-in-Law *** But Were Afraid to Ask"

Marcus Welby, M.D. "In My Father's House"

O'Hara, U.S. Treasury "Operation: Moonshine"

McMillan and Wife "The Fine Art of Staying Alive"

Fantasy Island "The Racer," "Rogues to Riches"

Flying High "Palm Springs Weekend"

Sweepstakes

The Love Boat "The Harder They Fall," "Meet the Author"

Simon and Simon "Rough Rider Rides Again," "For Old Crime's Sake"

Matt Houston "The Yacht Club Murders"

Murder, She Wrote "Trial By Error"

Magnum, P.I. "All Thieves on Deck"

Blacke's Magic "Vanishing Act"

Crazy Like a Fox "Just Another Fox in the Crowd"

The New Gidget "Gilligidge Island"

Growing Pains "This Is Your Life"

Law and Harry McGraw "Gilhooey's is History"

Alf "Somewhere Over the Rerun" (rerun as "The Ballad of Gilligan's Isle")

The Skipper

The Skipper is the glue that holds the Castaways together. He settles petty disputes, and is the only outdoorsman in the bunch though his career has been spent mainly at sea in the South Pacific. After playing football in high school, he joined the navy and served on a number of vessels, including several destroyers and a subchaser near Guadalcanal.

It was on one of these that the hapless Gilligan saved the life of Captain Jonas Grumby (we learn the Skipper's real name in the first season's Christmas episode) by knocking away a loose depth charge rolling down the deck toward the Skipper. He's superstitious, as are many seafaring men, and those fears get him into trouble frequently. But as a friend, shipwreck companion, and mediator, there's no match.

31.
Diogenes, Won't You Please Go Home?
May 1, 1964

Created by Sherwood
    Schwartz, Executive
    Producer
Produced by Jack Arnold
Written by David P.
    Harmon
Directed by Christian Nyby
Guest
Vito Scotti as . . . .
. . . . Japanese Sailor

Gilligan drives the Skipper nuts by locking something in the cupboard in his hut. When the Skipper breaks in that night, it's empty. Ginger and Mary Ann think he's hiding pearls. The Professor and the Skipper think it's diamonds or rubies. Mr. Howell thinks it's an

The title combines two very divergent stories. Diogenes was the original cynic (about 412–323 B.C.) who supposedly went around in the daytime carrying a lamp, searching for an honest man. It's also reported that he lived in a tub. The allusion in this title is, of course, to truth.

"Bill Bailey, Won't You Please Come Home" by Hughie Cannon was an early ragtime classic, first published in 1902, and is supposedly based on fact. The real Bailey was a vaudevillian who worked with a partner, Cowan. Locked out of his apartment one night by

his wife, he borrowed money for a hotel room from Cannon, a song and dance man at the time. Bobby Darin had a huge hit with the song in 1960, boosting its popularity even further.

When Mr. Howell says there isn't much difference between a bottle of Scotch and a diary to Dean Martin, he's referring to the famous singer, notorious (perhaps apocryphally) for his alcoholic consumption. Martin's variety show was a popular staple of weekly television from 1965 to 1974.

Christian Nyby is a legendary director who helmed films as diverse as The Thing *in 1952,* Operation C.I.A. *in 1965 and* Devlin Connection *in 1982. He worked extensively in television, directing episodes of* Perry Mason, I Spy, Rawhide, The Twilight Zone, *and* Emergency!

eight-year-old bottle of Scotch. None of them will let him out of their sight. Gilligan finally confesses to the Professor he's hiding his diary of their life on the island. Then everyone starts to worry about what he might have written about each of them.

The Skipper tries to bribe him with a job on the new ship he'll get when they're rescued. Ginger offers to get a movie made of his diary, with him as her romantic leading man. Mr. Howell promises him he'll publish it. In frustration, Gilligan dumps it in the lagoon, and everybody's watching. They all instantly start treating him badly, now that they think it doesn't matter.

Gilligan tells the Skipper his version of the time the Japanese sailor took them captive (episode number thirteen "So Sorry, My Island Now"). Gilligan remembers saving the others himself. The Skipper's amazed and says he's written down *his* version of the same event—where *he's* the hero. Mr. Howell's done the same thing. So has Ginger.

32.
Physical Fatness
May 8, 1965

Created by Sherwood
   Schwartz, Executive
   Producer
Produced by Jack Arnold
Written by Herbert Finn
   and Alan Dinehart
Directed by Gary Nelson

Gilligan interrupts the Professor at a chemical experiment. He's working on a phosphorescent dye marker similar to the ones the navy uses for distress signals. Planes flying anywhere near the island will see it, day or night. Gilligan's entranced with the "shiny junk." He tells the Skipper, who's overjoyed at their imminent rescue. Gilligan asks him what he'll do after they're rescued. The Skipper figures he'll be out of business with the *Minnow* wrecked, so he'll probably go back into the navy. Gilligan offers to join him, but Skipper's worried he's getting overweight. He keeps splitting his pants. The navy manual says a man six foot three should weight 199. He's at 221. He can't get back into the navy.

The Professor figures he'll

Anyone who doubts the notion that people believe what they see on television has only to hear this story from series creator Sherwood Schwartz. "I was in my office preparing one of the new shows and Commander Doyle of the coast guard phoned me and asked if he could come see me about something. Well, you don't say no to a commander of the coast guard. I said sure. He came in and put a stack of maybe sixteen to eighteen telegrams on my desk and said, 'Why don't you read some of these.' I picked up one of the telegrams and they all said essentially the same thing, 'The United States sends billions of dollars to help the far-flung parts of the world. We have now seen, for weeks, seven Americans stranded on a little island.' These people believed it. They don't believe things until *they see them on television."*

have the dye marker ready in about a week. The Skipper insists that Gilligan keep him from eating anything, but at the next meal, when Gilligan gives him one piece of lettuce, he's so hungry that that night, he can't sleep. "I've tried counting sheep but they keep turning into lamb chops."

The Skipper runs ten laps around the island. Then Ginger leads him in the exercises of the stars, but they're a little, well, feminine. Mrs. Howell gives him her reducing pills. At the next weigh-in, he's down to 201 pounds. Gilligan gets on and *he's* five pounds underweight for the navy. Ginger and Mary Ann fatten him up while the Skipper goes mad with envy.

When Mr. Howell suggests he and Gilligan might spend their days together like Tweedledee and Tweedledum, he's referring to the rotund servants of the Red Queen in Lewis Carroll's Alice in Wonderland.

In addition to his extensive television credits, Jack

33.
It's Magic
May 15, 1965

Created by Sherwood Schwartz, Executive Producer
Written by Al Schwartz and Bruce Howard
Produced and Directed by Jack Arnold

Gilligan catches something huge but when the Skipper comes to help him reel it in, it's a box. They haul it up and the crate says RAFT on it and they jump for joy. But they didn't see the whole stencil. It really says THE GREAT RAFTINI, and it's a magician's trunk. Ginger grabs his cape and does a great trick (she mentions she worked as a magician's assistant early in her career). The Professor thinks these magic tricks could save them if the headhunters come back. He suggests they all learn several tricks.

Mr. Howell dons Raftini's tux and practices with Mrs. Howell's help. Gilligan comes in to show them his trick and ends up handcuffed to Mr. Howell. They eventually get loose and Ginger shows them the trick. Gilligan ruins breakfast by pulling the tablecloth off the Castaways' dining table. The Skipper orders him to take all the tricks into the supply hut. Gilligan overhears everyone talking about his mistakes and later, when Ginger uses him in a trick and makes him disappear, he decides not to come back.

Everyone's devastated and they immediately launch a

Arnold directed one of the best bad movies of all time, High School Confidential!, a 1958 drug exposé done in the style of the sleaziest magazine of the fifties, Confidential. The cast included Jerry Lee Lewis, Jan Sterling, Russ Tamblyn, Jackie Coogan, and Mamie Van Doren. Arnold's wildly eclectic film career is peppered with classic schlock, blaxploitation, sex comedies, 3-D, and monster movies, including The Creature From the Black Lagoon, Girls in the Night, Black Eye, Tarantula, Space Children, The Lively Set, Monster on the Campus, It Came From Outer Space, and Revenge of the Creature. His more conventional work includes The Mouse That Roared, The Lady Takes a Flyer, Bachelor in Paradise, and Richard Matheson's sci-fi classic, The Incredible Shrinking Man.

search for Gilligan. The Skipper sees a sign, NO BODY IZ HOME, and believes Gilligan's in a nearby cave with a tiny opening. The Skipper apologizes and Gilligan comes out. Gilligan says he's got feelings too. And he's not going back to the others. Later, the Howells find him and Mr. Howell has a fistful of cash for him. Mr. Howell thinks they'll make great carpeting and tosses them into the cave. That night, the Skipper brings Gilligan some dinner, the Howells bring Mr. Howell's teddy, a blanket, and more food and later, so do the Professor, Ginger, and Mary Ann.

Dubov says "phooey" to the idea of Salvador Dali (1904–1989—an eccentric artist who was born in Spain. Dali invented the Surrealistic style, combining realistic objects in bizarre forms, such as perfectly-drawn pocket watches melting on a hellish landscape.

34.
Goodbye Old Paint
May 22, 1965

Created by Sherwood
  Schwartz, Executive
  Producer
Written by David P.
  Harmon
Produced and Directed by
  Jack Arnold
       Guest
Harold J. Stone as . . Dubov

The Castaways discover a famed Russian artist, Alexandri Gregor Dubov, on the island. He'd prefer they all leave as soon as possible. He pushes everybody around, but he's quite happy to gobble down as much of Mary Ann's cooking as she'll give him. He's been there for ten years, after he and the world decided they didn't like each other. He claims to have a transmitter to call a boat any time he wants. Trouble is, he doesn't want to right now.

Mr. Howell has a plan. He suggests they inspire Dubov to paint Ginger. Then they convince him it's brilliant and worth tons of money. Dubov will decide he's ready for the world. He is inspired, but Ginger claims she's saving herself for Salvador Dali. But he's determined and she gives in with grace. He decides to paint her as a Bali dancer. He finishes and after Ginger gets through screaming (it's wildly abstract), they convince him he's great. But then, Gilligan spills the beans and tells Dubov about their plan. Dubov has fits and stalks off.

After he learns Gilligan flunked art in third grade and

Ginger says she doesn't care if Dubov is Leonardo da Vinci (1452–1519), a Florentine painter, sculptor, architect, engineer, and scientist. He was the founder of the Classic style of painting and his masterpieces include "The Last Supper" and the "Mona Lisa." He lived and worked in Florence and Milan.

Other artists mentioned in this episode include:
Pablo Picasso (1881–1973)—the Spanish-born founder of the abstract movement who moved to Paris in 1900. He also founded the Cubist and Neoclassic styles and invented collage, the technique of pasting objects onto a canvas.
Marc Chagall (1887–1985)—a Russian-born French painter who used floating, dreamlike figures

in his work, which frequently had Russian folk art and Jewish themes. He was also known for his abstract stained-glass windows.

Henri de Toulouse-Lautrec (1864–1901)— a French painter and graphic artist best known for his posters of the denizens of the Moulin Rouge. A childhood accident left him permanently crippled. His life was the subject of a film, Moulin Rouge, which starred José Ferrer.

Dubov's idea of feminine perfection is Mae Busch, an American silent film star who later costarred as a foil for Laurel and Hardy in many of their short films.

Note: Guest star Harold J. Stone is uncredited on the Columbia House videotape of this episode.

is therefore unspoiled enough for abstract art, Mr. Howell comes up with another plan. He'll set Gilligan up as a rival genius. This should inspire Dubov to become so jealous he'll demand they go to civilization to have critics decide who's the greater genius. Mary Ann lures Dubov back with turtle soup and Gilligan puts a few daubs on a canvas.

The Howells "find" Gilligan's painting and "assume" Dubov painted it. They pretend to be wild about it. He immediately gets jealous as Gilligan shows up and claims it.

35.
My Fair Gilligan
June 5, 1965

Created by Sherwood
    Schwartz, Executive
    Producer
Produced by Jack Arnold
Written by Joanna Lee
Directed by Tony Leader

Gilligan saves Mrs. Howell's life and Mr. Howell is determined to reward him by adopting him. The Howells train him to be a credit to the Howell name. He proves to be an apt pupil, memorizing the Howell background, precepts, and even method of expression. Everyone else is slightly jealous.

All the other Castaways start treating Gilligan differently. The Skipper won't let him do anything. Ginger tries to talk him into becoming a movie producer. But Gilligan misses the camaraderie of the rest of the Castaways. Meanwhile, the Howells prepare for Gilligan's "debut" party as G. Thurston Howell IV.

DREAM SEQUENCE
That night, Gilligan dreams he's king in a Napoleonic court.

Note the style of Gilligan's (and Mr. Howell's) shirts. These sport shirts were meant to be worn over pants and are an extension of the Eisenhower jacket, named for U.S. President Dwight D. Eisenhower, who popularized the style born of military uniforms of the period.

"My Fair Gilligan" is a version of the story of Pygmalion (a woman-hating king in Greek legend). Though the story of the arrogant man who turns a peasant girl into a society lady is a popular one and has been used many times, it was probably done at this time because the film version of My Fair Lady *had just been released and was tremendously popular.* Noblesse oblige *means that with wealth and position come obligations.*

His Royal Daddy and Queen Mother join him seeing suppli-cants—the other Castaways. They each plead with him to grant them things—land, equipment, favors. He'd far rather be chasing butterflies. The irascible king demands they play with him, but they refuse and then the Queen Mother orders the guillotine.

THE PRESENT

Gilligan wakes yelling, "I don't want to be king." He goes out and starts working on the Skipper's hut. The Skipper comes out and Gilligan tells him he doesn't want to be anything other than himself. He definitely doesn't want to be a Howell—and he doesn't know how to tell them.

A number of celebrities are mentioned in this episode. In 1964, Cary Grant appeared in Father Goose, *Jimmy Stewart in* Cheyenne Autumn, *Jack Lemmon in* Good Neighbor Sam. *Julie Andrews starred in* Mary Poppins, *and* The Sound of Music *was out by the time this episode aired.*

36.
A Nose by Any Other Name
June 12, 1965

Created by Sherwood Schwartz, Executive Producer
Produced by Jack Arnold
Written by Elroy Schwartz
Directed by Hal Cooper

Gilligan's nose gets bashed by the Skipper's wild golf swing. It swells up horribly and Gilligan gets so depressed the others decide to try and make him feel better. Ginger tells him lots of attractive men throughout history had large noses, and the other women all try to convince him he's handsomer now. But he overhears their plan and it makes him even more depressed than before.

Finally, Gilligan tells the Professor he's got to fix it. The Professor knows when he's licked and tells Gilligan he'll operate. The Skipper suggests Gilligan could choose any nose he wants, even a celebrity's nose. They make a cast of Gilligan's face and Mary Ann and Ginger make some celebrity nose models.

Cyrano de Bergerac is the title character in an 1897 French drama by Edmond Rostand. The classic story concerns a romantic poet who woos the fair Roxanne for his tongue-tied friend. Cyrano had an exceedingly large nose and has given up on finding romance for himself, yet falls for his friend's lady love. Cyrano was a real person, a seventeenth-century poet. The story has been filmed multiple times, most recently as the modernized Roxanne, *starring Steve Martin.*

Michelangelo (whose last name was Buonarroti) was born in Florence, Italy, in 1475 and revolutionized the art of his time. He was an incredibly gifted painter, sculptor, architect, poet, and is responsible for beginning the Renaissance. His statue of David and his

*ceiling frescoes in the
Sistine Chapel are still
studied by art students the
world over.*

THE WORLD
1965

The Cold War got colder and the war in Vietnam got hotter in 1965. Both events were centered in Asia. Moscow and Peking (that's the way we spelled it then) were on the outs, and China loomed very large as the new leader of the Communist world and a major nuclear threat. Unlike China, the Soviets knew the responsibility of being a nuclear power. Policy in Moscow supported "wars of liberation," and that's what the conflict in Vietnam was. In fact, all of Southeast Asia was in turmoil and it wasn't hard for Western leaders to see the possibility (and threat) of a Communist sweep through the whole area. At a time when many people saw a Red under every bed, war with China or the Soviets was nuclear suicide, but war in tiny Vietnam was not.

No matter what we did, how much money, men, and materiel we poured into the region, the Vietcong refused to budge. And while Washington continued to see the threat as "Today Hanoi, tomorrow the world," it was blind to the burgeoning antiwar sentiment at home.

But in general, Vietnam hadn't yet become all-pervasive in our daily lives, despite fairly heavy television coverage. Civil rights and burgeoning civil disobedience were the topics most often on the evening news.

Other events of 1965 include:

- Hindi replaces English as the official language of India.
- Sir Winston Churchill, aged ninety-one, dies in London.
- Boeing announces a new short-range jet plane, the 737, to compete directly with Douglas's DC-9 (the 737 is still the workhorse of the nation's airline system).
- The British government announces a ten-year plan to convert to the metric system.
- Volkswagen introduces a new "fastback" model in addition to its popular "Beetle." Rolls Royce introduces the Silver Shadow.
- The year in films was dominated by the British. Richard Lester's second Beatles film, *Help!*, is a great success. Other British films capitalize on the British pop wave, including *The Knack*; *What's New, Pussycat?*; *Darling*; *The Ipcress File*; *The Yellow Rolls Royce*; and John Boorman's *Having a Wild Weekend*, starring another British pop group, the Dave Clark Five. Notable American films of 1965 include *The Great Race*, *Cat Ballou*, *The Sound of Music*, *Zorba the Greek*, *The Collector*, and *The Pawnbroker*.
- The first pacemakers are successfully implanted in heart patients at the VA Hospital in Buffalo, New York.
- A series of tornadoes strikes the Midwest in April, injuring five thousand and killing 270. Property damage estimated at $250 million. The Taal volcano in the Philippines erupts in September, killing at least 208 and blanketing

the southern part of the island with a thick layer of ash.

- Our cultural extremes were exhibited in books such as Norman Mailer's *An American Dream*—where a man brutally murders his wife to "find himself"—and Tom Wolfe's *The Kandy-Kolored Tangerine-Flake Streamline Baby*, a series of sketches of "pop" society.
- Vidal Sassoon of London makes headlines with his asymmetrical, angled haircuts.
- Liza Minnelli made her Broadway debut in *Flora, the Red Menace*, but the year was a weak one for the Great White Way. Two notable musicals for the year were British imports: *Half a Sixpence* and *The Roar of the Greasepaint, the Smell of the Crowd*. The year's only true hit, *The Man of La Mancha*, opened with little fanfare at a makeshift theatre on New York University's campus at the end of November.
- The unique, sculptural Sydney, Australia, opera house nears completion.
- East Germany agrees to allow West German residents to visit for two weeks at Christmastime.
- New types of music were spread all over the pop charts. Folk singers were all the rage and Bob Dylan's first single to be released in Britain, "The Times They Are A-Changing" was a smash. Joan Baez released her first singles in America, including the protest anthem, "We Shall Overcome," but the Beatles still ruled the world of pop. They played to fifty-six thousand shrieking fans in Shea Stadium. The Fab Four sold over 140 million records worldwide in 1965.

TELEVISION
1965

Nineteen sixty-five was a year of preparation for change in both society and in television. New things and new ways to do things were rapidly appearing. The Early Bird communications satellite was launched and on May 2, for the first time ever, three hundred million people in Europe and the Americas watched a live, one-hour special transmitted entirely by satellite. It was composed of news from the Dominican Republic, heart surgery in progress in Texas, Pope Paul VI speaking from the Vatican, Martin Luther King, Jr., in Philadelphia, a cricket match in Great Britain, a bullfight in Spain, and an on-air exchange of "most wanted" photos by the FBI, Scotland Yard, and the Canadian Mounties.

The reach of U.S. television was wide: *Bonanza* was seen in sixty countries, *Perry Mason* and *The Beverly Hillbillies* in fifty, *Dr. Kildare* in fifty-five, and *Gilligan's Island*, *F Troop*, and *Wackiest Ship in the Army* were rapidly expanding all over the globe. In all, *Broadcasting* magazine estimated that more than eighty U.S. television programs were being contemporaneously shown in foreign markets.

This was the year that color broadcasting exploded in the U.S., (but not yet in Europe).

The trend away from dramas and toward comedies continued and a new genre was introduced—the "spy spoof" with a bumbling secret agent.

- The three networks were spending approximately $10.1 million a week on prime time programming, up one million dollars from the prior year.
- ABC paid $15.5 million for two years of NCAA football.
- Major league baseball received more than $25 million for TV/radio rights during the year.
- In April, there were 3,280,000 color TV sets in the U.S., seventy-six percent more than one year earlier. Seventy-nine percent of U.S. stations could broadcast in color.
- Two million homes received cable TV.
- CBS had resisted the trend toward showing theatrical movies in prime time, but gave in this season, leading off with 1962's *The Manchurian Candidate.*
- *Supermarket Sweep* premiered on ABC. It's still running.
- *ABC Scope*, a news show, devoted itself exclusively to coverage of the Vietnam war until 1968.
- In the mistaken impression that game shows weren't good enough for evening audiences, NBC refused to put on a prime-time version of *Let's Make a Deal.* The show moved to ABC and NBC's entire daytime schedule self-destructed without its most popular show.

GILLIGAN'S ISLAND
1965

CBS's perception that *Gilligan's Island* was a critical failure was made clear when they moved the show from Saturday nights to Thursdays, something they rarely did at that time with a hit series. The show now followed *The Munsters* and led into *My Three Sons* and the Thursday night movie. ABC counterprogrammed with *Shindig*, *The Donna Reed Show* opposite *Gilligan*, then the new rural comedy, *O.K. Crackerby*, *Bewitched*, *Peyton Place*, and *The Long Hot Summer*. NBC broadcast *Daniel Boone*, *Laredo*, *Mona McCluskey* and *The Dean Martin Show*.

THURSDAY NIGHTS—FALL 1965

	ABC	CBS	NBC
7:30	Shindig	The Munsters	Daniel Boone
8:00	Donna Reed Show	GILLIGAN'S ISLAND	
8:30	O.K. Crackerby	My Three Sons	Laredo
9:00	Bewitched	CBS Thursday Movie	

9:30	Peyton Place	Mona McClusky
10:00	Long Hot	The Dean
	Summer	Martin Show
10:30		

The new shows this year included comedies *F Troop*, *Gidget*, *Green Acres*, *Tammy*, *Hogan's Heroes* (which would take a critical drubbing equal to *Gilligan*, but like *Gilligan*, would also be popular with TV viewers), *Camp Runamuck*, *Hank*, *I Dream of Jeannie*, *The Smothers Brothers Show* (this is a sitcom with Tom as an angel, *not* the later controversial variety hour), *Please Don't Eat the Daisies*, *Get Smart*, and a show that would make the reviews for *Gilligan's Island* last season look like raves, the infamous *My Mother the Car*, starring Jerry Van Dyke and Ann Sothern.

Dramas and action adventure shows premiering included a batch that would become classics: *Run For Your Life*, *I Spy*, *The FBI*, *The Big Valley*, *Lost in Space*, *Laredo*, and *Convoy*. Later that fall the networks added more shows destined to become classics: *The Avengers*, *Daktari*, and *Batman*.

Because this was *Gilligan's Island*'s first season in color, all the black-and-white footage shot in Hawaii and used in the opening was useless. So replacement footage of the *Minnow* leaving the harbor was shot in Southern California's new small boat harbor at Marina del Rey. The storm sequence was unrealistically tinted and the Skipper and Gilligan fighting the wheel in the storm was shot in a fake-looking mock-up of the *Minnow*'s bridge. But the new shots of the cast are vivid and great looking and, of course, the lush island looks beautiful in the new color shows.

Gilligan survived the move to a new night with only a slight loss in the ratings.

RATINGS
1965–1966 Season

1.	Bonanza	31.8
2.	Gomer Pyle, USMC	27.8
3.	The Lucy Show	27.7
4.	The Red Skelton Hour	27.6
5.	Batman (Thurs.)	27.0
6.	The Andy Griffith Show	26.9
7.	Bewitched	25.9
	The Beverly Hillbillies	25.9
9.	Hogan's Heroes	24.9
10.	Batman (Wed.)	24.7
11.	Green Acres	24.6
12.	Get Smart	24.5
13.	The Man from U.N.C.L.E.	24.0
14.	Daktari	23.9
15.	My Three Sons	23.8
16.	The Dick Van Dyke Show	23.6
17.	Walt Disney's Wonderful World of Color	23.2
	The Ed Sullivan Show	23.2
19.	The Lawrence Welk Show	22.4
	I've Got a Secret	22.4
21.	Petticoat Junction	22.3
22.	GILLIGAN'S ISLAND	22.1
23.	Wild, Wild West	22.0
	The Jackie Gleason Show	22.0
	The Virginian	22.0

COLOR

CBS was at the forefront of the development of color TV. The network had first come up with a color system in 1939 and it further refined it after World War II. This system placed a wheel composed of three color filters which rotated at high speed in front of a camera lens, producing the appearance of full color. In 1949, the FCC held formal hearings to set the color standard for the country. The CBS system was in competition with an inferior electronic system developed by RCA that required exacting adjustments and settings. But the CBS system wasn't compatible with the black-and-white system then in use.

The FCC chose the CBS system and the network began color broadcasts in 1951. But no one else in the industry adopted the system, because broadcasters wanted viewers with black-and-white sets to still get a good monochrome picture of a color telecast.

Later in 1953, the FCC formed the NTSC[1] (National Television Standards Committee), dumped the CBS system, and changed over to the RCA system with some modifications.

---

[1] Wags even today refer to NTSC as "never twice the same color," because of its touchy adjustments

With this advantage, RCA (the parent company of NBC) pushed its network into the forefront of color programming. RCA made the cameras the TV stations used as well as many of the TV sets we bought for our homes. By 1962, there were one million color sets in the U.S. In 1965, there were five million sets and CBS and NBC became all-color networks. CBS wasn't a sore loser—it jumped on the color bandwagon and pushed and promoted color as heavily as did NBC.

ABC[2] wasn't last in the race to color by choice. It was the smallest of the networks and had no corporate-giant parent to infuse it with cash. CBS's 1962 profits were $29 million, ABC's $10.7 million. ABC also did not have strong position to acquire the current motion pictures that were becoming such a programming staple (and whose price had quadrupled in three years) and it was also vulnerable to corporate takeovers. Network head Leonard Goldenson looked around for protection and settled on ITT, the International Telecommunications Company, as his savior and negotiated a merger in 1966.

But the government found a number of reasons to object to the merger and put a stop to it, throwing ABC into another couple of cash-strapped years. By 1968, the third network was still not broadcasting fully in color.

CBS had converted its drama programs to color first, then concentrated on the sitcoms. *Gilligan's Island* was a natural for color with all that tropical foliage, and it converted with the 1965–66 season. Many shows had special sea-

---

[2] For those who don't remember, the letters of the three networks stood for American Broadcasting Co., Columbia Broadcasting System, and National Broadcasting Co.

son openers to show off their new colors, such as *My Favorite Martian's* multi-part full-color flashback-to-riverboat-gambler's-days episode, but *Gilligan* just looked great every week anyway.

1965—SMOOTH SAILING

Bob Denver was astonished at how prepared Schwartz was for the second season. "Sherwood is a man who can create twenty-two minutes of plot, which is very difficult. I thought it was easy at the time I was doing it [the show]. I thought all producer/writers like Sherwood in town did this for a living and knew how to do it. As the years went by, I found out it was very few and mainly only one, who could take twenty-two minutes and create two acts, a teaser, and a tag, and put it together correctly so you watch it and don't even notice the twenty-two minutes went by and you laugh all the way.

"It's a God-given talent and the man is brilliant. I've watched television since then the last twenty-five years and I haven't seen a show written that well and constructed that well and I think one of the main reasons this show keeps rerunning because it's not dull and it's not repetitious. It's new. It's all due to Sherwood, who sat in the office by himself working many, many nights. I went in the second year and he had sixteen scripts on his desk and I said, 'What are you doing, going over last year's scripts to get some new ideas?' He said 'These are this year's.'

"I looked at him and I laughed. I said, 'C'mon

Sherwood, you've got sixteen finished scripts ready to go?' I took a couple and looked and they were. He'd given all these scripts to the prop department and the special effects department, all the people who need them to get ready and he said they'd been out there a couple of weeks. He gave lead time to the props, to the special effects, to the makeup—to everybody who had to do something where normally they get no time. They'd had a month to prepare. So every explosion or silly thing I did or anyone did was prepared so far in advance that it came off perfectly when we shot it. I credit almost all of it to him."

37.
Gilligan's Mother-in-Law
September 16, 1965

Created and Produced by
   Sherwood Schwartz
Executive Producer, Jack
   Arnold
Written by Budd Grossman
Produced and Directed by
   Jack Arnold
   Guests
Henny Backus as..........
.... Native Mother
Russ Grieve as Native Chief
Mary Foran as ....
.... Native Daughter
Eddie Little Sky as ....
.... Native Warrior

"Boola Boola," is probably the most famous of Yale's pep songs. It was written in 1901 by Allan Hirsch and is still one of the top four songs sung at Yale.

Henny Backus was married to Jim Backus. She was an actress, model, and sculptress when they met at the home of a sick friend.

WHAT'S MISSING?
If you are watching this episode in syndication on a local television channel which edits two

to five minutes out of most syndicated programs, the missing scenes might include: Ginger and Mary Ann doing the prospective bride's hair and makeup before the party; Gilligan and the Skipper in grass skirts, hurling insults at each other ("You look like a bowl of soggy shredded wheat." "I've seen whisk brooms that looked better than you."); and the Howells doing likewise ("You look like Miss Alfalfa, rotating her crops"). Mr. Howell ends up in black tie and grass skirt and the chief snatches Mr. Howell's top hat. In addition, at the feast, Gilligan's prospective mother-in-law wants him to eat more so he'll get big and fat, while Gilligan wonders if they plan to eat him. Mother and daughter dance with Gilligan (note Ms. Backus's hilarious Polynesian shimmy). The scenes have all been

Three very hefty natives arrive on the island and spot Gilligan. The youngest one tells her parents she wants Gilligan for a husband. But when the Castaways spot them, they think it's the Skipper she wants. Mr. Howell thinks it might be their salvation—if they go to the native island for the ceremony, they might be able to find their way back to civilization. The Skipper panics at the sight of the very large young woman, races to his hut and starts barricading the door. The Professor and Gilligan try to talk him into it.

But Gilligan flees when the Professor manages to communicate with the natives and learns it's Gilligan who's the intended bridegroom. The rest of the Castaways search the island for Gilligan (and encounter alligators and a bear) and he finally shows up at the lagoon. The intended bride's father is chief of his tribe and he informs Gilligan he must pass a test first. It includes carrying the young woman. He manages for a bit, but is nearly crushed when they fall.

Then Gilligan must pass the test of knives, which is quite

reminiscent of a circus side-show knife-throwing act, and then the chief tells the Castaways the groom's people must throw a party. This is something Mrs. Howell can really get into and she provides quite a bash for everyone. The Castaways are all dressed "native." They feast and then dance. Suddenly a tall, handsome native named Hiroki arrives and shrieks. The chief says he's a former suitor and he wants to compete with Gilligan for her hand. Gilligan tries to give Hiroki her hand—and all the rest, but the chief insists on a contest. Spears, in fact. The combatants will throw them at each other the next day.

Gilligan practices while Ginger goes to work on Hiroki. Hiroki's reaction to Ginger's advances astonishes her. He starts shrieking! The Professor translates that Hiroki likes her but she's "not the kind of girl he'd like to take home to Mother."

restored on the Turner networks.

38.
Beauty Is As Beauty Does
September 23, 1965

Tuesday Weld was a popular actress in the sixties and was Bob Denver's costar on The

Many Loves of Dobie Gillis. She played Dobie's unattainable love, Thalia Menninger.

"Paul Revere's Ride" is the famed Longfellow poem telling of the midnight ride of the Revolutionary patriot to alert the citizens about a British raid.

"Let Me Entertain You" has become the stripper's anthem since it was introduced on Broadway in Gypsy *in 1959. The splendid musical (music by Leonard Bernstein and lyrics by Stephen Sondheim) dramatizes the life of stripper Gypsy Rose Lee and her sister, actress June Havoc.*

Created and Produced by Sherwood Schwartz
Executive Producer Jack Arnold
Written by Joanna Lee
Produced and Directed by Jack Arnold

The Castaways hear on the radio that one of Ginger's rivals has won a beauty contest. The men toast the women Castaways in a show of feminine appreciation. Gilligan really puts his foot in it when he suggests they have a beauty contest. The women are all for it. The men know they're done for.

The Professor helps Mary Ann with makeup and exercise. Mr. Howell leads Lovey in old-fashioned calisthenics, and the Skipper helps Ginger. The only "uncommitted delegate" is Gilligan and into his lap the decision lands. Gilligan hangs out with Gladys the chimp, who's the only one who doesn't want anything from him. Except bananas. He tells her his problems.

39.
The Little Dictator
September 30, 1965

Created and Produced by
   Sherwood Schwartz
Written by Bob Rodgers
   and Sid Mandel
Produced and Directed by
   Jack Arnold
Music by Johnny Williams
Guest
Nehemiah Persoff as . . . . . .
. . . . Rodriguez

Pancho Hernando Gonzales Enrico Rodriguez, ex-*presidente de la Republica Ecuarico*, is unceremoniously dumped on the island and immediately takes over as "provisional president" ("He who has gun is the leader") and plans to turn the island into a new banana republic, "Ecuarico West." The island's twice as big as Ecuarico. He plans free, democratic elections ('You should live so long") and imposes his monetary system ("tree bark and my signature"). He plans for the country to "stay underdeveloped enough to get an American loan."

The "Gilligan the Great" spelling song is based on George M. Cohan's "Harrigan," written in 1907 and introduced in the musical Fifty Miles from Boston *a year later. It became an American standard, as did many of Cohan's songs, including "Over There," "You're a Grand Old Flag," and "Yankee Doodle Dandy."*

Ginger's role as "Agent 0036" is a parody of both the James Bond films and Get Smart, *which premiered in 1965. With the popularity of* Goldfinger, *everyone was getting into the act doing jokes about double-oh-whatever. The spy spoof with agents 86 and 99,* Get Smart, *had just premiered on television on September 18, 1965.*

Dramatists have been coming up with phony country names since the first man stepped upon the first stage. "Ecuarico" is a particularly clever one.

Composer John Williams returned to do the music for this episode.

The Castaways plot a coup, but when Rodriguez runs out of bullets, he's ready to be exiled by the Castaways. Mrs. Howell tells him he will become a member of their society.

Rodriguez convinces Gilligan he should take over, with Rodriguez as his "advisor."

DREAM SEQUENCE

Gilligan has a dream where he's a dictator. Mary Ann (as a beautiful señorita) tells him the people are rioting. Mr. Howell (as the minister of finance) announces that the economy is falling apart. The Skipper (as the secretary of the navy) tells him the navy's in even worse shape. Ginger (as secret agent 0036) tells him the country's in anarchy. Rodriguez shoots them all. "Puppet ruler" takes on a whole new meaning in Gilligan's dream.

The episode title refers to one of television's first and most successful programs, Allen Funt's Candid Camera, which ran from 1948 to 1950 on various networks, and was revived in 1953 and

40.
Smile, You're on Mars Camera
October 14, 1965

Created and Produced by
   Sherwood Schwartz
Executive Producer, Jack
   Arnold

Written by Al Schwartz
and Bruce Howard
Directed by Jack Arnold
Guests
Booth Colman as.. Corwell
Arthur Peterson as Bancroft
Larry Thor as ..Newscaster

Mr. Howell's got Gilligan looking for exotic feathers for a pillow for Mrs. Howell. Meanwhile, back at Cape Kennedy, a launch team is trying to figure out what part of Mars their probe has landed on. The TV camera aboard the probe goes on and the scientists are floored to see a tropical landscape with an obviously man-made hut. They're thrilled: "There's some form of life on Mars." Then the camera goes out.

Gilligan stumbles over the probe and runs for the Professor, who immediately figures out what it must be. He and the Skipper move it to the clearing where they can work on it. A radio bulletin about the lost Mars probe tells them what it is. If they can repair the camera, Cape Kennedy will know they're there. The lens is missing and they all look for it.

They've given up when Gilli-

again in 1960. This latest incarnation ran until 1967 on Gilligan's *network,* CBS, *and "Smile, you're on Candid Camera" became part of the language.*

We learn that Gilligan has a brother.

gan shows them the "neat" magnifying glass he found, which is, of course, the lens. Then he breaks it. The Professor tries to figure out what he can use to replace it. Perhaps some tree sap . . . Gilligan and the Skipper get stuck in the sap around the trees.

The Howell Private Country Club Motto: "I pledge allegiance to the spirit of money, the color for which it stands, one currency divisible by ten, with luxury and affluence for the fortunate few."

Prospector Howell's observation, "Is that all that's been bugging you?" is a tag line from a series of commercials of the day.

In the dream sequence, the group says they're playing three-card monte, but they're actually playing poker. Three-card monte is actually the variation of the old

41.
The Sweepstakes
October 21, 1965

Created and Produced by
    Sherwood Schwartz
Executive Producer, Jack
    Arnold
Written by Walter Black
Directed by Jack Arnold

There's a new addition to the island—the Howell *Private* Country Club. Gilligan's become the chief slave, as usual. While serving the Howells drinks, Gilligan overhears a radio bulletin about the Argentine Sweepstakes, with the winning number good for a tax-free million-dollar prize. Gilligan pulls out his ticket and it's the winner. He runs and tells the others. But soon things are back to normal, except that the Howells have voted Gilligan into their very private club. The initiation fee is fifty thousand dollars. They give him a drink, put his feet up, give him the pledge of club allegiance and a club blazer. He's playing golf with Mr. Howell when the Skipper wants him to build a wall. Mr. Howell tosses the nonmember out.

Mr. Howell teaches Gilligan about being one of the idle rich, including how to dream like a rich man. Gilligan says he wants to spend his money to make people happy. Mr. Howell insists the only use for money is to make more money. But Gilligan tells the Skipper he wants to give him fifty thousand dollars so he can join the club too. When he tries to do the same for Ginger, she thinks he's trying to buy her sexual favors.

That night, the others join the club, to the Howells' disgust. "The world is crumbling, Lovey! Betrayed by one of our own kind!" Mr. Howell insists Gilligan deposit his sweepstakes ticket in the club safe. Gilligan doesn't have it, and Mr. Howell tosses all the others out of his club. The group mounts a search for the ticket,

walnut-shells-and-pea scam used for years to fleece unsuspecting rubes at carnivals. Three-card monte is still popular on the sidewalks of New York.

As usual, the dream sequence has been shot on the Gunsmoke *sets, with the Castaways again playing their Dodge City counterparts.*

noting they've found everything else he's lost since they've been on the island. Mr. Howell tells his troubles to his teddy and starts to dream. . . .

DREAM SEQUENCE

He dreams he's a crusty old prospector in the old West, who has just struck the mother lode. He hands over his strike in the assay office where the Professor gives him a receipt for one million dollars. He gives the receipt to Marshal Gilligan for safekeeping, dispensing IOUs for fifty thousand dollars to Gilligan and the Professor.

He goes to Miss Ginger La Plante's Last Chance Gambling and Drinking Saloon, and toasts his good fortune in the best rotgut whisky. He gives her an IOU for fifty thousand dollars. He hasn't had a bath or a drink in forty years. Mary Ann, the girl of the golden west, whose entire family has been wiped out by various Indian tribes. She needs fifty thousand dollars to save her ranch. He gives her an IOU. Then he joins a cardsharp (the Skipper) for a little "three-card monte," which they play like poker. The Skipper deals himself four cards. "Everything's gone up."

They play poker and bet fifty thousand dollars on the hand. Mr. Howell has three aces. The Skipper pulls a gun and says he's got four. He demands payment and Prospector Howell claims he's lost the paper. A lynch mob arrives to prepare him for hanging.

42.
Quick Before It Sinks
October 28, 1965

Created and Produced by
  Sherwood Schwartz
Executive Producer, Jack
  Arnold
Written by Stan Burns and
  Mike Marmer
Directed by George M.
  Cahan

The Professor is sure their island is sinking. He's got a depth marker in the lagoon and each day it's lower and lower. Gilligan has the solution: stilts. Mrs. Howell wants the guys to landscape the area outside their huts and the men decide to keep the women in the dark about their imminent peril. But the demands of Mrs. Howell's decorating indecision wears

WHAT'S MISSING?
Trimmed for syndication in some markets is a cute little scene of Mr. Howell's idea of landscaping work: He lies on the grass with a mint julep, carefully trimming the grass one blade at a time with Lovey's nail clippers, scissors, and nail buffer. Instead of cutting the shows to insert more advertising time, the Turner networks have time-compressed them.

out the Professor, Gilligan, Mr. Howell, and the Skipper, who are lugging palm trees and heavy plants all day on the landscaping project while working to build a new hut on the island's highest ground during the night.

The men can't take it any more and elect Gilligan to tell Ginger the truth. But when he says they've only got a few days left on the island, she thinks he means rescue is imminent and is so excited he can't bear to correct her. The women all want to know what's happened and Gilligan lies and tells them the Professor's fixed the transmitter. As always, one lie leads to another.

Fifi LaFrance and Ricardo Laughingwell were not real silent film stars. The Castaways make reference to famed silent film stars Theda Bara (the first mystery woman of the screen who created the first "vamp" and whose name is an anagram for "Arab death"), the little tramp, Charlie

**43.
Castaways Pictures Presents**
November 4, 1965

Created and Produced by
  Sherwood Schwartz
Executive Producer, Jack
  Arnold
Written by Herbert Finn
  and Alan Dinehart
Directed by Jack Arnold

Gilligan spots a ship and the Professor and the Skipper race to see. Trouble is, it's a sunken ship. But maybe they can raise it and fix it. The Skipper goes down to look at it, and the whole starboard side is missing. But there are some boxes aboard that they might be able to use. The next day, the Skipper can't get into his wet suit so Gilligan will go down. The Professor sets up a primitive air system so he can stay down long enough to do the salvage work.

Gilligan dives and gets too much air, which inflates his wet suit too much. They finally get the crates up and they're full of costumes, film, and a motion picture camera. The markings on it tell the Howells it's silent picture equipment. The costumes bring to mind the classic silent stars.

The Castaways make a movie of their shipwreck and their life on the island, directed by Mr. Howell. They all wear the excessive makeup of silent stars. The Professor is very stilted and when Mr. Howell demands he give Ginger a big kiss, he's worried about germs. He finally does it and Ginger takes over and really

Chaplin, and beloved silent film ingenue, Mary Pickford. Canadian Pickford set the style for the wholesome girl next door and was known as "the world's sweetheart." She was even more beloved when she married handsome, swashbuckling Douglas Fairbanks, Sr., and they became Hollywood's premier couple, entertaining lavishly at their estate known as "Pickfair," now owned by actress Pia Zadora.

"Cecil B. Howell" is a reference to Cecil B. DeMille, probably the most famous film director in the world—at least until Steven Spielberg came along.

The opening of the Castaways' film with Gilligan hitting a gong is a parody of the films of the British J. Arthur Rank Organisation, which always

opened with a muscle-bound man, near-naked body heavily oiled, hitting a gong with a large mallet.

In the radio sports report, the "Slippery Rock teachers" really exist. Slippery Rock Teachers College, now known as Slippery Rock University of Pennsylvania, was founded in 1889.

The Cannes Film Festival judges compare the Castaways' movie to the work of several avant garde directors. Ingmar Bergman is the famed Swedish director. With Smiles of a Summer Night *in 1955 and* The Seventh Seal *a year later, Bergman became the king of films with mystical, unexplained themes. Vitorio De Sica was an Italian realist director who became well known worldwide with his films* Two Women *in 1961 and* Yesterday, Today and Tomorrow *in 1964.*

puts her heart in it. "No germ could live through that kiss."

In a scene about the "dangers" of their daily life, Mary Ann, who is threatened by a cannibal (played by Gilligan) also needs some direction—he says "boo" to scare her.

At the film premiere (Ginger says, "I've heard of previews in out-of-the-way places, but this is ridiculous."), the Professor warns them of technical problems.

44.
Agonized Labor
November 11, 1965

Created and Produced by
   Sherwood Schwartz
Executive Producer, Jack
   Arnold
Written by Roland
   MacLane
Directed by Jack Arnold

Gilligan turns on the radio to get some "going-to-sleep" music, but gets a physical fitness program instead. A bulletin tells of "the sudden collapse" of the Howell companies. Gilligan and the Skipper wonder when to give the dreadful news to Mr. Howell. The morning seems soon enough.

In the morning, they find the Howells planning the Howell Oil Company, including offshore oil rigs and a sixty-room cottage. They finally tell them. Mr. Howell insists he can't be poor—he doesn't know how. All they've got left is the "few hundred thousand" they brought with them. Another bulletin reports a government lien on all his assets including any cash he may have with him. He's distraught.

Mr. Howell's mention of Fredric March and James Mason wading into the ocean is a reference to the various versions of the film A Star is Born. March played alcoholic has-been actor Norman Main in the 1937 version. Mason played the same character in the 1954 remake with Judy Garland. Depressed at his wife's success, Main kills himself by walking into the ocean. Barbra Streisand and Kris Kristofferson remade the film again in 1976, with a contemporary setting.

This idea of the Howells becoming French domestic servants brings to mind the 1937 film, Tovarich, in which Charles Boyer and Claudette Colbert play impoverished Imperial Russian exiles reduced to working as a butler and maid in Paris. Unlike the Howells, however, they succeed admirably.

Mary Ann tells the Howells she'll always be their friend. She's brought them some flowers. They're very touched until a bee emerges from the bouquet.

Later, the Skipper spills water all over Mr. Howell, the Professor fixes his bamboo polo pony and it throws him, and Gilligan and Ginger hit him in the face with a fish. Mrs. Howell has hysterics when they find what they think is a suicide note. The Castaways organize a search party.

Meanwhile, Mr. Howell is looking for an appropriate way to end it all, but nothing seems right. The Castaways find them and Gilligan suggests they work, maybe as domestic servants. After some reflection, the Howells agree to try it. They vow to bring a new standard of living to the island. But the first meal is a disaster. The Howells head for the cliff. A radio bulletin comes just in time. It was the *Powell* Industries that collapsed.

When Mrs. Howell says she doubts Moscow has a blue book, she refers to

**45.
Nyet, Nyet, Not Yet**
November 18, 1965

Created and Produced by
Sherwood Schwartz
Executive Producer Jack
Arnold
Written by Adele T.
Strassfield and Robert
Riordan
Directed by Jack Arnold

Guests

Vincent Beck as . . . . Igor
Danny Klega as . . . . Ivan

*the social register, a
volume traditionally
published in blue binding.
In earlier times, people in
the social register rarely
socialized with anyone not
listed.*

In the middle of the night, Gilligan hears what he thinks sounds like "a jet plane with asthma." The Skipper insists it's a falling star, but in the morning, a Russian space capsule drifts into the lagoon. The Castaways are astonished when two cosmonauts emerge, Igor and Ivan.

Of course, the Castaways are just interested in rescue, but the cosmonauts are in no hurry to get back to mother Russia— Igor's entranced with Ginger. Mr. Howell convinces Ginger to lure Igor away from guarding the space capsule so Gilligan and the Professor can get inside and try to communicate with the outside, but Gilligan shorts out the capsule's electrical system and then the cosmonauts catch them.

They manage to fix the radio the next day and get word a submarine is heading to pick them up the following day. But the Soviet spacemen realize if the Castaways are also rescued, the whole world will know about their mistake which landed them on the island. They plan to get the Castaways drunk on vodka so they can't be rescued.

Dawn Wells is still amazed at the worldwide success of Gilligan's Island. *She remembers, "I'm kind of an adventurer and I've been to Africa and climbed up to see the gorillas, but from Stephens College, the president and a few of my friends from Stephens went to the Solomon Islands by canoe into villages that no women had ever been to before and slept on the floors on grass mats with chieftains in their huts and all this sort of stuff, and as we arrived on one of the islands by canoe in*

**46.
Hi-Fi Gilligan**
November 25, 1965

Created and Produced by Sherwood Schwartz
Executive Producer, Jack Arnold
Written by Mary C. McCall, Jr.
Directed by Jack Arnold

A typhoon is heading toward Gilligan's Island and to prepare, Gilligan and the Skipper are storing supplies in a cave. The Skipper hits Gilligan with a crate and suddenly radio music comes out of his mouth every time he opens it. The Professor figures out a molar has pressed against a filling and turned it into a radio receiver. The Skipper'd like to make him into a transmitter. The Professor shows Gilligan that the position of his skull and his body will change the station. One added problem: His signals are interfering with the real radio's reception.

Ginger and Mary Ann are using Gilligan to get their favorite programs, but he's getting tired of it. Mrs. Howell is dying to listen to the radio to hear the list of the ten best-dressed women, but the Professor is listening to the weather nonstop. The storm should hit the next afternoon.

That night, the Skipper has trouble sleeping because Gilligan opens his mouth when he sleeps. He tosses him out of the hut. Gilligan knocks over the radio and breaks it. When he falls, he breaks his own receiver too. The Professor's very worried. This could be their biggest storm ever.

The Castaways stuff the cave like forties' students stuffing a phone booth. But it's just not big enough for all seven of them.

a rainstorm with all these wonderful war dances going on that they gave for us to introduce us, we walked into the chief's hut and the chief's wife said, 'I know you.' Now there's no running water, no electricity, no anything! She had been on the island of Honiara [the capital of the Solomons] in the seventies and had gone to nursing school for a couple of years and used to come home and watch Gilligan's Island. *So you can't get away from it, no matter where you are."*

JIM BACKUS

Jim Backus was raised in a Cleveland suburb, the son of a mechanical engineer and his wife. One of his teachers was Margaret Hamilton, who would go on to film immortality as the Wicked Witch in *The Wizard of Oz*.

Jim Backus's upwardly mobile family was not too thrilled when he told them he wanted to act, but they grew to respect his talent, particularly when he became established in television. Backus attended a Kentucky Military Academy (with future actor Victor Mature) and learned to love the game of golf while caddying at a local golf course. Had Backus and not Thurston Howell III been marooned on an island, he would have made golf clubs and played too.

Backus was well grounded in the Howells' hoity-toity ways from his next educational stint at a Cleveland prep school designed to get its young men into Yale, Harvard, and Princeton. When his father finally bit the bullet and accepted that Backus was determined to become an actor, he made sure he got the best training possible at the American Academy of Dramatic Art.

After an intense two-year course, Backus couldn't find work. He eventually went home with his pride shattered and looked for a job. The Depression had hit the family hard and they couldn't give him enough money to return to New York in the fall of 1936. One of his father's friends owned a batch of radio stations and gave him a job as a radio announcer.

Two years later, Backus tried New York again, but the city was unimpressed with his Ohio credentials. However, thanks to AADA classmate Garson Kanin, he got a small part in a Broadway show which ran for a few months. He became friends with Keenan Wynn during the run and his father, Ed Wynn, became Jim's mentor, encouraging him to find one or two characters or types he did well and stick to them. He particularly liked his rich boy who sounded like F.D.R. and his bumbling old man. . . .

In 1941, Backus met and later married sculptress, photographer's model and actress Henriette Kaye and they moved into a hotel across the street from the famed Algonquin.

He was a big success in New York radio and when he was cast as a Harvard football captain in a radio program, his wife Henny suggested he use the rich-boy character he did at parties.

Then Alan Young took over as a summer replacement for Eddie Cantor and liked the stuffy character Backus had created and thus Hubert Updyke III was born.

Hubert Updyke III was lovable, pompous, had "thousands of Cadillacs," "a mansion in Beverly Hills" (that was air conditioned on the *outside*), and "all the money in the world."

He became a regular character on the radio show, which became a hit, and they all moved to Hollywood in 1946.

Tina Louise has told the story of giving up a

Broadway role to come to Hollywood many times; well, Backus did the same thing. Just before he got on the train for Los Angeles, friend Garson Kanin offered him the lead in his new play, which Backus turned down. The title? *Born Yesterday*, which became a huge hit (and eventually a movie starring the luminous Judy Holliday, who won an Oscar for a reprise of her Broadway role).

Henny and Jim Backus lived like gypsies for a while in postwar Los Angeles, which was clogged with veterans from all over the country who had glimpsed California on the way to the Pacific theatre of war and decided it was where they wanted to live. There were no cars, no apartments, no houses available.

But Backus had plenty of work. He piled up radio, television and film credits once he'd had the "treatment." Hollywood, as always, loved beauty and Backus was subjected to electrolysis, nose job, and caps on his teeth.

In one of his autobiographies—*Forgive Us Our Digressions*, Backus complains that he was typecast as the hero's best friend and didn't really break out of that mold until 1955's *Rebel Without a Cause*, the movie that made a star of James Dean.

He says that typecasting almost prevented him from getting his first lead in a successful television series, *I Married Joan*, costarring Joan Davis. Backus played Judge Bradley Stevens whose decisions from the bench were often based upon the antics of his deranged wife Joan.

The writers of the show included *Gilligan's Island* creator Sherwood Schwartz, Neil Simon, Abe Burrows, and Leon Uris.

Backus went on to make films despite his heavy television work. He did a number of summer variety shows—in the fifties and sixties, when regular series finished for the season in May or June, instead of reruns, the networks put on summer replacement shows, often variety or comedy, lighter fare for the summer months.

Backus won his stardom in *I Married Joan*, but he won his actor's stripes in *Rebel Without a Cause*, playing James Dean's father. Backus describes Dean's talent as "blazing" and the experience of making the movie an intense and rewarding one. Dean frequently delivered emotionally complex performances in one take, leaving the other actors and crew with mouths agape.

Rebel led to more meaty fare for Backus, including roles in the steamy and intense *Hurry Sundown*, and *Our Town* with Henry Fonda. He kept his comedy skills polished with films such as *Critic's Choice*, *Ask Any Girl*, *It's a Mad, Mad, Mad, Mad World*, *Sunday in New York*, and *Advance to the Rear*.

He also guest starred on many TV shows, including a classic performance on a *Maverick* parody of *Bonanza*. Backus played rich rancher Josh Wheelwright, who lived on the vast "Subrosa" with his three dumb sons, Moose, Henry, and Small Paul—a sendup of the other show's Ben, Hoss, Adam, and Little Joe Cartwright of the "Ponderosa."[3]

[3] *Bonanza* suffered another hilarious parody in *Mad* magazine. The satire of the show was called *Bananaz*, the ranch the Pawnderosa (which was the size of 90 percent of the U.S.), the three women-starved sons were Ox, Yves (say it out loud), and Short Mort Cartwheel. Ox ate continuously through the entire episode and Short Mort was always spouting aphorisms like, "The family that forecloses together gets neuroses together."

But many people in the fifties and sixties remember Jim Backus best as the nearsighted Mr. Magoo. Magoo appeared in print, on television, in the movies, and in commercials. The catch phrase, "By George, Magoo, you've done it again" entered the language.

Then Jim Backus brought back another of his voices and from Hubert Updyke III, Thurston Howell III was to the manor born. But Backus almost wasn't able to play the part Sherwood Schwartz wrote with him in mind. Schwartz says, "My main concern was that I didn't have Jim. Jim was unavailable and I diminished the role because I couldn't find anybody to play that part. Jim suddenly became available about two weeks before we were to do the pilot and I called him. Fortunately, I knew him for many years from many other shows and I said, 'Jim, I need you for this show to play a very, very wealthy man like only you can play it.' He said 'Send me the script.' And I said, 'No. If I send you the script, you won't do the show.' So he said, 'You expect me to go star in a show without me even seeing a script?' I said, 'Yes.' And he said, 'You talked me into it.' And as he himself has said, his original part was shorter than a wine list on an airline."

Backus himself adds, "It was in 1946, I had a character called Hubert Updyke III and it was very successful. They made me stop doing it because it sounded too much like FDR. He was the richest guy in the world, so now, I was doing a series with Don Rickles. I was playing a father with daughters and he was a policeman with sons. I couldn't see that I would be very good in that and when Sherwood called me, I said, 'I want to do that, what the hell.' And William Morris told me Sherwood didn't want me."

After the series, he went back to films and television, but he was indelibly Thurston Howell III for a new generation and then their children and grandchildren. After making the first two reunion films, Backus was struck with a type of Parkinson's disease, recovered enough to make a guest appearance in the last *Gilligan* TV movie and some talk shows, and passed away on July 3, 1989.

How did he feel about *Gilligan's Island*? "To me, I watch it on Saturdays—they run them back to back—I sit there crying a lot—but it's just pure nonsense. It was a joy to do and it's a joy to watch. You knew no one was going to get hurt. It was pure make believe. . . .

"I'd make another one in a minute. When we were making it, I used to cry about the hours, how late it was and when we were working in the lagoon, it was cold; that the lagoon was too cold. Looking back now, oh, brother, I wish we were doing it."

Credits

Broadway Theatre
Hitch Your Wagon! 1937
Too Many Heroes 1937

Films, TV specials, series, and pilots
The Pied Piper 1942
Father Was a Fullback 1948
Easy Living 1949
One Last Fling 1949
The Bail Bond Story 1949
The Great Lover 1949

A Dangerous Profession 1949
Hollywood House—variety series, 1949–50
Ma and Pa Kettle Go to Town 1950
Customs Agent 1950
Emergency Wedding 1950
I Want You 1951
Half Angel 1951
His Kind of Woman 1951
Bright Victory 1951
The Hollywood Story 1951
The Man with a Cloak 1951
The Iron Man 1951
The Rose Bowl Story 1952
Here Come the Nelsons 1952
I'll See You In My Dreams 1952
Deadline U.S.A. 1952
Androcles and the Lion 1952
Don't Bother to Knock 1952
Pat and Mike 1952
Above and Beyond 1952
I Married Joan—series, 1952–55
I Love Melvin 1953
Angel Face 1953
Geraldine 1953
The Human Jungle 1954
Deep in My Heart 1954
Francis in the Navy 1955
Rebel Without a Cause 1955
The Square Jungle 1955
Meet Me in Las Vegas 1956
Massacre 1956
The Naked Hills 1956
The Opposite Sex 1956
You Can't Run Away From It 1956
The Girl He Left Behind 1956
The Great Man 1956
Eighteen and Anxious 1957

Top Secret Affair 1957
The Man of a Thousand Faces 1957
High Cost of Living 1958
Macabre 1958
Ask Any Girl 1959
A Private's Affair 1959
The Big Operator 1959
A Thousand and One Arabian Nights—voice
    only, 1959
The Wild and the Innocent 1959
Ice Palace 1960
Horizontal Lieutenant 1962
Boys' Night Out 1962
Zotz! 1962
The Wonderful World of the Brothers Grimm 1962
Talent Scouts—TV variety series, 1962–63
Critic's Choice 1963
Sunday in New York 1963
Johnny Cool 1963
The Wheeler Dealers 1963
It's a Mad Mad Mad Mad World 1963
Operation Bikini 1963
My Six Loves 1963
John Goldfarb, Please Come Home 1964
Fluffy 1964
Advance to the Rear 1964
Gilligan's Island—series, 1964–67
The Famous Adventures of Mr. Magoo—animated
    series, 1964–65
Billie 1965
Continental Showcase—variety series, 1966
Hurry Sundown 1967
Damn Yankees—special, 1967
Don't Make Waves 1967
Where Were You When the Lights Went Out? 1968
Hello Down There 1969
A Woman for Charley—telefilm, 1969

Cockeyed Cowboys of Calico County 1970
Magic Carpet—telefilm, 1972
Getting Away from It All—telefilm, 1972
The Girl Most Likely To . . .—telefilm, 1973
Miracle on 34th Street—telefilm, 1973
New Adventures of Gilligan—animated series, 1974–1977
Yes, Virginia, There is a Santa Claus—special, 1974
Crazy Mama 1975
Friday Foster 1975
Happy Birthday, America—special 1976
What's New, Mr. Magoo?—animated series, 1977–1978
Rescue From Gilligan's Island—telefilm, 1978
Gift of the Magi—telefilm, 1978
Good Guys Wear Black 1979
There Goes the Bride 1979
Angel's Brigade 1979
The "Castaways" on Gilligan's Island—telefilm, 1979
The Harlem Globetrotters on Gilligan's Island—telefilm, 1981
Gilligan's Planet—animated series, 1982–1983
Prince Jack 1984
Slapstick (of Another Kind) 1984

Guest Starring Roles

TV Reader's Digest "If I Were Rich"
Front Row Center "Uncle Barney"
Warner Bros. Presents "Survival"
U.S. Steel Hour "Don't Shake the Family Tree"
Matinee Theater "A Family Affair"
Robert Montgomery Presents "Reclining Figure," "Wait for Me"
Climax "The Mad Bomber," "The Magic Brew"

Studio One "In Love with a Stranger," "The McTaggart Succession"
Playhouse 90 "Free Weekend"
Goodyear Theater "Success Story"
The Millionaire "Millionaire Henry Banning"
77 Sunset Strip "Collector's Item"
Untouchables "The Star Witness"
Danny Thomas Show "The Deerfield Story"
Person to Person
Maverick "Three Queens Full"
Cain's Hundred "Five for One"
Follow The Sun "The Inhuman Equation"
McKeever and the Colonel "The Neighbor"
Dick Powell Show "Charlie's Debt"
The Beverly Hillbillies "The Clampetts Entertain"
Burke's Law "Who Killed Mr. X?" "Who Killed Carrie Cornell," "Who Killed Vaudeville?"
DuPont Show of the Month "Jeremy Rabbit, the Secret Avenger"
Arrest and Trial "Birds of a Feather"
Espionage "A Tiny Drop of Poison"
Accidental Family "What Is This? Thanksgiving . . . or a Nightmare?"
Daniel Boone "The Scrimshaw Ivory Chest"
I Spy "Happy Birthday . . . Everybody"
Wild, Wild West "Night of the Sabatini Death"
The Good Guys
Love, American Style "Love and the Marriage Counselor," "Love and the Understanding"
Nanny and the Professor "The Tyranosaurus Tibia"
I Dream of Jeannie "Help, Help, a Shark"
The Brady Bunch "Ghost Town U.S.A.," "The Hustler"
Alias Smith and Jones "The Biggest Game in the West"

The Mod Squad "Death in High Places"
Medical Center
Marcus Welby, M.D. "Last Flight to Babylon"
Chico and the Man "The Beard"
Harry O "The Sound of Trumpets"
The Night Stalker "The Chopper"
Gunsmoke "Brides and Grooms"
Joe Forrester "Stake Out"
Mobile One "The Pawn"
Ellery Queen "The Adventure of the Mad Tea Party"
Police Story "Odyssey of Death"
Charlie's Angels "Angels on Ice"
The Feather and Father Gang "Never Con a Killer"
Chips
Hallmark Hall of Fame "Have I Got a Christmas for You"
The Love Boat "The Inspector"
Fantasy Island "Anniversary"
Flying High "Beautiful People"
Sweepstakes
Trapper John "It Only Hurts When I Love"

Books by Jim and Henny Backus

Rocks on the Roof (retitled *Only When I Laugh* in paperback)
What Are You Doing After the Orgy?
Backus Strikes Back, Stein and Day, 1984
Forgive Us Our Digressions, St. Martin's Press, 1988

Thurston Howell III

Thurston Howell III would have been right at home in the eighties when greed and money were the holy grail on Wall Street. Politically conservative, athletically inept, morally amoral, and with a 23-carat heart (his hands shake whenever he's near "anything over 24-carat"), Howell is the curmudgeon of the island who's positive money *is* everything.

He went to Harvard, belongs to all the best clubs, has a dozen houses and friends drawn exclusively from the social register. He plays all the rich men's games—golf, polo, sailing, and riding to hounds—yet you get the impression it's the ritual and the sheer class of them that appeal to him, not the athleticism.

Mr. Howell is always ready to contribute to the latest problem facing the Castaways, as long as it doesn't involve anything resembling physical labor. In fact, when putting bars on the window of their hut (episode number 3), one drop of perspiration appears on his forehead and both he and Mrs. Howell don't know what it is. During his extended stay on the island, Mr. Howell makes sure that never happens again. Despite the Skipper's objections, Mr. Howell appropriates Gilligan whenever he needs something done, the services of a caddy, some gold mined, a fresh drink, or something fetched from his hut.

He never spends money if he can help it, but makes more of it. He faces east and salutes Fort Knox upon rising each morning, believes a gentleman never trumps his partner's ace. He believes money is power and power is to be used. Mr. Howell notes "a Howell is astute, generous, charming, kind, and handsome. And above all, modest."

He brought "several hundred thousand" in cash on the excursion on the *Minnow*, along with a complete wardrobe, sporting gear, costumes, and other necessities.

But this is the man who offers five hundred thousand dollars' ransom for Gilligan, and when they're all rescued, dumps his business and social friends when they're rude about Gilligan and the Skipper. It's obvious that Thurston Howell's solid gold heart is in exactly the right place.

The Professor, when discussing the defense of the island from attack, mentions the Roman emperor Hadrian, who ruled the vast empire from 117 to 138 A.D. He established the Euphrates river as the eastern boundary of the empire and built his wall throughout England as protection from invasion. He also mentions the Tower of London, which is actually a collection of buildings on the banks of the Thames river, built at various times, all surrounded by a moat and a wall. William the Conqueror built the first building and the Tower has been used in different

47.
The Chain of Command
December 2, 1965

Created and Produced by
   Sherwood Schwartz
Executive Producer, Jack
   Arnold
Written by Arnold and Lois
   Peyser
Directed by Leslie
   Goodwins
   [Uncredited] Guest
Janos Prohaska [?] as The
   Ape

The Castaways find a headdress which they take to mean that tribes on neighboring islands may be on the warpath and are constructing coconut bombs to defend themselves. The Skipper and Professor discuss the larger defense plans while Gilligan makes weapons and the Howells decide what's proper to wear to a capture. "Somber, but sincere."

Mr. Howell suggests ransom money is the way to handle the savages. Ginger and Mary Ann are rolling bandages, but they're using them as curlers. The Skipper has a serious talk with Gilligan about taking over for him if anything happens. But he thinks Gilligan could use a little coaching on assuming command.

Gilligan's a disaster at a drill with the others, but he says it's because the Skipper's watching. The Skipper leaves, and it's just as bad. Gilligan goes to find the Skipper but only finds his cap on the beach and a note that says he's "completely surrounded by savages." Uh oh.

eras as a royal prison and the site of many famous executions.

48.
Don't Bug the
Mosquitoes
December 9, 1965

Created and Produced by
    Sherwood Schwartz
Executive Producer, Jack
    Arnold
Written by Brad Radnitz
Directed by Steve Binder

This whole episode is a tribute to the Beatles, who burst on the American music scene in December 1963, to the joy of their fans and the dismay of adults everywhere. They were criticized for their long hair, their manner of

*dress and the shrieking
and screaming of their fans.*

*When introducing the
Honeybees, Mr. Howell
imitates Ed Sullivan. The
Beatles' first American
TV appearance was on
Sullivan's long-running
Sunday evening show.*

*The Wellingtons (plus, in
this episode, Les Brown,
Jr.) who play the Mos-
quitoes in this show, sang
the title song for the first
season on* Gilligan's Island.
*The group was composed
of Kirby Johnson, Ed Wade,
and George Patterson.
When the show's theme
song was changed
slightly and rerecorded for
the second season,
another group was hired.
The Wellingtons made a few
records around this time,
including several
contributions to an album
by Mouseketeer Annette
Funicello (see
discography).*

Special Guest Stars
Les Brown, Jr., and the
  Wellingtons as The
  Mosquitoes

Gilligan's grooving to the latest singing group on the radio,
the Mosquitoes, and the music's
driving everyone else nuts. Mr.
Howell and the Skipper order
him to turn it off. He does, but
the music doesn't stop. There
they are—the Mosquitoes—
who have just been dropped by
a helicopter. The mop-headed
group (Bingo, Bango, Bongo,
and Irving) is on R&R (rest and
recuperation) to get away from
screaming fans. Mr. Howell is
dismayed—"If we had to be rescued by a musical group, why
couldn't it have been the New
York Philharmonic?"

Gilligan announces that the
Mosquitoes are giving them a
concert. They sing "Don't Bug
Me," to cheers from the
younger people. Then "He's a
Loser." They announce they're
going to be on the island
another month. Mr. Howell has
a goofy look on his face and
they discover he's been using
earplugs for the concert.

The Castaways don't want to
wait another month to be res-

cued, so they make the Mosquitoes' lives as miserable as possible. It works too well and in the morning, the Mosquitoes are gone.

"Tighter than Presley's pants" refers, of course, to Elvis Presley, whose tight pants and gyrations created such a scandal in 1959 that he was not allowed to be shown below the waist on The Ed Sullivan Show.

Ginger demonstrates the Watusi, a popular dance at the time.

Kirby Johnson, one of the Wellingtons, remembers that Carol Connor dubbed Dawn Wells's voice, but Dawn Wells herself thinks it was Jackie DeShannon. Both were popular sixties singers.

49.
Gilligan Gets Bugged
December 16, 1965

Created and Produced by
  Sherwood Schwartz
Executive Producer, Jack
  Arnold
Written by Jack Gross, Jr.,
  and Michael R. Stein
Directed by Gary Nelson

Dawn Wells is often questioned about romance on the island. She responds, "We had an episode where they tried to get us engaged but the censors wouldn't allow that either. You know, we were all on this island sort of unchaperoned. I wore shorts, but I had to have a little point to cover my navel. In that day and age, you couldn't show your navel and you couldn't show any cleavage. One of my favorite stories is Sherwood Schwartz coming home to his wife and saying he'd had a terrible day between the censors at CBS propping up my pants and Tina's neckline. Between the cleavage and the navels, they could hardly go on the air."

Gilligan thinks he's been bitten by a rare insect. The Skipper describes the bug and the Professor thinks it might be fatal within twenty-four hours. The Professor tells everyone to watch Gilligan for the symptoms: joint pain, loss of appetite, and itching. Due to a series of unrelated mishaps, Gilligan does in fact have all the symptoms.

The Castaways are sure Gilligan's dying and Mrs. Howell decides they should throw him a party. It's quite a shindig, but the group is hardly in the mood for revelry and Gilligan can't understand it when they all leave in tears.

Bob Denver dead?!? There once was a rumor going around that he had died. He remembers, "I'm home and the phone rings and I said 'Hello' and a voice says 'Is Bob Denver there?' and I said, 'Speaking.' 'No. Is Bob Denver there?' 'Speaking. Who is this?' It was UP, United Press. 'Is

50.
Mine Hero
December 23, 1965

Created and Produced by
    Sherwood Schwartz
Executive Producer, Jack
    Arnold
Written by David
    Braverman and Bob
    Marcus
Directed by Wilbur D'Arcy

Gilligan's trying to catch dinner but the fish are avoiding the lagoon because the Skipper's noisily hammering together a raft. The Professor's putting together a nifty time-delay anchor which will keep the unmanned raft from drifting once it makes it to the shipping lanes. The Howells are playing badminton.

Then Gilligan hauls in a huge barnacle-encrusted sphere which proves to be a mine, left-over from the war. He panics and yells for the Skipper, who's not really paying attention. He tells the Howells, who think he means a mine in the ground and Mr. Howell immediately appropriates a half interest.

Meanwhile, the Professor's collecting all the metal on the island to melt down for the anchor but Gilligan refuses to part with his solid steel four-leaf clover lucky charm. Ginger flirts with him and surreptitiously removes it from around his neck, but he's wise to it. Gilligan drags them to see the iron mine he reeled in. The Professor notes that it's ticking. They all flee.

But the Professor says running won't do them much good, since the island is com-

Bob Denver there?' 'Come on, I'm speaking.' 'Is Bob Denver there?' 'Who is this?' 'This is United Press. Are you dead?' I hung up and the other wire service called and we went through the same thing. 'I'm not dead!' They finally traced it to some high school in the midwest where some kid ran in in the morning and said 'Bob Denver was taking a bath and a radio fell into the tub and he was electrocuted.' It hit the wire services went all over the country in about two hours and for days afterward, I'd get on planes and people would scream.''

posed of coral and volcanic ash and there are undoubtedly underground gas deposits and if the mine explodes, the entire island is doomed. The men decide to try and disarm it. The Professor approaches the mine carefully and removes the seaweed. He can't find the timing device and figures it's under the mine. Gilligan and Mr. Howell go to help move it, but they are both wearing metal and are sucked against the mine.

The Professor uses the radio's UHF waves to demagnetize them and the mine. Gilligan is the only one small enough to crawl under the mine with a brass wrench to loosen the fitting as they tip it. But it's rusted closed. The Professor says they have no choice. They've got to attach it to the raft and tow it out to sea after they remove the metal rudder. But Gilligan's already in the lagoon towing the mine. They all rush to the lagoon and as Gilligan tows it past the opening to the sea, they tell him to cut the line and the mine sails out to sea.

But it floats back in and explodes. A large fish lands in Gilligan's arms.

51.
Erika Tiffany Smith to the Rescue
December 30, 1965

Created and Produced by
    Sherwood Schwartz
Executive Producer, Jack
    Arnold
Written by David P.
    Harmon
Directed by Jack Arnold
Guests
Zsa Zsa Gabor as . . . .
. . . . . . Erika Tiffany Smith
Michael Witney as . . Johnny

A very nice motor launch arrives in the lagoon. It's wealthy socialite Erika Tiffany Smith. She asks her boat pilot to pick her up at the cocktail hour. She's walking when she runs into the Skipper. Her yacht is anchored two miles offshore. She's looking for a deserted island to build a resort hotel. She's disappointed there are women among the Castaways. The Skipper takes her on a tour while Gilligan tells the others.

Mrs. Howell's not thrilled— Erika's name appears ahead of theirs in the social register.

How did Russell Johnson feel playing opposite the glamorous Zsa Zsa? "This was a very nicely-written show for the Professor. I kept hearing that Zsa Zsa was impossible to work with and that made it awkward for me because for the first time on the show, the Professor was to have a romantic entanglement. However, my apprehension vanished as soon as I met Zsa Zsa. She was really great. And easy to work with. As a matter of fact, we were the ones who made it difficult for her. You see, we were filming during the World Series." Evidently, every time they finished a scene, the cast and crew would rush over to a little black-and-white TV, leaving Zsa Zsa standing there alone until the next shot was set up. "And I'm sure when Zsa Zsa left, she said to herself, 'Dahling, these people are very difficult to work with.'"

And, after all, the "ink is scarcely dry" on her money. They have a acid-laced reunion. Mrs. Howell decides to go lie down and Erika and Mr. Howell talk turkey. Who does she deal with to buy the island? He tells her he's it. He tries to tell her the island's on the shipping lanes, but she doesn't believe it. "This island is so remote it never appeared on *Twilight Zone*." But that's okay—she's building a resort for the wealthy and remoteness is a plus.

She meets Mary Ann and the Professor, who fascinates her. He confesses he's always wanted to do research work and he wants someone by his side. She implies she's the one. He's besotted. He's looking forward to discovering the mating cycle of the angleworm. She'll build him a lab. Erika tells Mr. Howell they're engaged. The Professor's so confused, he calls Mary Ann "Ginger."

Erika hires the Skipper as captain of her yacht. He agrees if he can take Gilligan along. She reluctantly assents. She and the Professor stroll around while he tells her about the turtles and palm trees. She's more interested in moonlight swims.

Later, the Professor tells Ginger that he's worried Erika's not all that interested in his work. He doesn't know the first thing about hugging and kissing. Ginger offers to coach him. She lays a passionate kiss on him and tells him that's what Erika wants.

52.
Not Guilty
January 6, 1966

Created and Produced by
  Sherwood Schwartz
Jack Arnold, Executive
  Producer
Written by Roland
  MacLane
Directed by Stanley Z.
  Cherry

Gilligan's fishing and catches a crate marked COAST FOOD COMPANY. The Skipper's disappointed to find nothing but coconuts in it. But at least they're wrapped in Honolulu newspapers. One has an article about the Blake murder case, reading: "Survivors of the *Minnow*, which left the island immediately after the murder, are being sought for ques-

A local call from a pay telephone cost ten cents in 1966.

David Harmon, the show's story editor, remembers, "We did a lot of funny gags and slapstick on Gilligan's Island, but every time the Professor did any experiment on the island, it was one hundred percent accurate. He never said anything scientific that wasn't true. In fact, Gilligan's Island helped to start educational television. There was a public TV station in Philadelphia that showed a group of students segments of our show where the Professor was doing experiments, then showed them the same experiment conducted by one of their instructors. Afterwards, the kids were quizzed about what they learned. They retained a good deal more by watching the Professor than one of their own instructors. That was the beginning of educational television over twenty years ago. It was started by Gilligan's Island and educational television has gone on to become one of the great teaching and learning tools of this century."

tioning. All other suspects have been cleared and it is believed one of the seven persons aboard the missing *Minnow* is the killer."

Gilligan and the Skipper go to see the Professor, who's designed a guillotine—for coconuts. They leave. They go to warn Mary Ann and Ginger. They're cooking up wild oleander poison to get rid of the mice around the hut. "If it works, we're going to try to get rid of some other horrible creatures around here too."

Gilligan and the Skipper discuss telling the Howells. After all, how do they know they didn't steal all that money? They go to check out the Howells, who are asleep, but they awaken and are outraged at the intrusion. The Skipper drops the newspaper article. The Skipper and Gilligan go to bed, but they're both riddled with doubts about each other. The next morning, they look for the clipping and realize it's gone. The Howells find it and read about the murder of Randolph Blake.

Mary Ann and Ginger find the newspaper when they're cleaning the Howells' hut. They go to the Professor's hut where he's still playing with his guillotine. They panic, but he sees the article and he realizes why they're all so jittery.

53.
You've Been Disconnected
January 13, 1966

Created and Produced by
  Sherwood Schwartz
Executive Producer, Jack
  Arnold
Written by Elroy Schwartz
Directed by Jack Arnold
  [Uncredited] Guest
Sandra Gould as . . . .
. . . . . . Telephone Operator

A big storm sweeps the island and leaves everything in a mess. The next morning, Gilligan and the Skipper start to clean up. Gilligan trips over a large snakey thing and calls the Professor and the Skipper. The Professor realizes it's the trans-Pacific telephone cable. He's excited: "We can telephone for help."

Meanwhile, Ginger nearly faints when she hears a radio

The gossip columnist on the radio is imitating Hedda Hopper, one of the two legendary Hollywood columnists of the golden years of Hollywood.

Triangle Studios doesn't exist today, but it's a name with a lot of history behind it. Triangle Studios was one of the first motion picture companies in Los Angeles. The L.A. Music Center builds sets today at that location, near downtown. Silent film star Mabel Normand had her studio there and it was later used by cowboy star William S. Hart as his production facility.

CBS (the network which originally aired Gilligan's Island*) stands for Columbia Broadcasting System.*

WHAT'S MISSING?
When this episode airs in some markets, a scene with Mary Ann on duty at the makeshift telephone is cut. She interrupts a call between a couple, which causes the woman to think her boyfriend is seeing another woman. Then she and Gilligan reach a couple so busy kissing, they hang up the phone immediately after answering.

Sandra Gould, who plays the operator in this episode, also played nosy neighbor Gladys Kravitz on Bewitched.

bulletin that Triangle Studios is making Ginger's life into a movie, *The Ginger Grant Story.* She's thrilled. In an unrelated story, it's announced that CBS will star a hippo in a new sit-com. Upon hearing the news about the telephone, Ginger races down and insists she has to call her agent.

The Skipper suggests they simply cut the cable and then the phone company will come to repair it. [This is a splendid idea. Too bad they didn't do it.] The Professor insists he should be able to make a telephone. But he's got to cut through the metal casing first and the last saw blade breaks. Knowing that diamonds are the hardest thing, he sends Gilligan to get diamonds from Mrs. Howell.

But they can't get enough speed going for the necklace to work. While Ginger writes about events on the island for her movie, the Skipper looks for some natural gas on the island so they can make a blowtorch to use heat to get inside the casing. He finds it and the Professor cuts open the cable and starts stripping the wire. Gilligan backs into the blowtorch and sets his pants on fire.

54.
The Postman Cometh
January 20, 1966

Created and Produced by
Sherwood Schwartz
Jack Arnold, Executive
Producer
Written by Herbert Finn
and Alan Dinehart
Directed by Leslie
Goodwins

Mary Ann writes her daily letter to beau Horace Higgenbothem and has Gilligan load it into a bottle. Then the Skipper and Gilligan hear Horace has married a shipping heiress. Later, Mary Ann listens to her favorite soap, "Old Doctor Young." The Professor and the Skipper elect Gilligan to tell her but he can't. The Professor can't either and blurts out something about mushrooms being poisonous.

Ginger tells them the only way to help Mary Ann is to give her a "dream man" to make her forget Horace. She suggests the three single men woo her. She'll teach them. They all prepare and flirt with her, the Skipper as Marshal Dillon, Gilligan as Charles Boyer, while the

In the dream sequence, Mr. Howell's lovable Dr. Zorba Gillespie's wild hair is a parody of Sam Jaffe's equally wild 'do as Dr. Zorba on the hit ABC-TV series Ben Casey. *The Gillespie comes from Dr. Leonard Gillespie, mentor to NBC's medical drama,* Dr. Kildare. *Both medical shows had started in 1961 and were still on the air in 1966. Despite Jaffe's status as a respected actor, many jokes and parodies were made of his hair. This was years before anyone had seen boxing promoter Don King.*

Mary Ann's favorite radio program, "Old Doctor Young," is a parody on the long-running radio soap opera, Young Doctor Malone. *Coincidentally, Robert Young would play a doctor on* Marcus Welby, M.D. *in 1969.*

When Mr. Howell compares the Skipper's

*build to the Ponderosa,
he's referring to the vast
ranch owned by the
Cartwrights in the number
one TV show that year,
Bonanza.*

*The Skipper's
impersonation of
Marshal Dillon is a
reference to the show
that eventually would be
Gilligan's Island's nemesis,
Gunsmoke. James
Arness, brother of Peter
Graves, played the
lawman. The Skipper's
starfish badge is an
inspired touch.*

*When the Professor tries
to imitate Cary Grant,
he's impersonating the
best. Cary Grant was one
of the most gorgeous
leading men ever to be in
films. His suave good
looks and consummate
charm remain the
standard for the romantic
notions of millions of
women. Charles Boyer
(whom Gilligan imitates)
was also a model of suave,*

Professor pretends to be Cary Grant. She thinks they're all nuts.

Then Mary Ann overhears the Skipper and Gilligan talking and thinks she's eaten poison mushrooms and is about to die. That's why everyone's been so nice to her. She's horrified when she reveals that she's found out the secret and that all they can think of are parties and celebrating.

DREAM SEQUENCE

That night, Mary Ann has a dream where she's in a hospital and everyone's still in their silly characters except now they're doctors and nurses and she can't get anyone to pay any attention to her.

*European elegance. He
was an international film
star and was very visible
on TV, starring in and
producing* Four Star
Playhouse, *and
appearing on shows such
as* I Love Lucy, Climax,
and Hallmark Hall of
Fame. *He also starred in
the 1964 NBC series,* The
Rogues.

The title brings to mind
The Iceman Cometh, *an
innovative 1946 play by
Eugene O'Neill, famed
for his dark symbolism
and psychological
character studies. His
plays are often set on the
waterfront or near the sea,
and he was one of the
founders of the Theatre
Guild, the once-
prestigious production
company. Many critics
consider him the greatest
American dramatist
ever.* The Iceman Cometh
*was filmed in 1973 and
starred Lee Marvin,
Fredric March, and
Robert Ryan.*

If Horace Higgenbothem did marry the heiress, it didn't work out. In Rescue From Gilligan's Island, Mary Ann nearly marries Horace, who's been waiting for her for fifteen years.

When Mr. Howell says, "That kind of trust made Julius Caesar a pin cushion," he's referring to the betrayal and assassination of Julius Caesar by a group of conspirators led by Brutus and Cassius. He died of multiple stab wounds inflicted by the group in 44 B.C.

55.
Seer Gilligan
January 27, 1966

Created and Produced by
  Sherwood Schwartz
Executive Producer, Jack
  Arnold
Written by Elroy Schwartz
Directed by Leslie
  Goodwins

To his surprise, the sunflower seeds Gilligan's been munching on give him the ability to read the minds of the other Castaways. The Professor is, as usual, the doubter in the bunch. The Skipper tells him to think of something and Gilligan reels off a complicated scientific formula. The Professor is convinced. Gilligan repeats the trick for the others, and Mr. Howell muses on the commercial possibilities of the discovery.

Nobody knows what's causing it at first, but when Gilligan gives Ginger some of the seeds, she can do it too. They tell the others and the Professor realizes the plant the seeds came from was reported to have become extinct three hundred years ago. He tells the others that these seeds were used by the ancient mystics. Everyone wants the seeds and that night, they all try devious ways to get Gilligan to tell them where the bush is.

The next morning, Gilligan goes out to get the seeds. The Professor tells them the effect is only temporary. Gilligan returns with a large bag of seeds for each Castaway. They all rush off to test them. The Howells discover that mind reading between husband and wife is not an ideal situation. Gilligan and the Skipper try to work while mind reading and come to disaster, while Ginger and Mary Ann have a nonverbal fight.

Gilligan asks the Professor what to do. These are the first real fights the Castaways have had. He'd envisioned the seeds helping promote world peace. But Gilligan's thoughts about him are uncomplimentary and he stalks off.

Cotillions have gone the way of dinosaurs. Originally a formal dance where couples changed partners frequently, it came to mean simply a formal ball.

Mrs. Howell's reaction to the word and concept of "work" brings to mind the reaction of Bob Denver's character, Maynard G. Krebs, on The Many Loves of Dobie Gillis. *Work was a four-letter word to Dobie's beatnik buddy Maynard. The CBS comedy ran from 1959 to 1963.*

Mr. Howell compares his dancing ability to Jose Greco, a world-famous flamenco dancer. Mr. Howell's expression (and vocal impersonation) "How sweet it is," is the trademark of the "Great One," Jackie Gleason, who used the expression on The Honeymooners *as well as his popular*

56.
Love Me, Love My Skipper
February 3, 1966

Created and Produced by
  Sherwood Schwartz
Executive Producer, Jack
  Arnold
Written by Herbert Finn
  and Alan Dinehart
Directed by Tony Leader

Mr. Howell delivers envelopes to each hut. He doesn't realize he's dropped one. The Howells are having a cotillion, and everyone's gotten an invitation except the Skipper. He doesn't know whether the slight is unintentional or deliberate, and checks to see that everyone else got one. They did. The Howells (who think they've invited him) don't understand the Skipper's odd mood.

Gilligan tells the Skipper he won't go to the party if the Skipper doesn't. He's flattered and touched. The Professor, Mary Ann, and Ginger hear what Gilligan's doing and agree they'll boycott the How-

The *Gilligan's Island* lagoon as it was early in 1995 (the mill house is for a recent production). The old tank was torn out later in the year to make way for—what else?—a parking lot. (*Photo by author*)

The *Gilligan* production offices and soundstage at CBS Studio City as they are today—and in use by ABC's *Roseanne*. (*Photo by author*)

Gilligan tries to choose between the watermelon and Ginger while Alan Hale has no such dilemma in an early publicity photo. (*Photo courtesy of a private collection*)

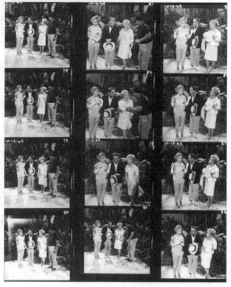

A rare contact sheet of various candid shots taken during the filming of "Erika Tiffany Smith to the Rescue," picturing Natalie Schafer, Jim Backus, Zsa Zsa Gabor and Alan Hale. (*Photo courtesy of a private collection*)

Dawn Wells checks out one of Sterling Holloway's birds in a publicity still from "The Pigeon." They never actually had a scene together. (*Photo courtesy of a private collection*)

Vito Scotti and Bob Denver in a publicity still for "So Sorry, My Island Now." (*Photo courtesy of a private collection*)

Tina Louise vamps Bob Denver, who becomes "The Dictator" in his dreams. (*Photo courtesy of a private collection*)

Bob Denver and Dawn Wells pose beside the battered *Minnow*. (*Photo courtesy of a private collection*)

Dawn Wells, Jim Backus and Tina Louise during rehearsal for "Lovey's Secret Admirer." (*Photo courtesy of a private collection*)

Bob Denver poses in the traditional sailor's stance—looking out to sea from the *Minnow*. (*Photo courtesy of a private collection*)

Russell Johnson, as The Professor. (*Photo courtesy of a private collection*)

The Castaways look pretty happy to be back on the mainland in *Rescue From Gilligan's Island*. Their smiles are partly due to the actual reception the film cast and crew received from locals who treated the filming as if it were reality. (*Photo courtesy of a private collection*)

Jim Backus adjusts Natalie Schafer's jewels in *The Castaways on Gilligan's Island*. (*Photo courtesy of a private collection*)

Mary Foran lusts after Bob Denver in "Gilligan's Mother-in-Law." (*Photo courtesy of a private collection*)

Bob Denver and Alan Hale in a publicity shot from the pilot, which was eventually used as part of "Birds Gotta Fly, Fish Gotta Talk." (*Photo courtesy of a private collection*)

ells' bash. They decide to have a party themselves, a masquerade in honor of the Skipper.

That night, the Howells read the R.S.V.P.s, which are all refusals. Mrs. Howell is devastated. Both of them are appalled when they realize they aren't invited to the other party. Mrs. Howell thinks Mr. Howell must have offended them. After all, he acts like a "ninny" on occasion. They fight and Mr. Howell moves out, saying he's going to his club and is *not* going to her party.

The Skipper decides on a pirate costume for the party. Gilligan finds the Skipper's lost invitation and the Skipper's mortified—he's got to apologize to the Howells. Gilligan informs him they're not living together. The Skipper tells Mrs. Howell what happened, and she's very gracious, but she's still peeved with "that man," (her husband) who is "arrogant, bigoted, childish, selfish, dreadful, and inconsiderate." She says those are his good points. She's thinking of joining the Foreign Legion.

variety show which ran from 1952 through 1970.

The title brings to mind a series on at the time this show was filmed, My Living Doll. Julie Newmar played a robot who was the perfect woman.

The song the Castaways sing as the robot sinks slowly into the lagoon is "Aloha Oe" (Farewell to Thee), the traditional Hawaiian song played for the departures of ships.

When Mr. Howell calls the robot "our answer to Lloyd Bridges," he's referring to the actor who starred in Sea Hunt from 1957–1961 and ran for many years in syndication. More than half the show took place underwater. A new version of the show, starring Ron Ely, ran for a season in 1987.

Bob Denver remembers one problem they had on Gilligan's Island. "When

57.
Gilligan's Living Doll
February 10, 1966

Created and Produced by
   Sherwood Schwartz
Executive Producer, Jack
   Arnold
Written by Bob Stevens
Directed by Leslie
   Goodwins

Gilligan wishes on his rabbit's foot and soon he and the Skipper see a parachutist heading for the island. They find a robot and the parachute. It talks. But it only repeats what they say. The Professor thinks it's a test robot for the air force. He notes that whoever sent it up will come looking for it and they'll be rescued.

The Professor does open heart surgery on the robot and reprograms it so that it obeys his commands. He says it will do all the work on the island. But they learn that instructing a non-thinking robot is tough. The robot breaks through a hut wall when Mary Ann tries to teach it to sweep and Ginger gets flying crockery when the robot does dishes. The Skipper has better luck having it do the laundry until Mr. Howell demands the robot for his caddie. Then Gilligan falls in the washing machine and . . .

The Professor programs the robot to help them get off the island. The robot says it can build a boat in "seventeen hours, four minutes, eleven seconds." He sends the robot off to do it. Everyone packs and goes to the lagoon to see the completed boat. It's a toy-sized, two-masted schooner. They ask the robot what full-sized boats it can build, and it answers, "a carrier, destroyer, or minesweeper." Mr. Howell orders up a destroyer and the robot notes it needs 412,000 tons of steel. They all go back to the drawing board.

Mrs. Howell asks the robot to build a bridge to Hawaii—all it will take is eighty-nine years. Mr. Howell asks for a search-light, but the robot says it can't make one without electric power.

Ginger tries flirting with the robot, but when she asks it to get her off the island, it says it isn't programmed to do that. But she persists and it starts steaming. Gilligan thinks they should ask it to build a radio station. But it gives the Skipper

Dawn Wells and I did a scene together, three and a half pages is supposed to run a minute and a half. We talk very quickly, both of us. We'd do the scene and they'd go, 'Well, that was about thirty seconds. We have to get four more pages of dialogue. Hold on.' And they'd have to call the office and Sherwood Schwartz would say, 'They did it again?' They'd say, 'Yeah, they did a minute-and-a-half scene in thirty seconds' and he'd sit down and type and the pages would come down and we'd do it fast and he'd say, 'Can you guys slow down a minute? My hands are getting tired in the typewriter.' It was always that way."

the idea of getting it to swim to Hawaii and programming the robot to tell the authorities about them.

58.
Forward March
February 17, 1966

Created and Produced by
  Sherwood Schwartz
Executive Producer, Jack
  Arnold
Written by Jack Raymond
Directed by Jerry Hopper
  [Uncredited] Guest
Janos Prohaska as the Ape

The Skipper's longing for some different food when Gilligan tells him an avocado just flew onto the island. They look for it and it's a grenade. The Professor dismantles it before it does any damage, but who threw it? What do they want? Mr. Howell suggests surrender. The Skipper wants to fight, but what about the women? He agrees to a white flag. But the Professor thinks they might not honor the white flag. Meanwhile, Gilligan's making the white flag.

Gilligan goes back to the

When Ginger announces she is ready to be "Mata Hari," she refers to the famous World War I spy. She was actually a dancer named Gertrude Margarete Zelle, who took Mata Hari as her stage name (it means "sun" in Malayan) and was executed by the French in 1917. Her story was filmed several times, beginning with Mata Hari in 1932, with Greta Garbo playing the beautiful spy.

We learn that the Howell family crest is crossed dollar bills on a field of Swiss banks.

Ginger sings "It Had to Be You," a pop standard written in 1924 by Gus Kahn and Isham Jones. The song was interpolated into lagoon and the other men tell him the surrender plan is off. A grenade lobs in and explodes. The men set up a command post, but the Skipper and Mr. Howell get into a spat about who's in charge. The Professor insists they have more important things to do—like scouting the island. Mr. Howell appoints himself general and puts himself in charge of the women. He's quite a tyrant.

The Skipper and Professor can find no one on the island. General Howell trains Gilligan in peashooting. Then the camp is strafed by machine-gun fire. Later, they find the gun under a bush. It's full of ammunition. Then they find a gorilla, who's the one that's been tossing the grenades. General Howell fires the machine gun into the air and it scares the ape off. They reconnoiter and find the ape's cave. They look for a back way in and dig it out. Gilligan goes in and finds there's an old ammo dump in the cave, but then the ape finds him and won't let him out.

a dozen films, including the biography of Gus Kahn, I'll See You in My Dreams (1951), where it was sung by Danny Thomas and was used in the underscoring as a recurring theme.

Bob Denver was not only typecast from playing Gilligan, it affected his recreation, too. "I've tried to rent boats sometimes, like a sailboat or a motorboat to go out for a day or two, and what I have to go through, and listen to all the jokes for an hour, 'You want this boat? How long are you taking it out for? Three hours, yuk, yuk, yuk.' You don't want to have to rent a boat when you're Gilligan. But I do like sailing."

This story is a version of a classic con, which grifters call "the Wire." This con was also the basis for the Paul Newman and Robert Redford film, The Sting, *which was released in 1973. It's also detailed in a "reality" show from the fifties,* Racket Squad.

Lyndon Baines Johnson was U.S. president when this episode was filmed. Ladybird Johnson was first lady.

Gilligan mentions he has an uncle John.

59.
Ship Ahoax
February 24, 1966

Created and Produced by
    Sherwood Schwartz
Executive Producer, Jack
    Arnold
Written by Charles Tannen
    and George O'Hanlon
Directed by Leslie
    Goodwins

The Skipper pulls rank on Gilligan, who's not happy about it. They argue and draw the proverbial line on the hut floor. Gilligan returns everyone's belongings he's been storing for them. He finds the Howells fighting and Ginger and Mary Ann at each other's throats.

Ginger's become a fortune teller. She spreads the cards and predicts an earthquake and one starts. Later, Ginger tells the Professor how it works: They have tremors all the time, and a pot in her hut begins to shake before anyone can feel the shaking, making her look like a seer.

The Professor asks her to find a way to predict that a ship will come for them pretty soon—to keep the Castaways from killing each other. The Professor steals the radio and lets Ginger listen to the news, so she can predict things later.

But it only foments more dissension. Gilligan tells the Skipper about Ginger's prediction of the outcome of the Army-Navy game, and he bets Gilligan two weeks of collecting firewood she's wrong. Mr. Howell bets Gilligan water collection duty for a week when he tells him of Ginger's stock prediction. Of course, they're both losers.

The Skipper and Mr. Howell beg Ginger for predictions. She holds a fortune-telling show that night and predicts lots of rescue ships. Then the radio reports a destroyer, the *U.S.S. York*, was last heard from somewhere near where the *Minnow* was lost. An admiral launches a full-scale rescue fleet. One hundred ships will be in the area starting at dawn. Ginger sends Gilligan out with flyers announcing her business.

The Professor confronts her but by now, she's very impressed with herself and her powers. Gilligan is her first appointment. He asks what will happen to him after they're rescued. She sees a ship—with him as captain and then a storm, a coral reef, and him saving her.

Mr. Howell, as usual, has plans to exploit Ginger's talent. The Howells invite her to tea and give her two mink coats. All he asks for are the stock prices an hour before the market opens. They all listen to the news and the *York* has been found. They ask Ginger what happens now. The Professor says she'll tell them tonight and drags her away.

NATALIE SCHAFER

Natalie Schafer, a native of Red Bank, New Jersey, studied acting with the great Katharine Cornell, despite her parents' objections. After a job in a bookstore, she started making the rounds of theatrical agents and producers. Her tenacity led to several small roles on Broadway, including one in Gertrude Lawrence's first dramatic vehicle, *Susan and God*.

She married matinee idol Louis Calhern in 1934, and they performed together in summer stock theatres. Calhern died in 1956. Natalie got leading roles in *The Show is On* and *Lady in the Dark*, another Gertrude Lawrence hit. She was discovered by an MGM talent scout in *The Doughgirls* and moved to Hollywood.

When she didn't want to sign a studio contract with MGM, Louis B. Mayer asked her, "Why aren't you signing? Why?" Schafer said, "Because I'm in love in New York. He lives in New York. Mr. Mayer said, 'So what? We'll bring him out here.' "

"I said, 'That's not possible. I don't think his wife would let him go.' And Mr. Mayer looked at me and said, 'A married man! A married man! I thought you were a lady. Get out of my office.' I get fan mail to this day all the time and that surprises me. People recognize me in markets and that really surprises me. It was twenty-five years ago, how can I still be recognizable? I kind of like that."

In addition to her fine stage career, Natalie appeared in some wonderful films along the way, including *Repeat Performance*, about a woman who kills her husband on New Year's Eve and then is given a chance to relive the previous year to try and change her life and her relationship with her husband. She plays a marvelous wealthy Russian expatriate in *Anastasia*, and appeared in Fannie Hurst's *Back Street* and *The Day of the Locust*.

She seems to have truly enjoyed her work on *Gilligan's Island.* "When I first saw the script, I thought it would lay an egg. It was such a surprise to have it go on and on and on. I still don't know why, except everybody relates in some way. Like my fan mail from children would say, 'My mother and father fight all the time. You and your husband never fight, do you?' Well, we did sometimes."

"Now, I wish we were still in production, but then, I was a New Yorker when they sent me this script. I thought 'This will never go.' It was so unlike anything I'd ever read, anything I'd ever been in, anything I'd ever seen. I didn't want to leave New York but my agent said, 'Oh, this will never go, but you want to go to Hawaii, it's a great chance. Go ahead and do it.' At Christmas time I was in Puerto Vallarta and my mother was very ill and I was very nervous about being there and a telegram was brought to me one evening, and I looked at it and burst into tears. Everybody came around thinking my mother had died. I said, 'No, the series sold!' But I loved it and I'd love to go right on doing it. I'd love another series. I never thought I'd say that.

"I liked Jim and working with Jim and he always ad-libbed and I grew up in the theatre and we never ad-libbed, so it was an exciting new adventure and then I had permission to design my own clothes and plan my own wardrobe and that was wonderful because it was very important that when this woman came on, you knew what kind of a woman she was. And slacks and gloves and pearls and hats and she wasn't exactly a Pasadena lady. We'd read on Sunday and rewrite and they were very nice about accepting it when we did it. Nobody ever said 'I didn't write that.'"

There are no records of a designer or shop in New York in the sixties called "Madame Swee-Lo." Since Schafer has said several times that she created many items of Mrs. Howell's wardrobe, it's possible that this credit was some inside joke.

Schafer did discover the downside of playing such a memorable character in millions of homes. "I think it changed your career. I was up for a lot of jobs that I didn't get because it was not like *Gilligan's Island*. They'd say, 'Oh, she's done *Gilligan's Island*, we can't put her on as something else.' I've been a sadistic killer lesbian in *The Killing of Sister George*, but they paid no attention to that.

"We were all typed, pretty strongly. Bob Denver, very much so, Jim and I, and there were an awful lot of jobs we couldn't have. The new young network people didn't approve. They didn't know that we'd ever done anything else. I had a young network boy interview me one day and he said, 'Now tell me, Miss Schafer, what have you done?' And I looked at him and said, 'You first,' and he spent twenty minutes telling me what he did at the Yale drama school. Then I said, 'Thank you very much,' and left."

Miss Schafer passed away on April 10, 1991. The *Los Angeles Times* said that she was survived by several nieces and nephews and her longtime companion, Maurice Hill.

Credits

Broadway Theatre
Trigger 1927
March Hares 1928
The Nut Farm 1929
Ada Beats the Drum 1930
The Rhapsody 1930
The Great Barrington 1931
Perfectly Scandalous 1931
New York to Cherbourg 1932
So Many Paths 1934
Why We Misbehave 1935
Lady in the Dark 1941
The Doughgirls 1942
Lady Precious Stream 1936
Goodbye in the Night 1940
A Joy Forever 1946
Forward the Heart 1949
Six Characters in Search of an Author—Phoenix, 1955 (Off-Broadway)
Romanoff and Juliet 1957
The Highest Tree—Longacre, 1959
The Killing of Sister George—national tour, 1967

Films, Telemovies, TV Series, and Specials
Marriage is a Private Affair 1944
Molly and Me 1945

Keep Your Powder Dry 1945
Masquerade in Mexico 1945
Wonder Man 1945
Dishonored Lady 1947
The Other Love 1947
Repeat Performance 1947
The Secret Beyond the Door 1947
The Snake Pit 1948
Caught 1949
Payment on Demand 1951
Take Care of My Little Girl 1951
The Law and the Lady 1951
Callaway Went Thataway 1951
Has Anyone Seen My Gal? 1952
Just Across the Street 1952
The Girl Next Door 1953
Female on the Beach 1955
The Petrified Forest—television special, 1955
Forever Darling 1956
Anastasia 1956
Oh Men! Oh Women! 1957
Bernadine 1957
Susan Slade 1961
Back Street 1961
Gilligan's Island—series, 1964–1967
The Survivors—series, 1966
40 Carats 1973
The Day of the Locust 1975
Rescue From Gilligan's Island—telemovie, 1978
The "Castaways" on Gilligan's Island—telefilm, 1979
The Harlem Globetrotters on Gilligan's Island—telefilm, 1981
Gilligan's Planet—animated series, 1982—1983
I'm Dangerous Tonight—telefilm, 1990

Guest Starring Roles

The Chevrolet Tel-Theater "Sham"
Kraft Television Theatre "The Miracle of Chick-
   erston"
Philco TV Playhouse
Studio One
Lux Video Theatre
Mr. & Mrs. North
Robert Montgomery Presents
Armstrong Circle Theatre
I Love Lucy "The Charm School"
Topper
The Phil Silvers Show "Bilko's Formula 7"
The Ann Sothern Show
Guestward Ho! "Babs's Mother"
The Beverly Hillbillies "The Dress Shop"
ABC Stage 67 "The Canterville Ghost"
Route 66
Love, American Style "Love and the Man of the
   Year"
The Brady Bunch "The Snooperstar"
Vegas! "Ladies in Blue" (pilot)
Three's Company "Jack in the Flower Shop"
CHiPs
Matt Houston
Trapper John M.D., "Candy Doctor"
Simon & Simon "The Secret of the Chrome
   Eagle"
The Love Boat

Lovey Wentworth Howell

Eunice Wentworth Howell (Sherwood Schwartz
says her real first name exists in the script for
episode number sixty-seven) went to Vassar

after a sheltered upbringing in Grosse Pointe, Michigan (also the birthplace of her husband).

She does all the society things a woman of her class usually does, attends and organizes benefits (though she does occasionally tire of these), balls, concerts, and the like, and avidly concerns herself with her husband's physical and fiscal health.

She loves the symphony, weddings, and jewelry and acting—particularly playing Lady Macbeth—but of course, she only does it for charity. She uses perfumes "Gold Dust No. 5," "Warm Afternoon," and "Tea Rose."

60.
Feed the Kitty
March 3, 1966

Created and Produced by
   Sherwood Schwartz
Jack Arnold, Executive
   Producer
Written by J. E. Selby and
   Dick Sanville
Directed by Leslie
   Goodwins

The Skipper is putting together some boards from a crate that washed up in the lagoon when he sees some writing on the boards. The Professor translates the Latin: "Lion." The crate was from a zoo. Gilligan's been hearing roars and growling all morning.

This is the single most-remembered episode among the cast members. Bob Denver had the most harrowing experience. "I had this five-hundred-fifty-pound African lion. It's six-thirty at night. He wasn't very happy. He's growling around. I explained to the trainer what I was going to do, but I don't think he heard me. The lion's lying on the twin beds in the hut, I rush in, I think he's outside and I run around like a little mouse and pile furniture up, sit down next to the lion, scream, and run. You don't do that in front of a

*lion. As I ran away, I heard
him roar. I said, 'He's
coming! He's in the air!'
I'm going, 'Oh, I'll catch
him. No. I'll punch him,
but my hand would have
gone down his throat up
to my elbow.' When the
lion pushed off, the twin
beds split apart and he
was back in a second
crouch and the trainer was
in midair, tackled him off
the bed, rolled him on the
floor. The whole crew
applauded. To this day,
I don't know why they
applauded. Because he
missed me? Of course,
about ten minutes later,
they said, 'Let's do it
again.' 'Sure . . . you tie
him down. I want to see
chains around him.'
When the lion roars, you
know he's coming."*

The men go out on the lion
hunt. They are—you should
pardon the expression—nervous as cats. The Skipper suggests Gilligan go back to guard
the women and he's only too
happy to comply. Meanwhile,
the women are sitting in the
clearing when Mrs. Howell
begins to sneeze. Indignant
when Ginger thinks a Howell
could catch a cold, she
explains she's got allergies—
to cats. The lion's right above
them on a rock.

The women trap him in the
Howell hut and flee. Gilligan
arrives and goes inside. When
the lion growls, he thinks the
lion's outside and barricades
the door. But the lion's right
behind him. He and the lion
become friends and Gilligan
removes a thorn from the
lion's paw. Gilligan calls him
Leo.

They eventually figure out
that the lion was in a circus and
responds to Mr. Howell's
booming ringmaster voice.

The Castaways decide to put
on a circus. Gilligan runs the
lion through its paces while
Ginger practices for her high-wire act. The Skipper practices
juggling but it's not going well.
He suggests to Mary Ann she

do a hatchet-throwing act with him but she declines. Then Gilligan, who's been feeding the lion canned corned beef, has run out of food. They'd better build a cage fast.

61.
Operation: Steam Heat
March 10, 1966

Produced and Created by
   Sherwood Schwartz
Executive Producer, Jack
   Arnold
Written by Terence and
   Joan Maples
Directed by Stanley Z.
   Cherry

Gilligan finds a steam vent in the island. The Skipper is thrilled—hot water! The Professor's more concerned that it means an active volcano. Sure enough, on the other side of their little rock, a volcano is spitting lava. The Professor goes to check, but doesn't tell the others.

Meanwhile, everybody wants the hot water. Gilligan builds a pipeline to the huts, promising everyone equal access to the hot water. But Mr. Howell

Ginger talks about a movie she was in where she played a beautiful woman who was thrown into a volcano, but she never tells us the name of the film.

Alan Hale remembered one drawback to playing a marooned character in a medium people take as seriously as they do television. "The only problem I ever had was when I'd go out to a restaurant. Someone would always ask me how I got off the island. I'd tell them the producer let me off if I promised to go back in the morning."

observes, "Leaving you in charge of a construction job is like leaving a lit match in charge of dynamite." Everybody's ready—the Skipper waits for a hot shower, Mr. Howell waits in a steamer trunk doubling for a bathtub (with a little sailboat), and the girls wait for hot dishwater. He turns it on and the pipeline develops over a hundred leaks.

Meanwhile, the volcanic eruption is getting worse. Mr. Howell, Ginger and Mary Ann, and the Skipper try to bribe Gilligan to deliver the wonderful stuff to them first. But when the professor comes back and volcanic ash is showering down on them all, it's clear hot baths are not their main concern. The Professor suggests he try to diffuse the volcano's power with an explosion. He prepares it and Gilligan drinks some of the Professor's liquid and then finds out it was nitroglycerin. He's positive he's going to explode if he moves. Ginger prepares to throw herself in the volcano.

62.
Will the Real Mr. Howell Please Stand Up?
March 17, 1966

Created by Sherwood
   Schwartz
Written by Budd Grossman
Produced and Directed by
   Jack Arnold

Gilligan and the Howells are floored to hear on the radio that "The Wolf of Wall Street," Thurston Howell III, has been rescued and is planning to sell off his major holdings. Mr. Howell is livid that an impostor is about to ruin his financial empire. Gilligan and the Skipper have to restrain Mr. Howell when he heads for the lagoon. Several times. He offers the Castaways one million dollars for whoever comes up with a way to get them off the island.

Their ideas are mostly of hot-air balloon and Icarus wings type. Gilligan even thinks they could shoot someone out of a cannon. They eventually go with the Professor's more reasonable suggestion of a raft on pontoons. They build it and send Mr. Howell off . . . to the bottom of the lagoon.

The title of this episode is taken from the phrase used a zillion times on the popular game show, To Tell the Truth, *which aired on CBS from 1956 to 1967. After three people each tried to convince the celebrity panelist they were Jane Doe, bricklayer, or astronaut, or whatever, host Bud Collier would say, "Will the real Jane Doe please stand up?"*

Natalie Schafer remembered, "Wherever I go, people always ask me the same question. Why on earth did I bring trunks full of clothes if I was only going on a three-hour cruise. As I explain, the answer is really quite simple. You have to be ready for everything. I just loved doing all sorts of crazy things on our show—jumping into the lagoon with my hat and my gloves and my pearls and oh, yes, my clothes too. And I adored sinking into quicksand. And even climbing trees. All sorts of crazy things. I wonder if I could become an astronaut. That's one thing I haven't done yet."

The next news bulletin reports that Mr. Howell will sail on around the world with a crew of forty-nine babes. Everyone's worried that Mr. Howell is going around the bend and the Professor tries a little elementary psychology, but it doesn't help much. Mr. Howell turns to his teddy. Then the radio says the impostor has fallen overboard while drinking champagne from a crew member's slipper. Guess where he ends up?

The impostor sneaks into camp, bonks Mr. Howell on the head with a coconut, and puts on his clothes. The real Mr. Howell regains consciousness and finds he's wearing the impostor's clothes. Gilligan's the first one who sees both men. He thinks he's dreaming.

When discotheques became all the rage in the sixties, they usually were called the Something a-Go-Go. One of the first of these clubs still survives—the Whisky a-Go-Go—now simply called the Whisky (on the Sunset Strip). At times in

63.
Ghost a-Go-Go
March 24, 1966

Created and Produced by
  Sherwood Schwartz
Jack Arnold, Executive
  Producer
Written by Roland
  MacLane

Directed by Leslie Goodwins

Guest
Richard Kiel as. . the Ghost

Gilligan thinks he's seen a ghost, and he's a wreck. Mary Ann's been hearing strange noises and the magazine Ginger was reading last night is missing—and so's the table. The Howells think Gilligan's playing practical jokes on them. Mr. Howell's polo pony is up in a tree and they think Gilligan did a little dance in their patio last night.

When the Professor reports hearing a "mournful cry" in the night, Gilligan freaks out. That night, he refuses to go to sleep. He wants the Skipper to stay up with him. The Skipper tries to convince Gilligan he's seeing things until he sees the ghost himself and faints. The Howells, Ginger, and Mary Ann rush in, refusing to be alone.

The next morning, the Professor tries to find a rational explanation. He asks if a sheet's missing. Mary Ann says there is one missing. They figure it blew off the line and has been blowing around the island ever since. They set out

1965–1967, there were dozens of go-go clubs, all of which usually had cages hung in the clubs where female go-go dancers in miniskirts and shiny white boots watusied and frugged their way to oblivion inside them. One of the more original names was a club in San Francisco's Chinatown, the Dragon a-Gong-Gong.

The very tall Richard Kiel, who plays the Ghost, starred in several James Bond films, including Moonraker *and* The Spy Who Loved Me.

to look for it. Gilligan hears the ghost and this time, it talks to him. The ghost says he's a good ghost. He scares them because they scare him. They must leave. Gilligan says they can't leave. The ghost says they must find a way. Then the ghost appears and Gilligan flees.

At the lagoon, the Skipper's found a fully-equipped boat with a note in it from the ghost. The Castaways gather and prepare to sail off in the boat. But they're still wary and decide to send the boat out with seven dummies first to test it. The ghost might want to kill them.

In addition to the telegrams and letters to the coast guard about the Castaways noted above, Bob Denver remembers another story. "There was a retired admiral in New Jersey in the seventies who watched the show when we gave out the longitude and latitude one time and he sent it to Washington, and said 'There are people stranded.' It went down

64.
Allergy Time
March 31, 1966

Created and Produced by
  Sherwood Schwartz
Executive Producer, Jack
  Arnold
Written by Budd Grossman
Directed by Jack Arnold

The Skipper develops a bad case of itching and sneezing and the Professor tries to diagnose his illness. He worries the

Skipper has a rare tropical disease but eventually decides it's only allergies. Everybody tries to figure out what he's allergic to. The Professor runs a couple of tests and decides the Skipper's allergic to Gilligan.

The Professor makes Gilligan a nonallergic soap and he scrubs down, but it's no use. The Professor wonders if it's psychological, but in a blindfolded test with all the Castaways, it's only Gilligan who sets off a sneezing fit. That night, Gilligan moves out of the hut he's shared with the Skipper and in with the Professor.

Gilligan has trouble sleeping—he misses the Skipper's snoring. The Professor promises to try to snore like the Skipper, but all he does is sneeze like the Skipper. Gilligan moves in with the Howells. Mr. Howell confesses that Mrs. Howell talks in her sleep and she retorts that Mr. Howell walks in his sleep. They both start to sneeze.

Ginger and Mary Ann hang up a blanket so Gilligan can sleep in their hut, but they soon start sneezing. He takes his blanket and pillow and heads into the jungle. In the morning, they all find a note from Washington all the way to Honolulu. They got it on the big coast guard cutter at sea, and a sailor walked up to the captain and said, 'Sir, I think it's a TV show.' "

from Gilligan, who has moved to the other side of the island to become a hermit. The Castaways set out to find him, using their noses.

Ginger finds him first and insists that despite their allergies, they want him back. But she can't complete her plea for her sneezing. The others have the same reaction. The Skipper even sneezes so hard he sneezes down a tree.

The Professor develops a Gilligan vaccine and the men go to retrieve the outcast. They all quail at the sight of the giant needle, but think Gilligan's the intended stickee—but, of course, it's them. They've got to get shots twice a week— perhaps for as long as they're on the island. They all refuse.

This is the only episode when the Castaways actually leave their island until they're rescued in 1978.

One of the most frequently asked questions about Gilligan's Island is why the Professor could make

65.
The Friendly Physician
April 7, 1966

Created and Produced by
   Sherwood Schwartz
Jack Arnold, Executive
   Producer
Written by Elroy Schwartz
Directed by Jack Arnold

Guest

Vito Scotti as the Physician
Mike Mazurki as . . . . . . Igor

You'd think the Castaways would be thrilled when Dr. Boris Balinkoff arrives. He'll take them to his island, then to civilization, but the trouble is, he's a little strange.

The doctor's only got a small launch, so Gilligan suggests he and the Skipper go with the doctor to pick up his yacht, then come back for the others.

But his house is the proverbial haunted mansion. They sit down to eat steak dinners with cutlery heaped with dust and spiderwebs. The doctor's dog comes in, but all he does is meow. The cat barks. Gilligan and the Skipper explore the doctor's foyer then Gilligan disappears into a hidden panel. The Skipper follows and is sucked in too. They go down a creepy staircase and find a medieval torture chamber, complete with a rack and a stock, and the Skipper gets stuck in the latter. Gilligan finally finds the hidden spring that releases it. There's also a skeleton in a cage. They go back to the hall and the doc-

every imaginable device out of two seashells and a mango, yet could not build a raft that would float for the Castaways, despite his six degrees. Sherwood Schwartz has a ready answer for that one. "None of the degrees was in boat building."

tor's waiting with his roaring parrot. He says he's been doing animal research. Switching a bunch of them around. He wants to do it with people. "Igor, take them into the play-room."

The rest of the Castaways arrive and find the house just as creepy. Mr. Howell gets sucked into another secret door and finds the doctor. "How would you like to rule the world?" Mr. Howell has an answer, "I'd rather buy it and hire someone to run it for me." The doctor proposes he replace all the world leaders with his own followers. Howell offers him twenty million dollars for his project. He refuses.

The Skipper's barber back home is named Sam.

People often ask Sherwood Schwartz about the dangerous stunts done in the show. Schwartz says, "In the entire time, not once, with all those beatings on the brain, did the Skipper ever really hurt Gilligan and I think that was one

66.
"V" for Vitamins
April 14, 1966

Created and Produced by
   Sherwood Schwartz
Jack Arnold, Executive
   Producer
Written by Barney Slater
Directed by Gary Nelson

The Skipper gets a haircut and suddenly he feels like Samson, unable to lift anything.

The Professor does some tests and finds that because of the lack of citrus fruits on the island, the Skipper lacks vitamins, particularly vitamin C. He says eventually they're all going to start suffering just like the Skipper.

That night, Gilligan is innocently eating an orange when the Skipper pounces on him. Gilligan says he got it in the jungle, but it's the last one. The Castaways all try to get it from him, using their usual ploys. Mr. Howell tries to buy it, Ginger tries tears, and Gilligan finally decides to be like Solomon and give each one a slice. But there's still dissension. While everyone argues over what's fair, the hot sun rots the orange. The Professor says it all: "Our greed has pushed us to the brink of disaster."

Gilligan suggests they "give it a decent burial" and the Professor realizes he's solved the problem. They'll plant the seeds and grow their own oranges. Each Castaway is given some of the pips and they all set out to plant them. But they don't really don't know how. Mary Ann's solution seems best: "One part sunshine, two parts water, and

of the most important things in the show. The fact that the love between these two men overcame all the dreadful things that Gilligan kept doing one week after another. Nothing was going to get them off the island."

three parts prayer." But a cold night endangers their project. They light tiki torches to keep the seeds warm and the Professor leaves Gilligan on guard to keep the fires burning. But he falls asleep.

DREAM SEQUENCE

Gilligan dreams he's Jack in the Beanstalk. Mrs. Howell (as his mother) gives him precious jewels to buy oranges. Mr. Howell plays a fast-talking con man who trades the jewels for some magic beans. His mother is furious and throws them out the window, where they grow into a giant beanstalk. Gilligan climbs and reaches the castle of a "mean, cruel giant."

Gilligan tells us his philosophy of life: "Life's like a game of marbles. No matter how pretty yours are, the other guy's are prettier."

We learn that Mrs. Howell's maiden name is Wentworth. Natalie Schafer adored playing Mrs. Howell. "I'm delighted when I'm

67.
Mr. and Mrs.?
April 21, 1966

Created and Produced by
    Sherwood Schwartz
Jack Arnold, Executive
    Producer
Written by Jack Gross, Jr.,
    and Mike Stein
Directed by Gary Nelson

The Howells try to sell Gilligan on the joys of marriage.

Then the radio reports an oddity in the news. Minister Buckley Norris in Massachusetts has been exposed as a fraud. He's the one who married the Howells. Mrs. Howell wants to know when he's going to marry her. He retreats to his teddy. She throws him out of the hut—after they've divided their possessions. She starts with the trunk of money.

Ginger suggests the Skipper marry them as was done in a movie she made. He agrees. The Professor says a captain has no authority on dry land, only at sea. Gilligan suggests they build a raft and marry them in the lagoon. Everyone thinks that's a good solution.

The wedding preparations proceed. Lovey Wentworth has her great grandmother's wedding ring and gives it to Gilligan to hold with some trepidation. While Gilligan and the Skipper build the raft, the Skipper recounts the only time he came close to marriage. Gilligan says marriage is not for him. The Skipper practices on Gilligan and Mary Ann. Gilligan refuses to say "I do." He drops the ring.

The wedding begins. Everybody looks lovely. The Skip-

recognized because I really didn't expect— twenty-five years later— to be recognized, so I think that's a lot of fun. I think kids today love us but adults, all my fan mail comes from adults. They have a hard time getting away from Gilligan's Island. It's on three times a day. All over the world. My word, fan mail comes from Japan and Australia, London, Germany. I think people relate in some way and also something I think is very important—there hasn't been enough laughter in the business. I think laughter is very important and I think people want to laugh. And with Gilligan's Island, you can't help laughing. When I first went into it, I didn't think I'd ever laugh at it. I thought it was dreadful then I got so that I really fell in love with it. And then we worked together, Jim Backus and I, on rewriting our parts and making them funnier and ad-libbing a lot. In the script I was written as a stuffy Pasadena lady who said 'Yes, dear' and 'No, dear,' and that's about all she said to her husband."

per's even buttoned his shirt. Ginger's the maid of honor and Gilligan poles them out into the lagoon and, of course, gets stuck on the pole. When the Skipper tries to abbreviate the ceremony, everyone complains. The Howells get into a fight, the ring gets stuck on Gilligan's finger, which only makes things worse. Mr. Howell hands the Skipper a cigar band. Miss Wentworth is outraged and refuses to marry him.

Mr. Howell, when writing his will, mentions his nephew Perry (who owes him $1.42) and Perry's wife Frances.

Mr. Howell also talks of his "polo pony Seabiscuit"—implying that he uses the most famous thoroughbred race horse in the world as his personal mount. Seabiscuit would have been pretty old for polo, though. As a four-year-old in 1937, Seabiscuit won $168,580, finishing first in eleven of fifteen starts, second

68.
Meet the Meteor
April 28, 1966

Created and Produced by
 Sherwood Schwartz
Written by Elroy Schwartz
Directed by Jack Arnold

The Skipper and Gilligan are shaken when a meteor falls and lands on the island. The Professor tells them to keep away from it because it could be dangerous. He makes a crude Geiger counter to check the meteor's radiation. He tells Gilligan and the Skipper not to tell the Howells or Ginger and Mary Ann. As usual, Gilligan trying to keep a secret confuses everyone. Ginger thinks they're planning a surprise birthday party for her; Mary Ann thinks they're planning a surprise Christmas party for everyone; the Howells think they're planning a surprise anniversary party for them.

The Professor finally tests the meteor. It isn't radioactive, but it does have "cosmic rays." He fashions a screen around it to protect the Castaways and reflect the rays upwards, where they might be detected by a weather plane. He insists they all dip their clothes in lead and put on lead makeup to protect them while they put the shield up. It works but only for a while. They go back and the screen's gone and there's been some explosive growth of the surrounding foliage. The Professor fears they'll all be prematurely aged by the rays. They've got to get rid of the meteor.

Later, they hear a weather report about a violent electrical storm approaching them. The meteor is composed primarily of metals and if they can attract a bolt of lightning to it, it might be destroyed. The Professor makes a lightning rod out of

place twice, and third place twice.

Mr. Howell jokes about his "matched golf clubs"—mentioning Wingfoot, Hillcrest, and Pebble Beach—all exclusive private country clubs.

lead—the only metal they've got. It's late when they've finished and Gilligan's fallen asleep.

DREAM SEQUENCE

Gilligan dreams they're all fifty years older. The Castaways are preparing for a party celebrating their fiftieth anniversary on the island. Mr. Howell offers a toast to fifty years "out of the smog," and some of them dance. The radio (whose announcer is also fifty years older!) tells them about a violent storm approaching.

The POW! OOOF! *and* BUH-ROOOOOM! *supers are a parody of* Batman, *the latest sensation at the time. College dorms and fraternity houses across the nation changed their dinner hours so students could watch the Caped Crusader and Robin battle the evil forces of Gotham City.*

Bob Denver enjoyed making this episode. "I loved my makeup because I always wanted

69.
Up at Bat
May 5, 1966

Created and Produced by
  Sherwood Schwartz
Written by Ron Friedman
Directed by Jerry Hopper

Gilligan and the Skipper are harvesting coconuts and stop to rest. Some of Gilligan's coconuts roll into a cave and when he goes after them, he's bitten by a vampire bat. The Skipper rushes him back to camp to get patched up. The Professor warns Gilligan not to tell Ginger and Mary Ann what bit him.

Gilligan panics when he looks in Ginger's mirror and doesn't see himself. He doesn't know she's been complaining that the silvering is gone and it's only glass now.

Gilligan is worried he's turning into a vampire and spooks the Skipper to the point where he wraps a muffler around his own neck.

Gilligan rises in a trance to a full moon and stalks the Howells. He tries to bite Mrs. Howell, but her diamonds protect her. He awakens and is horrified. The Professor tells the Skipper there are no such things as vampires, but he realizes Gilligan will worry himself sick about this and prepares an antivampire potion—some natural tranquilizing herbs—and makes Gilligan drink it. He and the Professor carry him back to the hut. But in the morning, the only thing in Gilligan's hammock is a bat.

The Professor captures the bat when it flies into the girls' hut and tells them it isn't a vampire bat, but a red fruit bat and it's definitely *not* Gilligan. So where's Gilligan? He's gone to live in a cave. The Castaways search for him. Gilligan falls asleep and dreams he's in:

to be Dracula and when our makeup man, Keester Sweeney, finished with me, I had the best time playing the part because I looked so good with the fangs and the black hair."

*DREAM SEQUENCE—
TRANSYLVANIA 1895*

The Howells are weary travelers who have the misfortune to knock on the door of Belfry Hall. The mistress of the hall (Ginger) awakens the vampire Gilligan, who "can't wait to put the bite on them." But he's an inept vampire, his wife long suffering. Ginger puts the Howells up, despite their nasty comments about the accommodations.

TINA LOUISE

The statuesque Tina Louise was born in New York City and has spent decades trying to get roles that didn't hinge on her measurements. Her search for approval isn't hard to understand. She had a pretty lousy childhood which ran the gamut from divorce and boarding school to high society. A drama teacher selected "Louise" as a middle name for Tina N.M.I. Blacker and she eventually adopted it as her professional name. When Tina was a teenager, her mother married well and she became a society debutante and gained a fair amount of notoriety as a "millionaire chorus girl."

She was a chorus girl for a while. She appeared in a musical revue with Bette Davis, *Two's Company*, where the songs and sketches were all linked by the common theme of romance. It only ran for ninety performances and she segued into *John Murray Anderson's Almanac*, a lavish throwback to the splendid revues of the twenties.

Tina was also a regular on *The Jackie Gleason Show* in the years before he made sixteen beauties into the regular "Glea-girls" who graced his show.

She became tabloid fodder, but then she tried

to break out of the bimbo category where
actresses with her looks usually find themselves
locked. She studied at the famed Lee Strasburg's
actor's Studio in New York and hoped to become
a respected dramatic actress.

But when you've got a body that doesn't quit,
you're just plain going to get roles that utilize
that. Since she also sang and could dance, she
was cast in the Broadway production of *Li'l
Abner*, based on the long-running Al Capp comic
strip. She played the scurrilous Apassionata Von
Climax, aide to General Bullmoose, who wants
to throw the denizens off their land so he can
bulldoze Dogpatch into a missile base. Apassionata seduces Li'l Abner away from Daisy Mae so
the general can work his evil plan.[4]

By 1958, Brigitte Bardot was the hot new
French sex kitten and U.S. studios were on the
prowl for an American Bardot. Tina was cast in
the steamy *God's Little Acre* based on Erskine
Caldwell's scandalous novel and it seemed she
was on her way. She made a trio of intense, melo-
dramatic films in 1959 and a group of dramatic
television shows, including episodes of *Climax*,
Checkmate, *The Doctors*, *Burke's Law*, *Route 66*,
and *Kraft Suspense Theatre*.

So when Tina took a role in the musical spoof
of Hollywood, *Fade Out—Fade In*, she returned
to Broadway with some solid dramatic acting
credits behind her. It was from this show that
she was cast in *Gilligan's Island*.

---

[4] *Li'l Abner* was also the Broadway debut of another actress
with brains, talent, and an incredible body, Julie Newmar,
who played "Stupifyin' Jones." She and Tina shared a dressing room.

Tina avoided marriage until after she was thirty, then wed actor Les Crane during the filming of *Gilligan's Island*. The entire cast turned out at the elaborate wedding, which was documented by a photographer from a movie magazine. But the marriage only lasted three years, and they parted while she was pregnant with their daughter, Caprice.

After *Gilligan's Island*, Tina had trouble returning to dramatic roles. She did five episodes of *Love, American Style* and *It Takes a Thief*, and several films.

Drama and legitimacy returned as Tina finally started getting roles in dramatic shows and not just comedies. She played a drug addict in an episode of *Kojak*, a hooker in trouble in *Police Story*, and guest starred on *Kung Fu*, *Ironside*, *Mannix*, *Cannon*, and *Marcus Welby, M.D.* Her role in the hit film *The Stepford Wives* didn't hurt.

She also moved into telefilms, where so many actresses typecast like her—Farrah Fawcett, Leslie Ann Warren, Elizabeth Montgomery—break out of their molds. In fact, in one week in 1976, two of Tina's most dramatic roles aired nearly back to back. She played a sadistic trustee in a women's prison farm in *Nightmare in Badham County* and starred in *Look What's Happened to Rosemary's Baby*, a sequel to the hit film.

She appeared in *Call to Danger*, a crime series pilot with Peter Graves and Diana Muldaur, with Graves as a Dept. of Justice investigator.

She recently played a cameo as Brad Pitt's girlfriend's seductive mother in *Johnny Suede*.

Tina formed a health care company, TLC, and marketed a parasol a few years ago to help women guard their skin from the sun. She's

spent several years working on an autobiograph-
ical book, *Sundays*, about her boarding school
years.

Fade Out-Fade In

One story many people know is how Tina Louise was starring in a Broadway show when she
auditioned for *Gilligan's Island* and left Broadway because she thought she would be the star
of the TV series. What few people know is that
her part in the musical wasn't so hot and the
show itself would become one of the most troubled in Broadway history.

Originally titled *A Girl to Remember*, *Fade
Out—Fade In* is a musical spoof of thirties Hollywood written for Carol Burnett. She played Hope
Springfield, a plain, clumsy, star-struck usher-
ette discovered by a movie mogul and sent to
Hollywood for a screen test. But Hope is the
wrong girl. The mogul really wanted the statuesque floozy next to her in line, Gloria Curry—
the part played by Tina Louise. The film is
remade with Gloria, who is a disaster. She can't
even speak a line properly. Hope's version is
shown at a preview, is a hit, and it's the one
released. She becomes a star.

Fade Out was a jinxed show from the beginning. Burnett became pregnant and delayed the
opening by seven months. Soon after the opening, she was in a car accident and then had to
start filming a TV variety show. She started missing performances and tried to buy her way out
of the show. The show closed, the producers
sued her and it reopened months later, by which
time, Tina Louise had left for *Gilligan's Island*.

She'd bought out her *Fade Out* contract for ten thousand dollars.

Tina's part of Gloria was small (she isn't even in the first act), her character is an uninteresting stereotype, and she didn't even have a song of her own. Her big comedy scene was that Gloria thinks WPA (for Works Progress Administration) is pronounced "Wupah."

Tina's career was probably helped much more by *Gilligan's Island* than it might have been had she stayed in *Fade Out*. Ginger Grant is far more interesting than Gloria Currie. And as for the rumors that she and the rest of the *Gilligan's Island* cast weren't friendly, she now says, "Like everyone says, we were a family . . . and we had a lot of fun and when we had problems, we solved them."

As for her decision to avoid the reunion movies, she says, "I camped so well, it was kind of difficult for me to get back to doing what I'd been doing before. I'd just become a member of the Actor's Studio when I took the job. I just thought it would run a year and I'd get back to doing what I'd been doing. After three years, it was kind of hard. Finally I started getting to get dramatic roles but I didn't want to confuse all these casting agents. I just knew that one person I wanted to impress would tune in the night I was in that charming movie of the week. But I do think the tune-in value and being on the air all the time every day is wonderful for me when I'm doing the dramatic work I like to do."

Credits

Broadway and Regional Theatre
Two's Company—Alvin Theatre, 1952
The Fifth Season 1953
John Murray Anderson's Almanac—Imperial Theatre, 1953
Will Success Spoil Rock Hunter? 1955
Li'l Abner—St. James Theatre, 1956
Fade Out—Fade In—Mark Hellinger Theatre, 1964
Come Back to the Five and Dime, Jimmy Dean, Jimmy Dean—Columbus, Ohio, 1989

Films, TV Series, Specials, and Pilots
Kismet 1955
The Jackie Gleason Show—variety series, 1952–1955
Jan Murray Time—live variety, 1955
God's Little Acre 1958
The Hangman 1959
Day of the Outlaw 1959
The Trap 1959
Armored Command 1961
Garibaldi (Italian) 1961
Siege of Syracuse (Italian) 1962
For Those Who Think Young 1964
Gilligan's Island—series, 1964–1967
A Salute to Stan Laurel—variety special, 1965
The Red Skelton Show—variety special, 1966
The Wrecking Crew 1968
The Bob Hope Show—variety special, 1969
House of Seven Joys 1969
How to Commit Marriage 1969
The Good Guys and the Bad Guys 1969
The Happy Ending 1969
But I Don't Want to Get Married—telefilm, 1970

Call to Danger—pilot, 1973
Death Scream—telefilm, 1975
The Stepford Wives 1975
Don't Call Us—pilot, 1976
Look What Happened to Rosemary's Baby—telefilm, 1976
Nightmare in Badham County—telefilm, 1976
SST—Death Flight—telefilm, 1977
Mean Dog Blues 1978
Friendships, Secrets and Lies—telefilm, 1979
The Day the Women Got Even—telefilm, 1980
Advice to the Lovelorn 1981
Hellriders 1984
Rituals—series 1984–1985
Evils of the Night 1985
O.C. and Stiggs 1987
Dixie Lanes 1988
Miss Hollywood Talent Search—special, 1989
Johnny Suede 1992
Mihola 1992

Guest Starring Roles

Studio One "Johnny August"
Appointment with Adventure "All Through the Night"
Producers Showcase "Happy Birthday"
The Phil Silvers Show "Bilko Goes South"
Climax "A Matter of Life and Death"
Tales of Wells Fargo "New Orleans Trackdown"
The New Breed "I Remember Murder"
Checkmate "A Funny Thing Happened to Me on the Way to the Game"
The Real McCoys "Grandpa Pygmalion"
The Doctors "A March for Three Lovers"
Burke's Law "Who Killed Billy Jo?"
Route 66 "Tex, I'm Here to Kill a King"

Kraft Suspense Theater "The Deep End"

Mr. Broadway "Something Like a Rose"

Bonanza "Desperate Passage"

It Takes a Thief "Totally By Design"

Love, American Style "Love and the Advice Givers," "Love and the Duel," "Love and the Lady Athlete," "Love and the See-Through Mind"

Mannix "Missing: Sun and Sky," "The Face of Murder"

Ironside "Beware the Wiles of the Stranger"

Police Story "Death on Credit," "Requiem for C.Z. Smith"

Kung Fu "A Dream Within a Dream"

Kojak "Die Before They Wake"

Movin' On "Cowhands"

Cannon "The Wedding March"

Marcus Welby, M.D. "All Passions Spent"

Dallas "Digger's Daughter," "The Lesson," "Spy in the House," "Jule Returns," "The Red File"

The Love Boat "The Second Time Around," "Who Killed Maxwell Thorn?"

CHiPs "Chips Goes Roller Disco," "The Great K-5 Race and Boulder Wrap Party"

Fantasy Island "Elizabeth"

Matt Houston "The Kidnapping"

Knight Rider "The Topaz Connection"

Blacke's Magic "Death Goes to the Movies"

Simon & Simon "Act Five"

Married ... With Children "Kelly Bounced Back"

Roseanne "Sherwood Schwartz: A Tribute"

Ginger Grant

Ginger Grant is the archetypical "B" movie star, appearing in such epics as *Mohawk Over the Moon*, *Sing a Song of Sing Sing*, *San Quentin Blues*, three sci-fi films, *Belly Dancers From Bali Bali*, *The Rain Dancers of Rango Rango*, *The Bird People Meet the Chicken Pluckers*, *The Hula Girl and the Fullback*.

Though Ginger had no shortage of male companionship while in Hollywood, you sense she's far more interested in her career than a relationship. She doesn't seem any more obsessed with her personal appearance than anyone else who bases a career on his or her looks.

She lived in Hollywood with another actress named Debbie Dawson, and was scheduled to play Cleopatra in a Broadway play entitled *Pyramid for Two*. She's devastated when she learns via the radio that Dawson has been given the part. She also has a sister.

How does Tina Louise describe Ginger? "Ginger was the ultimate flirt. I flirted with everything from an astronaut to a robot."

THE WORLD
1966

It was hard not to believe the country was coming apart at the seams in 1966. There were civil rights riots in many major cities; antiwar demonstrations became ever more violent and crime more pervasive. Africa seemed likely to erupt into flames, Southeast Asia continued in turmoil, thousands of American men were dying in a country most of us had barely heard of, fighting in support of a regime the people who lived there didn't seem to want. The British Empire was crumbling, the Middle East was filled with wars small and large, and yet, these were all just things most people saw on the evening news.

For most Americans, life went on as usual. Of course, the optimism and booming economy of the postwar years was pretty much gone and with it, our innocence. But it was still a time when we could look forward to a better life for our children than we'd had, a secure retirement, and many bright things on the horizon.

We might have become a bit blasé about our achievements in space by now, and there were so many astronauts who'd been there, it was hard to remember them all, but it sure looked like men—our men—would walk on the moon before the end of the decade.

Technology was exciting too, thanks to new developments in silicon chips, printed circuits, and semiconductors; computers were cheaper, faster, and more powerful, and engineers were starting to use them as design tools to create things more easily, more rapidly, and more accurately. The Japanese were using lasers in automobile design.

Education—even college—seemed possible for everyone who wanted it, unemployment was low, job stability was high, and the industrial output of the country at an all-time high.

And then there was the miniskirt. Part of the youth-oriented fashion trend from London's Carnaby Street, miniskirts swept the fashion world. In addition to plastic and vinyl clothing, the other new look was Courrèges's androgynous or unisex styles—clothes that blurred the distinction between the sexes.

Other 1966 milestones:

- Indira Gandhi is elected as India's third prime minister.
- The first hovercraft begins service across the English Channel. The trip takes about twenty minutes.
- The U.S. resumes air raids over North Vietnam. Many Western nations issue a protest. Communist nations call it naked aggression.
- There is massive internal strife in South Vietnam as students and dissident Buddhists demonstrate against the government of Premier Ky. U.S. facilities in are Huè are burned. The South Vietnamese Labor Confederation calls general strike in Saigon and fifty thousand workers participate. Ky calls for the U.S. to invade North Vietnam. The U.S. refuses.

- The American spacecraft Surveyor 1 lands on the moon and begins sending pictures back to earth.
- James Meredith, the first black graduate of the University of Mississippi, is shot and wounded during a voting rights march from Memphis to Jackson.
- The year in films was rather lackluster except for Richard Burton and Liz Taylor in Mike Nichols's *Who's Afraid of Virginia Wolfe?*, *Doctor Zhivago*, Britain's *Fahrenheit 451*, and the latest James Bond installment, *Thunderball*. Sean Connery broke loose from his 007 role and appeared in *A Fine Madness*. The number of Bond imitators grew with *Our Man Flint*, *The Silencers*, *Arabesque* and *The Man from Istanbul*.
- Five U.S. airlines are grounded by a machinists' strike.
- Robert Kennedy was received by large crowds for a speaking tour in South Africa, despite the government's lack of cooperation and general civil disturbances in a number of emerging African nations, including the assassination of South African Prime Minister Verwoerd on the Parliament steps for "doing too much to aid nonwhites."
- Alabama Governor George Wallace signs a bill declaring U.S. school desegregation orders null and void in his state.
- Jack Ruby's murder conviction for killing accused JFK assassin Lee Harvey Oswald is overturned by a Texas appeals court.
- The new Metropolitan Opera House opens in New York's Lincoln Center.
- Frank Robinson leads the Baltimore Orioles to defeat defending champions the Los Angeles

Dodgers in the World Series. The Dodgers had nearly lost stars Sandy Koufax and Don Drysdale in salary disputes early in the year, but both signed for salaries of $130,000 for Koufax and $115,000 for Drysdale.

- The Boston Celtics won their unprecedented eighth consecutive NBA title by defeating the Los Angeles Lakers in a best-of-seven series.
- Seventy nations prepare to gather in Montreal for Expo '67.
- Medicare, the first health program for senior citizens, takes effect in July.
- The massive joint Egyptian/Swedish/West German/Finnish/Italian project to move the Abu Simbel Temples constructed by Ramses II was nearly completed. The 3,200-year-old structures were moved to higher ground to make way for the elevated waters of the Nile after the completion of the Aswan High Dam in 1967.
- *Time* magazine called London "The City of the Decade" for its contributions to pop music, fashion, and discotheques.
- The most notable football game of the collegiate season was a Notre Dame/Michigan contest in November. Both teams were undefeated and untied, but settled nothing, playing to a 10–10 tie.
- Two of the biggest-selling books of the year were true crime books: *In Cold Blood* by Truman Capote and Gerold Frank's *The Boston Strangler*. Capote called his a "nonfiction novel" and claimed to have established a new genre. Mark Lane's *Rush to Judgment* and Edward Jay Epstein's *Inquest* fueled growing national dissatisfaction with the Warren Report on the assassination of President Kennedy. Other bestsellers of 1966: *Valley of the Dolls* by Jacque-

line Susann, Robert Crichton's *The Secret of Santa Vittoria*, James Clavell's *Tai-Pan*, and Roderick Thorpe's first novel, *The Detective*. Each of these would become a major motion picture.

- The Whitney Museum of American Art opens in New York City.
- The treasures of Florentine museums were threatened when the Arno River overflowed its banks in November. A UNESCO-sponsored salvage effort succeeded in reopening all but one of the museums but experts felt it would be years before the damage to artifacts could be assessed.
- The most popular show on Broadway was *Mame*, starring Angela Lansbury.
- The sun sets on the British Empire: Spain and Britain have talks over the future of Gibraltar. Argentina and Britain have talks over the future of the Falkland Islands. Britain announces the independence of former colony Barbados. Prime Minister Harold Wilson suspends talks with Rhodesia.
- Britain and France agree to build a tunnel across the English Channel.
- Astronomers discover and name quasars, short for quasi-stellar radio sources.
- Japan, Britain, and Thailand launch efforts to establish peace talks about Vietnam. All efforts fail.
- LBJ's daughter, Luci Baines Johnson, marries Patrick Nugent in Washington, D.C.
- A peace accord ends the three-year-long undeclared war between Indonesia and Malaysia.

TELEVISION
1966

News, sports, and specials continued to be the top programming around the world in 1966. The Vietnam war and President Johnson's trip to Southeast Asia, the space flights, and elections were highlights of the year's telecasts. Sports was the biggest draw and the prices went up and up. The networks paid more than $27.5 million to broadcast the 1966 baseball season and $44.5 million for pro and college football.

The new shows that fall weren't a stellar bunch—whatever happened to *The Pruitts of Southampton*; *Run, Buddy Run*; *Pistols 'N' Petticoats*; *The Rounders*; *Love on a Rooftop*; *Hey Landlord*; *Hawk*; *The Hero*; and *Iron Horse*? *Hey Landlord* may have been ahead of its time—it starred Will Hutchins (*Sugarfoot*) as a sweet, trusting guy named Woody who had blind faith in everyone. Sounds a lot like the Woody in *Cheers*. Among the few successes were Marlo Thomas's *That Girl*, *Mission: Impossible*, *The Green Hornet*, *The Girl From U.N.C.L.E.*, *The Monkees*, and *Star Trek*.

The international appeal of American television continued unabated. *Bonanza* was seen in sixty-two countries, *Dr. Kildare* in fifty-two, *Get Smart* in thirty-five, and *I Spy* in twenty-four.

Other shows with increasing overseas exposure were *I Love Lucy*, *The Rogues*, *Honey West*, *The Big Valley*, *The FBI*, *F Troop*, *Mr. Roberts*, *Mission: Impossible*, and *Star Trek*. The French loved *Green Acres*, the Japanese adored *Lost in Space* and *Tarzan*.

Other events during the 1966–67 season:

- There were 193 million television sets in the world, 75 million in the U.S. A color TV cost less than three-hundred dollars. Sony marketed its "Tummy TV" in the U.S. in 1965, and a tiny 4″ by 2″ by 2–½″ set which received thirteen channels was on display at an electronics show in London.
- A new group announced plans to start a fourth TV network, the Overmyer Network, which planned to start broadcasting eight hours of programming per day to one hundred affiliates in September 1967.
- On June 2, the first telecast from the moon is broadcast via the Jet Propulsion Lab in Pasadena, California.
- A new Pacific satellite, Lani Bird, brings daily live broadcasts from the battlefields of Vietnam into American homes.
- In the summer, ABC's new show, *The Dating Game*, soars in the ratings when the other two networks preempt their regular shows to air a live press conference with defense chief Robert McNamara about Vietnam.
- ABC premieres its fall shows weeks earlier than NBC and CBS.
- Milton Berle, whose new show premieres on third-place ABC, quips, "If they wanted to shorten the Vietnam war, they ought to play

it on ABC. Nothing lasts longer than thirteen weeks there."

- *NBC World Premiere Movie* ushers in the age of the made-for-television film.
- CBS censors force the Rolling Stones to change their song lyrics on *The Ed Sullivan Show* from "Let's Spend the Night Together" to "Let's Spend Some Time Together."
- February 5, 1967, *The Smothers Brothers Comedy Hour* on CBS knocks NBC's *Bonanza* from the number one spot.

GILLIGAN'S ISLAND
1966

Yep, they moved it again. Everyone knows—
even the networks *say* they know—that audiences have to know where to find a show in order
to watch it, and the way to establish an audience
is to leave a show where it is, especially if it's a
success. But *Gilligan's Island* packed its bags
once more and moved to Mondays.

Gilligan began the evening on CBS, leading into
a new comedy, *Run, Buddy Run*, which starred
Jack Sheldon, an actor who was usually a supporting player. The show was based on a one-
joke premise—average guy overhears plans for
a mob killing and the inept mobsters spend the
rest of the season chasing him—and the show
was gone by January.

It was replaced by another new show, *Mr. Terrific*, starring the even less well-known Stephen
Strimpell [with the talented John McGiver and
Dick Gautier in supporting roles!] as a bumbling
gas station operator who gets some pills from a
secret government agency that turn him into a
caped crime fighter. The trouble was, the pill
only lasted an hour. The show only lasted thirteen weeks.

As part of this uninspiring comedy block on
CBS, *Gilligan's Island* dropped out of the top

twenty shows. Its ratings were still respectable, though, and it usually managed to win its time slot.

MONDAY NIGHTS-FALL 1966

	ABC	CBS	NBC
7:30	Iron Horse	GILLIGAN'S ISLAND	The Monkees
8:00		Run Buddy Run	I Dream of Jeannie
8:30	Rat Patrol	The Lucy Show	Roger Miller Show
9:00	Felony Squad	Andy Griffith Show	The Road West
9:30	Peyton Place	Family Affair	
10:00	The Big Valley	Jean Arthur Show	Run For Your Life
10:30		I've Got a Secret	

At the end of the season, Mike Dann, CBS head of programming, called Sherwood Schwartz with the good news that *Gilligan's Island* was renewed for a fourth year. Dann was still at CBS but Jim Aubrey was not, nor was Schwartz's main nemesis, Hunt Stromberg. This should have been good news (remember that Aubrey hated the show; Stromberg hated every character in the show except the Skipper and Gilligan, and he wanted their relationship changed), but there was still no one at CBS who really liked the show.

Schwartz called the cast and took them to lunch to celebrate, then waited for official con-

firmation from CBS business affairs. Whatever
dealings you have with a network, studio or production company, it's not really official until
business affairs does the paperwork. Schwartz
had plans to use more guest stars in the 1967–68
season, and CBS seemed enthusiastic about the
storylines he'd proposed. Schwartz began putting together storylines for the 1967–1968
season.

RATINGS
1966–1967 Season

1.	Bonanza	29.1
2.	The Red Skelton Hour	28.2
3.	The Andy Griffith Show	27.4
4.	The Lucy Show	26.2
5.	The Jackie Gleason Show	25.3
6.	Green Acres	24.6
7.	Daktari	23.4
	Bewitched	23.4
	The Beverly Hillbillies	23.4
10.	Gomer Pyle, USMC	22.8
	The Virginian	22.8
	The Lawrence Welk Show	22.8
	The Ed Sullivan Show	22.8
14.	The Dean Martin Show	22.6
	Family Affair	22.6
16.	The Smothers Brothers Hour	22.2
17.	Friday Night Movies	21.8
	Hogan's Heroes	21.8
19.	Walt Disney's Wonderful World of Color	21.5
20.	Saturday Night at the Movies	21.4
21.	Dragnet	21.2

22.	Get Smart	21.0
23.	Petticoat Junction	20.9
	Rat Patrol	20.9
25.	Daniel Boone	20.8

Though the show still won its time slot, *Gilligan's Island* dropped out of the season's top twenty-five shows for the first time.

1966—CUT ADRIFT

Just a note on Ginger's hairstyles during the years. You'll notice that she begins to wear her hair more casually by this time in the show, but the early bouffant and topknot of orange juice can–sized curls were not exaggerations or some movie star affectation. Women really wore their hair that way. Most women still went to a beauty salon every week, and you had your hair set in huge rollers, sat under a dryer for an hour, then the beautician teased it and lacquered and it wouldn't move until your next appointment.

70.
Gilligan vs. Gilligan
September 12, 1966

Created and Produced by
  Sherwood Schwartz
Written by Joanna Lee
Directed by Jerry Hopper

The Skipper and Professor are dying for Mary Ann's coconut pineapple pie, and they're pretty steamed when Gilligan wanders in licking the empty pie plate. He swears the pie was already gone and he was only licking up the crumbs. No one believes him. He goes in search of the pie thief, thinking it's a monkey. Suddenly he comes face to face with . . . himself. The Gilligan clone rushes off and goes to the lagoon, where he speaks—in Russian—into a spoon from his gold pocketknife to a nearby sub. He's a spy, especially prepared for this mission by plastic surgery.

No one believes Gilligan isn't performing a series of pranks. Ginger and Mrs. Howell blame him for cutting the clothesline. Meanwhile, the agent makes plans to kidnap the real Gilligan. When Gilligan mentions the gold pocketknife, the Professor, Skipper, and Mr. Howell start to believe him. They search for the look-alike. Gilligan finds a knapsack and calls the others. But before they can get there, the Russian captures him, ties him up and takes his place.

The Russian fools the others and tries to get the Skipper to talk about "why we're here" until the Skipper tosses him out of the hut for blaming him for their shipwreck. Ginger and Mary Ann discuss Gilligan's slightly off behavior but Ginger puts it down to "growing pains" until the look-alike tries to seduce her the next day. His commandant suggests he talk to "wealthy capitalists." He plays chess with Mr. Howell and quizzes them about "their orders." The look-alike accuses Mr. Howell of cheating and is thrown out. The Professor thinks he's suffering from delusions. He tells the others to humor Gilligan.

Gilligan's favorite vegetable is spinach, Mary Ann loves carrots, Mrs. Howell adores sugar beets. Ginger says the two things she misses most are vegetables and dates— but not the kind you eat.

Mr. Howell tells us his chef's name is Herman.

Bob Denver comments on the reason the cast was always fresh. "Each week was a different show so it never got boring. Each week we thought we'd done the silliest, stupidest thing we could have done and then we'd read the next week's script, and we'd go 'Oh no, here we go again.' Each episode was fun, it really was."

71.
Pass the Vegetables Please
September 26, 1966

Created and Produced by Sherwood Schwartz
Jack Arnold, Executive Producer
Written by Elroy Schwartz
Directed by Leslie Goodwins

Gilligan's catch of the day is a crate of vegetable seeds. Everyone's very excited. No one notices the outer lid says DANGER—EXPERIMENTAL RADIOACTIVE SEEDS. Mary Ann, raised on a farm, is a big help to the planting, but, of course, it's Gilligan who does all the work.

The vegetables sprout. Like crazy. After three days, they've got plants that are almost fully grown. The Howells plan a vegetarian do. At the first harvest, all the veggies look quite strange. The corn grows in a circle, the string beans look like pretzels and the carrots look like cow's udders. Oh well; Mary Ann and Ginger prepare their feast.

As soon as they've eaten their fill, the radio reports the loss of the radioactive seeds from a research lab in Honolulu. The seeds are dangerous. This ruins their appetites. Gilligan finds the cover of the box. The Professor's books don't help much. He's not sure if the veggies are dangerous or not.

The Professor concludes they're dead meat if they don't move around. They all walk until they drop. Mary Ann sees a boat with people on it but the Skipper and Professor can't see it. She's got super vision from the nuked carrots. They build a signal fire. Then Gilligan turns into Mr. America and can lift whole trees. Must be all the spinach. Mrs. Howell's racing around like a crazed cleaning machine from her sugar beets. Mary Ann reports the boat's gone.

72.
The Producer
September 26, 1966

Phil Silvers headed the production company that produced Gilligan's Island,

*Gladasya Productions—
named after Silvers'
slurred signature greeting
from his earlier TV roles.
Silvers had a long and
glorious career in nearly all
phases of the enter-
tainment business. The
Brooklyn-born comedian
began in vaudeville as a
singer at the age of thirteen,
then took his comedy act
to burlesque—at Minksy's,
the top spot of the day. He
made musical films,
appeared on Broadway,
was very active in radio,
and had his fist TV series
in 1948. He hosted a number
of game shows and had
several variety shows, but
his greatest success came
playing Sgt. Bilko from
1955 to 1959. He made
many guest appearance
on TV from the sixties
through eighties.*

*"To be or not to be" is sung
to the tune of the
"Habanera" from Bizet's
opera,* Carmen. *Polonius*

Created and Produced by
   Sherwood Schwartz
Jack Arnold, Executive
   Producer
Written by Gerald Gardner
   and Dee Caruso
Directed by Ida Lupino and
   George M. Cahan
Special Guest Star
Phil Silvers as The Producer

The radio reports a film producer, Mr. Harold Hecuba, is
circling the globe in his private
plane looking for new talent for
his musical extravaganza. He
crash lands on the island and
starts ordering them all
around. He says a couple of his
flunkies are following him in
another plane. If they want a
ride back to civilization, they
can just follow his orders. He
takes over the Howells' hut. He
wants a butler and a maid, and
the Howells will do nicely.

Ginger has a solution for his
abuse. She serves his dinner as
a broke Italian woman who
shares her one dress with her
four sisters. Then she's Marilyn
Monroe. She tells him she just
wanted to show him her versa-
tility. He howls, saying she was
painfully over the top. She tells
the Skipper she won't go with

them when they're rescued. They try to remind her of her public, but she's sure she's been forgotten.

The Professor is worried about Ginger's mental health. Gilligan suggests they do a musical starring Ginger. The Skipper thinks it's a lousy idea. They have no musical to do and HH runs them off their feet all day. The Professor suggests they use the Howells' records and one of their books and rehearse at night. The only book they've got is *Hamlet*.

sings "To Thine Ownself Be True" to the toreador song, "Couplets d'Escamillo" also from Carmen. Ophelia sings "Hamlet, Dear" to the "Barcarolle" from The Tales of Hoffman by Offenbach.

Dawn Wells says, "The New York Shakespeare Festival this year [1993] wanted to do this Hamlet segment before they opened their season but the royalties became a problem so they couldn't do it. Wouldn't the critics love that? Gilligan's Island and Shakespeare in the same evening?"

73.
Voodoo
October 10, 1966

Created and Produced by
    Sherwood Schwartz
Jack Arnold, Executive
    Producer
Written by Herbert Finn
    and Alan Dinehart

A zombie was a popular exotic rum drink in the years when mixed cocktails were more in vogue.

Sherwood Schwartz remembers one time when Alan Hale was injured. "Alan fell out of a *tree backwards and broke his wrist and didn't say a word. We had three more shows to do that season and he never said a word and he had many physical things to do during those last three shows. The only way I found out about it was at the wrap party at the end. He said, 'It'll be nice now because I can go to a doctor and get my arm fixed.' And I said 'Why?' And he said, 'Because it's broken.' I said, 'Why didn't you tell me?' And he said 'Because I didn't want to upset the show.' How often do you get that kind of dedication from any employee in any business, particularly the entertainment world where there are so many prima donnas. There's a man who went through the last three episodes with a broken arm because he didn't want to upset the show.''*

Directed by George M. Cahan

Guest

Eddie Little Sky as . . . . Witch Doctor

Gilligan's been digging up ancient artifacts from the cave. The Skipper's sure he's going to be cursed by the gods. What they don't know is a witch doctor is in the back of the cave. He sticks a pin in a voodoo doll and Gilligan feels a twinge in his neck. He's also lost his lucky rabbit's foot in the cave.

The Professor's thrilled with the artifacts and takes Ginger and Mary Ann to see the cave, though they're afraid. The Howells plan to open a museum with the relics, particularly a solid gold idol. Meanwhile, the witch doctor has made a voodoo doll of each Castaway and they suddenly start moving strangely as the savage plays with each doll. The Professor turns into a zombie. Everyone tries their best to bring him out of it, but fails.

74.

Where There's a Will

October 17, 1966

Created by Sherwood
  Schwartz, Executive
  Producer
Produced by Robert L.
  Rosen
Written by Sid Mandel and
  Roy Kammerman
Directed by Charles
  Norton

Mary Ann picks some flowers for Mr. Howell, who's ailing, but she is so upset she runs out of the Howells' hut in tears. The Professor tries to diagnose his ailment, and finally says he's suffering from a common bellyache. But Mr. Howell's so grateful that it's not serious, he decides to rewrite his will, leaving his entire estate to the Castaways.

When he's back to normal, he passes out copies of the will. Ginger's been given a diamond mine, the Professor a railroad, Mary Ann is given both a cotton and a sugar plantation—and a fleet of cars to go from one to the other. Gilligan is given an oil well and the Skip-

What do the Castaways want if money's no object? Gilligan's wants are the simplest: a skateboard, ten pounds of licorice, a door, to restring his tennis racquet, a new hockey puck, a new beanie, hip boots, a harpoon, a jar of pickles, a treehouse, a maple tree.

The Skipper's going to buy a new boat—a luxury yacht with a pool. Maybe a fleet of yachts. Maybe an aircraft carrier. Maybe a whole 7th Fleet.

Ginger's going to back her own Broadway play while Mary Ann tries to figure out whether to live in London and summer on the Riviera or the reverse. The Professor can't decide whether to build his new research lab on the East or West Coast, and is excited by the thought of his very own nuclear reactor.

per is given forty acres in Colorado—downtown Denver. They're all terrifically excited.

Gilligan can't sleep that night, thinking of all the things he's going to buy with the oil proceeds. Ginger and Mary Ann are doing the same thing. So's the Skipper, and even the Professor.

Mr. Howell goes looking for the Skipper, but Gilligan says he hasn't seen him, though he was just talking to him. Then an arrow nearly hits Mr. Howell. He tells Mrs. Howell he thinks someone's trying to kill him. He thinks he new will is the culprit. He goes looking for Ginger and Mary Ann, but they run off and he falls into a hidden pit they were building.

He figures the Professor is the only one he can trust, but when he goes looking for him, he's nearly flattened by a falling rock the Professor set up on a hill. The battered millionaire barricades himself in his hut.

But the Castaways are really only putting together a surprise party for Mr. Howell. The Professor shifted the rock to get some rare mushrooms for their dinner, Ginger and Mary Ann trapped a wild boar in the pit after they missed him with the arrow. Meanwhile, Mr. Howell is preparing for a siege. But what will they do for food? He decides to confront the "scoundrels." But as he approaches the hut, the Castaways are discussing slaughtering the boar. No one wants to do it. Mr. Howell thinks they're talking about killing him. He races back to the hut and packs a suitcase to live on the other side of the island. Alone.

75.
Man with a Net
October 24, 1966

Created and Produced by
  Sherwood Schwartz
Written by Budd Grossman
Directed by Leslie
  Goodwins
Special Guest Star
John McGiver as . . . .
. . . . .Lord Beasley

A mad British butterfly collector is loose on the island and Gilligan's the first thing he catches. The Skipper tries to talk to him, but he's got one thing on his mind—the

John McGiver had a long and illustrious career in films and television. He was a schoolteacher in New York when bitten by the acting bug and appeared in an Off-Broadway play which led to a role on television's prestigious anthology, show, Studio One. Television viewers saw him on The Front Page, The Jimmy Stewart Show, The Patty Duke Show, The Pruitts of Southampton, and Harvey. His films include Breakfast at Tiffany's;

The Gazebo; Mr. Hobbs Takes a Vacation; Who's Got the Action?; My Six Loves; Take Her, She's Mine; Who's Minding the Store?; A Global Affair; Man's Favorite Sport?; Made in Paris; The Manchurian Candidate; The Glass Bottom Boat; Fitzwilly; Midnight Cowboy; and Mame.

Captain Bligh was master of the H.M.S. Bounty on its infamous 1789 voyage when the crew mutinied, led by Fletcher Christian. He was set adrift in a rowboat with eighteen of the crew who refused to join the rebels. Descendants of the Bounty crew still live on Pitcairn Island in the South Pacific. Charles Laughton played Bligh in the 1935 Academy Award–winning film, Mutiny on the Bounty, Trevor Howard in the 1962 version, and Anthony Hopkins in the 1984 film, The Bounty.

pussycat swallowtail. It's the only butterfly in the world that has escaped him. He does manage to say they can go with him when he leaves. He's got a flare gun by which he'll summon a boat when he's through.

The Professor tells the others not to get too excited. Sometimes lepidopterists will take months or years netting their specimens. He suggests everyone help. Lord Beasley keeps falling off cliffs and over logs. The Castaways are exhausted from stomping all over the island, including climbing its tallest mountain.

The Castaways try their usual stuff to convince him to fire his flare gun. Ginger vamps, Mr. Howell bribes. He's oblivious. The Professor memorizes facts about rare butterflies to impress Lord Beasley. Mary Ann suggests he use crib notes and the six-degreed academician is insulted. Until he thinks about it. He goes searching with Beasley and they examine butterfly eggs and caterpillars together. Lord Beasley figures out the Professor is faking his interest.

The Castaways have a meeting. Gilligan suggests they just fire the flare gun. In fact, he's got it. But Lord Beasley has the flares. He is outraged and says they'll stay on the island and catch the butterfly, "even if it takes *forever*!"

The Skipper and Gilligan have a plan. They paint a butterfly to look like the pussycat swallowtail. The Professor thinks it won't fool Beasley, but it does—until he takes it outside to examine it more closely and is caught in a sudden downpour. "If this was England, I'd have you put in jail for butterfly forgery."

76.
Hair Today, Gone Tomorrow
October 31, 1966

Created by Sherwood
    Schwartz, Executive
    Producer
Produced by Robert L.
    Rosen
Written by Brad Radnitz
Directed by Tony Leader

Gilligan's doing everybody's laundry and he's pooped. Even the Skipper tells him he's got to quit doing so much; he'll be old before his time. In the

Note the music when the Castaways all go to see Gilligan. It's an old song about aging, "The Grandfather Clock." It was used in extensively in an episode of The Twilight Zone, *"Ninety Years Without Slumbering," starring Ed Wynn, and was first aired at the end of 1963.*

The Skipper cites Yul Brynner as one of the good-looking men who are bald. Brynner was

the handsome, bald star
of The King and I (on stage
and screen), Anastasia,
Solomon and Sheba, The
Ten Commandments, and
many other great films.

Ginger reveals she has a
beautiful sister.

The Skipper compares his
and Gilligan's bald heads
to "two-thirds of a
pawnshop sign."
Pawnshops once had
figural signs over their
doors consisting of three
gold balls.

morning, Gilligan's hair's turned white. He's very upset. He goes to see the Professor. He's got no idea what happened. The Professor tells him to just go about his business as usual.

The Skipper demands the Professor tell him what's really wrong with Gilligan, but the Professor insists he's fine. There's only one chance in a million he could be suffering from a disease where a person turns old overnight. Old. Ninety-eight years old. Gilligan overhears this and is sure that's what ails him.

He makes out his will. He gives away his jewelry, his comic books, his laundry business, and his body. Ginger and Mary Ann try to think how to make him feel young. Mary Ann tells him she's in love with him. She kisses him and all he feels are his arteries hardening.

Mrs. Howell suggests Gilligan dye his hair. The Professor agrees and he mixes the dye. Mrs. Howell puts it on that night. But the Professor miscalculated and all Gilligan's hair falls out. He's bald as a billiard ball. He spends the day in his rocker with his head under a quilt.

77.
Ring Around Gilligan
November 7, 1966

Created by Sherwood
   Schwartz, Executive
   Producer
Produced by Robert L.
   Rosen
Written by John Fenton
   Murray
Directed by George M.
   Cahan
Special Guest Star
Vito Scotti as . . . .
. . . . Dr. Boris Balinkoff

The Skipper and Gilligan are building a raft because there's been a shift in the ocean currents. Meanwhile, a nasty-looking man with a monkey called Igor arrives on the island. He's mad scientist Dr. Boris Balinkoff. He views the two Castaways as potential "guinea pigs." He puts his magic ring on Gilligan's finger and makes him into a robot that will do anything he asks. He uses a radio control to communicate with Gilligan. But during the day, Gilligan is normal, and he isn't concerned when Mrs. Howell takes a fancy

When the mad doctor sends Gilligan "back to your little grass shack," it brings to mind the classic song, "I Want to Go Back to My Little Grass Shack," one of the most frequently recorded songs of Hawaii. It was written in 1933 by Bill Cogswell, Johnny Noble, and Tommy Harrison. It was one of the two songs (the other was "The Hukilau Song") most mainland visitors learned to dance to in the hula classes held on the big Matson ships which sailed weekly to Honolulu from the west coast.

to the ring and asks if she can wear it. That night, Mr. Howell finds his Lovey under the control of the mad scientist and packing a suitcase full of money and when he tries to stop her, she flips him with expert judo.

The next morning, Mrs. Howell convinces her husband it was all a nightmare. Unknowing, she gives the Skipper the ring to return to Gilligan. Dr. Boris tells him to destroy the raft. He does, then comes out of it and gives Gilligan the ring. Later, he asks Ginger to hold the ring so he doesn't damage it while he's working. She comes and destroys the raft, then reports to Dr. Boris (who thinks aerobics have transformed Mrs. Howell into Ginger!).

Ginger returns the ring and is mystified when Gilligan tells her she destroyed the raft. Then the monkey, Igor, gets the radio control and Gilligan starts behaving like Igor, to the consternation of Mr. Howell and the Professor. In his cave, Dr. Boris wakens from a nap and finds Igor with the radio control and takes it away. That night, Dr. Boris has Igor deliver a bag of six more rings to Gilligan. He activates the remote and tells Gilligan to put one on each sleeping Castaway's finger. They're all robots now and ready to execute his "brilliant caper"—the theft of all the gold from Fort Knox.

78.
Topsy-Turvy
November 14, 1966

Created and Produced by
 Sherwood Schwartz
Written by Elroy Schwartz
Directed by Gary Nelson
Guests
Eddie Little Sky, Allen Jaffe, Roman Gabriel as . .Natives

The Castaways are going nuts with the sound of war drums from a neighboring island. They fear an imminent invasion and the Professor finds a cave large enough for all of them as well as some supplies, where they can weather the headhunters' attack. Then Gilligan falls and hits his head and suddenly, his vision has rotated 180 degrees—everything's upside down. To say the least, it's disorienting.

Meanwhile, Mr. Howell's

When Mr. Howell is practicing his fencing, and compares his prowess to that of the Count of Monte Cristo, he refers to the hero of Alexandre Dumas's classic novel, Edmund Dantes. The nobleman is wrongly accused and imprisoned. After some years, he stages a daring escape and spends the rest of his life as a mysterious figure who exacts revenge on all who wronged him.

When Gilligan tries to help the Professor make a cure for what ails him, the Skipper calls him Dr. Kildare. Dr. Kildare was originally a series of books by Max Brand, then a very successful series *of films from 1937 to 1947, which starred Lew Ayres and Lionel Barrymore. Next, it became a popular medical show on NBC from 1961 to 1966. It starred Richard Chamberlain as Kildare and Raymond Massey as Dr. Leonard Gillespie. By its third season, the show became more serial in nature and ran two half-hour shows per week. Some stories extended over many episodes, others were completed in one.*

practicing his fencing. Mrs. Howell thinks they should sit down with the headhunters and reason with them. "My dear, you reason with men at the Harvard Club, not with men who carry clubs." But then she comes up with an idea he likes—to dazzle them with trinkets. Of course she has no rhinestones, only diamonds, but Mr. Howell says they won't notice the difference.

The Professor thinks some native berries will help Gilligan but Ginger and Mary Ann are afraid to go scavenging because of the threat of headhunters. Meanwhile, the headhunters have landed (the drums have stopped because their drum broke) and are stalking the Castaways. The Professor cooks up some medicine from the berries and gives it to Gilligan to drink. He opens his eyes and they're right side up. All four of them. Now he's seeing double.

The Professor sends the Howells out for more berries and then he and the Skipper go off in another direction. The Professor tells Gilligan he might hallucinate and not to believe everything he sees. When the headhunters come into camp, Gilligan figures they're a figment of his imagination. They're about to lop off his head when Ginger and Mary Ann return from a berry hunt. The women go to look for more berries and are captured by the headhunters. Then the Howells suffer the same fate. The captives are all herded into a bamboo cage.

79.
The Invasion
November 21, 1966

Created by Sherwood Schwartz, Executive Producer
Produced by Robert L. Rosen
Written by Sam Locke and Joel Rapp
Directed by Leslie Goodwins

The Skipper and Gilligan are fishing in the lagoon when the Skipper snags an attaché case marked PROPERTY OF U.S. GOVERNMENT, DO NOT OPEN. A rusted set of handcuffs dangle from the handle. They take it to the Professor, who's thrilled. He's sure it contains State Department

There are parodies of most of the popular spy films and TV shows of the day in Gilligan's dream sequence. Of course, they're all based on Ian Fleming's James Bond character, 007, and his evil counterparts at S.P.E.C.T.R.E. and S.M.E.R.S.H. Goldfinger was released in 1964, Thunderball in 1965, and You Only Live Twice in 1967. Michael Caine starred in 1965's The Ipcress File and James Coburn headlined as Our Man Flint in 1966. Additional hits at the time were TV shows Man from Interpol (1960),

The Man from U.N.C.L.E. *(1964)*, Secret Agent *(1965)*, I Spy *(1965)*, Get Smart *(1965)*, The Avengers *(1966)*, and The Girl from U.N.C.L.E. *(1966)*.

secrets that were handcuffed to a secret agent. He thinks the government will spare no expense to track it down. He makes the Castaways all swear they won't open it.

That night, none of them can sleep because they're dying of curiosity. They all perform a wild variety of sneaky tricks and ruses to grab a peek into the case, but the Professor catches them. But the next day, he's pounding on the case and it pops open. It contains "United States Defense Plans Against Secret Attack." The Professor swears them all to secrecy. If enemy agents found they had it or knew what was in it, they'd be killed. Then Gilligan slips the rusty handcuffs around his wrist and they snap shut.

The Professor tries everything and can't get them off. He works for three unsuccessful hours. The Howells have an entire suitcase full of keys (for all their properties) but they're all the wrong type. That night, Gilligan goes to sleep with the briefcase handcuffed to his wrist.

DREAM SEQUENCE

Gilligan dreams he's a spy with the "Good Guy Spy Outfit." The Chief (the Professor) calls in Agent 014 (Gilligan as Maxwell Smart). His mission is to take the attaché case to the ministry of defense. Gilligan has a number of tools at his disposal—a radio telephone comb, a pistol razor, and an antibullet shield nail file. He must watch out for their arch enemies from E.V.I.L. The case blows up (along with the agent) if a button is pressed.

RUSSELL JOHNSON

Russell Johnson's father died when he was eight and, in the custom of the time, his widowed mother placed him and his brothers in a Philadelphia school that was one step away from an orphanage. They did get to go home for holidays, but today he wishes he had been closer to his mother. He was not a superior student, and in his autobiography, relates that he flunked algebra and was held back a year.

This punishment had the right effect on Russell and he became a National Honor Society student from then on. He vividly remembers the top student in his school and perhaps based the Professor a little on that boy.

Russell Johnson joined the Army Air Corps at eighteen and was shot down in the Philippines in March 1945. Later, the beribboned bombardier-navigator used the G.I. Bill to enroll in Hollywood's Actors Lab, where he (like Tina Louise) learned the Stanislavski method of acting.

The Actors Lab helped him make connections and he made his film debut four years later (after working at a ballpoint pen plant, driving a cab, and doing new car prep work) in *For Men Only*, playing the heavy. He continued to play villains, a few scientists in what have become classic sci-fi flicks (such as *It Came from Outer Space*, *This Island Earth*, and *Attack of the Crab Monsters*), and other roles in television.

Russell appeared in the best of the anthology shows, including two *Twilight Zone* episodes, "Back There," and "Execution." He made a lot of Westerns (there were a lot of Westerns on the air at the time) and starred in a series, *Black Saddle*, about New Mexico lawmen right after the Civil War.

The pilot of *Gilligan's Island* was made without him, but it's not hard to see why he was chosen to replace John Gabriel. Gabriel was almost too handsome and too macho to be believable as a scientist. Johnson was also a handsome man, but he's got a much less sexually threatening type of good looks. Johnson recalls other casting which wouldn't have worked. "Carroll O'Connor tested for the part of the Skipper and Dabney Coleman tested for the Professor and believe it or not, Raquel Welch tried out for the part of Mary Ann."

But Russell almost didn't take the part of the Professor. "It came back to me three times. The first time I thought I was going to be Ben Casey, but that didn't work out. I was considered. The second time it came around, I'd made a pilot film with Jane Powell and in the meantime, they had cast the show. They made it and CBS bought it but they said they'd like to have somebody else playing the Professor and the two girls. But I'd done this other pilot film with Jane Powell and I thought that was going to sell. It didn't sell."

Johnson, having one series lead under his belt, was really waiting for his shot at the big time. Then, he says, "The third time, about a month later, my agent called and said they're still interested. I said, 'Let me get out there and I'll test.' And I did and that was it."

Gilligan's Island wasn't the financial boon for its actors a show with its staying power would be today. "We were at the very beginning of the residual idea. We were paid for six runs on a very minimal scale. None of us have received anything for the last twenty-seven, twenty-eight years."

Russell went on working, in the workmanlike jobs that keep actors going. He guested on some TV shows, and the *Gilligan* cartoons got him into voice-over work. "Old actors never die, they don't even fade away. They're always available."

Credits

Theater
MGMT—Center Theatre Group, Los Angeles, 1977–1978

Films, Telemovies, TV Series, and Specials
Back at the Front 1952
For Men Only 1952
Loan Shark 1952
Turning Point 1952
Column South 1953
Law and Order 1953
It Came from Outer Space 1953
Seminole 1953
Stand at Apache River 1953
Tumbleweed 1953
Rogue Cop 1954
Johnny Dark 1954
This Island Earth 1954
Black Tuesday 1954
Ride Clear of Diablo 1954
This Island Earth 1954
Ma and Pa Kettle at Waikiki 1955
Strange Lady in Town 1955

Many Rivers to Cross 1955
Attack of the Crab Monsters 1957
Courage of Black Beauty 1957
Rock All Night 1957
Badman's Country 1958
Saga of Hemp Brown 1958
Space Children 1958
Black Saddle—series, 1959–1960
Great Adventure—series (narrator), 1964
Gilligan's Island—series 1964–1967
A Distant Trumpet 1964
The Movie Murderer—telefilm, 1970
Vanished—telefilm, 1971
Terror at 30,000 Feet—telefilm, 1973
Beg, Borrow . . . Or Steal 1973
Aloha Means Goodbye—telefilm, 1974
New Adventures of Gilligan—animated series, 1974–1977
Collision Course 1975
Adventures of the Queen—telefilm, 1975
You Lie So Deep, My Love—telefilm, 1975
Nowhere to Hide—telefilm, 1977
Hitchhike to Hell 1978
The Ghost of Flight 401—telefilm, 1978
The Bastard/Kent Family Chronicles—miniseries, 1978
Rescue From Gilligan's Island—telefilm, 1979
The "Castaways" on Gilligan's Island—telefilm, 1979
The Harlem Globetrotters on Gilligan's Island—telefilm, 1981

Guest Starring Roles

The Lone Ranger "Counterfeit Redskins"
Circus Boy "Corky and the Circus Doctor"
DuPont Theatre "Dan Marshall's Brat"

Crossroads "The Unholy Trio," "A Holiday for Father"

Casey Jones "Track Walker"

Adventures of Rin Tin Tin "Rin Tin Tin and the Soldier"

Medic

Lawman "The Encounter"

The Californians "Overland Mail"

Gunsmoke "Bloody Hands," "The Bear," "The Long Night," "The Fugitives"

Rescue 8 "The Bells of Fear"

The Twilight Zone "Back There," "Execution"

June Allyson Show "Inter Mission"

Thriller "The Hungry Glass"

Laramie "Badge of Glory" "Killer's Odds," "Double Eagles," "The Perfect Gift," "The Dynamiters"

Hawaiian Eye "Kapua of Coconut Bay," "Go for Baroque"

Ben Casey "Go Not Gently Into the Night"

The Detectives "The Queen of Craven Point"

Adventures in Paradise "Survival"

Tales of Wells Fargo "To Kill a Town"

Wide Country "Who Killed Eddie Gannon?"

The Dakotas "Mutiny at Fort Mercy"

77 Sunset Strip "The Toy Jungle"

The Farmer's Daughter "The Stand-In"

The Deputy "Lawman's Conscience"

It's a Man's World "Night Beat of the Tom-Tom"

General Electric True

Empire "Arrow in the Blue"

Rawhide "Incident at Alkali Sinc"

Greatest Show on Earth "Man in a Hole"

Big Valley "The Good Thieves"

Tales of Wells Fargo "To Kill a Town"

Wide Country "Who Killed Eddie Gannon?"

Empire "Arrow in the Blue"

The Outer Limits "Specimen Unknown"
The FBI "The Dynasty," "Caesar's Wife"
The Felony Squad "The Human Target"
That Girl "Fly by Night," "Ugh Wilderness"
Invaders "The Trial"
San Francisco International Airport "Crisis"
The Young Lawyers "The Bradbury War"
O'Hara, U.S. Treasury "Operation: Bribery"
Marcus Welby, M.D. "I Can Hardly Tell You Apart"
Owen Marshall, Counselor at Law "Words of Summer," "Journey Through Limbo," "Once a Lion"
Ironside "Programmed for Panic"
Mannix "The Green Men"
Cannon "Lady on the Run"
Mobile One "The Informant," "Californium"
ABC Afterschool Special "Hewitt's Just Different"
Lou Grant "Babies"
Hagen "Trauma"
Alf "Somewhere Over the Rerun" (renamed "The Ballad of Gilligan's Isle")
Roseanne "Sherwood Schwartz: A Tribute"

Book by Russell Johnson

Here on Gilligan's Isle (with Steve Cox), HarperPerennial, 1992.

Roy Hinkley—The Professor

The Professor's a high school teacher and "well-known scout leader," has six degrees, and is nearly asexual. He was on the *Minnow* to write a book, *Fun With Ferns*. It's never explained how a three-hour tour on a small boat could help with either the research or solitude needed for such a book.

He speaks a number of languages, and has little trouble communicating with the assorted savages, cannibals, and headhunters he encounters on the island.

Though he manages to create a wide variety of inventions to aid the Castaways, his inability to create a long-distance, sea-going craft is due to the lack of iron on the island.

The Professor has a number of handy reference books with him on the island, including *The History of Tree Surgery* and *Volcanoes and Their Destructive Powers*.

When Wiley calls Ginger's most recent film Moon Over the Mohawk, *she corrects him—it was about a Native American astronaut and was titled* Mohawk Over the Moon.

Don Rickles was a popular and accomplished actor, and appeared in many TV series. He guest starred in The Twilight Zone, Burke's Law, The Dick Van Dyke Show, I Spy, Medical Center, The Munsters, *and* Wild, Wild West. *In the sixties, he became a frequent*

80.
The Kidnapper
November 28, 1966

Created by Sherwood
  Schwartz Executive
  Producer
Produced by Robert L.
  Rosen
Written by Ray Singer
Directed by Jerry Hopper
Special Guest Star
Don Rickles as. . . . .
. . . . .Norbett Wiley

  Mrs. Howell's been kidnapped and the Skipper and Gilligan get a ransom note. They have an hour to put ten thousand dollars in a hollow log. The Professor searches and finds no one else on the island. Mr. Howell gives Gilligan and the Professor the money (he kisses it goodbye) and they put the money in the log. The Professor hides to see if he can see the kidnapper, but Gilligan gets stuck in the log.

The men find Mrs. Howell blindfolded on a tree stump. She's fine. Then Mary Ann is kidnapped and the ransom note arrives. This time, the Howells are to deliver twenty thousand dollars into the mouth of the idol. They accomplish this and two hours pass with no word from the kidnapper. But then Mary Ann appears, and she's fine.

Then Ginger is taken and the note demands thirty thousand dollars, to be delivered by Gilligan and Mary Ann. She's returned safely. She dramatizes her ordeal for the others. She says he's going to kidnap everybody else, then start all over again.

The Castaways set a trap for the kidnapper and plan to use Gilligan as bait. Of course, Gilligan ends up in the trap, but eventually, the Skipper gets the kidnapper and the Castaways build a jail. Norbett

headliner in Las Vegas and refined his "insult humor" stand-up act. He also seemed to turn up at every roast that the Friars Club gave and always delivered the snappiest zinger of the evening. There were a number of attempts to build a TV show around him, including the 1965 pilot, Kibbee Hates Fitch. *ABC gave him* The Don Rickles Show *in 1968, but his insults and offensive comic persona didn't work very well on the small screen and the show only lasted a few months. CBS tried with another* Don Rickles Show *in 1972, but with a more conventional sitcom premise. He played a New York advertising man with a wife, daughter, and a nice Long Island house. But again, viewers tired of his insults and the show was canceled after four months.*

Wiley claims he gets an itch whenever he's around money, which is why he left civilization. Then he got caught in a storm and his boat washed up on the beach. They all come alive at the mention of a boat.

The Howells talk to Wiley, a high society kidnapper who's taken a number of their friends. He's very flattering to them, which they appreciate, despite the fact that he got fifty thousand dollars for one of Mrs. Howell's social rivals. In fact, he's very cordial and flattering to everyone. Soon everyone wants to let him out of the jail. The Professor refuses to consider it. Ginger played a psychiatrist in a movie and offers to analyze Wiley.

He had a terrible childhood. His father was out of work. They were terribly poor. Ginger tells the others he's a "victim of his environment." They have to welcome him back to society. She and Mary Ann convince the Professor to let Wiley out.

The title brings to mind Agatha Christie's famous mystery novel, And Then There Were None, which

81.
And Then There Were None
December 5, 1966

Created by Sherwood
   Schwartz, Executive
   Producer
Produced by Robert L.
   Rosen
Written by Ron Friedman
Directed by Jerry Hopper

Mary Ann's hanging out the washing and Gilligan's entertaining her with his knot knowledge when she suddenly disappears. He finds the Skipper and the Professor and they figure out she's been abducted, probably by natives.

Mr. Howell prepares to protect Mrs. Howell with his "sword cane," but he's brought his "flask cane" by mistake. The others all search for Mary Ann and the headhunters and then Ginger's captured.

The Castaways have a meeting and the Professor thinks perhaps the natives are looking for brides and that's why they kidnapped Ginger and Mary Ann. Mrs. Howell panics, thinking they're going to sacrifice her in order to draw out the savages, but it's Gilligan's dignity that's sacrificed. They stick him in Mrs. Howell's best clothes, wig, hat, and lor-

has been filmed four times (twice as Ten Little Indians). *If you've never seen it, go rent the video of the 1945 original, beautifully directed by René Clair. The script and acting are superb and the whole thing is terrifically scary. It stars Walter Huston, Barry Fitzgerald, Louis Hayward, Roland Young* (Topper), *and Dame Judith Anderson (the brilliant actress who played Mrs. Danvers in* Rebecca). *The story is about a group of ten people stranded together on an island trying to guess the identity of the killer in their midst as one by one, the ten are murdered. The 1966 remake took place in an alpine village and starred Hugh O'Brian, Shirley Eaton (the girl who gets painted in* Goldfinger), *pop singing idol Fabian, and Stanley Holloway* (My Fair Lady).

Robert Louis Stevenson's famed horror story, The Strange Case of Dr. Jekyll and Mr. Hyde, *was first published in 1886. The philanthropic Dr. Jekyll discovers a potion which unleashes "the evil that is present" in his soul and becomes murderer Mr. Hyde. When he can no longer effect the change back into the good Dr., Hyde kills himself. The story has been filmed numerous times, both seriously and humorously. The most famous versions are a 1920 silent film starring the great John Barrymore, a 1932 version starring Fredric March and one from 1941 starring Spencer Tracy.*

Frankenstein *refers to Mary Shelley's famous mad scientist, (also filmed numerous times).* Bluebeard *is a famous ogre from Charles Perrault's story. Jack the Ripper is another classic*

gnette. The masquerade fails, and Mrs. Howell is missing.

The men rush to the lagoon, hoping to sabotage the savages' canoe. Professor puts on his Freud hat and says he thinks there never were any headhunters—one of the Castaways has been driven nuts by their isolation and is doing this. Gilligan is afraid he's the one. He's been alone with each of the women right before she's disappeared.

DREAM SEQUENCE

Gilligan sees the *London Times*'s headline: DR. GILLIGAN LOVED BY ALL. Under the photo of a very Victorian Gilligan is the caption, "Couldn't you just kiss him?" Then another headline: IS DR. GILLIGAN MR. HYDE? TRIAL BEGINS TODAY.

In a London courtroom (with the handlebarred Skipper as the bailiff), Dr. Gilligan waltzes in, calla lily in his hand [he looks more like Oscar Wilde than Dr. Jekyll]. Mary Ann, as a "poor Cockney fla'ar girl" says she owes "everything" to Dr. Gilligan. He was her 'Enry 'Iggins. The Bailiff isn't impressed with her "improved" manners. Mary Ann has found Dr. Gilligan someone to take his case —egad! It's Mary Poppins! Well, Mrs. Howell in full Julie Andrews-rig. Mr. Howell is the crusty old judge.

The Professor is the prosecuting barrister (and the judge's nephew) and swats Dr. Gilligan with his own flowers and calls him a swine, "Frankenstein, Bluebeard, and Jack the Ripper all rolled into one." The eyewitness, the Lady in Red (Ginger, of course), testifies. She claims he's Dr. Gilligan until he sees or thinks of food, then becomes Mr. Hyde.

horror story, based on an unsolved series of grisly murders in London from 1888 through 1889.

Mary Ann's "fla'ar girl" is a direct homage to the big film of 1964, My Fair Lady, *based on the musical (itself based on George Bernard Shaw's play,* Pygmalion) *that starred Julie Andrews on Broadway. It was a minor scandal at the time that the nonsinging Audrey Hepburn took the role of Eliza Doolittle in the film (the vocals by premier song-dubber Marni Nixon). All of which accounts for the appearance of Mrs. Howell as* Mary Poppins. *Brit Julie Andrews wasn't thought to be well known enough in America when the film of* My Fair Lady *was cast, but she became a huge star thanks to* Mary Poppins, *which was also released in 1964.*

The title brings to mind the famous Bette Davis film, All About Eve, *where the scheming, ambitious understudy (played by Anne Baxter) usurps the star's role, her friends, and her lover.*

Dawn Wells comments on Bob Denver's work, "This man is so talented. You see him play Gilligan and you see all the wonderful comedy happen with him. A little light goes on and he just does it. When you see all these different episodes where he played all those other characters, it's just phenomenal. You don't realize it when you're doing it. At the moment. Going back and watching some of the reruns, you realize some of the great stuff Bob has done."

82.
All About Eva
December 12, 1966

Created by Sherwood Schwartz, Executive Producer
Executive Producer Jack Arnold
Written by Joanna Lee
Directed by Jerry Hopper
Tina Louise as . . Eva Grubb

A motor boat pulls into the lagoon and a woman gets out. The Castaways search the island for the woman (they can tell by her high-heeled footprints and one shoe she's lost). Gilligan finds her. She tries to run, but the Skipper traps her. She tells them they can have the boat and bursts into tears.

Her name is Eva Grubb and she's plain and wears glasses. She never wants to see another human being as long as she lives. Men don't know she exists. She'll give them the boat key if they promise to leave her there alone.

The Professor thinks they shouldn't leave her there in her emotional state. The Skipper says they can send a boat back for her. Later, she steals the spark plugs after Gilligan tells her their plans.

The Howells have the answer. As Mrs. Howell observes, "Anyone who thinks money can't buy happiness just doesn't know where to shop." But Eva refuses Mr. Howell's bribe. The Castaways have a meeting and Ginger has the right idea: a makeover for Eva.

The women open their beauty shop and start with a henna rinse, Ginger's clothes, and makeup. Eva is transformed into a clone of Ginger. She's a knockout. She gives them back the spark plugs and the Castaways prepare provisions for their journey. Eva overhears Ginger and Mary Ann talking. Ginger fears when they get home, Eva will become insecure again. Then Mrs. Howell tells Eva that no one could tell her apart from Ginger if she ever showed up in Hollywood. That night, Eva knocks out Ginger and ties her up.

83.
Gilligan Goes Gung Ho
December 26, 1966

Ginger made some prison films, including San Quentin Blues *and a musical,* Sing a Song of Sing Sing.

Gilligan makes a reference to Gunsmoke *when he calls the Skipper "Mr. Dillon," the marshal's name on the other series.*

When asked which was his favorite episode, Bob Denver says, "I think all the dream sequences were the most fun where we got to play different characters. I never had a favorite episode though. They're all pretty silly."

Created and Produced by Sherwood Schwartz
Written by Bruce Howard
Directed by Robert Scheerer

[Uncredited] Guests

George Neise . . . . Pilot
Jim Spencer . . . . Copilot

Gilligan is sure Ginger has killed the Professor and runs off yelling for a policeman, but they were only rehearsing a play. But the Castaways think maybe they do need some kind of legal authority. The Professor says they should elect a sheriff. The Skipper and Mr. Howell get into their usual fight over who's in charge, but the Skipper is chosen. He makes Gilligan his deputy.

Gilligan finds a phosphorescent rock and the Professor has the Castaways collect more. He says they can make a wonderful rescue message out of those rocks that'll be visible even at night.

Sure enough, a search plane *is* in the area, after they've had another report of "people living on a deserted island."

Gilligan arrests Mr. Howell for theft and bribery and puts him in jail. The Skipper and Pro-

fessor go out all day to collect
more rocks and Skipper leaves
Gilligan in charge. He goes
overboard and arrests Ginger
and Mary Ann. Mrs. Howell
bakes them a cake with a file
in it and Gilligan discovers it
and arrests Mrs. Howell. The
Skipper and Professor return
and Gilligan arrests them too.

84.
Take a Dare
January 2, 1967

Created and Produced by
  Sherwood Schwartz
Written by Roland
  MacLane
Directed by Stanley Z.
  Cherry
  Special Guest Star
Strother Martin as. . . . .
. . . . George Barkley

Gilligan listens to a radio program called "Take a Dare,"
which offers anyone ten thousand dollars to spend a week
on a deserted island with no
help and nothing but the
clothes on his back. Gilligan's
disgusted—he's doing it for
nothing. The program's con-
testant, George Barkley, has

*Originally a diving
champion from Indiana,
Strother Martin made a
career out of playing nasty
bad guys in one hundred
classic films, including*
The Man Who Shot Liberty
Valance, McLintock!,
Invitation to a Gunfighter,
Shenandoah, Harper,
Cool Hand Luke, Butch
Cassidy and the
Sundance Kid, The Wild
Bunch, True Grit, Rooster
Cogburn, *and* Slap Shot.
*His television
appearances included* 77
Sunset Strip, Perry
Mason, Ben Casey, *and*
The Rockford Files.

been dropped on an island. Their island. As Gilligan and the Skipper go banana picking, Barkley steals their buckets of fish.

They ask around and nobody took the fish. Later, they're listening to the program and Barkley reports by shortwave that he's doing fine. He sure is, he's stolen a bunch of stuff from the Castaways, including a hammock, plates, Skipper's magazine, and a frying pan. Gilligan and the Skipper find Barkley, who's lounging around eating bananas. The show calls and Barkley lies and the Skipper and Gilligan can't stand it and attack him. The Skipper grabs the shortwave and they all try to get it to work but Barkley's stolen a vital part.

The Professor tries without success to fix the shortwave. The Howells have the answer: money. If he won't report their presence on the island because he'll lose the ten thousand dollars they'll offer him that much or more. They do, but he thinks all the Howells' money is bogus, as well as their checks and Lovey's jewels.

Ginger vamps him, and though he rises to the bait, he still refuses to supply the missing part. The next day, Barkley and the shortwave are gone. They search the island and find Barkley transmitting. Gilligan and the Skipper yell so they can be heard but Barkley foils them. The next day after his transmission, Barkley throws the transmitter over a cliff into the ocean.

85.
Court Martial
January 9, 1967

Created by Sherwood Schwartz, Executive Producer
Produced by Robert L. Rosen
Written by Roland MacLane
Directed by Gary Nelson

On the radio, the *Minnow* is in the news. The Maritime Board has a hearing into the disaster and affixes blame squarely on the captain's papers if he ever returns. The Skipper is distraught at this news and runs away. Gilligan fears he's suicidal and gets the rest to help him look for the Skipper. Gilligan finds his

The R.M.S. Queen Mary was the largest passenger liner in the world at the time. It made its final transatlantic crossing in 1967 and was purchased by the city of Long Beach, California, which made it into a tourist attraction and it is permanently berthed there today.

Of the pirates mentioned by Gilligan, one was a real man, the other two are from fiction. Captain Kidd was a legendary pirate who is supposed to have buried his ill-gotten gains in many places around the world. He was caught and executed in

*London in 1701. He
became a popular
character in pulp fiction
and was the subject of
a popular melodrama in
the 1830s. Captain Hook is
the one-handed
antagonist in Sir James
M. Barrie's* Peter Pan, *and
Long John Silver is the
one-legged pirate in
Robert Louis Stevenson's*
Treasure Island.

buddy as he's making a noose out of vines. Ginger and Mary Ann save him from jumping off a cliff. He shuts himself in his hut and broods.

The Castaways try to think of something to help and Ginger remembers that in her movies, they solve a mystery by recreating the crime. The Professor thinks that's a great idea—recreate the sinking of the *Minnow*. They build a replica of the *Minnow* and the Professor says he remembers every single order the Skipper gave. Gilligan and the Skipper go through their actions, with the Professor rocking the replica, Mary Ann providing wind and thunder, and Ginger the waves. It's pretty realistic.

The Skipper figures out exactly what happened: When Gilligan threw the anchor overboard, the anchor line was not attached.

Now Gilligan's depressed and making a vine hangman's noose. The Skipper insists they both failed and there's only one thing left for them to do. They decide to move to the other side of the island. The Howells insist they reconsider. They'll give them anything. But the two stand firm and leave over protestations from Ginger, Mary Ann, and the Professor.

DREAM SEQUENCE

Gilligan and the Skipper build a small lean-to and that night, Gilligan dreams they're on a schooner in the days of the pirates. Gilligan is an admiral and Mrs. Howell, Ginger, and Mary Ann are the queen and princesses who are afraid of pirates. Sure enough the pirates (Mr. Howell, the Skipper, and Professor) are climbing the rigging. They overpower Lord Admiral Gilligan and seize the ship. They lock the women below and Gilligan in an iron cage on deck.

86.
The Hunter
January 16, 1967

Created by Sherwood Schwartz, Executive Producer
Produced by Robert L. Rosen
Written by Ben Gershman and William Freedman
Directed by Leslie Goodwins

Swashbuckling Rory Calhoun starred in more than two dozen western films, including Rogue River, A Bullet is Waiting, Powder River, The Hired Gun, Apache Territory, Ride Out for Revenge, The Domino Kid, The Treasure of Pancho Villa, *and* The Gun Hawk. *He also appeared in* Secret of Monte Christo, Nob Hill,

The Great John L., That Hagen Girl, How to Marry a Millionaire, The Spoilers, Colossus of Rhodes, *and* Marco Polo. *He also starred in a television series,* The Texan, *from 1958 to 1960 and was the host of* Western Star Theatre *in 1963. He appeared in many television shows, including* Bonanza, Death Valley Days, I Spy, Gentle Ben, Police Story, Hec Ramsey, Petrocelli, Starsky and Hutch, Hawaii Five-O, Hart to Hart, *and the miniseries* The Blue and the Gray.

Harold Sakata became famous as Oddjob, the vicious servant in Goldfinger, *which premiered in 1964. He has made a number of appearances since then in movies and television, usually as the taciturn aide to the bad guy.*

Special Guest Star

Rory Calhoun as . . . .
. . . . Jonathan Kincaid
and
Harold Sakata as . . . Ramoo

Gilligan's dozing on the beach when a helicopter lands in the lagoon. He rushes to the passenger, Jonathan Kincaid. While Gilligan babbles about not having television, hot dogs, or licorice whips, Kincaid wants to know if there's wild game on the island. When he learns there isn't—but that no one knows the seven Castaways are there—he gets an idea to hunt something other than his usual prey. Gilligan introduces the rest of the Castaways and Kincaid tells them a boat's picking him up at 10 A.M. the next morning. The excited Skipper dreams of going to an Italian restaurant and having "eight or ten pizzas and six dozen meatballs, then eight or ten miles of spaghetti, and then I'm gonna have dinner!" After the thrilled Castaways rush off to pack, Kincaid consults with his man, Ramoo, as to which Castaway would be the most challenging to hunt. Mrs. Howell's concerned their friends won't understand how they could have "spent seven years with people who aren't even in the social register." Kincaid interviews each Castaway to determine his or her physical condition. Looks like Gilligan is the likeliest candidate. That night, the Castaways have a "Goodbye to our Island" party, but Kincaid puts a damper on things by telling them exactly what he plans for tomorrow. They're all horrified. He promises that if the selected candidate eludes him for twenty-four hours, he'll make sure they're all rescued. Kincaid selects Gilligan.

87.
Lovey's Secret Admirer
January 23, 1967

Created by Sherwood
    Schwartz, Executive
    Producer
Produced by Robert L.
    Rosen
Written by Herbert Finn
    and Alan Dinehart
Directed by David
    McDearmon

The Professor enumerates his degrees: BA from U.S.C., BS from U.C.L.A., MA from S.M.U. (Southern Methodist University), PhD from T.C.U. (Texas Christian University). It's doubtful the writers were trying to imply the Professor was especially religious—all these initials simply set up Mr. Howell's joke about alphabet soup.

Cinderella, *a musical version by Rodgers and Hammerstein and starring Leslie Ann Warren, was a popular telecast on CBS every year.*

Mrs. Howell dreams she's kissed on the cheek during the night and wakes bemused. Then Mr. Howell sees a love note tucked under her pillow. He rages around, accusing Gilligan, Skipper, and the Professor of harboring a secret desire for his wife. For her part, Mrs. Howell is thrilled and flattered.

Mrs. Howell, Ginger, and Mary Ann decide to try to find out who the secret admirer is. Ginger and Mary Ann stage a fight outside the Skipper's hut supposedly about him, and he confesses that if he wrote anyone a note, it would be Ginger.

The Professor invents a lie detector for Mr. Howell. The first subject is the Skipper, who insists he has no interest in Mrs. Howell. Gilligan confesses to being in love with his turtle, Herman. They all decide there must be someone else on the island. "You mean a total stranger in love with *my* wife?!"

That night, the rest of the Castaways hide around the Howell cabin and catch the culprit—Mr. Howell. He says he had no idea it would get out of hand. He talks himself into trouble when he implies Mrs. Howell would never have a secret admirer if it wasn't for

him. She throws him out. That
night, Mrs. Howell listens to a
Cinderella story on the radio
and it pervades her dreams.

DREAM SEQUENCE

In the dream, the Skipper is
the evil stepmother to Mrs.
Howell's Cinderella when a
knight arrives with a message
from the palace: It's their invitation to the ball. Stepmother
calls his her two ugly daughters, Frederica and Giselle—
Mary Ann and Ginger (obviously having a wonderful time
playing hags) to tell them of
the ball. Of course, Cinderella
can't go.

Later, her fairy godfather
(Gilligan) appears and conjures
up a mule, then the right stuff.
Cinderella is coifed, gowned,
and excited. After another
abortive try, he manages a car-
riage (his first try sounds like
a Volkswagen).

88.
Our Vines Have Tender Apes
January 30, 1967

Created by Sherwood
   Schwartz, Executive
   Producer

Gilligan's Island *was a
very physical show. Bob
Denver remembers, "I've
got to be honest. I did
almost get hurt in a stunt
was when we did one of
the hammock gags, when
I fall out of the top*

hammock and Alan would get out of the bottom one and get in the top one and I would get in the bottom one, he'd get in the top one and we kept doing this, you can't rehearse it— and one time, I was in the bottom hammock and I was going to roll out and Alan passed me, midair, and hit the floor and I thought well, I was very lucky that time. I did a lot of my own stunts but I wouldn't do the high falls like twenty-five feet off the palm tree, I just wouldn't do those. And I always let my stunt double do it first or otherwise he wouldn't get paid. So except for those really dangerous ones, I did them."

Produced by Robert L. Rosen
Written by Sid Mandel and Roy Kammerman
Directed by David McDearmon

Guest

Billy Curtis as . . . . . . Tongo

Gilligan discovers a modern-day Tarzan sleeping in his hammock. The man proceeds to lead the Castaways on a merry chase as he swings from trees and uses vines to evade pursuit. At first he terrorizes them, then begins to be a nuisance as he destroys their property and lobs coconuts at them.

They think he's after one of the women. Mary Ann uses makeup to make herself unattractive, but Ginger is caught and captured. She tries to communicate with the savage and learns his name is Tongo. She tries to win his confidence and eventually manages to bash him with a coconut and escapes.

Mary Ann is drafted to lure the ape man, though she's not too pleased about it. She lets him chase her—right into a trap. The Castaways have prepared a cage and he's caught in it. While unobserved, this Tarzan reveals his true stripe by using a tape recorder to chronicle his adventures. He's an actor who's up for the lead in a new jungle movie and he's in training. He expected the island to be uninhabited but when he ran into the Castaways, he thought they'd be an ideal test for his thespian skills.

Meanwhile, the Castaways are working at civilizing him and the Skipper takes pity on the poor beast and lets him out of the cage. Just then, a real gorilla arrives on the scene and snatches the would-be Tarzan. The Castaways find the tape recorder and the jig is up.

89.
Gilligan's Personal Magnetism
February 6, 1967

Created by Sherwood Schwartz, Executive Producer
Produced by Robert L. Rosen
Written by Bruce Howard
Directed by Hal Cooper

Note that the brown and white printed cloth the Howells use for blankets and around their hut is authentic tapa cloth. This bark cloth is made by natives of many South Pacific islands. It's created by pounding the bark of the taro plant (the same root that is pounded into poi, that gray-

purple, bubbly, pasty stuff that makes tourists cringe) into flat strips. The strips are then criss-crossed and pounded together until they form a sturdy cloth. It is then decorated and used for clothing, sails, and decoration. The cloth is stiff at first, but with use, it becomes soft and pliable. The native patterns are made with inks from plants that are put on carved blocks and stamped into the bark cloth.

Gilligan and the Skipper are bowling when an electrical storm begins. Gilligan is about to roll one more when the ball is struck by lightning, sending him crashing into the pins. The Skipper gets the Professor and Gilligan seems okay, though dazed. But when he tries to put down the ball, he can't. When the Skipper tries to help, he gets an electric shock. The Professor examines the ball and finds the rock it's made of has a high iron content and when struck by lightning, it created a magnetic field and . . . well, it's stuck on Gilligan's hand.

Gilligan's pretty depressed to be stuck dragging around the rock. Mrs. Howell tries to psychoanalyze it off his hand while the Professor works on a more practical solution. Later, getting into his hammock proves to be a problem.

The next day, the Professor gets an electrical force field going that he's sure will shatter Gilligan's rock. They start the mechanism going despite another electrical storm. Lightning strikes Gilligan and brings down the hut, tossing the others around the beach. When they come to, the rock's gone from Gilligan's hand, but there's only one problem: Gilligan's invisible.

Again, the Professor sets his mind to the problem, but he strikes out. The rest of the Castaways try to cope and cheer up Gilligan, but it's difficult. The Professor takes a leaf from the pages of *The Invisible Man* and wraps Gilligan in strips of cloth. These are impregnated with lead, though, to reestablish the molecular balance in Gilligan's body. He wanders around looking like a mummy and scares Ginger, who flees, catching the cloth strips and unraveling him.

Gilligan leaves the Castaways a note—he's moved to the other side of the island.

DAWN WELLS

Whenever the talk at a party turns to the attractive women of classic TV, someone usually asks "Ginger or Mary Ann?" A nineties' Budweiser commercial even posed that question. The result of most polls seems to be Mary Ann.

Dawn Wells was the youngest member of the *Gilligan's Island* gang when she was hired to do the series. She not only was pretty much the girl next door she portrayed, she has grown into the kind of woman most fans of *Gilligan's Island* would want Mary Ann to become.

Invariably charming, friendly to fans, and still lovely, Dawn Wells does a little acting, attends *Gilligan's* events with Russell Johnson and Bob Denver, and does interviews as an icon of the sixties. She recently has published *Mary Ann's "Gilligan's Island" Cookbook* (Rutledge Hill Press, 1993).

Dawn Wells may not have come from Kansas, but she is good pioneer stock, just the same. She grew up in Reno, a fourth-generation Nevadan. Her great-great-grandfather was a stagecoach driver during the 1849 gold rush. Her father founded a company called Wells Cargo and was one of the original owners of the Las Vegas Thunderbird Hotel.

When she was young, she shared two dreams with many of her contemporaries: to be a ballerina and Miss America. Bad knees ended her dancing aspirations, but she did become Miss Nevada and went to the Miss America pageant in 1960. She went on to college, where she majored in drama after starting in chemistry.

After some stock company work, she came to Los Angeles and got an agent and work fairly easily. She appeared in most of the popular TV shows of the early sixties.

After CBS decided to recast The Professor and the two women from the pilot, Dawn was cast as Mary Ann—the character was called "Bunny" in the pilot—and, despite the critical drubbing the premiere of *Gilligan's Island* took, easily won America's hearts.

She remembers, "We had to go in and audition for a series that was sold already with a time slot and an advertiser. I had no idea how lucky we were. And I auditioned for about a week, about two hundred and fifty girls coming and going all the time. And they were auditioning in New York at the same time; in fact, I think Tina Louise was cast in New York."

Dawn wasn't a shoo-in for the part. In fact, Raquel Welch auditioned for Mary Ann. Dawn is still amazed, "Isn't that something? I can't imagine her as Mary Ann. She should have auditioned for Ginger. They kept telling me I had the role, and yet they kept having me come back tomorrow to audition with somebody else and no contracts were signed, and you know how tenuous that position is. So I think on a Thursday afternoon, this gorgeous girl with a gorgeous figure came in to test for Mary Ann and I thought, 'That's it.' But she didn't get it.

She might not have wanted it. I don't know. They might not have offered it to her."

Today, she does television, legitimate theatre, and personal appearances, but her primary occupation is running her company, Wishing Wells, which makes clothing for the disabled.

Dawn seems to have had a wonderful time working on *Gilligan's Island*. She remembers her favorite episodes: "I think we all liked the dream sequences because we got to be other roles. My favorite was the Dr. Jekyll/Mr. Hyde one when I got to do a Mary Poppins with accents. Guest stars were fun, when you got to do something other than just the seven of you trying to get off the island."

She has her own theory why the show is still so popular. "I think *Gilligan* is very special. *Gilligan* was sort of a composite of family. The family unit is sort of breaking up today—you don't have a mom and a dad and two kids anymore. It was the first kind of sitcom that was taken out of the living room. We are not dated. You can't tell when we were filmed. So what you're telling little kids about what's good and what's right and what's wrong, is talked about in a sarong and a boat. You don't know if it's 1964 or 1984."

She thinks the gorgeous scenery also played a part. "We were the first with a pretty picture. Most situation comedies those days were living room comedies. It was beautiful to look at. The palm trees, the beautiful setting. I also think the blend of chemistry of people."

Credits

Theatre
Barefoot in the Park
The Star-Spangled Girl
Romantic Comedy
Mary, Mary—Drury Lane, Chicago
Bus Stop—Drury Lane, Chicago
Gaslight
Vanities
The Owl and the Pussycat
The Effect of Gamma-Rays on Man-in-the-Moon Marigolds
Same Time, Next Year
Fatal Attraction—Center Stage Co., Toronto, Canada
Chapter Two—National Touring Company, 1979–80
They're Playing Our Song—National Touring Company, 1982
Fire Escape—Richmond Shepard Theatre, Hollywood, 1984
Surprise, Surprise—Victory Theatre (Burbank, CA), 1994

Films, TV Series, Telemovies
The New Interns 1964
The Night of the Iguana 1964
Gilligan's Island—series 1964–1967
Winterhawk 1976
Return to Boggy Creek 1977
The Town That Dreaded Sundown 1977
Rescue From Gilligan's Island—telefilm, 1978
The "Castaways" on Gilligan's Island—telefilm, 1979
The Harlem Globetrotters on Gilligan's Island—telefilm, 1981

Gilligan's Planet—animated series, 1982–1983
High Rollers—game show, 1974–1980
High School, USA—telefilm, 1983

Guest Starring Roles

The Roaring 20s "War with the Night Hawkers"
Maverick "The Deadly Image"
Tales of Wells Fargo "Kelly's Clover Girls"
87th Precinct "Out of Order"
Lawman "No Contest"
Joey Bishop Show "A Young Man's Fancy"
Surfside 6 "A Private Eye for Beauty"
Bonanza "The Way Station," "The Burning Sky"
It's a Man's World "The Bravest Man in Cordella," "Chicago Gains a Number"
Hawaiian Eye "The Sign-Off"
Laramie "The Violent Ones"
Redigo "Papa-San"
Channing "Swing for the Moon"
The Invaders "Dark Outpost"
Wild, Wild West "Night of the Headless Woman"
The FBI "The Attorney"
Hagen "More Deadly Poison"
The Love Boat "The Judges"
Fantasy Island "The Way We Weren't"
Matt Houston "The Visitors"
Vega$
Matlock "The Therapist"
Growing Pains "Carnival," "Broadway Bound"
Baywatch "Now, Sit Right Back and You'll Hear a Tale"
Alf "Somewhere Over the Rerun" (rerun as "The Ballad of Gilligan's Isle")
Roseanne "Sherwood Schwartz: A Tribute"
Columbo "It's All in the Game"

Book by Dawn Wells

Mary Ann's Gilligan's Island Cookbook by Dawn Wells, Ken Beck, & Jim Clark (Rutledge Hill Press) 1993.

Mary Ann Summers

Despite her innocence and seeming naiveté, Mary Ann is a young woman with a firm backbone, high ideals, and an unshakable confidence in the permanence of things in the world she knows.

She comes from Winfield, Kansas, and there's more than a little pioneer spirit inside her small frame. She grew up on a farm (probably raised by her aunt and uncle, just as was Dorothy in *The Wizard of Oz*), has the pioneer's innate resourcefulness, ability to provide hearty meals and optimism.

She'd like to think Horace Higgenbottham is at home pining away for her, but she secretly suspects he's not. Yet, when she is finally rescued, he's there, waiting with an engagement ring.

90. Splashdown
February 20, 1967

Created by Sherwood Schwartz, Executive Producer
Produced by Robert L. Rosen
Written by John Fenton Murray
Directed by Jerry Hopper

Ginger's reaction to being caught in the space capsule— "Would you believe . . .?"—was an extremely popular phrase at the time. It came from the television show, Get Smart, *which premiered in 1965.*

Gemini V, the seventeenth manned space flight,

was launched August 21, 1965, with astronauts L. Gordon Cooper, Jr., and Charles Conrad, Jr., aboard. It was the longest flight to date, with 120 orbits in 190 hours, fifty-six minutes. U.S. manned spacecraft kept the Gemini name until it was replaced by the Apollo missions in 1968.

Mrs. Howell says she only uses one kind of perfume—"Gold Dust No. 5"—but in the first season's "Diamonds Are an Ape's Best Friend," we see Mrs. Howell has a number of different perfumes, including the one used to lure the ape, "Warm Afternoon."

Ginger says she's been in three sci-fi films.

Guests

Chick Hearn as . . . .
. . . . .Commentator
George Neise as . . . .
. . . . NASA Official
Scott Graham as . . . Tobias
Jim Spencer as . . . . Ryan

The Castaways learn of an impending space capsule launch which might be useful to them. A manned space capsule will be sent up to rendezvous with an unmanned capsule already in orbit. The Professor calculates when the capsule will be directly over them. He rigs up a boosted transmitter and they try to interrupt communications between the capsule and mission control in Houston. They all try like crazy, but all they produce is some static that only lasts for a minute or two. But the space mission isn't over yet and the Professor calculates the manned capsule will be over them on its sixteenth orbit. He tells the others to spell out S.O.S. with tree trunks on the beach, then they'll set fire to them, making them visible from the capsule. It'll work much better if they have something to make the trunks more flammable. All they've got is Mr. Howell's best brandy. He sacrifices it grudgingly.

Gilligan sets the logs alight (and his pants). The astronauts are on the radio and report what they see. "S.O.L.," astronaut Sol Tobias's name. He thinks it's a hello message to him. The next day, mission control loses contact with the capsule and a little later, the capsule lands in the lagoon. The Skipper and Gilligan run over to it, but it's the unmanned capsule, Scorpio EX-1. The Professor checks and the entire communication system has shorted out and it is useless. But the radio reports that a team of navy destroyers are looking for the capsule. The Castaways are happy, but the Professor notes the navy thinks the capsule came down in the ocean and may never look on the island. They try to push it out, but there's an argument about who will go on the capsule. The Professor insists the Skipper and Gilligan must be the ones.

Writer Brad Radnitz went on to write for Supertrain; Nurse; Harper Valley; Trapper John, M.D.; Matt Houston; Call to Glory; The Wizard, *and* High Mountain Rangers.

91.
High Man on the Totem Pole
February 27, 1967

Created by Sherwood Schwartz Executive Producer
Produced by Robert L. Rosen
Written by Brad Radnitz
Directed by Herbert Coleman

Guests
Jim Lefebvre, Al Ferrara, and Pete Sotos.. as Natives

Gilligan and the Skipper are lost in the jungles of their island. While trying to find the beach, Gilligan finds a totem pole. The pole's top head looks exactly like Gilligan. The Professor helps them clear the area around the totem and says it was carved by the Kupakai, the tribes that inhabit the islands near them.

That night, Gilligan wonders if he's related to the man who is represented by the head on the totem. He's worried that he's descended from a long line of headhunters. Gilligan's depressed by the whole idea and the Castaways are worried. The Howells try to cheer him up, but it seems everything they say has the word "head" in it.

Ginger tries to vamp him out of his depression, but she fails. The Skipper makes him a boomerang, but when Gilligan throws it, he nearly decapitates the Skipper. Then Mary Ann reports that Gilligan's running around with an axe. The Skipper and Professor find him chopping off the head from the totem.

Gilligan packs to move to the other side of the island because he doesn't trust himself, but the Skipper and Professor talk him out of it. Then some Kupakai warriors come and are shocked when they see their king's head lying on the ground. They replace it. Gilligan goes to get the head, planning to keep it in his hut, and is surprised when he sees it back on the totem. The Professor and Skipper see the headhunters.

The headhunters kidnap the Howells and start boiling water in a cauldron. The Skipper and Professor see them and decide Gilligan could stop them by convincing them he's their dead king.

"I Wanna Be Loved by You" was the song that made "boop-boop-a-doop" girl Helen Kane famous. The song was written in 1928 for her first musical on Broadway, Good Boy. *Debbie Reynolds played Helen Kane in the film* Three Little Words, *but when she sang the song, Kane herself dubbed the song on the soundtrack.*

But by far the most famous rendition today is Marilyn Monroe's in the 1959 film, Some Like It Hot. *Tina Louise sings it very much in the Monroe style.*

Dawn Wells says this was the toughest episode for her. "It was an extremely difficult role because I had to concentrate on staying in somebody else's character. In other words, Mary Ann had to become Ginger Grant, movie star, instead of Dawn Wells becoming Tina Louise. Is that right?" The impersonation becomes

92.
The Second Ginger Grant
March 6, 1967

Created by Sherwood
  Schwartz, Executive
  Producer
Produced by Robert L.
  Rosen
Written by Rob Friedman
Directed by Steve Binder

Ginger's entertaining the Castaways (she sings "I Wanna Be Loved By You"). Mary Ann's mesmerized and says she'd give anything to be like her. After Ginger's finished, Mary Ann trips and hits her head on a rock. When Gilligan helps her up, she thinks she's Ginger. The Professor checks her out and says there's no evidence of a concussion. Then he tries a little psychological testing. He tells the others it's a common occurrence but, until he can come up with a treatment, Mary Ann will expect to see a Mary Ann among them. Ginger's the logical one. She borrows a brown wig from Mrs. Howell.

At dinner that night, the hazards of the impersonation

become obvious. Ginger's a lousy cook. Later, Mary Ann's trying on all of Ginger's dresses and doesn't understand why all her clothes are too large. She starts cutting them all down to fit. The next morning, Mary Ann sees Ginger doing the laundry without the wig on and she faints. The Professor says she's in a traumatic shock. He tries hypnosis. Gilligan watches through the window and gets hypnotized by mistake. The Professor instructs Mary Ann (and Gilligan) that she's Mary Ann. But it doesn't work. Mary Ann thinks she's still Ginger, but Gilligan thinks he's Mary Ann.

really complicated when Dawn Wells imitates Mary Ann imitating Tina Louise's Ginger Grant imitating Marilyn Monroe's Sugar (from Some Like It Hot) imitating cartoon character Betty Boop's song.

Mr. Howell, as emcee of the show, imitates Ed Sullivan, wooden host of the longest-running variety show on television.

93.
The Secret of Gilligan's Island
March 13, 1967

Created by Sherwood Schwartz, Executive Producer
Produced by Robert L. Rosen
Teleplay by Bruce Howard
Story by Bruce Howard and Arne Sultan
Directed by Gary Nelson

The Professor reveals that he spent two years in Egypt.

Many people ask why the theme song didn't have Mary Ann and the Professor's names in it the first season, calling them "the rest." Dawn Wells explains, "There was a billing problem at the beginning when we originally went on the air.

There were three replacements— Ginger, the Professor, and Mary Ann came in after the pilot and we did a lot of negotiations and I guess Tina's contract came out first, and she was negotiated to be the last of the five being billed so we were 'the rest' for a while." Bob Denver solved the dilemma. "I said to the producers, 'It's not really fair. There were seven people on the island, you shouldn't have "the rest," two people stuck in back, put them in front.' And they said, 'No, contractually, they're stuck back there.' And I said 'Contractually, I get first billing and I have a choice where I want to go.' And they went, 'Yeah,' and I said 'So put me last.' They said, 'All right, we'll put them in.'"

The Professor and Skipper look for Gilligan, who missed reakfast. He's found some petroglyphs — hieroglyphics carved in stone. The Professor gets very excited and thinks the discovery may help them get off the island. The drawings show people leaving the island. The Professor wants them to look for the rest of the tablet. The Skipper and Gilligan search through other caves.

Meanwhile, the Professor is cleaning off the first piece when the Skipper and Gilligan bring another one. Ginger and Mary Ann are making some acid for the Professor to do further cleaning (of course, Gilligan almost drinks some). Gilligan's been using the missing piece for months as a tray. He drops it and breaks it, but the Professor pieces it together. It contains a map for a route to Hawaii. The Professor suggests they send the Skipper and Gilligan out on a raft to follow the route.

That night, Gilligan dreams of being the caveman who carved the stone. He's an artist who wastes time carving scenic pictures of "evil place on other side of hill." Despite

Chief Howell's insistence they not do it, the group is preparing for a trip on the other side of the hill, where there is snow. Mary Ann and Ginger are husband-hungry cavewomen. The Professor's inventing the wheel. Then Chief Howell locks up Gilligan and Skipper.

94.
Slave Girl
March 20, 1967

Created by Sherwood
  Schwartz, Executive
  Producer
Produced by Robert L.
  Rosen
Written by Michael Fessier
Directed by Wilbur D'Arcy
Guests
Midori as . . . . Kalani
Michael Forest as . . Ugundi

Gilligan rescues a beautiful young native woman from the lagoon. When she is revived, she pledges to be his slave for saving her life. The Professor speaks a few words of her language and explains that her honor is at stake. If Gilligan doesn't accept her service, the whole tribe will attack them.

Again, Mr. Howell says, "Hmmmm. How sweet it is," recalling the great man Jackie Gleason's signature expression. Gleason had gorgeous girls who drifted around the set on his variety show. He frequently said this as a particularly well-endowed lady strolled by.

Bob Denver laughs when he thinks of all the things they did with the radio on the show. "It was a great radio. A one-dollar-ninety-five radio that never broke down. The Professor was always going in and taking out pieces to make stuff but there was always more stuff in there."

But Gilligan really hates being followed around and watching her do all the work.

The Professor says the only way out is a fight to the death—Gilligan's. Mr. Howell has an idea. He will pretend to kill Gilligan in a duel, then Kalani will belong to the Howells. Gilligan is inept with the épée but he dies fairly convincingly. Mr. Howell only savors his victory for a moment. Several of her people arrive and challenge him to fight for Kalani. They're strapping lads and Mr. Howell is sure he'll be killed.

Then Gilligan appears and Ugundi challenges Gilligan for Kalani. The Professor has the solution. He's seen a plant which paralyzes the muscles and stops the breathing for a while. They will convince Ugundi Gilligan's dead. But the Howells aren't in on the scheme and overhear the Professor and Skipper and think they really mean to kill Gilligan.

Buck Rogers was a hero first in comic books, then radio, movie serials, then in a television series, Buck

**95.
It's a Bird, It's a Plane, It's Gilligan**
March 27, 1967

Created by Sherwood
   Schwartz, Executive
   Producer
Produced by Robert L.
   Rosen
Written by Sam Locke and
   Joel Rapp
Directed by Gary Nelson
Guests
Frank Maxwell as . General
Edward Faulkner as ......
.... Colonel
Walt Hazzard as Lieutenant
[Uncredited] Guest
Chick Hearn as ....
.... Radio Announcer

An army general and colonel watch a demonstration film of the personal jet pack, which allows men to fly like a bird. A lieutenant arrives with bad news. A ship in the Pacific has lost the test model. The general orders the fleet to search for it, as it might get into "the wrong hands" (this *was* the Cold War).

The general hasn't been seen anything like this jet pack since he was a boy reading Buck Rogers.

Gilligan feels the same way when he finds the errant jet pack. The Skipper insists Buck Rogers wasn't a real person.

Rogers, *on ABC from 1950 to 1951. He was played by actor Kem Dibbs. The idea was revitalized in another television series,* Buck Rogers in the 25th Century, *on NBC from 1979 to 1981. Gil Gerard played the superhero this time. The pilot for this series was first released theatrically, filled with special effects and outtakes from the sci-fi television series,* Battlestar Galactica. *The original movie serials were reedited into a feature-length film,* Destination Saturn, *in 1939, starring Buster Crabbe.*

Ginger tells everyone she was in the film, The Bird People Meet the Chicken Pluckers.

Chick Hearn (playing himself as the radio reporter) was a Los Angeles television and radio sportscaster and was the voice of the Los

Angeles Lakers basketball team. He won a 1965 Emmy Award for his work on KTTV, now the Fox TV affiliate station in Southern California.

The Professor thinks there may be enough fuel in it to get one of them back to Hawaii. The fuel has a short shelf life and he doesn't know how long it will keep its potency.

Nobody wants to do it, so they make a dummy to fly to Hawaii. Mary Ann and Ginger make the dummy and the Professor rigs a launch pad to send the dummy in the proper direction. Gilligan breaks the launch pad and the dummy takes off in the wrong direction, with Gilligan aboard, without the note. It comes back to the beach out of fuel.

The Howells tell the others the radio reported there will be a final big search for the jet pack tomorrow. The Professor suggests there's fifteen minutes of fuel left and someone can soar up in the air and be spotted by the rescue fleet. No one wants to do it.

We learn that the island is "three hundred miles southeast of Honolulu."

96.
The Pigeon
April 3, 1967

Sterling Holloway made his name in the thirties playing hillbillies and

Created by Sherwood Schwartz, Executive Producer

Produced by Robert L. Rosen

Teleplay by Brad Radnitz

Story by Jack Raymond and Joel Hammil

Directed by Michael J. Kane

Special Guest Star

Sterling Holloway as .. Burt

Gilligan finds a pigeon and the Professor says he's a homing pigeon—also a carrier pigeon. They can strap a message on his leg and send him home. But the bird was obviously blown off course by a storm and he's low in weight and feathers. The Professor starts a program of vitamins and food and says he'll be able to fly in two weeks.

The Skipper thinks he knows a way to fatten up the pigeon faster. He and Gilligan sneak into the Professor's hut and feed the pigeon a whole mango pie. Then Ginger and Mary Ann sneak in and give him some coconut milk. Then the Howells sneak in and feed him too. In the morning, the Professor brings out the pigeon, now a candidate for Jane Fonda's Workout. It's too fat to fly. It will take *three weeks* to slim it down.

yokels in films. Later on, he supplied voices for many Disney characters, including Winnie the Pooh. He appeared in over one hundred films, including The Merry Widow, Alice in Wonderland, Gold Diggers of 1933, Meet John Doe, Little Men, A Walk in the Sun, Sioux City Sue, The Beautiful Blonde from Bashful Bend, Shake Rattle and Rock, The Adventures of Huckleberry Finn, It's a Mad Mad Mad Mad World, The Aristocats, *and* Thunder and Lightning.

They put the bird on a strenuous exercise program. Gilligan's named the bird Walter, and Mary Ann thinks it's terribly clever that he named him after the actor, Walter Pigeon. Gilligan says he named him after Walter Stuckmeyer, his best friend in grammar school, who was pigeon-toed! Three weeks later, they put a message on his leg and send him off. Walter goes home and a man removes the message. He thinks the message is a joke from a Mrs. Hawkins, the place his pigeons usually go.

Walter arrives back on the island with a note that "Birdy" enjoyed the funny note. Mr. Howell takes charge and offers Birdy one million dollars for rescuing them, signs his name, and encloses a thousand-dollar bill. The man gets it and again thinks Mrs. Hawkins is pulling his leg. He responds that everyone knows Mr. Howell was lost in a shipwreck. He used the bill for a pigeon nest.

The Professor suggests they send a picture of them all and sends Gilligan to get the pigeon from the cave where he left him. There's a giant six-foot spider in the cave.

97.
Bang! Bang! Bang!
April 10, 1967

Created by Sherwood
   Schwartz, Executive
   Producer
Produced by Robert L.
   Rosen
Written by Leonard
   Goldstein
Directed by Charles
   Norton
Guests
Rudy LaRusso as. Michaels
Barlett Robinson as Hartley
Kirk Duncan as . . . Parsons

Explosive thermoplastics in
everyday forms are a new tool
of American spies. A scienytist,
Parsons, shows Agent Michaels
film of an explosion from an
ashtray. They have about fifty
pounds of this plastic. Another
twenty-five pound crate washed
overboard in the Pacific.

Gilligan finds it and the Professor's quite excited. There
are many things they need
(they don't know it's explosive). Ginger and Mary Ann
want jewelry, Gilligan molds a
bunny rabbit. Mr. Howell is
excited to have the first item,
a plastic golf ball. Thanks to

*The Howells' chauffeur at
home is named Charles.*

*When Gilligan loses some
fillings, he says "Now I
have twenty-two percent
more cavities." This
parodies a pervasive
series of ads running at the
time for Crest toothpaste,
where some schoolchildren
are pleased that "our
group has thirty-four
percent fewer cavities."*

Mrs. Howell's lousy stance and Gilligan's monkey's curiosity, the ball explodes harmlessly.

Ginger and Mary Ann make dinner plates and jewelry, and the monkey steals a plate. The Professor gives the Skipper some plastic nails which he suggests are of use for nailing thatch. The monkey tosses a plate in the jungle and it explodes, but again, no one notices. Gilligan lost a filling while trying to get the plate from the monkey and the Professor fills his tooth with the plastic.

The Castaways are all admiring their new plastic items when the monkey runs up and grabs another piece, tosses it, and it explodes. It's plastic explosive!

98.
Gilligan, the Goddess
April 17, 1967

Created and Produced by
   Sherwood Schwartz
Written by Jack Paritz and
   Bob Rodgers
Directed by Gary Nelson
Special Guest Star
Stanley Adams as ....
............King Kaliwani

Gilligan's astonished to see some natives chasing Mary

Again, Mrs. Howell refers to Grace and Prince Rainier, Princess Grace and Prince Rainier of Monaco, everyone's number one royal couple at the time.

When the Skipper tells Ginger he killed her living girdle, he refers to a product of the Playtex Company, whose "living girdle" was famous—

Ann and Ginger. King Kaliwani introduces himself as Emperor of Eternal Night, Knight of Eternal Day, Seeker of Eternal Truth, and Lord of Eternal Eternalty. Oh, and Keeper of Eternal Flame. The king is there seeking a "white goddess" which legend has foretold. He bows low when Mrs. Howell arrives, very impressed with yet a third white goddess. Gilligan nets the three tribesmen. Mr. Howell tells him to cease, "These savages are civilized."

The Professor's intrigued by their contact with civilization (the king has a Zippo lighter— "the eternal flame"). But the natives are intent on their mission. But faced with three goddess, the king selects Mrs. Howell. Until he tells them his selection will be "married to volcano." She refuses, and so do Mary Ann and Ginger. The tribesmen say they will take one by force.

The men decide the best approach is for one of them to dress as a woman and go with the tribesmen. The others can follow secretly. Mr. Howell, the Skipper, and the Professor all squeeze into some of the women's clothes, but the results are ghastly.

and was the butt (pun intended) of many, many jokes.

Mr. Howell's reference to Maxine and Laverne when they're all in drag is, of course, to Patty, Maxine, and Laverne, the Andrews Sisters, famed World War II singing trio.

Greta Garbo, legendary screen beauty and mystery woman, became permanently linked to her line from the 1929 film, Grand Hotel, "I want to be alone." As she was playing a Russian ballerina, the line came out, "I vant to be alone."

WHAT'S MISSING? If you're watching this episode in syndication on a local station where the episodes are edited, you will miss the wonderfully funny scenes where the other men first dress in drag before selecting Gilligan to be the white goddess for the natives.

ABANDONED

The first hint of trouble came from Jim Backus, who was in New York to tape a new television version of the hit Broadway show, *Damn Yankees*, with Lee Remick as Lola and Phil Silvers as the devil. He had a meeting with close friend and CBS VP Perry Lafferty, who confirmed the show's pick-up. But later in the day, Lafferty called Backus and said they were off the schedule.

Sherwood Schwartz remembers: "When I originally heard from the network that we were renewed for another year, I called the cast . . . I had great news. The show was renewed and I called everybody personally and told them that. Two of them bought houses as a result of that call. Actually. Then a funny thing happened. I didn't get official confirmation. As a producer, I didn't get confirmation from business affairs. Business affairs waits until the last moment, as they're supposed to do, because anything can happen before the contractual last moment. The star can get hurt, the ratings can slip, there's a lot that can happen. And I never got official confirmation from business affairs."

In his book, *Inside Gilligan's Island*, Schwartz says he never really found out what happened. From Lafferty and Dann, he pieced the story together that nobody ever wanted to cancel *Gilligan's Island*. But they *had* meant to cancel *Gunsmoke*. After many illustrious years (and four years as number one), the eleven-year-old warhorse had lost ratings and its younger viewers.

However, when CBS head William Paley got the news while on his annual Caribbean vacation, he freaked. *Gunsmoke* was his favorite show. *Gunsmoke* was Mrs. Paley's favorite show. It had to go back on the schedule. The team putting together the fall schedule had only one place to put it. Into the Monday night 7:30–8:30 hour reserved for *Gilligan's Island* and a new comedy, *Doc*. Mr. Paley hadn't been a supporter of *Gilligan's Island* since the critics savaged it. In his eyes, it was a low-class show.

Schwartz was shocked. "All of a sudden, the second shoe dropped and it was a result of this *Gunsmoke* mix-up. We were off the air all of a sudden. And I had to make a terrible phone call to these people I'd called just a month earlier to tell them the good news and I had to tell them some really bad news. Because we were a family by that time. We cared about each other, we cared about the show. The audience loved the show. It had everything going for it. And I had to call and tell them there was no next year."

Bob Denver remembers that day. "Sherwood had to call all of us and tell us. That must have been the most fun for him. 'Hello, we're canceled.'"

The *Gilligan's Island* cast dispersed without a final episode, no rescue, not even a chance to get together one more time to say goodbye. The entire cast wouldn't be together again until they were reunited on the Fox network's *Late Show*, on May 18, 1988.

After eleven years on Saturday nights at ten o'clock, *Gunsmoke* moved to the Monday seven-thirty *Gilligan's Island* time slot and jumped in the ratings to number four. The western drama attracted its youngest viewers in years and moved into the top ten for the next five years.

It's hard to say why CBS didn't just put *Gilligan's Island* into production and use it to plug into a slot vacated by the first failure of the season, but the answer is no one cared enough. There never really was anyone at the network who loved the show passionately enough to fight for it.

Today, it seems unthinkable that any network would cancel a successful show, but you might remember the case of *Chicken Soup* in 1989, a rather tasteless sitcom put in the golden time slot behind the number one *Roseanne*. It got fabulous ratings, but they weren't quite as fabulous as ABC thought they should have been for a show following their number one hit, and it was canceled. *Sic transit gloria.*

ANIMALS ABOARD

Since human guest stars were rare due to the very nature of *Gilligan's Island*, there were a lot of episodes featuring animals (both real and fake), whose presence was much easier to explain.

First, of course, CBS had a great idea. Bob Denver remembers, "Sherwood Schwartz, our dear creator, went over to CBS and they said, 'We have a great idea for a new character on the island. A dinosaur becomes Gilligan's best friend. He finds him on the other side of the island and brings him home.' I said, 'Sherwood, how are we going to do that?' He said, 'I'll take care of it.' I said, 'In a two-shot, I'll be holding the dinosaur's leash. You'll see me and part of a leg. And if you want to see the dinosaur, I'm going to be this big [indicates a half-inch high] and the dinosaur will be huge.' He said, 'Don't worry, I'll take care of it.' He found out it cost seventy-five thousand dollars a minute to put the dinosaur in the shot and that was the end of the dinosaur idea. Goodbye."

The misadventures with animals used in *Gilligan's Island* are among the favorite stories told by the cast members.

In episode number one, "Two on a Raft," Gilligan and the Skipper are terrorized by a shark when they attempt to go for help on a raft the Castaways build.

A thieving monkey appears in episode number three and a duck in number seven which is christened Everett by Gilligan until it lays an egg and the Castaways decide Emily is a better name.

A frog makes a brief appearance in episode number fourteen and helps the Castaways find a new water source, and Janos Prohaska plays a womanizing ape in episode number twenty-two, "Diamonds Are an Ape's Best Friend."

Sam the parrot makes the Castaways think a group of gangsters is on the island plotting a murder in episode number twenty-seven, and the Castaways stage a race with two large tortoises in the next show.

Bob Denver remembers, "Because we were on a tropical island, we occasionally had to deal with various animals and some animals naturally were harder to deal with than others but that wasn't always the case. I remember when we were using a monkey. We all thought he was real cute and we really liked having him around until one day he climbed up a tree and wouldn't come down. I even climbed up after him and tried to get him to come down by bribing him with a banana but he wouldn't come down. Then the monkey's trainer yelled up at me that he didn't like bananas, this monkey likes spaghetti. I looked down and Jim Backus, who played Mr. Howell, said, 'It's just our luck to get an Italian monkey.' I'll never forget that monkey, especially when he wouldn't come down until his trainer made him a plate of spaghetti."

In the second season opener, the Castaways encounter alligators and a bear while searching for Gilligan, and Gilligan acquires a chimp, Gladys, in episode number thirty-eight, crowning her Miss Castaway in a contest fraught with political peril. The ape makes a brief return appearance in "The Chain of Command."

There's a grenade-lobbing gorilla in episode number fifty-seven who takes a shine to Gilligan, and a lion terrorizes them all in episode number sixty, "Feed the Kitty."

Bob remembers another animal, a parrot (episode number sixty-five, "The Friendly Physician"). "I remember Jim Backus having to work with a parrot—a big, live parrot. He didn't really want to work with him too much, but by morning, he had him on his shoulder with sunflower seeds. By the end of the morning, he was out of seeds and the parrot took his thumb. I never heard language like that in my life."

There are pigeons in episode number ninety-six, as well as a giant, moldy old fake spider that looks like a refugee from a cheap fifties horror flick—or a grammar school Halloween haunted room. You can even see the wires in several scenes!

An equally cheesy papier-mâché bat makes an appearance in episode number sixty-nine and monkeys appear in episode number seventy-seven, "Ring Around Gilligan," and number ninety-six, "Bang! Bang! Bang!" There's a near-sighted gorilla (probably Prohaska again) in number eighty-eight "Our Vines Have Tender Apes," who mistakes Gilligan in a suit made from Mrs. Howell's furs for another gorilla.

Then, of course, there's Mr. Howell's teddy. . . .

SEARCH AND RESCUE
Life After Cancellation

In the years following the sudden cancellation of *Gilligan's Island*, Schwartz assumed it was only a matter of time before they'd be put back on the air. It was a logical assumption. The show was still a bonafide hit when it was taken off.

But as time passed, the three networks refused to even consider a special where the Castaways get rescued. In his book, Schwartz says that he'd never intentionally have let the series end without that rescue.

He'd been approached numerous times about doing an animated version and as the possibility of renewal of the live-action show dimmed, he finally agreed. In 1974, Schwartz, working with Filmation, sold *The New Adventures of Gilligan* to ABC for its Saturday morning lineup.

The shows are enjoyable and fun, and since most of the original actors do the voices of their *Gilligan's Island* characters (Dawn Wells and Tina Louise did not participate), the shows give you a funny feeling that they are real episodes of the show you must have missed. There are the usual assortment of dilemmas, savages, wild animals, and visitors to the island, and life on the rock goes on without a break. Note that Ginger has become a blonde. This was done in case Tina Louise objected to them using her image.

Then, in 1982, Schwartz developed another animated series, *Gilligan's Planet*, where the hapless Castaways modify a space capsule that's landed in a lagoon and try to get back on the mainland, only to be propelled into outer space, where they are marooned on a deserted planet far from Earth. In this series, Dawn Wells did the voices of both Ginger and Mary Ann.

Meanwhile, in 1973, Schwartz found he was getting constant calls from newspapers all over the country asking if the Castaways were ever rescued. He reckoned it was because the series had replayed many times in reruns by then and somehow, people felt there *had* been a rescue show and they'd missed it.

Schwartz again tried to peddle his idea of a TV movie called *Rescue From Gilligan's Island*. The networks refused. He tried for four more years to sell it, always meeting with refusals, until he had a chance meeting with an agent. The project was suddenly "hot." NBC bought the idea within a few days and the Castaways were finally rescued in October 1978.

Rescue From Gilligan's Island

October 14 and 21, 1978

Starring   Bob Denver
           Alan Hale
Also Starring
Jim Backus as Thurston
  Howell III

Alan Hale remembers how the Castaways' homecoming actually happened: "It was during the scene when we were in our huts and we were being towed into the harbor by the coast guard. All around the docks, there were literally hundreds of people cheering and yelling out our names. The strangest thing was that these people weren't hired to be there, it was a crowd that had gathered to see what was going on. A lot of people honestly thought the Castaways were finally being rescued. It gave us goosebumps. Some of us even had tears in our eyes. We began to feel like we were really being rescued. It was a strange case of fiction turning into fact."

Tina Louise elected not to join the Castaways for this rescue, or for the other TV movies. She did, however, seriously consider doing each of the movies as they were offered to her. Russell Johnson thinks he figured out the reason for her declining to do them: "It's probably because she wanted to divorce herself from that character. In

Natalie Schafer
And Also Starring
Judith Baldwin as Ginger
Russell Johnson
Dawn Wells
Costarring
Vincent Schiavelli .. Dimitri
Art LaFleur .... Ivan
Featuring
Norman Bartold.. Producer
Barbara Mallory ....
.... Cindy Smith
June Whitley Taylor ....
.... Miss Ainsworth
Martin Rudy .... Dean
Mary Gregory ....
.... Mrs. Devonshire
Glenn Robards ....
.... Mr. Devonshire
Diana Chesney ....
.... Mrs. Fellows
And
Victor Rogers.. Mr. Fellows
Michael Flanagan . Director
Martin Ashe .... Butler
Robert Wood .... Tony
John Wheeler Studio Guard
Alex Rodine ....1st Officer
Don Marshall ..... FBI Man
Mel Prestidge ....
.... Governor's Aide
Lewis Arquette ..... Judge
Judd Laurence . Technician

Michael Macready......... FBI Man #2

Richard Rorke .... Helicopter Pilot

Marcus K. Mukai .... Hawaiian Man

Snag Werris .. Camera Man

Micki Waugh. Pom Pom Girl

Alisa Powell . Pom Pom Girl

Portia Stevens .... Pom Pom Girl

Candace Bowen........... Pom Pom Girl

Executive Producer, Sherwood Schwartz

Director of Photography, Robert Primes

Created by Sherwood Schwartz

Written by Sherwood Schwartz, Elroy Schwartz, Al Schwartz, David P. Harmon

Directed by Leslie H. Martinson

Producer, Lloyd J. Schwartz

Associate Producer, Valton Lee Taylor

Production Designer, Stan Jolley

Film Editor, Marshall Neilan

one sense, right after the show was dropped in '67, all of us suffered from what you might call typecasting. I had worked for fifteen years doing all kinds of things before Gilligan's Island, mostly playing heavies. After Gilligan's Island, people didn't see me that way at all but I had done it for years. We all suffered a kind of typecasting of being put in a box by people, and it took a while to get out of it."

NBC nearly sabotaged this telemovie when it was aired. It was originally supposed to be shown from 8–10 P.M. on October 14. Then the head of programming decided to split it into two one-hour segments. Despite this, the first part got a rating of 30.2 (percent of television homes) and a share of 52 (percentage of homes watching TV at that *time). The second half dropped a bit because people thought it was a rerun of the previous week's show, since it had the same title.*

Gilligan's having nightmares about the island breaking loose, sinking, and melting. His shouts are so loud, he wakes all the other Castaways. The Professor reassures everyone. Meanwhile, at a Soviet space center, one of their spy satellites goes berserk. The scientists panic, as there is sensitive information encoded on a metal disk which, if it fell into the other side's hands, would revoke their treaties. They destroy the satellite, but the disk falls to earth.

Gilligan finds it and shows it to the Professor. He's intrigued, not recognizing the new alloy it's made of. It helps him fashion a working barometer, which predicts a large storm and a tidal wave which will wash over the island. It could also sweep a boat into their area. The news being mostly bad, the Professor tells Gilligan to keep quiet about it. Of course, the Skipper gets it out of him, and rushes off to the Professor and soon the word's out to everyone. As usual, Mrs. Howell's worried about what to wear to a rescue.

Everyone gathers around the Professor and he tells them the

bad news about the tidal wave. The Professor thinks there might be a way. If they lash their huts together, they might weather it. They've got three or four days. They have to move the huts together and tie them and assemble provisions. They build a winch to raise the huts, then they (*everyone*, for a change), push them into position. They end up with what is very like a Tahitian longhouse as the storm arrives.

The Professor tries to convince Mrs. Howell that tying herself to the supports is more important than wrinkling her clothes. Suddenly, Mrs. Howell remembers her poodle, Fifi. They can't leave her out in the storm. Gilligan runs out to look for her before Mr. Howell reminds her they left Fifi at home fifteen years ago. Gilligan's caught outside as the storm blows up something terrible. He grips a tree for his very life.

The storm finally clears and the hut-boat makes it, though most of its thatching is gone. The Castaways are all asleep, exhausted, and still lashed to their poles. Mr. Howell awakens first and steps outside—into the Pacific Ocean. The Professor rescues him and then they all realize Gilligan's not there. They are all miserable. They're having a moment of silence when they see Gilligan—and his tree—trailed by one of the vine-ropes from the hut-boat. After a run-in with a shark, everybody's back aboard and the Castaways start rowing and singing. For two days.

They decide to use their clothes as a sail and plan what they'll do when they get home. Gilligan has caught dinner and he's put a fire under it. The whole hut-boat immediately catches fire, but it's that that saves them. The smoke is spotted by a Coast Guard chopper. The Castaways look up in amazement. The pilot says he'd have never spotted them without the smoke.

It's an incredible sight as the strange craft is escorted into Honolulu harbor amid streamers, officials, crowds, bands, planes, and fireboats. Gilligan's at the helm. There's even a telegram from the president (Carter), except they've never heard of him. Or Gerald Ford. Or Watergate.

The Castaways get a ticker-tape parade back in Los Angeles. Things aren't so cheerful in the Soviet embassy until they see Gilligan on television, wearing the metal disk around his neck as a good luck charm. Two agents are immediately alert. The Castaways are all ready to "go their separate ways" when they're suddenly reluctant to part.

Gilligan and the Skipper put the finishing touches on the *Minnow II* while they're awaiting the insurance check (the Skipper's given Gilligan a "tiny piece" of the *Minnow II*). The Soviet agents try to talk Gilligan into trading them the disk, but he refuses. The Skipper's furious to get a letter saying the insurance company won't issue a check until he proves he didn't cause the accident. They've got to get everyone to sign an affidavit.

Ginger's making a movie, but the producer isn't pleased with her performance or her wardrobe. They want a nude scene. She's appalled by what the producer calls "modern writing" and walks off the set. When Gilligan and the Skipper arrive, Ginger's really glad to see them. She moans that they don't make "beautiful movies with beautiful costumes" anymore. Gilligan says he's seen *Star Wars*, *Jaws*, and *Julia* and he liked them. She wistfully notes there were no dirty words or nude scenes in those pictures. He asks if they weren't successful and she says they were all hits. The producer is listening and has a change of heart. He tells Ginger the sex and language is history. She signs the Skipper's affidavit. The Soviet agents continue to stage phony situations to get the disk, but they're even more inept than Gilligan.

The Professor is infuriated at the attention he's getting from the coeds at his school. He's become a romantic figure and the cheerleaders want him to be homecoming king and the trustees want him to sweet talk the alumni out of money. He signs the affidavit for the Skipper and Gilligan.

Mr. and Mrs. Howell are entertaining several couples from their New York social set when Gilligan and the Skipper arrive. The Howells' butler treats them much more kindly than the Howells' guests. They're happy to sign the affidavit, but Mr. Howell is hurt that they didn't ask him for the money first. Then the Howells overhear their other guests insulting Gilligan and the Skipper and Mr. Howell storms into the dining room and orders them all out of their house.

Mary Ann is dressing for her wedding to her longtime sweetheart Herbert, but she's in tears. Her childhood best friend Cindy tries to help her. Mary Ann says they've both changed and she doesn't love him.

The "Castaways" on Gilligan's Island
March 3, 1979

Starring   Bob Denver
           Alan Hale
Also Starring
Jim Backus as Thurston Howell III
Natalie Schafer
And Also Starring
Judith Baldwin as Ginger
Russell Johnson
Dawn Wells
Special Appearance by Tom Bosley as Henry Elliot

The Flight of the Phoenix, *a 1966 film starring James Stewart, Richard Attenborough, Peter Finch, and Ernest Borgnine, is a superb survival movie, where a group of men crash in an Arabian desert and though starving and dying of thirst, reconstruct their crippled plane by making a sort of flying wing out of one wing, and escape their certain fate.*

"The Wreck of the Hesperus" is a famous

ballad poem, by Henry Wadsworth Longfellow. It was published in 1841.

Shangri-La is the archtypical paradise as envisioned by James Hilton in his novel, Lost Horizon. *It is supposedly situated in the Tibetan interior and is a land of eternal youth. Some people still believe it really exists, partly because Franklin Roosevelt facetiously gave Shangri-La as the location of a secret air base from which originated an American bombing raid on Japan.* Lost Horizon *was filmed in 1937 with Ronald Coleman, Jane Wyatt, and John Howard, with Frank Capra directing, and again in 1973 with Peter Finch, Liv Ullmann, and Sally Kellerman. The beautiful 1937 version has recently been restored, though a few scenes are still missing.*

Marcia Wallace as Myra
  Elliot
Ronnie Scribner as Robbie
Costarring
Peter MacLean as ....
.............Fred Sloan
Judith Searle as .Mrs. Sloan
Rod Browning as..........
..........Dr. Tom Larsen
Joan Roberts as...........
............Laura Larsen
With
Natasha Ryan....Little Girl
Mokihana .... Naheeti
Sonny Craver..Navy Captain
Robert Jon Carlson........
.... Navy Crewman
Denise Cheshire ...... Girl
Directors of Photography,
  Joe Jackman, Keith
  Smith
Executive Producer,
  Sherwood Schwartz
Written by Sherwood
  Schwartz, Al Schwartz,
  Elroy Schwartz
Directed by Earl Bellamy
Produced by.............
.... Lloyd J. Schwartz
Associate Producer,
  Valton L. Taylor
Music .... Gerald Fried
Art Director ....
.... Vince Cresciman

Film Editor.. Albert J. Zuniga

The Castaways have been stranded on the island for nearly two weeks. Gilligan and the Skipper are looking for fresh water. A recent tidal wave has ruined the underground springs they've been using. The Howells play golf while the Professor tries to fix the radio. The first broadcast isn't good news: There's a storm due and the coast guard is abandoning its search for the *Minnow II*. The group is pretty depressed.

But shortly, Gilligan discovers several World War II planes in the jungle. There's a machine shop too and the as the Castaways clear the area around them, the Professor pieces together the history. He thinks there might have been an emergency airstrip there during the war. Gilligan asks him if he could combine the two planes and fly them out.

The Professor thinks it's a good idea. He saw *The Flight of the Phoenix* when on the mainland and he thinks they could do the same. Gilligan checks out the plane and sets the machine guns going, nearly wiping out his fellow Castaways.

This telemovie bears a striking resemblance to two shows that were popular at the time, The Love Boat and Fantasy Island. It would have been a fun premise for the show—all your favorite characters from Gilligan's Island with guest stars visiting them each week. Bet they could have gotten a season's run out of it.

Most of this film was shot at the backlot at Universal Studios, in the lagoon which has been used a zillion times on TV and in films, including Weird Science and Tales of the Gold Monkey.

The song Henry sings, "Lazybones," was written in 1933 by Hoagy Carmichael and Johnny Mercer, and was first popularized by Rudy Vallee.

The Professor and Mr. Howell work up plans to combine the planes, while Ginger and Mary Ann work on seats. The Professor rigs a winch and they hoist the wings into place and some time later, they finish. The Castaways decide who stays and who goes. They all decide to go. The Professor gets behind the controls while the others try to generate enough power on their crude generator to ignite the engines. It works. They all get aboard.

The plane (christened the *Minnow III*) actually takes off and they're airborne, although the old crate is shaking like mad. The Professor tells Gilligan of his fears and the others panic when he goes to the back and passes out parachutes.

One engine gives out and the Professor shuts it off. He orders the others to jettison everything they don't need. They start tossing luggage. Mrs. Howell doesn't want to give up her clothes, but they finally pry her suitcase loose and Gilligan goes with it when he tosses it out. The others watch as he plummets, then opens his chute. The Skipper tells the Professor they have to go back. The Professor says "of course," but they won't be able to take off again. They return to the island.

They disembark and the only working engine falls off. The Professor says, "Coming back for Gilligan saved our lives." They find Gilligan stuck in a tree. They're discussing their plight when two naval officers appear. They saw the plane on the radar. Mr. Howell announces he's going to build "a tropical Shangri-La" on the island. Money is no object and the others are minor partners.

SAME ISLAND, NEXT YEAR

The resort is beautiful, though remote and with no phones, no television, no electricity. There's a launch, the *Minnow IV*, to pick up guests from passing cruise ships. Gilligan and the Skipper pick up the latest group, which includes real estate developer Henry and Myra Elliot, Dr. and Mrs. Larsen, and a young boy.

The Professor finds some ancient Polynesian masks on the other side of the island, and he wants to use them to decorate for the luau, despite the superstitious objections of the front desk clerk, Naheeti. Meanwhile, the Skipper and

Gilligan get the Larsens and
Elliots settled in, and are surprised to hear the boy belongs
to neither couple. Myra has a
tough time getting Henry to
wind down. He wears his suit
to the beach. The Larsens are
having no such trouble. Dr.
Larsen is a dentist and says he
can't live without these two
weeks every year. But Henry's
incorrigible. He knows there
has to be a phone hidden
somewhere and he searches
until he finds it—in a tree trunk
in the lobby. He calls his office
in Cleveland. He panics when
there's no answer. The entire
staff of the "Castaways" tries
to get him to relax. After a massage from Ginger and Mary
Ann, he is inspired—but only
by a business plan he comes
up with.

The Skipper and Gilligan take
him fishing. He panics when he
thinks he's lost his briefcase.
Gilligan, of course, tips over
the boat and dunks them all.
Henry nearly drowns when he
tries harder to save his briefcase than himself. The Professor takes him skindiving.
Henry finds Myra to tell her
they've got to go back. But he
overhears her swearing they'll

stay there until he learns to relax.

Meanwhile the boy, Robbie, is getting hungry and pilfers the Skipper's burger. The Skipper asks Naheeti to check all the guests. No one sent for the boy. The Professor discovers the masks were made in Chicago. He also thinks they should find the boy immediately. Gilligan spots him, but he runs. The kid's like a monkey, climbing trees, swinging on branches and vaulting from stump to rock. When an exhausted Gilligan collapses, Robbie relents and talks to him. Gilligan promises not to tell anyone he found him.

Third TV Movie
The Harlem Globetrotters on Gilligan's Island
May 15, 1981

Starring   Bob Denver
           Alan Hale
           Jim Backus as
              Thurston
              Howell III
           Natalie Schafer
           as Mrs.

The map J.J. Pierson has of the Castaways' island looks nothing like previous maps used on the series, and suspiciously like Oahu, Hawaii, mountains and all.

This episode planned to use the Dallas Cowboys Cheerleaders, but they were unavailable and the Globetrotters were substituted.

*Jim Backus was seriously
ill when this was first
planned and it was
thought he couldn't appear
in this TV movie at all,
which is why a hitherto-
unheard-of son was
inserted. But he was a little
better near the end of
filming and makes a cameo
appearance at the end.*

Howell
Constance
Forslund as
Ginger
Russell Johnson
Dawn Wells
Special Guest Stars
The Harlem Globetrotters
Martin Landau as . . . .
. . . . J. J. Pierson
Barbara Bain as . . . . . . Olga
Guest Stars
Scatman Crothers . . Dewey
Dreama Denver
Stu Nahan
Chick Hearn
Rosalind Chao
George the Robot
and
The New Invincibles
Costarring
Cindee Appleton as . Linda
Wendy Hoffman as . . Jackie
Whitney Rydbeck as
    George The Robot
With
Bruce Briggs . . . . . . Referee

Executive Producer,
    Sherwood Schwartz
Film Editors, Albert J. J.
    Zuniga, Beryl Gelfond
Art Director, Robert Crawley

Director of Photography,
   K. C. Smith
Produced by Hap
   Weyman, Lloyd J.
   Schwartz
Based on *Gilligan's Island*,
   Created by Sherwood
   Schwartz
Written by Sherwood
   Schwartz, Al Schwartz,
   David P. Harmon,
   Gordon Mitchell
Directed by Peter Baldwin

Gilligan is out looking for a comic book as the Harlem Globetrotters fly overhead. There's something wrong with the plane. Their radio's out as well as the electrical system. They're heading for a tiny island Dewey, their coach and pilot, found on the map.

Meanwhile, a mad billionaire, J.J. Pierson, is hiding on another part of the island. While at the Castaways resort on vacation the previous year, he discovered a new substance in one of the island caves. Further research by his scientist, Olga Smetna, showed it was the only trace of the substance in the world. He has christened it "Supremium," and has brought his lab, a group of robots, and a ton of scientific stuff to the island with the goal of stealing all the Supremium, which has proved to be an amazing power source. Their first goal is to frighten the Castaways and all their guests off the island.

George, head robot, does the dirty work. His tricks are pretty lethal, and several would kill the Castaways but they're all lucky, and find the various poisons, spiders, and what-not the not-very-bright robot uses. J.J. and Olga register at the hotel and plan trickery to get each Castaway to sign away the deed to the island.

Meanwhile, the Globetrotters have ditched their plane and float to another part of the island, where they occupy themselves playing basketball with coconuts. Gilligan finds them and brings them back to the resort, where Mrs. Howell and her son, Thurston Howell IV, reign supreme.

J.J. and Olga trick each of the Castaways into signing the document until only the Howells are left. He bets the deed to the island with Thur-

ston IV on a basketball game
between the Globetrotters
and the Invincibles, a team of
dribbling robots made by
Olga.

SAILING UNDER A NEW FLAG

Tributes, Satires, Dreams, and Parodies of Gilligan's Island

Gilligan's Island has had its share of parodies and tributes as is often the case with things that become cultural icons. The legion of Schwartz family members has also taken the characters with them as they moved on to other shows. These parodies are generally affectionate, and several have been hilariously brilliant.

The Tonight Show with Jay Leno

Jay Leno's *Tonight Show* recently picked up the gauntlet dropped by *Saturday Night Live* in terms of doing sketch comedy about topical issues. The show turned the O.J. Simpson trial and its personalities into a series of sixties sitcom parodies, including spoofs of *Gilligan's Island*, *The Patty Duke Show*, *The Monkees*, and *The Brady Bunch*.

The show recreated the original *Gilligan's* opening credits, writing new words for the theme song and placing the Simpson trial participants in the ship's wheel frames. The lyrics were very funny, telling of a "fateful drive" going from O.J.'s "Brentwood house, then up the 405." The audience ate it up.

SCTV Network

This 1981–1983 comedy sketch show did a brief parody of *Gilligan*, called *Cretin's Island*, where after one more boneheaded mistake, the Skipper throttles Gilligan. The announcer warns it's a "low-brow rip-off of a cheap comedy show."

The New Gidget

(Syndicated—
1986–1988)
"Gillingidge Island"
September 24, 1987

Executive Boom-A-Locka
  Harry Ackerman
Produced by Kenneth R.
  Koch and George
  Zateslo
Teleplay by Deanne
  Stillman
Story by Larry Mollin
Based on Characters
  Created by Frederick
  Kohner
Directed by Doug Rogers
Starring
Caryn Richman as.. Gidget
Dean Butler as Moondoggie

The Poseidon Adventure is a 1972 movie starring Gene Hackman, Ernest Borgnine, Red Buttons, Carol Lynley, and Shelley Winters. After the liner is overturned in a huge tidal wave, Hackman's character leads one group of survivors on a harrowing escape through the wreck. Shelley Winters plays a very heavy woman who insists she be left behind when the going gets tough. The others insist on helping her along, and she saves everyone's bacon by swimming through a long flooded compartment, thanks to her training as a long-distance swimmer.

Jesse White played the lonely Maytag repairman in commercials for many years.

Bob Denver does his Maynard G. Krebs from Dobie Gillis take on the word work, then notes it's the "wrong show."

Mr. Whipple tells everyone not to squeeze the Charmin in a recreation of a long-running commercial which introduced the product. The commercial was a frequent subject of parodies and jokes.

When Gidget doesn't think "anything could gross out Quincy," she refers to Jack Klugman's series about a medical examiner, Quincy, which ran on NBC from 1976 to 1983.

Sydney Penny as . . . .
. . . . Danni Collins
and
William Schallert as . . Russ
Also Starring
Lili Haydn as . . . . Gail
Guest Starring
Alan Hale as . . Captain Hale
**Special Guest
Appearance by**
Bob Denver as . . . . Gilligan
Costarring
Branscombe Richmond as
  Native Chief
Leon Fan as . . . .
. . . . Native Teenager
and
Jesse White as the Washing
  Machine Repairman
(Filmed on location in
  Hawaii)

Gidget writes her memoirs, including a "bizarre day trip from Kauai" with her husband, niece, and friend. They get on a battered ship called the *Minnow II*, a charter boat skippered (but he tells them *not* to call him "Skipper") by a familiar face who asks them to call him "Captain Hale." Of course, they are caught in a storm and washed up on the beach of a tropical island. . . .

Gidget's niece and Gail are not thrilled to be stranded. Captain Hale mentions this has happened to him before— except this time, the radio doesn't work. Moondoggie finally recognizes the captain as actor Alan Hale (he notes the president is an actor). That night, Hale tells them about the other cast members of *Gilligan's Island*: Backus collecting *Mr. Magoo* residuals, Bob Denver spilling pudding in his lap on the People's Choice Awards. Gidget suggests that Moondoggie and Hale put their heads together and get them rescued. Hale suggests an all-night signal fire. They concur.

In the morning, they hear a plane and run out of the cave but the fire's out. Hale and Moondoggie got their signals crossed and start bickering. They send the women out "gathering" while they rebuild the fire. Danni hears a radio playing hard rock and follow the sound of "either Bon Jovi or Motley Crue" and find a deserted village with the detritus of island life. But then they see a skull and a javelin flies at them. They flee. But they are caught in a trap by three savages.

They try to communicate but the natives don't seem to speak English. Gail rushes back to the beach and tells Moondoggie and Captain Hale to rescue them. The captain isn't worried: "These episodes always have a happy ending." Moondoggie and Hale plan to toss coconuts at the natives while Gail creates a diversion. Meanwhile, the girls draw a happy face in the sand and the natives spear it and say "Boom-a-locka." The captain, Gail, and Moondoggie are captured.

When the Professor says, "Who died and made you King Kamehameha?" he's referring to King Kamehameha I (1758–1819), the Polynesian warrior who conquered all the islands of Hawaii and united them into one nation. He put in place the first government and his heirs ruled for many years.

Alf (NBC—1986–1990)
"Somewhere Over the Rerun" (later renamed "The Ballad of Gilligan's Isle")
September 28, 1987

Created by Tom Patchett
 and Paul Fusco
Executive Producer Tom
 Patchett and Bernie
 Brillstein
Produced by Paul Fusco
Written by Scott Spencer
 Gorden
Directed by Nick Havinga

Starring

Max Wright.. Willie Tanner
Anne Schedeen ....
.... Kate Tanner
Andrea Elson .Lynn Tanner
Benji Gregory.Brian Tanner

Also Starring

Bob Denver..,.... Gilligan
Alan Hale......... Skipper
Russell Johnson..Professor
Dawn Wells..... Mary Ann

Alf is obsessed with *Gilligan's Island* and it's taken over his life. He wears a Hawaiian shirt, mixes "Skipper Colada" drinks, and orders bamboo furniture. He sings along with the theme song when he and Brian watch the show. Alf wants to know why life is so much less fun in their house than on *Gilligan's Island*. He wants coconut cream pie, not apple pie. Later, he keeps Willie and Kate up by telling the plot of "Gilligan's Mother-in-Law." He tries to flatter Kate by telling her she reminds him of Ginger.

He can't sleep. He tries "counting Castaways jumping over palm trees. But the Skipper's not the best of leapers." Willie wants some sleep and promises he'll build Alf a lagoon. The next morning, Alf has already built the lagoon and a hut. It fills the whole back yard. Willie falls in. He orders Alf to fill it in. The work goes slowly. He falls asleep and wakes up on Gilligan's island. The Skipper and Gilligan are there. Alf's in "rerun heaven."

Alf introduces himself and asks where the others are. Gilligan says Ginger and the Howells built a country club on the other side of the island and they won't let them in. The Professor and Mary Ann are around somewhere. Mary Ann announces lunch. The Professor says he doesn't let her make coconut cream pie anymore because of their blood cholesterol. They're all sick of the place and each other. They bicker. Alf is disappointed.

Melcombe/Mr. Howell's answer to the question of how the Howells had all their clothes on a three-hour tour is the same as Sherwood Schwartz's: The rich always seem to manage better than anyone else.

Safe at Home
(Syndicated)
"Gilligan's Island"
June 30, 1986

Executive Producer Arthur L. Annecharico
Created by Arthur L. Annecharico
Coordinating Producer, Mike Fierman

Producer, Arthur J. Epstein
Written by Lloyd J.
  Schwartz
Directed by Lee Lochhead
Starring
Michael J. Cutt . . . Dan Ford
Katherine Britton . . Caroline
Jeanna Micheals . . . .
. . . . Tatum McCoy
Richard Steven Horvitz . . . .
. . . . Gary
Gary Hudson . . . . Roger
Brenda Lynn Klemme . Amy
and
Steve Franken as Richard
  Melcombe

Caroline tells Gary about school career day and he doesn't know what he wants to be when he grows up. He's an assistant to an assistant at a cable TV station and a *Gilligan's Island* fan. Dan calls and the station is a mess and everyone's panicked because bigwig Richard Melcombe is around. Gary falls off the ladder and dreams he's Gilligan.

On the island, Tatum's Mrs. Howell, Melcombe is Mr. Howell, Roger is the Professor, Caroline's Mary Ann, Dan's the Skipper, and Amy is Ginger.

The Howells are planning a

When "Ginger" says "Nice driving, Ahab" to the Skipper, she's referring to Captain Ahab of Moby Dick, *whose boat landed in an even worse spot than the* Minnow, *inside the whale's stomach.*

In a truly inside joke, the youngest headhunter says "Boola, Boola, Boola," the Yale fighting cry. Harvard alumnus Mr. Howell would have a fit.

party to celebrating their safe arrival on the island. But the Professor says a big storm is coming and advises them to seek higher ground. Mr. Howell says, "The rich get the highest ground."

Gary comes to, and tells them who they all were in his dream. He makes the mistake of telling Melcombe he was the "greedy" Mr. Howell. He fires him. Dan and Tatum plead his case, without any luck. They tell him they're not coming to his party Saturday night. Dan says, in fact, they'll quit. Melcombe gives them until the party to reconsider.

Later, Gary packs and tells Caroline he's leaving and to tell Dan and Tatum not to quit over him. But they come home suddenly and Gary gets another knock on the head. He's back on the island.

The Castaways are all sympathetic about his fall. They're all still preparing for both the hurricane and the party. They talk about the problems of fifteen years on the island. The Professor succumbs to Ginger's advances at last. Gary/Gilligan wants to know where the bathroom is. And it hurts when the Skipper hits him with his hat. They finally get around to storm preparations. Gary/Gilligan thinks they should post a sign for the hurricane that says NO VACANCY. The Professor says if they could make it rain, the small storm will deflect the bigger one. Mary Ann seeds the clouds with popcorn, the Howells count their money ("It's what we do on a rainy day."). Ginger lies out in the sun, Gilligan does an Indian rain dance while the Skipper beats a drum. The Professor builds a coconut satellite. It begins to rain.

Baywatch (NBC/Syndicated 1989–present)
"Now, Sit Right Back and You'll Hear a Tale"
February 26, 1992

Executive Producers,
    Douglas Schwartz and
    Michael Berk
Executive Producers,
    David Hasselhoff,
    Gregory J. Bonann
Created by Michael Berk,
    and Douglas Schwartz,
    and Gregory J. Bonann
Producer, Paul Cajero

Producer, James Pergola
Written by Lloyd J.
  Schwartz
Directed by Douglas
  Schwartz
Starring
David Hasselhoff ....
.......Lt. Mitch Bucannon
Billy Warlock. Eddie Kramer
Erika Eleniak. . . . .
. . . . Shauni McLain
Jeremy Jackson . . . .
. . . . Hobie Bucannon
Tom McTigue. . . . .
. . . . Harvey Miller
Monte Markham . . . .
. . . . . Captain Don Thorpe
Richard Jaeckel as. . . . .
. . Lieutenant Ben Edwards
Special Guest
Appearance
Bob Denver as . . . . Gilligan
Dawn Wells as . . Mary Ann
Guest Starring
Gregory Alan-William. . . . . .
. . . . Garner Ellerbee

  In traditional tribute-show
style, after overdosing on *Gilligan's Island* reruns, Eddie falls
and hits his head. From then
on, the show is his dream/
delusion.
  Eddie and Shauni are

stranded by a dead engine after helping a stalled jet skier. They're not far from Anacapa Island and Eddie suggests there are worse things than being stranded together on an island. They take a life raft ashore. Eddie is searching for food when he sees Gilligan and Mary Ann. They tell Eddie and Shauni they really were shipwrecked all these years. The Professor finally built them a raft but it would only hold two, so they sailed and sailed and landed on yet another island. They're rescued and taken to Baywatch headquarters, where they create quite a sensation.

Eddie is entranced with Mary Ann and takes her on a tour of the beach but all Gilligan really wants is a hamburger and fries. Then they encounter Captain Thorpe, who has won the lottery and has acquired a yacht called the *Minnow II* (and a Thurston Howell accent). He's also lavishly redecorated headquarters. He announces they're going to rescue the other Castaways. They set sail with Gilligan, Mary Ann, Harvey acquires a lot of scientific knowledge, Garner dons the Skipper's cap, Eddie puts on a Gilligan hat, Shauni acquires a slinky gown and a red wig and asks Thorpe for a part in the miniseries about the rescue. Of course, she sails with them. Eddie confesses his love for Mary Ann, but Gilligan says he loves her too and it's about time he told her.

A terrible storm comes up. Suddenly, the credits roll (Eddie is the millionaire's wife) and the Professor assigns them all duties after they land. It's a silent comedy of errors and disasters, but they get the hut built.

That night, it's a crowded hut with the hammocks stacked three-deep. The inevitable happens and the hut collapses. The next day, Eddie shows Mary Ann mouth-to-mouth resuscitation. She can't wait to try it on Gilligan. But Gilligan and Shauni misinterpret, and Shauni decides to make him jealous by kissing Gilligan. This goes back and forth until the two mismatched couples demand the Skipper marry them.

The Gilligan's Island *cast was right at home on* Roseanne's *set—it's shot at CBS Radford on the soundstage where their*

Roseanne (ABC 1988–Present)
"Sherwood Schwartz: A Loving Tribute"
May 24, 1995

Executive Producers,
    Marcy Carsey, Tom
    Werner
Executive Producer, Eric
    Gilliland
Executive Producer,
    Roseanne
Created by Matt Williams
Supervising Producer,
    Kevin Abbott
Supervising Producer,
    Miriam Trogdon
Producer, Michael Borkow
Producer, Tim Doyle
Producer, Dusty Kay
Producer, Sid Youngers
Produced by Al
    Lowenstein
Teleplay by William Lucas
    Walker
Story by William Lucas
    Walker & Allan Stephan
Directed by Gail Mancuso
Starring
Roseanne . Roseanne Conner
John Goodman . Dan Conner
Laurie Metcalf . . . .
. . . . . Jackie Conner Harris
Sara Gilbert . . . .
. . . . Darlene Conner
Sarah Chalke . Becky Conner
Michael Fishman . . . .
. . . . D.J. Conner

*old series was shot as
well.*

Also Starring
Johnny Galecki . . . . . . David
Estelle Parsons . Mrs. Howell
Glenn Quinn . . . . Mark
Guest Star
Martin Mull . . . . Mr. Howell
Uncredited Cameos
Bob Denver as . . . . . . Jackie
Tina Louise . . . . . Roseanne
Russell Johnson . . . . . . Mark
Dawn Wells . . . . Darlene
Sherwood Schwartz . . . .
. . . . Himself

David is worried about his plans to go to Paris to study art and leave Darlene alone for a month.

Dan's decided to build a boat and Roseanne thinks it's stupid. He'll never finish it, and if he does, there's better ways to spend a thousand dollars. But he regales her with tales of a glorious cruise. He dreams they're on the deck with champagne, elegant clothes, and a passing pizza boat.

Roseanne says what will *really* happen is they'll get lost, then shipwrecked. On a deserted island. A very familiar island . . .

The Skipper (Dan) and Gilligan (Jackie) help the Howells

(Martin Mull and Estelle Parsons) out of the boat. The Professor (Mark) and Mary Ann (Darlene) are along, too. And David, who doesn't know what he's doing there—he wanted to be on *Friends*. Then the Movie Star appears (Roseanne) and chews out the Skipper for his driving and cussing out Kathie Lee Gifford (in her role as Carnival Cruises spokeswoman).

The radio reports the search has been called off. Gilligan's tooth receives a coast guard signal about a storm brewing. Then the volcano erupts. An earthquake shakes things up. Then natives arrive and take them prisoner.

RECORDS TO PLAY ON A TROPICAL NIGHT

As you wander the flea markets and garage sales of this great land of ours, you might find:

The theme song as recorded for the TV series was never released on record. All recordings of it were done by other singers.

"The Ballad of Gilligan's Isle"

Television's Greatest Hits, Vol. 1
Teevee Toons: TVT 1100
This is a newly-recorded version of the song.

Star Trek and Other TV Songs
Kid Stuff Records: KS 147
A 1978 rerecording of the theme song.

Rerun Rock Presents
Rhino CD:R2 70199
A rap version of the theme song.

"Gilligan's Island (Stairway)"
Splash Records
Uses theme song lyrics to tune of Led Zepplin's "Stairway to Heaven."
Littel Roger and the Goosebumps

"Sea Cruise Gilligan's Island"
Rogelletti Records: RR-002
Canadian punk rock version
Rude Norton

"Isle Thing"
UHF Original Motion Picture Soundtrack
Parody to the tune of "Wild Thing"
"Weird Al" Yankovic

**"The Ballad of
Gilligan's Oil"**
Artist/Record Company
unknown
Reprinted in Sierra Club
newsletters at the time
of the Exxon *Valdez* oil
spill:

*Sit right back and you'll
  hear a tale
A tale of a fateful trip
That started from an
  Alaskan port
Aboard an Exxon ship*

*Third mate wasn't much of
  a sailing man
But the skipper liked to
  booze
So the mate steered the
  giant oil barge
While the skipper took a
  snooze*

Large icebergs filled the
  shipping lane
The mighty ship was slowed
If not for the innovative
  Exxon crew,
Their oil would not get sold

The helmsman was heard
  shouting out
"Clear sailing straight
  ahead!"
As the jolt of the vessel's
  grounding
Knocked the skipper out of
  bed

The ship set ground on a
  shallow reef
That pierced its single skin
Ten million gallons of oil
  spilled out
And a case or two of gin

No booms, no skimmers, no
  dispersants
Not a single contingency
The oil clean-up effort
Proved primitive as can be

The local folk and fishermen
Heard Exxon take the blame
They dreamed about vast
  riches
As they ran to file their claim

But their lawyers called it an
  "Act of God"

So the company can't be sued
And Exxon makes a profit
From the jacked-up price of
   crude

So now we leave Prince
   William Sound
Its shores mucked-up with oil
And sail off to more northern
   ports
More pristine lands to spoil

Jim Backus

Albums
1001 Arabian Nights
ColPix: CP/SCP 410
Cartoon film soundtrack

Dr. Demento's 20th Anniversary Collection
Rhino: R2–70743

Mr. Magoo in Hi-Fi
RCA: LP-1362

Color Along with Me, with Jim Backus
Burnell Entertainment: BE-460

The Dirty Old Man
Dore

Singles
"I Was a Teenage Reindeer"/"The Office
   Party"
Dico: 101

"The Dirty Old Man"/"Frigid"
Dore: 899

"Delicious"/"I Need a Vacation"
Jubilee: 5330

"Caveman"/"Why Don't You Go Home for
    Christmas?"
Jubilee: 5351

"Rocks on the Roof"/"Caveman"
Jubilee: 5361

Les Brown, Jr.

Played one of the Mosquitoes in episode number
    forty-eight, "Don't Bug the Mosquitoes."

Wildest Drums
GNP Crescendo, 1963

Tina Louise

Albums
Li'l Abner
original cast
Columbia: OL 5150
Sony Special Products: A-5150 (reissue)

Tina: Her Portrait in Hi-Fi
Marco Gregory and his Orchestra
Concert Hall: CHS 1503
A strange 1957 release of instrumental classics,
    supposedly Tina Louise's favorite music she
    plays in her "little apartment just off Gra-
    mercy Park." The cover photo, however, is a
    knockout.

It's Time For Tina
Concert Hall H-1521 (on CD in Japan)
Urania USD 2005 (stereo reissue)

Melody of Love, Vol. 2
Waldorf Music Hall: 1HK 33-1232
Tina doesn't sing on this album, but is the model
on the cover.

Fade Out–Fade In
Original Broadway cast album
ABC Paramount ABCS-OC-3
Tina's two duets in the show, one with Carol
Burnett, one with Jack Cassidy, were both cut
in New Haven. She has a few lines in various
other group songs.

Singles
"I'll be Yours"/"In the Evening"
United Artists: UA-127-X

Natalie Schafer

Album
Our Television Musicals
Blue Pear: BP 1019
Schafer sings a song from *The Canterville Ghost*.

The Wellingtons

(Sang the theme song the first year of the show
and also played the Mosquitoes in episode number forty-eight, "Don't Bug the Mosquitoes.")

Album
Annette on Campus (five songs by the Welling-
tons)
Buena Vista: 3320

Singles

"Savage Sam and Me"/"Just Say Auf Wieder-
sehen"
Buena Vista: F-421

"Merlin Jones" (Annette and the Wellingtons)
Buena Vista: F-431

"Thomasina"/"Jesse James"
Buena Vista: F-430

"The Ballad of Davy Crocket"/"A Whale of a
Tale"
Disneyland Records: DL-557

"The Scarecrow of Romney Marsh"
Disneyland Records: LG-774

"Go Ahead and Cry"/"Take My Hand"
Ascot: AS-2217

"For All We Know"/"Let's Fall in Love"
Capitol: 5315

Note that the four songs heard in episode number forty-eight, "Don't Bug the Mosquitoes,"—
"Don't Bug Me," "He's a Loser," "I Wanna Go Back
to Pago Pago with You (Yeah, Yeah, Yeah)," and
an instrumental—are also heard in a number of
episodes as the Castaways tune their radio. They
were never released on vinyl.

THE COLLECTIBLE CASTAWAYS

The entire field of TV collectibles has skyrocketed in recent years. Baby Boomers and nostalgia seekers looking for part of their youth have driven the price of many items to auction-house levels.

Lunchboxes are particularly desired, only in mint condition, thermos intact, and the highest prices are for only a few shows, such as *Lost in Space*, *The Brady Bunch*, and *Star Trek*, which are all in the five-hundred-to-seven-hundred-dollar range.

But there is no *Gilligan's Island* lunchbox. In fact, considering its appeal, *Gilligan's Island* merchandising was remarkably limited at best. When asked why there was so little done, Sherwood Schwartz recently told a fan, "We were stupid!" The following items are very hard to find, and all are expensive.

Matchbooks.
Props from the pilot. "From the Deck of the *S.S. Minnow*" printed on covers. 1963.

Commemorative Ashtray.
Presented to the cast and crew while series was in production. Only fifty to sixty made.

Topps Gum Cards.
   Very, very hard to find, and not very attractive. Black and white photos with comic-style balloon dialogue from the first fifteen episodes. Complete set of fifty-five cards. Most cards are extremely rare, except for number thirty-seven, which is nearly impossible to find at any price. 1965.

Gilligan's Island Board Game by Game Gems.
   This rather indifferent (and boring) game is extremely scarce. The Castaways should sue— the only characters on the island are Gilligan, Mr. Howell, the Skipper, and a monkey. 1965.

Whitman 128-page Coloring Book.
   Color artwork on cover. 1965.

TV Guide issues.
   With *Gilligan's Island* covers June 11, 1965, and May 8, 1966.

Whitman Storybook.
   By William Johnston. Story using characters but unrelated to any episodes. 1966.

11-page Notepad.
   With color photo of the Skipper and Gilligan on 8-½ by 11 cover. A cache of sixties TV show notepads was found several years ago, but as they were all in mint condition and unused, the price remained high.

The New Adventures of Gilligan Board Game.
   Milton Bradley. From cartoon series. 1974.

Gilligan's Floating Island Playskool Game.
A marvelous bathtub toy with island, trees, boat, raft, anchor, treasure chest and three figures. 1980.

The Adventures of Gilligan's Island.
Nintendo Game from Bandal America. 1989.

Gilligan's Island Pinball Machine
Bally/Midway. 1991.

Vinyl Figures.
Skipper and Gilligan. Hamilton Gifts. Also smaller PVC version of two figures. 1991.

Because of the ongoing popularity of *Gilligan's Island*, new collectibles keep coming. The dolls listed above are one recent example. There has been a rumor for some time that the collectible cards will be reprinted, and the show's fan club (see below) recently commissioned and sells a new lithograph of, and personally signed by, the surviving cast members.

Ads for TV collectibles can be found in several collector's newspapers, especially *Toy Shop*, Krause Publications, 700 E. State St., Iola, WI 54990; and *Toy Trader*, P.O. Box 1050, Dubuque, IA 52004.

The only price guide available is *Hake's Guide to TV Collectibles*, by Ted Hake (Wallace-Homestead), 1990. This book is an excellent reference, though the prices are a bit outdated. Hake also sponsors a quarterly auction of TV collectibles. Hakes, P.O. Box 1444Z, York, PA 17405.

Another good source for TV collectibles is Casey's Collectible Corner (HCR Box 31, Rte. 30, No. Blenheim, NY 12131, 607/588-6464)..

You might also enjoy *Board Games*, by Desi Scarpone (Schiffer), 1995. It contains color photos of nearly every TV show board game ever made.

News, auctions, and stories about the various collectibles can also be found in *Island News*, published by The Original Gilligan's Island Fan Club, P.O. Box 25311, Salt Lake City, UT 84125-0311.

BOOKS FOR A DESERTED ISLAND

America on the Rerun, David Story (Citadel), 1993.

Backus Strikes Back, Jim Backus and Henny Backus (Stein and Day), 1984.

Bad TV: The Very Best of the Very Worst, Craig Nelson (Delta), 1995.

The Best of 60s TV, Michael McCall (Ballard Press), 1992.

The Best of TV Sitcoms, John Javna (Harmony Books), 1988.

The Complete Directory to Prime Time Network TV Shows (5th ed.), Tim Brooks and Earle Marsh (Ballantine), 1992.

Forgive Us Our Digressions: An Autobiography, Jim and Henny Backus (St. Martin's Press), 1988.

Here on Gilligan's Isle, Russell Johnson with Steve Cox (HarperPerennial), 1992.

Inside Gilligan's Island, Sherwood Schwartz (St. Martin's Press), 1994.

Mary Ann's Gilligan's Island Cookbook, Dawn Wells, Ken Beck, and Jim Clark (Rutledge Hill Press) 1993.

Sweethearts of '60's TV, Ronald L. Smith, (St. Martin's Press), 1989.

The Unofficial Gilligan's Island Handbook, Joey
    Green (Warner Books), 1988.
What Are You Doing After the Orgy? Jim and
    Henny Backus.

ANOTHER THREE-HOUR TOUR?

The TV movies ended with the deaths of Jim Backus, Natalie Schafer, and Alan Hale, Jr.

In 1992, Sherwood Schwartz collaborated on *Gilligan's Island: The Musical*. It was first performed at the Flat Rock Playhouse in Flat Rock, North Carolina, then played in Chicago and San Diego. It has twenty songs (including "The Ballad of Gilligan's Isle") and was a new story, though it used many of the standard elements of the original TV series.

There have been reports from various cast members for several years that there might be a big-screen *Gilligan's Island*. A script evidently exists, but no plot details are available. However, since the success of *The Brady Bunch Movie* in 1995, there's no question that this is still a distinct possibility.

On a 1993 talk show, Bob Denver said, "We've got another two-hour script for a TV movie that Sherwood's written. It's for *Gilligan: The Second Generation* and I marry Mary Ann and the Professor marries Ginger and we all have little children until there are seven like there were before and they grow up and they want to go back to see where Gilligan's Island was and they get a boat and they go out and there's a big storm . . . and

they land on the island and they do the things
we did on the island and we're back on the mainland—the original cast—trying to find out where
they are."

Sounds like a good movie premise, doesn't it?

INDEX

His inventive, off-the-wall humor made America laugh out loud in movies like *Big, Turner and Hooch*, and *A League of Their Own*. His charm and boyish good looks won over Darryl Hannah in *Splash* and Meg Ryan in *Sleepless in Seattle*. His genius for breathing life into a character made *Forrest Gump* a household name. And his haunting Oscar-winning performance in *Philadelphia* established him as one of today's hottest leading men.

Warm, witty and vulnerable, Tom Hanks is both the everyman we can all identify with and an actor with stunning star quality. Now, Roy Trakin traces Hanks' life and career in this honest, no-holds-barred biography.

TOM HANKS
JOURNEY TO STARDOM

ROY TRAKIN

TOM HANKS
Roy Trakin
_____ 95596-0 $4.99 U.S./$5.99 Can.